Special EDITION

Believe in love. Overcome obstacles. Find happiness.

Taking The Long Way Home
Christine Rimmer

Snowed In With A Stranger
Brenda Harlen

MILLS & BOON

TAKING THE LONG WAY HOME
© 2024 by Christine Rimmer
Philippine Copyright 2024
Australian Copyright 2024
New Zealand Copyright 2024

First Published 2024
First Australian Paperback Edition 2024
ISBN 978 1 038 90556 7

SNOWED IN WITH A STRANGER
© 2024 by Brenda Harlen
Philippine Copyright 2024
Australian Copyright 2024
New Zealand Copyright 2024

First Published 2024
First Australian Paperback Edition 2024
ISBN 978 1 038 90556 7

This is a work of fiction. Names, characters, places, and incidents are either the
product of the author's imagination or are used fictitiously, and any resemblance to
actual persons, living or dead, business establishments, events, or locales is entirely
coincidental.

Published by
Harlequin Mills & Boon
An imprint of Harlequin Enterprises (Australia) Pty Limited
(ABN 47 001 180 918), a subsidiary of HarperCollins
Publishers Australia Pty Limited
(ABN 36 009 913 517)
Level 19, 201 Elizabeth Street
SYDNEY NSW 2000 AUSTRALIA

MIX
Paper | Supporting
responsible forestry
FSC® C001695
FSC
www.fsc.org

Printed and bound in Australia by McPherson's Printing Group

Taking The Long Way Home
Christine Rimmer

MILLS & BOON

Christine Rimmer came to her profession the long way around. She tried everything from acting to teaching to telephone sales. Now she's finally found work that suits her perfectly. She insists she never had a problem keeping a job—she was merely gaining "life experience" for her future as a novelist. Christine lives with her family in Oregon. Visit her at christinerimmer.com.

Visit the Author Profile page
at millsandboon.com.au for more titles.

Dear Reader,

A little happy hour good cheer on a rainy Friday night. That's all librarian Piper Wallace is looking for. But as fate would have it, she's going to get so much more, including a little quality time with a hot younger man. No, Piper's not looking for love. In fact, she's put love in the Never Again category.

But just for one night? She's never done that before, and she tries to be open to new experiences. Really, what could go wrong?

Rancher and chain saw artist Jason Bravo has always had something of a secret crush on the pretty librarian, starting way back when she first began working at the local library. He was thirteen then. Now he's a grown man—and he is not passing up his one chance with Piper.

The deal is that they'll both walk away when their one night is over. But a deal like that is made to be broken. Especially when a good man refuses to give up on the woman of his dreams.

I hope Jason and Piper's story keeps you turning pages, that it makes you smile and sigh and maybe shed a tear or two.

Happy reading, everyone.

Christine

DEDICATION

This one's for my older son Matt
and my grandson, Milo.

Matt, you're a wonderful father and a fine man who
takes loving care of his family. You step up to help
whenever it's needed. Plus, you're smart and funny
and thoughtful, too. A mum couldn't ask for more.

And, Milo, how have the years passed so swiftly?
Wasn't it just yesterday you were running through the
sprinklers in the backyard? Watching you grow up
is an honour and a pure delight.

Chapter One

People always thought of libraries as quiet, even peaceful. But in Piper Wallace's experience, no way.

The Legos at the Library event was in full swing when four-year-old Bobby Trueblood stuck the plastic spaceman in his mouth and swallowed—or tried to. Piper, newly promoted to the top position of library director, saw him do it.

As Bobby grabbed his throat and attempted to cough, Piper stepped in close, bent down to his height and spoke to him calmly. "Bobby, can you breathe at all?"

Frantic, Bobby shook his head, held his throat with both hands and continued his desperate, soundless effort to cough.

"Okay," Piper said softly, "I'm going to help you get that spaceman out of there…"

A few feet away, Lacey Beaufort, the children's librarian, had noticed the problem. "I'm calling 911," she said in a near whisper and whipped out her phone.

Moving directly behind the little boy, Piper dropped to one knee. "Bobby, I'm just going to put my arm around you now…" She drew his small, heaving body back against her and tried like hell to remember her first aid training.

Slap it out first, right?

Dear God in heaven, she hoped so.

With her fist just above his navel, Piper bent him at the waist. As he continued desperately clutching his throat and struggling to draw even a bit of a breath, she struck him five times between his shoulder blades with the heel of her right hand, being careful with each strike to pound upward in an effort to help him expel the object.

Nothing. Poor Bobby continued to hold his throat and shake his head.

About then, his mother, Maxine Trueblood, turned and saw what was happening.

"Oh, my Lord!" Maxine shouted in horror. "Bobby! Bobby, are you all right?!"

Bobby was most definitely *not* all right. Lacey had the 911 dispatcher on the phone now. As for Piper, she moved on to perform abdominal thrusts. Wrapping her other arm around the boy, locking her right hand on her left wrist, she squeezed sharply in and up, five times in succession.

The fifth squeeze finally did it. The small plastic figure shot out of the child's open mouth, hitting seven-year-old Milo Nevins in the chest.

"Holy smokes!" exclaimed Milo as Bobby finally sucked in a long, wheezing breath.

"It's out," Lacey reported to the 911 dispatcher. "…Yes, that's right. The toy is out. And he's breathing now…Yes. That's what I said. He's getting air, breathing normally. The obstruction is out." She listened for a moment and replied, "I think he's all right, just really shaken up…Yes. Of course. I'll tell them…"

About then, Maxine scooped her son up into her arms. The little boy grabbed his mom around the neck and started crying.

Piper rose to her feet. "He'll be okay," she reassured

the terrified Maxine. She asked Lacey, "Are they send-ing an ambulance?"

"Since he seems fine, no. But he should go straight up to the hospital in Sheridan so that they can look him over."

Maxine nodded. "Yes, okay. We'll go right now." She was crying by then, too. Her other child, a little girl, clung to her coat and sobbed right along with her mom and her brother. In the meantime, two other mothers had moved in close. One offered a travel packet of tissues as they both patted Maxine's back and whispered reassurances. "Thank you," sobbed Maxine, holding Bobby on one arm while swiping at her own tears with her free hand. And then she spoke directly to Piper. "Thank you so much!"

"Of course," Piper replied. "Bobby is going to be fine." She said that at full volume, for everyone to hear. Then she turned to Lacey. "I'm going to walk them out to the car..."

The other moms stepped out of the way and Piper moved in. With a light hand at Maxine's back, she guided the sniffling mom forward.

As they left the children's section, Lacey continued to assure the crowd that Bobby was all right. Faintly, when Piper, Maxine and the two children went through the re-ception atrium toward the main entrance, Piper heard Lacey announce the next group of entries. She kept moving forward, guiding the shell-shocked mom and her kids out the wide glass doors into the stormy mid-April afternoon.

It was cold out there and pouring down rain. At least Maxine, Bobby and the little girl were wearing hooded coats. Piper hadn't stopped for hers. "Would you like me to go with you?" she asked as they reached Maxine's bat-tered Subaru.

Maxine drew a slow breath. "We'll be all right. I can manage."

"You're sure?"

"Yes. He's okay now. We'll be fine—and I don't know how to thank you. If you hadn't known what to do…"

"Happy to help." Piper pulled Maxine into a quick side hug. "Now, let's get you guys out of the rain, huh?"

Maxine blinked and looked Piper up and down. "But what about you? You're dripping wet."

"I'm fine." Piper lifted the little girl up into her car seat and buckled her in as Maxine did the same for Bobby.

Two minutes later, Piper stood shivering in the downpour watching the Subaru leave the library parking lot. Once the car disappeared from sight, she whirled and ran for the shelter of the building.

Inside, she ducked into her office to grab her purse and the change of clothes she kept in the closet there just in case. Because you just never knew at the Medicine Creek Library.

A couple of years ago, Tootie Gracely, technical services librarian, had bumped into Piper in the staff room and spilled half a strawberry smoothie down the front of Piper's sky blue silk dress. Another time someone had left an enormous wad of bubble gum on the chair at the reference desk. Piper's tan pencil skirt had not survived the incident.

Which was why she was always prepared for a wardrobe disaster.

Today, after ten minutes in the restroom, she looked— well, better than she had any right to expect, given the circumstances. She'd changed into slim gray pants, a white shirt, a gray jacket and black pumps. She'd also mopped up her smeared mascara, put on fresh lip gloss and smoothed her wet hair up into a ponytail. As for the green wool dress she'd worn out into the rain, she left it in her office to deal with later.

Drawing her shoulders back and aiming her chin high, Piper reentered the children's section just as Lacey announced a new group of winners.

Half an hour after that, Legos at the Library wrapped up. Everyone declared the event a big success, even if little Bobby Trueblood *had* gotten a plastic spaceman temporarily stuck in his throat.

The really great news was that Maxine had called from the hospital and left Piper a message full of thanks and relief. Bobby was fine. The doctor in the ER had examined him, delivered a gentle lecture about what *not* to put in his mouth—and sent the Truebloods home.

Potential tragedy averted. Bobby Trueblood had come through his ordeal in good shape. And hey, it was Friday. Piper had the weekend off.

Tonight of all nights, she wanted to blow off a little steam. She wanted some happy-hour good cheer, to enjoy a drink at Arlington's Steakhouse bar in the company of friends and colleagues.

And if she couldn't get a group together on the spur of the moment, no problem. Just one friend or colleague would do it. Because if happy-hour good cheer wasn't happening, someone to confide in would be great.

That morning, she'd received a second invitation to share information from one of her 23andMe DNA matches—and this was no second-or-third-cousin kind of match. This was someone she'd given up on years ago.

Way back in her teens, she'd put all that hope and heartbreak behind her. So much so that, when the match was miraculously made, she couldn't bring herself to deal with it. A few days after the notice from 23andMe, the match himself had reached out for the first time.

How hard could it have been to respond to the guy?

Harder than she'd ever imagined, definitely. Her mother had been on her case about it way too much the past month or so. So far, she'd backed her mom off.

But now she was at the point where she would love to have a friend to talk to about the situation. Tonight, a drink and a long conversation with someone she trusted, well, that would be even better than going out with a group to celebrate Bobby Trueblood's continued good health.

As it turned out, none of her coworkers could join her tonight. And when she called a few friends, she got regretful refusals, which didn't really surprise her. Most of her friends were in their late thirties to early forties. They had spouses, kids of varying ages and jobs, too. They juggled hectic schedules as best they could. That night, no one could get away.

Piper put on her red raincoat, grabbed her soggy green dress and hurried out to her Volkswagen Tiguan. Behind the wheel, she turned the car toward home.

But halfway there, she changed her mind.

She wanted to go out. And why shouldn't she? Widowed four years ago with no children, Piper had zero reason to rush home. Plus, she made it a point to be open to first-time experiences. Really, tonight was as good a night as any to try happy hour solo.

Five minutes later, she was parking on the street outside Arlington's Steakhouse. Inside, she refused the host's offer of a small table to herself and claimed an empty stool at the bar, where she ordered a cosmo.

As she slowly sipped her drink, the fiftyish cowboy to her left mounted a half-hearted attempt to pick her up. She answered politely but took care to give the man zero encouragement. After a few minutes of awkward conversation, he gave up and left her alone.

She turned around on her stool. Every table in the bar area was occupied. She waved and smiled at a few people she knew. They waved back, but none of them approached her or signaled her over.

Which was fine.

Except, well, she did feel a little uncomfortable. Everybody else seemed to be on a date or out with friends.

Sipping a cosmo alone? It felt kind of sad now she was doing it.

Fair enough, she thought, and sat up straighter. She would finish her drink and be on her way—and in the meantime, she would people-watch.

For the next few minutes, she casually observed a couple at a two-top not far from the bar. They were adorable, kind of shy but obviously crushing on each other. Pretty young, too. They looked barely old enough to order a real drink.

She turned her powers of observation on another couple at the next table over from the shy lovebirds. No flirty, excited glances were zipping back and forth there. Those two hardly looked at each other, let alone spoke.

The cowboy she'd discouraged a few minutes before got up from his stool. "Have a nice night." He tipped his hat to her.

She gave him a smile. "You, too." He headed for the door. Piper resumed her people-watching.

"Hey, Mrs. . . .er, Piper. How are you?"

Hiding a grin at the way he'd stumbled over what to call her, she smiled at the young man who stood behind the stool the older cowboy had vacated. Piper had known Jason Bravo for fourteen years. She'd met him when she first came to work at the library.

Jason was in middle school then, wasn't he?

Back then, he used to check out books on things like woodworking and saddle making. She'd been twenty-six at that time, a librarian for two years and absolutely thrilled to have snagged a position in her hometown library.

Jason had been a good kid, one who'd grown into a fine, handsome man—and thoughtful, too, stepping up now to check on her, to make sure she was okay on her own.

"Piper?" He watched her face expectantly.

She realized she'd failed to respond to his greeting. "Uh, hi, Jason. Good to see you. And yeah, I'm. . .fine."

He gave her the kind of smile that should probably come with a warning label. "You don't sound so sure about that."

"Sorry, just thinking back."

"To. . .?"

"My first year at the library. You were in middle school then, right?"

"Eighth grade," he replied without even having to think about it. For a moment, they just looked at each other. Finally, he asked, "Want some company?"

Why not? "Have a seat."

He claimed the empty stool, signaled the bartender and asked Piper, "Another drink?"

"Sure."

The bartender poured Jason a beer and quickly whipped up a second cosmo for Piper.

Jason took off his hat, hung it from one of the hooks under the bar and then raised his glass. "Are you waiting for someone?"

She tapped her drink to his. "No, I'm on my own."

"You like drinking alone?"

"Not exactly. But tonight, all my friends had somewhere else to be. I almost went home, but then I had this idea that I…" She shrugged. "It doesn't really matter."

"Sure, it does—come on. Tell me." He had thick, dark hair and blue-gray eyes. And that smile of his made all her menopause-adjacent hormones sit up and take notice.

Don't be ridiculous, she reminded herself. *He's a nice boy just trying to look out for you.* "I, uh, do my best to be open to new experiences, that's all. Tonight, I decided to try drinking alone at a bar."

He laughed then. The rich, deep sound tugged on something forbidden down inside her. "And how'd that work out for you?"

She sighed. "Well, it's not something I'm going to be doing on a regular basis. Honestly, it's lonely and it made me a little bit sad. But I needed to get out, you know? It was a rough afternoon at the library."

His gaze stayed locked on her face. "What happened?"

"Well, today was our Legos at the Library event. Everything was going great. Until Bobby Trueblood tried to swallow a plastic astronaut…"

"That's scary. Is he okay?"

"He's fine now, but I had to perform the Heimlich maneuver. And I was terrified while it was happening…"

"Of course you were." Jason leaned a fraction closer.

His big shoulder brushed hers and a little shiver vibrated through her. He raised his beer again. "To you, Piper. You saved the day."

"I wouldn't go that far."

"I would. And I'll bet Bobby would, too."

"He's okay. That's what matters—and the sheer relief that he came through it just fine had me wanting to get out with friends, to uh, celebrate life and all that. And then when no one could come out with me, I decided to try the whole being-alone-at-a-bar experience."

He chuckled. "Being-alone-at-a-bar. That's a thing?"

She gave a silly little snort-laugh and felt comfortable enough with him right then that she wasn't even embarrassed. "It's not a thing to anyone but me and as I said, it's not fun in the least. I am never choosing to be alone at a bar again—I mean unless I desperately need a drink for some reason. I kind of settled on people-watching, trying to make the time go faster." She tipped her head at the couple who looked like they wanted to be anywhere but together and whispered, "I believe they're fighting."

He watched them for a moment. "Never seen them before. But you're right. They don't look happy."

"You think maybe he cheated?"

"Hmm." Jason took a moment to consider the possibilities. "Nah. She probably wants to go to counseling to work on their issues and he's one of those guys who doesn't believe in that crap."

"Harsh," she said with a grin.

"Hey, it was just a guess." He tipped his head at another couple and then leaned close again to ask, "That blonde and the guy with the mullet. What about them?"

Piper gave a half shrug and whispered, "She loves him despite his unfortunate grooming choices."

"What? You're judging a man's mullet?"

She assumed a remorseful expression. "You're right. That was over the line."

Jason looked at her as if... Well, as if he found her fascinating. Was he actually flirting with her?

No way.

And that second cosmo? It made her bold. "Jason Bravo, are you flirting with me?" The words were out of her mouth before she could think how silly they might sound. "Um, I mean, you wouldn't, right?" Shutting her eyes, she drew a slow, calming breath and muttered, "Just shoot me now..."

He leaned close again. "Of course I'm flirting with you."

"But...why?" she asked because tonight she couldn't seem to keep all the uncool things from popping out of her mouth.

"You're a very pretty woman and flirting is fun."

How did he do that? Every time she put her foot in it, he managed to make it all okay. It was lovely of him. "You have salvaged this evening for me. Thank you."

"Anytime." Those dusky blue eyes seemed to suggest things she knew she shouldn't take seriously. He asked, "How's your mom? Haven't seen her in a week or two."

"Same as always." Piper's mom, Emmaline Stokely, was opinionated, outspoken, lively and fun. An artist, Emmaline painted psychedelic landscapes and made boho jewelry. She also took surveys and babysat other people's pets among other things, all in the interest of making ends meet in her own special, creative way. "I think she's deep into a new series of landscapes. When she's lost in her work, even I don't see much of her."

"She's remarkable." Jason was an artist, too. He not only ran the family ranch alongside his mom and dad and younger brother, but he was also a talented chain saw carver. Piper's mom always spoke highly of his work.

Piper made a noise of agreement to the wonderfulness that was Emmaline. "She's one of a kind, all right."

"That she is." One side of his fine mouth quirked up. "She told me once that for the first nine years of your life, the two of you lived on the road in a Volkswagen bus."

"It's true. She homeschooled me in that bus. I met a whole bunch of interesting people, very few of whom were anywhere near my age. Then my grandfather died, and we came home to help out my grandmother."

"And you stayed?"

She nodded. "I fell in love with Medicine Creek. I wanted to go to a real school and have a 'normal' life. Mom seemed to know how much I needed that. So she sold the bus, and we moved in with my grandmother."

The bartender asked, "Can I get either of you another drink?"

"No more for me." Piper gave him a smile. "Thank you."

Jason said, "I'll have one more." He asked Piper, "Hungry?"

"Really, I should get going."

He pinned her with those beautiful eyes of his. "Got a menu?" he asked the bartender.

"You bet."

So they ate sliders and sweet potato fries, and another hour flew by. Her sad, solo evening had magically turned wonderful. Now, she didn't want the evening to end.

But really, it was time to say good-night to this beautiful, attentive man who was several years too young for her—not that it mattered how young or old he was. Piper wasn't getting anything going with a man. Not now. Probably never.

Jason put his hand over hers and said, "Don't."

Her breath caught. And suddenly her heart was racing.

With the hand he hadn't captured, she picked up her water glass and drank it down. "What's going on here?" she whispered, her voice oddly breathless.

He leaned in again and she wondered how in the world any man could smell that good. Like red cedar shavings, saddle soap and…something else. Ferns, maybe, something moist and green and fresh.

Their gazes locked.

And she asked, "Jason, are you trying to pick me up?"

His eyes didn't waver. "Oh, you bet I am. The question is, will you say yes?"

She should pull her hand away. But she didn't. "Hmm. This is not the kind of situation I normally find myself in. To be brutally honest, I'm boring."

He just shook his head. Slowly.

She insisted, "No, really. I am. I always say I'm open to trying new things, but the truth is, I'm a creature of habit. I like my routines."

"Such as?"

"Well, every Thursday, without fail, I eat lunch at Henry's." The diner was a Medicine Creek landmark.

"Henry's is great. Everybody loves Henry's."

"But Jason, *every* Thursday?"

"Absolutely. Why not?" He looked at her so steadily.

She asked in a shaky whisper, "Do you pick up women in bars all the time?"

He laughed then, a low, rueful, oddly tender sound. "No. To tell you the truth, I'm more of a relationship kind of guy."

For most of her life, Piper had considered herself a relationship kind of girl. She'd grown up wanting what her grandparents had shared—that special someone, her very own soulmate.

But not anymore. Never again. "I hope you find what you're looking for, Jason."

"You're saying you're not interested?"

"In a relationship...with you?"

"Well, I was thinking more that we might see each other again."

Was he kidding? He must be. But she answered him honestly. "Nope. Not going there. I'm single and happy that way."

He drew a slow breath. "So, then, Piper. Do you think you could be interested...just for tonight?"

The question shocked her. She was, what? Thirteen on the day he was born. And the age gap aside, going home just for the night with any man was not, and never had been, her style.

She blurted, "I've never done that, had a one-night stand."

He leaned a fraction closer. "First time for everything."

The breath had mysteriously fled her lungs. She dragged in air. And shocked herself by admitting in a goofy little squeak, "Okay, I'm intrigued."

"Good. And right now, I think I should probably up my game a little." He gave her a slow grin.

She frowned. "What does that mean?"

"This…"

She gasped as his soft lips touched hers. And then she sighed.

Because Jason Bravo definitely knew how to kiss. So much so that it didn't even occur to her to pull away.

The bar and everyone around them receded. It was just the two of them sharing a lovely, leisurely kiss. A light kiss—but so sweet. He didn't touch her, except with those wonderful lips of his.

"Wow," she whispered when he finally pulled away.

His gaze tracked—from her mouth to her eyes and back to her mouth again. "Piper, come home with me. I'm out at the family ranch, the Double-K. I have my own place there."

She wanted to say yes. She wanted that so much.

And why shouldn't she?

They were both grown-ups, after all.

And they were both single…weren't they? "Got a special girl, Jason?"

His gaze remained steady, focused on her. "Absolutely not."

She stared at him. He was fun and kind and she knew she could trust him.

Plus, he was one hot cowboy.

"All right," she said. "I'll follow you to your place."

He insisted on picking up the check. At the door, he helped her into her raincoat and offered his arm. She took it, grinning to herself, thinking that the kiss they'd shared back there at the bar might get a few busybodies whispering.

Not that she cared, really. She'd been raised by a single

mom who never let the opinions of others dictate her behavior. If Emmaline ever learned that her only child had
spent a night with Jason Bravo, her response would be a
proud smile and an enthusiastic *Good for you, my love.*

It was still raining out. Piper pulled up the hood of her
raincoat. They were both parked right there on Main. He
walked her to her car and then ran through the rain to his
big pickup.

When he eased out onto the street, she followed him.

In no time they left the lights of town behind. Overhead, the clouds were a curtain of gray blotting out the
stars, obscuring the peaks of the mountains. The rain came
down hard enough that the windshield wipers could hardly
keep up with it.

Twenty minutes or so from town, they turned off the
highway onto a well-tended gravel road. By the time she
pulled to a stop behind him at a wide, wooden gate, she was
feeling pretty nervous, second-guessing the wisdom of this
completely uncharacteristic decision she'd made.

Going home with Jason Bravo? This was not like her
at all.

He got out, opened the gate and signaled her through
under a big iron sign depicting two Ks back-to-back—
two Ks for the Double-K Ranch, which had belonged to
his mother, Megan Kane, before she married Nate Bravo.
Piper knew this because she enjoyed reading books about
Wyoming history—including *Brands of the Bighorns* by
Chester T. Sedgwick, which offered detailed accounts of
all the local ranches and their owners over the years.

Once through the gate, she pulled to the side and waited
as he drove through, got out of his truck again, shut the

gate and then jumped up behind the wheel to lead the way once more.

They passed a Victorian-style house on the left. From there, the road wove through a stand of cottonwoods. When they emerged onto open land again, Jason pulled to a stop in front of a two-story log cabin with a pair of small one-story wings branching off to either side. At the back of the house she could see what looked like an attached barn.

Jason jumped out of his truck and jogged to her side window. She rolled it down. "This is it," he said, the rain running off his hat, making a stream of water between them. "Pull up beside the deck."

He stepped back and she drove forward, stopping a few feet to the left of the deck steps. A moment later, he pulled open her door for her.

When she stepped out of the car, he said, "You'll ruin your shoes." And then he put one arm at her back, the other under her knees and scooped her high against his broad chest.

She laughed in surprise. Clutching her purse in one hand, she grabbed him around the neck with the other as he carried her up the short run of stairs and under the shelter of the overhang above the door.

Once he reached the doormat, he set her on her feet. She pushed back the hood of her coat and blinked up at him as a sense of complete unreality assailed her. She was about to have a one-night stand with Jason Bravo. Never in her life had she imagined this might happen.

He gazed down at her from under the dripping brim of his hat. "You okay?"

She gave him a big smile. "Yes, I am."

"Come on in." He unlocked the door, ushered her ahead of him and flipped a switch on the wall. The rustic chandelier overhead lit up the big living area.

"Your house is beautiful, Jason."

"It's pretty simple," he said. "A couple thousand square feet. Great room in the middle, bedrooms to either side."

"But what's with the attached barn?"

"I have my workshop back there."

"Ah. So that's where the chain saw art happens?"

"Yeah. You want a tour?"

She did, but getting a tour of his workshop would make tonight feel more like a date. This was not that and boundaries mattered. "Better not."

He tossed his hat onto a rough-hewn bench by the door and then took her face between his big, wet hands. "Please don't change your mind."

She gazed up at him, breathless. "I won't."

He seemed relieved. "Good."

Her poor heart was going a mile a minute. "Do I look terrified?"

One corner of his mouth ticked up. "No way. Not you."

"Liar," she said, feeling nothing short of fond of him right at that moment.

"Piper…"

"Hmm?"

"I can't believe you're here."

"I understand. Because neither can I."

He took her mouth, gently at first. And then more deeply, more…hungrily. His lips went from cool and rain-wet to scorching hot.

She gasped at the wonder of that kiss and let her purse

drop to the rug at their feet. Talk about being open to new experiences...

Twining both arms around his neck, she silently vowed to give herself up to him and to the magic of this one special night.

Chapter Two

Utterly limp and completely satisfied, Piper stared dreamily up at Jason's beamed bedroom ceiling.

"That was…" She raised her voice a little to be certain he could hear her in the other room. "Jason, I have no words!"

Idly, she twined a long swatch of her hair around her index finger like she used to do back when she was a kid. Before tonight, there had been only two men in her life—her college boyfriend, Brandon. And her husband, Walter. Until Brandon almost killed her and turned her love to hate, she'd been head over heels for him. As for Walter, he was the opposite of her college lover. Walter was quiet and safe. He'd died of a heart attack when he was only forty-one.

As gloriously naked as when he went in there, Jason emerged from the bathroom. The man was every bit as gorgeous coming toward her as he'd been when he walked away. Without a word, he lifted the blankets and got back into the bed with her. His expression was much too serious.

"Jason. What's wrong?"

Bracing up on an elbow, he looked at her solemnly. "I should be asking you the same question. I can't believe you're not upset."

She let out a slow, happy sigh and twirled her hair some

more. "I just had four orgasms in three hours. I'm swimming in endorphins right now. I don't think I could be upset if I tried."

For a moment, she thought he might give her a smile—but no. His eyes remained serious, and the corners of that wonderful mouth refused to tip up.

"Okay," she conceded. "I get it. It's not good that the last condom broke."

He touched the side of her face, a light caress that warmed her deep down inside. "You did say you're not on birth control…"

"Jason, I promise you. I'm not going to get pregnant."

"Are you telling me that you can't have kids?"

"It's possible that I can't—more than possible. I'll go further. It's very likely that I can't."

The skin was all scrunched up between his eyebrows. "You don't know for sure?"

"No, I don't. But I do know that it's not the right time in my cycle for me to get pregnant. My period just ended. Also, Walter and I were married for eight years. We never once used birth control and I never got pregnant in all that time." She waited for him to say something. But he just kept on looking at her.

Assuming he wanted more details, she went ahead and overshared. "We, uh, always agreed we wanted children, Walter and me. Now and then, we would talk about checking into fertility tests and all that, but we failed to actually do anything about it."

The truth was, she and Walter had talked about a lot of things. But there'd always been a lack of urgency between them, a certain distance that at first had felt so sane and real and comfortable. Walter had been safe, and safety was what she'd needed at the time. She hadn't let herself admit until quite a while after her husband's unexpected death that she'd never been in love with him.

"So, really," she concluded, more than ready to be done with this particular conversation. "A broken condom is not a big deal to me. If by some impossible miracle I really did get pregnant, I would be thrilled. I would love to have a baby and the prospect of being a single mom doesn't bother me in the least. My mom had me without a man around and it worked out just fine."

He looked at her as though he wasn't sure what to make of her. "You're way too calm about this."

She waved a dismissing hand—and then realized that he might be worried about STDs. "Listen, I mean it. I'm not pregnant and I promise that you won't be getting any sexually transmitted diseases from me. Until tonight, I haven't had sex with another person in years—since a good while before Walter died, to tell you the embarrassing truth."

He gave her a slow nod. "I haven't been with anyone since my last relationship ended almost a year ago—and she and I always used condoms."

"Okay, then. We're good, I'm sure." And she truly wanted to be finished with this conversation. Talk about awkward—and what time was it anyway? "Listen. I really should pull myself together and head back into town."

She didn't wait for a response from him, but instead slid to the edge on her side of the bed and slipped out from under the covers. It felt weird being naked now that the good times were done.

But so what?

"Be right back," she said as she headed for his bathroom. Once she'd used the toilet and freshened up a bit, she returned to the bedroom to find him back in the bed, sitting against the carved headboard, the sheet pulled up to his waist, the ridges and hollows of his broad chest and lean belly on glorious display.

Her clothes were right there on the bedside chair. She got busy putting them on, starting with her white lace bikini panties and matching bra. Piper loved good lingerie. All her underwear was pretty. Good lingerie made her feel attractive and feminine, whether any man ever saw it or not. She stifled a smug little grin as she realized that tonight of all nights, wearing nice underwear had been an excellent idea.

Jason watched her as she buttoned up her white shirt. When she reached for her gray trousers, he said, "I want to see you again."

That couldn't happen. They had an agreement and she fully intended to stick by it. "Jason, you are amazing. Tonight was perfect. But, sweetie, we agreed. It was just this one time."

His gorgeous face looked carved from stone. "Please don't talk to me like I'm a child."

She winced. "I'm sorry. It's just...listen. I had a beautiful night and I promise I do not see you as a child. I see you as a very sexy man—and I do have to go."

For a long, painful string of seconds, he just looked at her through those eyes she knew would be haunting her secret dreams. Then he pushed back the covers and swung his feet to the floor. "All right, then." He reached for his own clothes. "I'll put on some pants and walk you out."

* * *

Outside, the rain had stopped.

Jason pulled open the door of her little SUV for her. He knew better than to try to kiss her. She thought she was done with him. He got that.

They had an agreement. He wasn't going to break it—at least, not right now.

"Good night," she said as she settled into the driver's seat and reached for her seat belt.

"I'll be happy to follow you to the gate and open it for you, so you don't have to get out of the car."

Her eyes were wary. "Is there something complicated about getting it open?"

He shook his head. "It's a simple butterfly latch, but you'd have get out of the car twice, to open the gate and then again to shut it behind you."

"No problem. I can manage."

"All right, then. Night, Piper." He closed her door.

She met his eyes through her side window. As she granted him a quick wave, he resisted the wild need to fling the door wide again and drag her back out and into his arms.

With a nod, he stepped away from the car. A moment later, he was watching her taillights disappear into the stand of cottonwoods between his place and the main house.

Overhead, the last wisps of storm clouds drifted way up there in the starry sky. To the west, Cloud Peak poked up toward heaven, more threads of cloud caught on the crest. All was right with the world.

Just not with Jason.

He heard a whine and his dog, Kenzo, a German She-prador, came wiggling out from under the deck. "Hey, boy!" Kenzo trotted on over. Jason knelt to scratch him behind the ears and tell him what a good boy he was.

Back in the cabin, Jason knew he wouldn't sleep. A month ago, he would have headed out to see if the night calver needed him. But calving season was winding down on the Double-K and it wasn't cold enough to worry about any newborn calves freezing before they could latch on.

With Kenzo at his heels, he walked on through the house to his workshop in back, where a beautiful red cedar stump waited for him to discover what waited inside. Kenzo lapped up a long drink from the water bowl in the corner and then flopped down near the door that led back into the cabin as Jason geared up, grabbed a hatchet and started peeling bark.

An hour or so before dawn, he and Kenzo reentered the house. He fed the dog, put on his work clothes and went out to join his dad and his younger brother, Joe, for morning chores.

As it turned out, his mom's cousin Sonny and his wife, Farrah, had driven up yesterday from Buffalo. This morning, Sonny pitched in with the chores, too.

Sonny and Farrah and their kids used to live and work full-time on the Double-K. The kids were grown up now and on their own. About a decade ago, Farrah had inherited a motel in nearby Buffalo from her mom. Nowadays, the couple ran the Cottonwood Inn for a living.

They still showed up to pitch in whenever they were needed—and sometimes, like this weekend, they left a manager to run the motel and came out to the ranch for a visit. Both Sonny and Farrah liked the motel business. But they also missed life on the Double-K.

After the chores were done, the men converged on the

main house for breakfast. Jason's mom and Farrah had done the cooking this morning.

Jason took his turn washing up in the half bath off the front hall and joined the group around the breakfast nook table. He hadn't realized how hungry he was until he started shoveling it in—hungry and kind of tired, too. Even with more than one cup of coffee, he wouldn't mind heading back to his place for a nap after the meal. Staying up all night was starting to catch up with him.

The talk around the table was the same as always—about moving cattle and what equipment needed repair. He kind of tuned it out in favor of recalling the night before. Smiling to himself, he pictured that sweet dusting of freckles across Piper's pale shoulders and all that long, red hair on his white pillowcase.

He'd had fantasies of Piper since the first time he set eyes on her when he was thirteen and she came to work at the Medicine Creek Library. She'd been single then, though right away she'd started going out with Mr. Wallace, who taught history at the high school. They'd gotten married eventually. He was a nice guy, Walter Wallace. But not good enough for Piper.

Nobody was.

And never in a thousand years would Jason have guessed that last night might ever really happen.

But then he'd walked into Arlington's, taken a seat at a four-top in the bar area with a few guys he grew up with and ordered a beer. He was just about to pick up the check and head back to the ranch for the night when Piper appeared and hopped up on a stool in the middle of the bar.

All of a sudden, he'd had zero desire to leave. He'd stayed right where he was, half-heartedly holding up his end of the conversation with the other guys, keeping an eye on his favorite librarian while trying to be cool about it.

She always looked so pulled together—not like a city girl, exactly. But close, in her trim gray pants, matching jacket and white button-up shirt. Everything tailored and crisp. And with little black pumps on her narrow feet, too. She had that red hair pulled up in a high ponytail and he tried not to let himself imagine wrapping that tail of hair around his hand, or maybe taking it down so it fell loose and messy on her shoulders.

But he did imagine. In detail. It was a longtime habit with him, imagining doing sexy things to Piper Wallace.

And when the cowboy beside her had gotten up to go, Jason saw his chance and took it. .

"Wild night, huh?" Joe was watching him—and wearing a smirk. Twenty-three now, Joe thought he knew everything.

Jason set down his coffee cup and looked his little brother square in the eye. "I got no idea what you're talking about."

Joe smirked all the harder. "Noticed that little VW SUV sitting out in front of your place till all hours last night."

"And this is your business, how?"

Joe could be a smart-ass, but he was a good guy at heart. He knew when he'd stepped in it. Backing down, he put up both hands as though Jason held a gun on him. "Okay, okay. You're right. I didn't see a thing.'

"Boys," said their mom. "Not at the table."

Both Jason and Joe chuckled at that. It was one of Meggie Bravo's hard-and-fast rules when they were growing up—no fighting at the table. "Sorry, Mom," they replied in unison, just like when they were kids.

And the talk turned to the new research on sunn hemp as an alternative to alfalfa.

All the rest of that day, as he checked on the last of the newborn calves and pitched in to move cattle to fresher pastures, he thought about Piper.

And that night in bed, he faced the truth.

Yeah, he'd agreed that last night was the only night he would share with her. And at first, it had seemed only right to let some time go by before trying to get her to see things a different way.

But hell. Life was too short. No man could afford to sit around on his ass waiting for the right woman to see the light.

Now that he'd had a little time to think it over, he realized that the least he could do would be to check in with her. No matter what she'd said last night about it being the *only* night, well, a woman had a right to change her mind. He needed to tell her again that he really would like to spend more time with her—and as soon as she was ready to look at the situation in a more hopeful light, well, all she had to do was give him a call.

He made himself wait until Tuesday to seek her out at the library.

And he got lucky, too. He walked in and she was right there near the entrance hugging Mrs. Copely, who had been the director for years until her retirement last December, when Piper had stepped up to fill her shoes.

Piper caught sight of him over Mrs. Copely's shoulder. She didn't frown or anything, but she didn't look all that happy to see him.

Mrs. Copely let Piper go. "Well, I'll be on my way. Just had to stop in to see how you were doing."

"It's always good to see you, June."

Mrs. Copely sighed. "I miss you all. But Andre and I are heading off on another cruise next week. The Caribbean this time."

"Sounds wonderful."

"We do enjoy a little travel—but we'll be back in plenty of time to help out with the live auction in July."

"We're counting on it," said Piper.

Mrs. Copely spotted him as she turned to go. "Jason Bravo! How are you, young man?"

"Real good, Mrs. Copely."

She grabbed him in a hug, and he was engulfed in her powdery scent. June Copely was a big woman. When she hugged you, you felt it. "It's such a perfect coincidence that I walked right into you, Jason." She took him by the shoulders and beamed a giant smile at him. "Piper and I were just talking about the annual auction this summer." She looked over her shoulder at Piper, who nodded and smiled back.

He shot Piper a look—mostly to make sure she stayed put until he could have a word with her. She forced a smile for him, too.

Mrs. Copely said, "Jason, do you think you might possibly consider donating one of your chain saw sculptures to this very important cause?"

"I would be honored, Mrs. Copely."

"Wonderful!" She clapped her plump, age-spotted hands. "Do you have a card?"

"Of course." He pulled out his battered wallet and handed one over.

"Fantastic." She took the card, went on tiptoe and kissed his cheek.

He said, "I'll make sure Piper has my number, too."

"Please do." Mrs. Copely lifted the flap of her shoulder bag and slipped the card inside. "And now, I am out of here. I'll be in touch." With a perfectly executed pageant wave, Mrs. Copely sailed out the main doors.

"I'll give you all my information," he said to Piper before she could rush off.

"Of course." Her smile was reluctant. "This way." Turning, she set off toward the children's section.

He fell in step behind her.

Today, she wore a yellow skirt and a short blue-green jacket. Her little pumps were blue with pointy toes. And her hair, contained in a loose, low knot at the back of her head, made his hands itch to undo that knot so he could run his fingers through the long red strands.

At the children's section, she veered right. It wasn't far to the office with her name on the door. "Come on in," she said, and stood to the side, ushering him forward. "Have a seat." She shut the door and gestured at the pair of guest chairs on the far side of her desk.

"Thanks." He took one.

She circled around and sat in a big, black swivel chair, placing the expanse of her tidy desk between them. "It's very generous of you to donate one of your carvings. Thank you, Jason."

"Always happy to contribute to a good cause." He pulled another card from his wallet. She reached across the desk for it—and he changed his mind.

Slipping the card back into his wallet, he took out his

phone. "Just give me your number. I'll send you a text. That way we can easily keep in touch."

"Jason. Just call the library and ask to speak to me."

"I mean your cell number."

She bit her lip and asked in an adorably worried tone, "What are you doing?"

He got it. She really didn't want to give him her number. "All right, Piper," he said wearily as he pulled out the damn card again and handed it over.

"Thank you."

"Sure."

She popped to her feet. "Well…"

He kept his butt in the seat, though he'd never been the pushy kind. Until now. With her. He cast about for a friendly, neutral topic of conversation—just to kind of get the ball rolling.

There was a handmade card on her desk. A stick figure with spiky brown hair and a wide, red-crayon smile adorned the front of it. "Cute. Looks like it's handmade just for you."

She was smiling again—somewhat cautiously, but still. A smile was a smile. "Bobby Trueblood sent me that."

"Ah. The boy you saved at the Lego event."

"Yes, well. He's doing great. They came in yesterday, Bobby, his mom and his little sister. He was smiling and talking a mile a minute. No ill effects from almost swallowing a plastic astronaut."

"Glad to hear it."

She nodded. "He's the sweetest little guy…" As her voice trailed off, she looked at him reproachfully. "Jason. We had an agreement."

He went for it. "Go out with me.'

"Please. We've been through this."

"I was thinking a picnic. Saturday. I'll pick you up at noon. Wear jeans and sturdy shoes or boots. And a swimsuit underneath. I'll bring everything we need, and I know the perfect spot along Crystal Creek."

She just stood there, staring down at him, waiting for him to give up. The woman had no idea how long he could keep on like this.

Forever. Longer.

But it wasn't working.

He knew it was time to go. "Hey. Can't blame a man for trying." He got up. "You haven't seen my workshop. Now that I'm contributing to the auction, I would appreciate your help deciding what to donate. Plus, I've finished a new carving I'd like you to see. Just drop by when you can. Evenings are good, any night the rest of this week. My days are mostly about what needs doing on the Double-K..."

"I understand," she said. Whatever the hell that meant.

And he supposed he'd struck out enough for one day. "See you, Piper."

"I'll walk you out." She started to come around the desk.

He put up a hand. "No need. You take care, now."

Piper watched his fine backside walking away from her. The man had the broadest shoulders and the narrowest hips.

And she really needed to stop thinking about Friday night.

When the door shut silently behind him, she sank to her chair and tried not to get wistful about that picnic he'd wanted to share with her. She wished things were different. She truly did.

But one night was the deal they'd made. Better to stick to that. All the reasons *not* to say yes to him still applied.

However...

It was good of him to donate one of his carvings to the auction. And as the library's director, she had an obligation to show her appreciation for both his work and his generosity.

That evening she stayed late preparing for the upcoming board meeting. The Medicine Creek Library got a lot of backing from town leaders and from the chamber of commerce. They were an independent library, but they had the enthusiastic support of the community and some big private donors. With everyone helping out, they were able to run a great program.

Much of the credit for the library's longtime success went to June Copely, who'd been the director for decades. Piper knew she had big shoes to fill, and she worked hard to be as productive and innovative as her predecessor.

June had overseen the renovations accomplished last year by the hit home improvement TV show *Rebuilt by Bartley*. The project had expanded the library—and not only by adding more space for books, but also by making the library more beautiful, more welcoming, with a more open, inviting floor plan.

Really, Piper owed so much to June. And June was thrilled to have gotten Jason on board for the auction. Piper needed to be sure that Jason felt appreciated for his contribution and that meant she really should accept his invitation to visit his workshop.

That night, she got home around ten, ate a light meal and went straight to bed.

Wednesday, she woke up thinking of Jason—the kind

of thoughts she really shouldn't be allowing herself to have of him. Sexy thoughts. Fond thoughts.

And curious thoughts, too.

Beyond her obligations as director, she did want to see that workshop of his. And he'd said that he had a new carving he wanted to show her.

What kind of director would she be if she failed to gracefully accept the invitation of a respected local artist who'd agreed to donate his work to an important fund-raising event?

She had his card, but he'd said just to drop by any evening. Why not tonight?

After work, she went home and changed into jeans and a pair of comfortable walking shoes. It was a little after seven when she got to the gate with the ironwork Double-K sign above it. Nobody came out to see what she was up to as she opened the gate and then closed it once she'd driven her car through.

When she reached the cabin, a black dog sat on the front deck. The dog barked twice, then trotted down the steps toward her, tail wagging. The animal seemed friendly, so she dipped to a crouch.

"Hey there," she said.

The dog dropped to his haunches and tipped its head from side to side with a low, questioning whine. Cautiously, she offered a hand, palm up.

The cabin door opened and there was Jason in heavy-duty orange pants, a worn Cheyenne Frontier Days T-shirt and steel-toed boots. "His name's Kenzo. He's cautious, but friendly."

The dog sniffed her hand and allowed her to give him a quick scratch under the chin.

"It's good to see you," Jason said.

Her heart kind of juddered in her chest and then skipped a beat or two as she went up the steps to meet him. He watched her come toward him, his eyes never leaving her face.

For a moment, they just stood there a foot apart, staring at each other.

He broke the spell. "Come on in..." And he turned and led her into the house. She followed him across the living area into the open kitchen. From there, they went through a door on the back wall and directly into a barn with bright industrial-style lamps overhead.

They descended the five steps to ground level, where sawdust was thick on the floor. There were rough tables of varying heights and tools everywhere—on the shelves that lined walls and also hanging from hooks. She looked around at tree stumps of different sizes and admired a gorgeous five-foot carving of a rearing dragon and another of an eagle taking flight.

"Still working on those two," he said, noting the direction of her gaze.

He picked up a remote from a workbench, pushed a button and the garage-style door on the opposite wall rumbled up onto a grassy space. It was still light out. About twenty yards away a barbed-wire fence stretched away in both directions. In the pasture beyond, cattle grazed.

"Now the weather's getting better and daylight lasts longer, I'll be doing more work outside," he explained. Then he sent the door rolling down again. Dropping the remote back onto the bench, he turned toward another door to the right. "This way..."

Beyond that door were finished carvings, a lot of them.

"I carve on-site for people at times, and I take commissions to carve what the buyer wants," he said. "But whenever I get the chance, I carve whatever I see waiting in the wood."

"They are beautiful, Jason." And they were. She admired a giant owl and a couple of frisky-looking bear cubs.

He gestured to the right. "Any of the carvings along that wall are available for the auction. I would also be happy to carve something on request."

"I was thinking it would be nice to let June Copely choose…"

"Works for me. Have her give me a call when she's back in town."

"I will, I…" The words died in her throat as she spotted a red cedar mermaid near the wall to her left, a mermaid who appeared to emerge from the wood, her tail curling around the base of the stump, her long hair trailing down the curves of her bare back—a mermaid wearing Piper's face.

Piper took a slow breath and made herself look at him squarely. "When did you carve that one?" Her voice came out brittle sounding as she gestured toward the mermaid.

His gaze never shifted but stayed locked on her face. Apparently, he didn't have to check where she pointed to know which carving she meant. "That's the one I wanted you to see. I started it after you left the other night and finished it before dawn on Sunday morning."

She went ahead and stated the obvious. "It looks like me…"

He grinned. "You noticed."

"You see me as a mermaid?"

"No. I saw a mermaid in that hunk of wood. And I happened to be thinking about you at the time, picturing your face." He stuck his hands in the pockets of his heavy-duty pants. "Maybe I went too far. Should I have asked you first?"

"No. Of course not. I'm flattered. It's very beautiful, Jason."

"Thank you."

"But…"

He frowned. "Whatever's bothering you, just say it."

"Well, I would appreciate it if you didn't offer it for the auction."

His expression relaxed. "Don't worry. I wasn't planning to. That one's mine. It has…personal significance."

She dragged in another slow, careful breath. "Jason, I…"

"Yeah?"

What was there to say, really? Yes, he'd invited her to see his workshop, but she shouldn't have come. Even considering that June would have wanted her to come—uh-uh.

She should not be here. "I know you were working. I should let you get back to it, so I'm going to go." When he said nothing, she turned for the door that led back into the workshop.

He followed behind her all the way to the front door, where she paused and faced him. "Your work is so good."

"Thank you." His expression gave her nothing.

"I'll have June call you…"

"All right."

"Great. Good night, then."

He nodded.

She turned and got out of there.

Chapter Three

Jason watched her drive away.

She'd seemed pretty eager to leave.

He didn't get it. He wanted to be with her. And when he looked in her eyes, he saw that she wanted to get closer to him, too. Was that just wishful thinking and an overactive imagination on his part?

Maybe.

But the fact remained that he wasn't ready to give up on her.

The next day was Thursday. And thanks to their conversation at Arlington's Friday night, Jason knew where to find her on Thursday at lunchtime.

"Jason!" Mona McBride greeted him with a big smile. Mona, her husband, Henry, and their daughter, Sadie, owned the diner jointly. As of last December, Sadie was also the fiancée of Jason's second cousin, Ty Bravo.

"Hey, Mona!" Jason gave her a wave and hung his hat on the tree by the door. The place was packed.

Mona said, "It might be a few minutes…"

"Not a problem." He'd spotted Piper seated alone at a deuce in the back corner near the swinging doors to the kitchen. "You know what, Mona? I'll just go say hi to Piper Wallace, maybe join her if she doesn't mind."

"All right, then. Be with you in a flash." Mona bustled off to take an order.

He headed on back to join his favorite librarian, who had her nose in a book and seemed oblivious to the noise and bustle around her. "Is this seat taken?" he asked when he reached the empty seat across from her.

She glanced up to grant him one of those looks—the ones she'd perfected from years at the library. This particular look said, *You are skating on very thin ice, young man.* "Make yourself comfortable," she said, heavy on the irony.

"'Preciate it, Piper. I was worried I might never get a seat."

That brought a knowing grin from her. "Oh, I'll bet you were."

Mona appeared. She offered him a menu. When he shook his head, she turned to Piper. "What'll you have?"

Piper closed her book and slipped it, spine down, between her purse and the wall. "Avocado BLT, wheat toast, with cucumber salad and iced tea."

"Done," replied Mona. "Jason, do you need a minute?"

"No. That sounds good. Give me the same, but I'll have fries with the sandwich."

"You got it." Mona marched off.

Once it was just the two of them again, he leaned forward. "Tell me you've changed your mind about going out with me."

She didn't reply, only gazed at him steadily.

Hey. It wasn't a no. He leaned even closer and whispered, "Piper. I like you. I want to spend more time with you."

She looked at him solemnly for several seconds. "Jason…" She said his name slowly. Thoughtfully. And then nothing.

He waited. That went on for a while—the two of them, just sitting there staring at each other, with all the noise and bustle of the busy restaurant going on around them.

Then Zeb, the dishwasher, who also helped out wherever he was needed, came hurrying over with Jason's place setting and two iced teas.

Piper gave Zeb a smile and waited for him to go before leaning across the table and admitting, "All right. I admit I've been thinking about you, too."

Jason quelled a giant grin. "Did you just give me a yes?"

She hesitated. That couldn't be good. And then she said very quietly, "I would be open to friendship."

Friend-zoned? Not what he'd hoped for. Not by a long shot. "Any chance of more?"

"Jason, it wouldn't be wise."

"Who cares?" He kept his voice low with effort, so that none of what they said would escape the confines of their booth. "I want you. I really do get the feeling that you want me. I can't stop thinking about last Friday night."

She started to speak. "I…"

Their food came. Mona set the plates down with a flourish. "What else can I get you two?"

"This is great," he replied.

Piper said, "It looks perfect, thank you." As soon as Mona left them alone again, Piper whispered for his ears alone, "I like you, too. And Friday night was…" She seemed at a loss for the right words.

He suggested, "Life-changing? World-shaking? Like

nothing that has ever happened before in the history of time and space?"

She laughed and suddenly he was the happiest guy alive. And then she tried to be serious. "Yes. It was so good. But it's over now and I meant what I said. Being more than friends won't work for me."

Being just friends didn't work for *him*.

He sent a quick glance around the diner. Every booth was full and so were all the classic bolt-down stainless steel stools with the green pleather seats that lined the long counter. The noise level was high enough that they could make their own private world in the corner booth.

"What are you afraid of?" he dared to ask.

She sat back from him. "Jason, I didn't say I was afraid." He kept his big mouth shut that time and was rewarded with, "I've had two serious relationships. Neither worked out. I have no interest in trying again."

"Give me a chance to change your mind."

She shook her head, ate a bite of her sandwich and set it down. "I don't think so…"

Again, she hadn't given him a real no. "So, then. You've had two serious relationships. I've had three."

Piper tipped her head to the side and made a thoughtful sound. "As I recall, you used to come into the library to study with Jennifer Rosario when you two were in high school…"

"That's right. Remember that time you caught us kissing in the US history section?"

"I do remember." She sipped her tea and added with a grin, "You two weren't the only ones."

He ate a French fry. "Jenny was so embarrassed. She worried that you would think less of her."

"I didn't. I always liked Jennifer."

He nodded. "Everybody liked Jenny. She used to make friendship bracelets, the ones with the beads strung on colored embroidery floss. She gave them out to everyone because she was everybody's friend."

"Didn't she move away?"

"Yeah. She and I broke up senior year. She moved to Cody, met another guy and got married. But back in high school, I really thought it was true love with Jenny. I told her so. I swore that I would love her forever."

"Did she say it back?"

"Yes—but it didn't work out."

Piper seemed to be studying him.

He went on, "After Jenny, I decided I needed to wait, to be certain, before ever saying those three words again."

Piper asked, "And since then?"

"I've had two more serious girlfriends since Jenny. I never said the words, though. It never felt right."

Piper seemed thoughtful. "I said the words to my college boyfriend." Her eyes were far away, focused on another place, another time. "And to Walter. I still feel guilty about that."

"About saying I love you to your husband?"

"No. About marrying Walter in the first place. He made me feel...safe. Too safe, really."

"You're saying he was the wrong guy for you?"

"I don't think there is a guy for me. I think I'm one of those people who's just happier on her own."

"There's someone out there for everyone, Piper."

"Jason, you are entitled to your opinion."

He studied the delicate shape of her face for a long, appreciative moment before asking, "What about if we try friends with benefits?"

"No. I did mean what I just said. The whole relationship thing is not for me."

"Friends with benefits isn't a relationship."

"Maybe not. But it's close enough that I don't want to go there. Honestly, I don't know what my problem is. Maybe I'm somehow doing relationships wrong. Or maybe it's that I grew up with my mom for my role model—and she never had any desire to get married and settle down. For those first nine years, when we lived on the road, traveling around the country to art fairs where Mom sold her paintings, we made our own rules—and that's why I think, somehow, I'm missing the couple gene. Or whatever it is that makes people want to find the 'one' to spend forever with. I'm happy being single and I don't need a husband or a lover or any other kind of special relationship with a man to make my life work."

He focused on the last of his sandwich as he decided how to respond. Finally he said, "So, then. Friends, and that's all?"

"That's right. Jason, I do like being with you. I like talking to you."

"And I like doing those things with you." *And I would love to do a lot of other things with you*, he thought but had the good sense not to say.

"So, then," she replied in a brisk tone, "if you want to be friends, I'm in. But I will completely understand if you say no." She poked at a cucumber with her fork. "I mean, it doesn't sound all that exciting for you."

She was so wrong. It sounded just great to him. Simply getting her to agree to see him again—as friends, if that was all she was ready for—would constitute a step in the right direction.

The right direction for what?

Hadn't she made it painfully clear that friendship was as far as the two of them could go together? And could he settle for that in the long run?

Doubtful. There was just something about her. Since last Friday night, this thing with her had become more than a crush for him.

He was half in love with her. And that scared him—because she really did seem determined not to let him get too close.

He pushed his plate away, dug in his pocket and laid enough bills on the table to cover both of their meals and a decent tip.

She was watching him closely. "What'd I do wrong?" she asked softly.

"Not a damn thing."

"But…?"

He eased his napkin in at the side of his plate. "I've been pushing for any way to get closer to you. But you're right. I'm not sure that being 'just friends' with you is going to work for me. I need a little time to think it over."

"Oh. Well, of course. I understand…"

He was about to get up and get out when he remembered the broken condom. "Listen." He leaned in and kept his voice very low. "I meant what I said the other night. Piper, I *will* need to know if you're pregnant."

She scoffed. "I told you that there is no way I could be."

"I remember what you said. And I'll still need to know for sure."

"All right. Let me, uh, check the calendar?"

"Sure."

She took her phone and poked at the screen a few times. "Okay, so my period is due in ten days, on May fifth, and—"

"Wait. That can't be right. Last Friday night you said your period had *just* ended."

She shot him a cool glance and whispered, "Stop. Really. I am not pregnant—but yes, you have a point. *Just* is a relative word. I meant recently, but looking at the calendar now, I see that it wasn't as *recently* as I implied on Friday night."

"Bottom line, the chances are greater than you thought that you could be pregnant and—"

"Jason, I really had no idea you were such an expert on a woman's cycle." Was she making a joke?

Because this was not funny in the least. He explained, "Back in high school, Jenny was more than a week late once. It was a false alarm, but at the time, I got real interested in just how likely it was that we were going to be having a baby."

Beneath those sweet freckles, her pale cheeks flushed red. "I'm sorry to make light of something that must have been scary."

"Yes, it was scary. We were seventeen and not in any way prepared for parenthood."

"Listen." She spoke gently now. "How about this? If my period doesn't come right on time, I'll take a home test the next day."

"That'll work. You still have my number?"

"Yes. I have that card you gave me."

"And you'll call me—either way."

"Yes, Jason. Of course I will."

Piper tried not to anticipate hearing from Jason again. But she did.

And when he failed to call, she felt let down. It was totally unreasonable of her to feel that way. He'd chased her until he tired of her unwillingness to give him a chance. She couldn't blame him for giving up and leaving her alone.

Really, it was for the best. They had too much chemistry to go the friends-only route. And getting something romantic going with him would be such a bad idea. As soon as her period made its appearance, she would call him and tell him he had nothing to worry about. And that would be it.

But then the day came.

And her period didn't.

She felt like a fool. She never should have agreed to call him if her period was a single day late. After all, she was forty years old. There were a number of reasons her period wouldn't necessarily appear like clockwork every time. She should have insisted on waiting at least a week more before having to contact him.

But she'd named the terms of this agreement and she would stick by them. Tomorrow morning, she would take a home test and then call him to let him know that the test was negative.

So why was she so…on edge about the whole thing?

She felt like a teenager all over again—and not in a good way.

All day long, she kept popping into the restroom just to check for spotting. It was nerve-racking to be so obsessed with a biological function.

She got home at six. Still no period. By eight in the evening, she couldn't stand it anymore. She needed to talk to someone trustworthy, so she gave her mom a call.

Emmaline answered on the second ring. "Hello, my love. How are you?"

"Are you working?" Her mom often painted late into the night.

"Nope. I'm all yours. Talk to me, Piper."

So she went ahead and put it right out there. "My period's late—well, not really late. But it's due today and it hasn't come yet."

As usual, her mom cut right to the point. "Are you saying you have reason to believe you might be pregnant?"

"I suppose it's possible," she grudgingly confessed. "Barely. It was one night last month. I'm not on any kind of birth control."

"But you did use a condom…"

"Yes, of course. We used condoms and one of them broke."

"I see—and one night with whom?"

"You're so nosy, Mom."

"Oh, yes I am." She could hear the shrug in Emmaline's voice. "I am the nosiest."

"Fine. I spent a night with Jason Bravo."

"Wow. I adore Jason."

"Yes, Mom. You've mentioned that."

"He's smart, sensitive and really good with his hands— not to mention he can make beautiful things with a big hunk of wood and a chain saw. Allow me to congratulate you on your excellent taste in one-night stands. I'm so proud of you."

Piper couldn't help but smile. "I knew you would be."

"And, sweetheart, you've always said you wanted children."

"I have, yes. I *do* want a child. I'd just reconciled myself to the fact that it wasn't going to happen."

"So, then, one way or another, it's all good. If you're not pregnant, life goes on as planned. If you are, everything changes and isn't that fabulous?"

"You make it all sound so simple."

"It is simple. Huge. But simple."

When they said good-night twenty minutes later, Piper felt pretty good about everything.

The good feeling didn't last, though. She went to bed and couldn't sleep. At 3:00 a.m., she realized that she needed to get to a pharmacy as soon as one opened and buy herself a home test.

Six hours later, a few minutes after she'd called the library to say she was taking a family day, the doorbell rang.

Her mom, in paint-spattered skinny pants, a big white shirt and polka-dot sneakers, her curly, white-streaked red hair tied back pirate-style with a green satin scarf, greeted her with, "Hello, my love. You look exhausted. Rough night?"

"You could say that."

"It's the not knowing, right? You need to find out."

"I do, yes."

"And that's why I made a quick trip to the State Street Pharmacy." Cheeks dimpling with a proud smile, Emmaline held up the white bag with the drugstore logo on it. "Ten home tests."

Piper blinked at the bag. "Do I need ten?"

"It seemed like a nice, even number—plus, if you doubt the results, you can wait a few days and take another. And another. Until you're satisfied that you are, or you aren't."

"Get in here." Piper grabbed her hand, yanked her inside and hugged her good and tight.

"Let's go upstairs and get started," Emmaline said briskly when Piper finally released her.

"I don't know…"

Her mom frowned. "What? Just come out with it."

"Mom, I love you harder than ever for showing up this morning with just what I needed, but some things I have to do on my own."

Emmaline took Piper's hand and put the bag in it. "You want me to leave?"

"No, I don't."

"How about if I hang out down here while you pee on one of those sticks in the privacy of your en suite?"

"Would you?"

"Of course. You go on up. I'll be right here when you need me."

An hour later, Piper dropped to the little teak stool in the corner of her bathroom and put her head in her hands. By then, three used test sticks littered the counter between the twin sinks.

"I do not believe that this could have happened," Piper moaned into her hands. "A baby…"

I am having Jason Bravo's baby.

"It's okay," she whispered to the bathroom floor. "It's more than okay. I've always wanted a baby…"

It was true. Because the reality of the life inside her? That part was nothing short of astounding. It was so wonderful it felt like it couldn't be real. And that had her feeling slightly queasy.

She picked up one of the used sticks and stared at the

result window. *Pregnant.* Her breath caught again at the enormity of that one word.

A baby. She was going to be a mom.

Doing it alone? Not a problem. It was a giant shock right now, true, but underneath the astonishment, she could already feel joy welling.

A baby.

She'd never realized how much she wanted a child.

Until now. Until it was happening.

A baby, a little person to help grow up. They would be a family of two—well, three, counting her mom.

Emmaline chose that moment to tap on the bathroom door. "Piper? How are you doing in there?"

Tossing the stick back on the counter, Piper put her head in her hands again. Her stomach churned with equal parts shock and joy.

There was another light tap on the door. "It's been over an hour. Just say you're all right, my love."

Swallowing down a big lump of combined terror and excitement, Piper got up, went over there and swung the door wide. "Come on in."

Her mom saw the sticks. "You took three? You're supposed to wait a week between tests for the pregnancy hormones to build up again. Did you read the instructions?"

"I did, yes. And you're right. But after the first one, I was a bit stunned. I kept thinking I had to be sure, somehow. So I took another one. And then another. And guess what? They all three came out the same."

Emmaline picked one up, peered in the little window and let out a whoop of delight. "This one's positive!"

"Exactly."

"So all three...?"

"Yeah, Mom. It looks like I'm pregnant. It really does."

Emmaline beamed at Piper and held out her arms. "Come on, now. Give this future grandma the sugar!"

Piper swayed forward.

Emmaline gathered her close and kissed the side of her head. "This is wonderful news. Wonderful!"

Piper held on tight and breathed in Emmaline's familiar scents of lemony shampoo and mint from the artist's soap she used to wash off stubborn ink and paint. "I can't believe this is happening," she whispered raggedly. "I just can't…"

Her mom took her by the shoulders and looked straight in her eyes. "What? Talk to me. You're not happy?"

Piper blinked in surprise at the question. "Yes! I'm happy. Very. But I'm also kind of wondering if this is all some crazy dream. For years, I've been telling myself that the chance to have a child has passed me by…"

Emmaline took both her hands. "Let's go downstairs. I'll brew you some of that masala chai you love, and you can relax. Catch your breath."

Piper nodded. "Chai. Yes. All right."

Downstairs, Piper took a stool at the island as her mother got busy with the electric kettle. When the tea was ready, they carried their mugs to the living area and sat on the sofa together.

Emmaline got right to the hard part. "How much does Jason know?"

"Well, he was there when the condom broke, so pretty much everything. Except that three home tests just came out positive." She took a careful sip of the hot chai.

"He's young."

"Yes, Mom. He is. Too young for me."

"I didn't say that."

"That doesn't make it any less true."

"Wait. Think again. Look at it this way. It's a fact that women tend to outlive their men. But probably not if the woman is at least a decade older. And ageism is a crock anyway. As long as two people are both functioning adults, more power to them. Jason is a good man. He's very grounded. And he's superhot, too."

Piper tried not to groan. "Mom. Please."

Smiling way too sweetly, Emmaline shrugged. "I'm only trying to make you see that Jason just might make a good match for you."

"No. Wrong. I don't need a good match. I don't even want one. I'm perfectly happy to raise my baby on my own, the same way you did."

"Of course you are, but that doesn't mean you wouldn't be happier with the right man beside you."

"I don't get it. What's up with you? Where is this coming from?"

"You're not me, my love. You really do want to connect."

"As though you don't?"

Her mom smiled so sweetly. "Of course I do."

"You're making zero sense. You have to know that."

"What I'm trying to say is that *you* want a family."

"I have a family."

"You know what I mean. A family that includes a man you can count on, one you adore."

"I can count on myself, my friends—and on you, Mom. I am fully self-supporting. There's nothing a man can give me that I don't already have."

Emmaline smirked. "Well, there's at least one thing that springs instantly to mind."

Piper groaned. "I can't believe you went there."

"Sorry, I couldn't resist." Emmaline put on her sweetest expression. "And back to the main point. We came home to stay when you were nine years old because you wanted friends your age and you wanted a settled-down life in this charming hometown of ours. Don't lie to yourself. You also want a partner in this settled-down life."

"I had a partner. He died."

Emmaline scoffed. "We both know that Walter was a terrible disappointment to you."

Piper gaped. "Wait a minute. I thought you liked Walter!"

"He was a perfectly nice man, but not the man for you. Nothing about your marriage was what a marriage is supposed to be—and don't pretend you don't know what I'm talking about. There was no spark, no passion. You were only going through the motions. And I get it. After Brandon, you—"

"Mom. Please can we *not* talk about Brandon McAdams?"

"Fine. My point is, don't kid yourself. You are not me. You don't want to be a single mom and you *do* want the right man. Yes, you've been disappointed. Twice. But please don't give up now."

Piper wished she might be magically transported to anywhere but here—someplace she wouldn't have to think about the things that had just come out of her mother's mouth. "You never said a word about all this before."

"You weren't pregnant before. Now you need to make important decisions and you should be honest with yourself and with Jason when you do. Piper, you're going to have to tell him."

"Of course I'm going to tell him. Give me a little credit, will you?"

"*When* are you going to tell him?"

"As it happens, I promised I would reach out to him by today. And I will."

"Good. And you should also respond to the request you got from your father. How long has it been since he got in touch with you?"

Piper gulped. "Which time?"

"He's tried to contact you twice?" Emmaline wore a disbelieving frown. At Piper's nod, she asked. "How recently?"

"A few weeks." Piper glared down into her nearly empty mug and wondered when her mother would get off her case. "I never should have let you talk me into signing up with 23andMe in the first place."

"Of course you should have. And you did. And after all these years, you've found your father. He's reached out to you twice now. Reach back."

"It's too late."

"As long as you're both still breathing, it's never too late. And I just don't get it. You know it's not his fault that I had no idea where to find him."

"Of course I know that."

"And you wanted desperately to know all about him when you were younger."

"Well, I'm over it now."

Emmaline pinned her with a hard glare for an endless string of edgy seconds before finally throwing up her hands. "I don't believe you. But be that as it may, even if *you're* over wanting to contact the man who contributed half your DNA, how can you deprive your baby of a grandfather?"

Piper had no comeback for that one. "Okay, Mom. I know you're right—but come on. One huge and intimidating task at a time, okay?"

Emmaline sighed. "Of course." Her tone was conciliatory now. "And I apologize for piling more on your already full plate. Sometimes I do get a bit carried away."

"Yes, you do. But in this case, you're not wrong," Piper said grudgingly.

Emmaline hooked an arm around her and kissed her on the forehead. "More chai?"

"No. I really should call Jason. I guess."

"Could you be more ambivalent?"

She shrugged and answered honestly. "Probably not."

With a low, wry chuckle and a shake of her curly head of hair, Emmaline picked up their empty mugs and carried them to the sink. Piper trailed after her. She felt lost, cast adrift, all her usual calm confidence blown to bits by that one word in three test stick windows.

Her mother put the mugs in the sink and turned to her. "Shall I stay?"

"Thank you. For everything. But no. Reaching out to Jason is another one of those things I need to do on my own."

Emmaline touched her cheek. "You're brave and strong and good." She guided a straight swatch of hair behind Piper's ear. "Beautiful, too."

Piper almost smiled. "Brave? I'm not so sure. But as for the rest of it, I take after my mother." They both reached out for one last hug and then Piper followed her mom to the door.

"Call me," Emmaline commanded. "Whatever you need."

"Thanks, Mom. You're a champion."

Emmaline reached for the doorknob just as somebody knocked. She pulled it wide.

It was Jason, in a crisp Western shirt and dark-wash jeans. He swiped his white hat off his head. "Emmaline. Hello." He spotted Piper behind her mom. She felt an actual *zap*, like an electric shock, as their eyes met.

"Hello, Jason," said Emmaline. "Have we got some news for you…"

Chapter Four

Two minutes later, Emmaline had driven off, leaving Jason and Piper facing each other in her open doorway. He wasn't sure how to proceed here.

"Come in." She gestured him forward into her small entryway and then indicated the coatrack in the corner. "You can hang your hat there." He hooked the hat on a peg and followed her into the great room, which had a fireplace on one wall, light-colored furniture and a quartz-topped island that marked off the kitchen area. "Have a seat." She swept out a hand toward the sofa. "Can I get you—"

"I'm good, thanks." He eased around the wood-topped, iron-framed coffee table and sat.

She perched on the chair across from him. More awkwardness followed. He wasn't sure what to say. She sat there so straight and careful, like she had no more idea where to start with this than he did.

He drank in the sight of her, in old jeans, black Keds and a sage-green T-shirt with Make America Read Again printed just above the soft curves of her breasts. Her face was scrubbed clean of makeup. Her hair, loose and messy, trailed over her shoulders.

Finally, he said, "I, uh, guess I got a little impatient. I should have waited for your call."

She waved a hand. "It's okay. Really. I was about to call *you*."

"Yeah?" That made him smile.

She nodded. "I took a home test this morning—well, three, actually."

Now he sat forward. "And?"

She sucked in a big breath and pushed the words out fast. "I'm pregnant, Jason…" For a moment, the words made no sense. He felt light-headed. She kept on talking. "I mean, I'm completely, ridiculously surprised about this. I keep wondering, how did this happen? I honestly never in a million years…" She kind of ran out of steam about then.

"Piper."

"What?"

And he was on his feet, circling the coffee table, pulling her out of her chair and up into his arms. Miraculously, she didn't object. Instead, with a long sigh, she sagged against him.

He cradled her close and whispered, "We're having a baby."

She stiffened in his hold. "Wait." Her slim hands came up to push at his chest as she craned her head back to meet his eyes. "No…"

He didn't get it. "No, what?"

"Jason, *I'm* having a baby."

Okay, fine. Yeah, *she* was the one having the baby. But he'd helped—and he intended to continue doing so. Unless… "Are you saying you were with someone else?"

A strangled laugh escaped her. "No! Just you. Only you."

He bit the inside of his lip to keep from grinning in relief. But then his urge to smile over this situation vanished. Because if there wasn't some other guy in this equation, then what was she getting at here? "I understand that for the next eight and a half months or so, you'll have to do all the work in this deal. But still, the baby is mine, so we're *both* going to be parents."

She blinked. "Oh! Well, I get that you might feel responsible."

"I am responsible, every bit as much as you are."

"Yes, but I'm just saying, I promise, you don't have to be involved at all."

As if. "Stop it, Piper. Of course I will be involved in raising our baby. This is a lifetime partnership we're talking about here."

Two frown lines appeared between those jade green eyes. "What does that even mean?"

"It means that no matter what happens between you and me, we will always be the parents of this child—both of us."

She pushed harder at his chest. "Please let me go." He dropped his arms to his sides and went back to the sofa. She sat down again, too. "Now," she said. "Let's just... slow down a little here."

"All right."

"I mean, first of all, we don't want to get ahead of ourselves. Maybe I got a false positive today..."

"Three times?"

"I'm just saying that we can't make assumptions or jump to conclusions. Please."

"How many more tests do you plan on taking?"

"Well, I was thinking I would make an appointment with my doctor, get a test there, just to be sure. Maybe next week?"

"Fair enough. I'll go with you."

"Jason, I..." She seemed to run out of words.

He leaned in and braced his elbows on his spread knees. "Be straight with me. Do you honestly have any doubt that you're pregnant?"

She swallowed. Hard. "No. No, I don't. But that doesn't mean we shouldn't be absolutely sure. And really, it's not as if we know each other all that well. We should arrange for a paternity test."

"If I'm the only one you've been with, then I don't see how a paternity test is necessary."

"Jason, I just think that you need to know. For certain."

"I do know for certain." When she scoffed at that, he added, "You're not a liar, Piper. Maybe I don't know you that well on some levels. But I *have* known you for fourteen years. And I know that you are honest. Everyone in town knows that about you. No way you would tell a man you're having his child if you weren't."

She looked so damn miserable. "I just... I guess I assumed you wouldn't be that eager to take on the endless responsibilities of being a father."

"Well, you assumed wrong."

She folded her hands together and stuck them between her knees. "I'm sorry. This is a lot, you know—and I've insulted you, haven't I?"

"I'll live. And I get it. Look, we both just found out. It's a shock for me, too." He wanted to comfort her, but he knew better than to try that again at this point. "Do you want me to go?"

She slid him a wary glance and answered carefully, "I would appreciate a little time to...process all this."

"All right." He wanted to ask for her number again but decided against it. She'd refused to give it to him more than once already—and if she failed to reach out, she wouldn't be all that hard to track down. He got to his feet.

She rose, too. "You have your phone with you?"

"Out in my truck, yeah."

"Hold on just a minute?"

"Sure." He waited as she went to the kitchen area and got her cell off the back counter. "I do still have your card," she said, as though to reassure him that she hadn't tossed it in the trash. "But I haven't entered your number yet."

"No problem." He rattled it off.

She typed it into her phone. "Okay. I have you in my contacts. I'll just send you a quick text." Her thumbs flew over the keys. "There. So now you can reach me anytime you, uh, need to."

It lightened his mood a little, that this time she'd given him the number without his even asking. "'Preciate that."

"No problem." She looked at him expectantly.

It took him a moment to realize she was hoping he would go. He headed for the foyer.

"I'll make the appointment with my doctor today," she said, "and text you to let you know where and when."

"Thank you." He grabbed his hat and went out the door.

Once in his truck, he took his phone from the console. She'd texted, It's me, Piper.

He smiled as he put her in his contacts. She was the strangest bundle of contradictions. Forty years old, if he'd done the math correctly, smart and capable and well educated. The kind of person who would always keep her head in a crisis and know what to do in any emergency. At the same time, as a woman, she was wary as a high school virgin at a keg party.

His amusement lasted until he'd rounded the corner

onto the next street. About then, he had to pull to the shoulder, put it in Park and take a few slow, deep breaths.

A baby.

Piper Wallace was having his baby.

He'd been crystal clear that he needed to know if it turned out she was pregnant. But had he actually believed it would happen?

No.

He gripped the wheel to keep his hands from shaking as he decided that he really needed someone to talk to.

A few minutes later, he parked around the corner from Cash Enterprises on Main Street, got out his phone again and texted his second cousin Tyler Ross Bravo. You busy? I'm around the corner from your office.

A minute later, Ty replied, Come on in.

Ty and his dad—the "Cash" of Cash Enterprises—ran the business together. They were mostly in property and land deals.

Ramona Teague, their longtime secretary and receptionist, smiled at Jason when he walked in the door. "Go right on through." She tipped her head toward Ty's office.

Jason tapped on Ty's door. From the other side, his cousin called, "It's open."

When Jason pushed the door wide, Ty was getting up from behind his big desk. They greeted each other with a quick hug and some backslapping. Then Ty gestured toward the sitting area across the room. They got comfortable there.

"Coffee? Something stronger?"

"No. I just need advice."

Ty chuckled. "And you came to me for that?" Divorced from his first wife, Ty had two kids and a fiancée, Sadie

McBride. For a year or two after his divorce, Ty had run a little wild, hooking up with a different woman just about every weekend. But those days were over now. He and Sadie were living together, and Ty was the happiest he'd ever been.

"Yeah, well." Jason was nodding. "You'll be an old married man before you know it. These days, you're downright dependable. I figure you're the one to give me solid feedback when I need it."

"Damn. You make me sound dead boring." Ty was grinning. He shrugged. "Probably because I am. And I like it that way. I would marry Sadie tomorrow, but she wants a summer wedding out at the Rising Sun." The Rising Sun had been in the Bravo family for several generations. It was jointly owned by three Bravo cousins—Ty's dad, Jason's dad and Zach Bravo, who lived on the ranch and ran the Rising Sun Cattle Company. "So then," said Ty. "What's going on?"

Jason thought of Piper. How reserved she could be. She wouldn't want her business on the street. Plus, it was way too soon to tell anyone that she was pregnant. Still, he had to talk to someone and he trusted Ty to keep a confidence. "This conversation has to stay between the two of us."

"As long as it's got nothing to do with Sadie or my kids, you got it. I'm a vault." Ty stretched out an arm along the back of the sofa.

Jason got to the point. "Piper Wallace is pregnant—and it's mine."

His cousin leaned forward, cleared his throat and sat back again. "Well."

Jason groaned. "That's it? That's all you got?"

Ty slanted him a wary glance. "I suppose I need to

admit up front that I already knew something was going on with you and Piper."

Jason did not like the sound of that. "How?"

"You were seen with her at Arlington's a while back. And then Sadie told me that her mom told her that you and Piper had lunch together at Henry's about a week and a half ago."

"You're saying everybody's talking about us?" Piper wouldn't like that. And if she didn't like it, Jason didn't, either.

"No. Everybody is *not* talking about you. It's just that they're bound to notice that you and Piper have been hanging out together. I mean, from what I've heard, she hasn't been out with anyone since her husband died. So it's news that she's seen around town with you, who just happens to be quite a bit younger than she is."

"So what?"

"No judgment—but face it. Nobody would have picked you as a match for the hot librarian."

Jason leveled his coldest stare on his cousin. "Are you *trying* to piss me off?"

Ty put up both hands. "Hold your fire, man. No offense. Lighten up a little."

"Yeah, well, show some respect."

"Got it."

Jason rose, went to the window and looked out at Main Street. A couple of cowhands, a skinny long-haired guy in a ball cap and a woman with a take-out bag from the Stagecoach Grill went by. Still staring out the window, he laid it right out there. "I have a thing for her, okay? I always have. When I was kid, it was a crush, something I never thought would be more than my own secret fantasy. But now, since that night she and I got together at Arlington's, it's turned into something more. I don't care if she's older. I just don't." He turned and faced his cousin. "I care about *her*."

Ty got up and joined him at the window. "You want my take?"

"That's what I'm here for."

"All right, then. The way I see it, more power to you. Yeah, she's a little older than you, but… Hey, man. We've all seen her ass." As Jason considered popping him a good one, Tyler stepped back and put his hands up again. "Honestly, cousin, I mean that in a way of complete respect and admiration. The truth is, I get it. There really is something about her. Come on. You're not the only one who ever had a crush on her."

"Are you telling me that *you*—"

"I'm just saying she made all of us willing to go the library back in the day."

"You are not helping," Jason grumbled. "And right now, I have no clue why I came to you for advice."

Ty laughed out loud then. "Sorry. I never could resist yanking your chain. And we both know I'm no expert on women, let alone on love. Took me way too many years to get it right with Sadie."

"But you did," Jason said. "You finally did. I admire that you worked it out, that you found a way to get what matters. I honestly do."

Ty clapped him on the shoulder. "What can I tell you? Except to say, figure out what you really want, get out of your own damn way and go for it. If Piper's the one for you, show her, make sure she knows it. I mean, no, you can't make a woman love you. But you can take a chance. You can put yourself out there. You can show her who you really are and prove to her that you're there for her, that she can count on you to step up for her no matter what goes down."

Jason let all that sink in for a minute. "Damn. That's really good advice."

Ty gave him a slow smile. "Glad I could help."

Jason did want to find a way to get closer to Piper—and not only as her baby daddy. Too bad he had no idea how to make that happen. After all, aside from the night they met up at Arlington's, she'd resisted every attempt he'd made so far. He returned to the Double-K that day with no clear idea of what his next move should be.

That night, he ate at the main house with the family. It was him, his mom, his dad and Joe. His sister, Sarah Ellen, was in Ohio, a student at Ohio State. She'd found a good-paying summer job there, so she wouldn't be home much this year except maybe for Christmas, or whenever she could steal a few days for a visit.

He loaded up his plate and dug in. The food, slow-cooker chicken, melted off the bone. And he'd always liked his mom's garlic mashed potatoes.

It was relaxing, listening to the murmur of voices around the table. Being with the family helped to take his mind off the phone in his shirt pocket that hadn't rung once all day.

He thought of the carving he was working on, a ten-foot-tall grizzly bear commissioned by a guy who owned a dude ranch in Jackson Hole. When it came to chain saw art, bears were real moneymakers.

"You're quiet, Jay," said his mom. Meggie May Kane Bravo was like that, observant. Attentive to him, to his siblings and his dad. And she could work circles around all of them. The Double-K had come down to her through her father. "Everything okay?" she asked.

"It's all good, Mom," he lied. "Pass me the chicken, please?"

She gave him that look, the one that said she knew he had something on his mind. But she didn't press. She handed him the platter and he helped himself to more.

He'd just picked up his fork again when his phone buzzed. As a rule, phones were forbidden at the dinner table.

Too bad. This was a special situation—or so he hoped. He didn't go so far as to check to see who'd texted him while he was sitting right there at the table. He might be a grown man, but in Meggie Bravo's house, even grown men lived by her rules.

Instead, he sent her an apologetic glance and said, "Sorry, Mom. Excuse me, I need to check this."

To his left, his dad was hiding a smile.

His brother muttered out of the side of his mouth, "We got a damn rule-breaker around here..."

Meggie held Jason's gaze for a moment. "All right," she said at last in a tone of great patience.

He tucked his napkin in at the side of his plate and pushed back his chair. Out on the front porch, he pulled the phone from his pocket and smiled when he saw he had a text from Piper.

I have an appointment with my doctor on Thursday at four in the afternoon.

He called her.

She answered on the second ring. "Hello, Jason."

"Hey. Just got your text. How about if I pick you up and we go together?"

"Better not. I'll be leaving from the library. And really, there's no need for you to be at the appointment anyway. I'll call you Thursday night—but I won't have the results then. It takes a couple of days for the lab to run the test. We probably won't know until Monday."

He almost let it be, almost agreed that he would wait for her call. But he couldn't quite keep himself from asking, "Are you embarrassed to be seen going to your doctor with me?"

"I…" A soft sigh escaped her. "Jason, I'm sorry. I should be braver. Believe me, I know that, given who raised me." She had it right about that. Emmaline Stokely could not have cared less what fools said behind her back.

"So you're nervous about it, about everybody talking?"

"I am. After all, I'm the director now. People have… expectations of the library director."

"You're good at your job. Your personal life is your own."

"I know, but—"

"Look, Piper. Chances are, they're all going to find out anyway. Might as well just go ahead and do what we need to do. Sneaking around will only make the situation worse. It's not anyone's business but ours and everyone else will just have to get over it."

"You're right. I know it."

"Piper, it's my baby, too." He said it gently, as a reminder. "I really do want to be there with you. I want to be at every doctor's appointment. My cousin Ty missed the ultrasounds for both of his kids. I'm not missing those. And I'm going with you to the birthing classes, to all of it. And when the baby comes, I'll be your coach.

"That's why there's no way around it, people are going to know eventually—that you're having a baby and that your baby is mine."

She said nothing for several seconds. He kept his mouth shut with effort. Finally she chuckled. It was a soft, rueful sound. "You couldn't just be one of those guys who's happy to walk away, now could you?"

"If I was one of those guys, you wouldn't have gone home with me that night."

"Hmm. Fair point."

He said, "You do know the blood test result is highly unlikely to be any different than the home test you took."

"Yes. I know. But it's very early. We don't know what might happen. Something could so easily go wrong and then we'll have gotten everyone talking when no one ever had to know."

"And then you would be, what? Relieved?" He kept his tone neutral, but it took effort.

"No! No, I wouldn't be relieved. I meant what I said that night we were together. I never in a million years expected to get pregnant, but I want this baby, I do. So much." He could hear the yearning in her voice. It did his heart good.

"I want our baby, too. Please let me go with you to the doctor."

Again, she hesitated. But when she did speak, she gave him the answer he needed. "All right. Pick me up at the library Thursday at a quarter to four."

Piper was just about to leave her office Thursday afternoon when the text came through from Jason.

I'm here. Waiting by the circulation desk.

She reminded herself that he was going to be involved and she needed to stop worrying about what people might think.

On my way, she replied.

Shrugging into her lightweight jacket and hooking her purse on her shoulder, she drew herself up to her full five-foot-five-in-practical-pumps and headed for reception.

He was right there waiting, heartbreaker-handsome in a fresh-looking plaid shirt tucked into dark-wash jeans. He had his hat in his hand and his dark hair was wet from a recent shower.

Behind the circulation desk, Marnie Fox, one of the assistants, pushed a stack of children's books across the desk toward the little girl on the other side. "Enjoy," she said.

"Thank you," said the child and gathered the books into her arms.

Marnie turned to Jason and asked way too hopefully, "What can I help you with?"

About then, he spotted Piper. "Thanks," he said to Marnie. "I was waiting for Piper and here she is."

Marnie blinked. "Oh! Well, I see…"

Which was a perfectly normal reaction, Piper reminded herself. And even if it hadn't been, so what? Jason had it right. People would think what people would think. Piper would keep her chin up and do what had to be done, same as always.

Piper nodded at Marnie. "See you tomorrow."

"Have a good night." Marnie waved as Piper and Jason started down the wide hallway to the main entrance.

Piper's doctor, Levi Hayes, was new in town. He'd taken over for old Dr. Crandall, who had finally retired.

Piper checked in with the friendly receptionist. Then she and Jason took a seat in the waiting room with a couple of young moms and three kids who were playing with blocks at a low central table.

One of the women smiled and nodded at her. Piper was pretty sure she was a regular at the library.

Jason leaned close. "Nervous?"

"A little."

"Are you just getting the blood drawn?"

"That's about the size of it. I think there's a brief consultation with Dr. Hayes."

"Want me to go in with you?" His eyes, more gray than blue in the bright waiting room light, seemed full of mischief right then.

"I think I can manage that part on my own."

He didn't push. Apparently, just being there in Dr. Hayes's office with her was enough for him right now. It wasn't as though having blood drawn was an event a prospective father longed to witness.

And really, it was kind of nice having him here. Now that he'd pushed her to live her brand-new pregnancy out in the open, she found that a lot of her nervous tension and worry had dissipated. It was the right way to go.

She touched his hand. He met her eyes.

"Thanks," she said. "For keeping after me until I agreed you could come with me today."

"You're welcome." He leaned closer. "After we're done here, how about getting something to eat? We can go to the Grill or to Arlington's. Or drive up to Sheridan if you'd rather."

He smelled amazing, of soap and something woodsy. *We are doing this out in the open*, she reminded herself.

She was going to be a mom and Jason wanted to be their baby's dad. He intended to be a real dad, the kind who was there for his child. That her baby would have a real dad was a good thing—a wonderful thing, something she'd never had as a child.

"Let's go to the Grill," she said.

"Sounds good to me."

It was only a little past five when Piper and Jason arrived at the Grill.

They got a small table by the big window in front. As they ate, she asked him about himself. He said he'd always wanted to live and work on the Double-K. "It's a good life, a healthy life. You get up early and you work hard and what you have you know you helped to build with your own two hands."

"Did you go away to college?"

"Yeah. I went to Santa Monica College in Southern California. It's a two-year community college. I took mostly art classes and got to spend a lot of time with my grandma Sharilyn. She's my dad's mom. She lives in Los Angeles with her second husband. Hector—the second husband— is a real sweetheart. He's nothing like Grandma Sharilyn's first husband, my dad's father, who was known as Bad Clint."

"So you're saying, your grandfather was as bad as his name implies?"

"According to my dad, he was the worst."

"You never met him?"

"Nope. Bad Clint Bravo died of blood poisoning after being bitten in a bar fight when my dad was fourteen."

"That must have been hard on your dad."

"He doesn't talk a lot about his father, but I think he was mostly relieved when Bad Clint died."

"So then, your grandmother ended up raising your dad alone?"

"No. My dad went to live with my great-grandfather. Then, when my dad grew up, he moved to LA and became a private investigator. My mother went after him there."

"You mean, she went to Los Angeles to find him."

"That's right. The way they both tell it, she finally convinced him they were made for each other. They've been happily married for almost thirty years."

"Well, all right, then. Here's to your mom and dad." She raised her glass of sparkling water.

He tapped it with his.

When they left the restaurant, he asked, "Do you need to get your car at the library?"

"No, I knew you would be picking me up, so I walked to work."

He drove her home. She started to invite him in, but then kept her mouth shut about that. They probably shouldn't get too carried away with this co-parenting thing. It was very early days.

But she did have one point she needed to get his agreement on. Unbuckling her seat belt, she turned toward him in her seat.

His dark eyebrows drew together. "You have that look."

She pulled back a little. "Which look is that?"

"You're about to say something you're not sure I'll go for."

A goofy squeak of laughter escaped her. She shook her head. "How did you guess?"

"So then it's true?"

"You didn't answer my question."

He gave her a one-shouldered shrug. "You didn't answer mine."

She put up both hands. "Fine. It's like this. I don't want to tell anyone about the baby, not for a while yet. It still hardly seems real to me and, well, most people wait to spread the word for at least a couple of months. Usually three months when they're in my situation."

He shot her an oblique sort of glance. "You have a situation?"

"Yes, I do. I brought home some books from the library, and I've been researching online, learning everything I can about pregnancy and childbirth. My age is a factor. It can't be ignored. Being over thirty-five makes me what they call *of advanced maternal age.*"

"Wow. No kidding?" He seemed kind of amused.

But she wasn't joking. "I'm completely serious. In some of my reading, they used the term *geriatric pregnancy.* I can't decide which description is worse, but whatever words you use, this pregnancy is considered high risk." She put a protective palm against her flat belly.

"Piper." He said her name almost tenderly. As she lifted her palm from her stomach, he claimed it.

"What?" she demanded as he rubbed his thumb slowly across the back of her hand. It felt good, that light touch of his. It soothed her. She prompted, "Just say whatever's on your mind."

He looked at her so steadily. "My mom was thirty-five when she had me—and even older when she had Joe and Sarah. A lot of older women have successful pregnancies that result in healthy babies."

She nodded as his thumb continued to brush back and

forth over her skin. She felt so close to him right then, intimate with him in a way she couldn't remember ever being with any man before. Like they were connected somehow, as though they shared a mutual understanding, the kind that made it possible to communicate without using words.

Thoughts of that one night they'd shared filled her head. It wasn't that long ago. But right now, it felt like forever ago. She wanted to sway a little closer to him, lift her face to his. She longed to feel the sweet, hot pressure of his mouth on hers...

Bad idea, she reminded herself.

Carefully, she eased her hand from his hold.

What were they talking about?

Right. He'd said his mother was close to Piper's age when she'd had both of his siblings...

"You make a valid point," she agreed. "I'm in excellent health and I plan to take good care of myself throughout this pregnancy. Dr. Hayes said that as long as I take good care of myself, this pregnancy should be uneventful. But I still think we should wait until I'm through the first trimester before we start telling everyone I'm pregnant."

"I get it. Agreed."

Relief made her smile. "Whew. Thank you."

"Don't thank me yet," he warned, that beautiful smile of his reminding her again of all the foolish things she shouldn't do—like jump into his lap and wrap herself around him or grab his hand and drag him out of the pickup, into her house and straight to her bedroom. But then he added, "I have something I want from you."

Those hot, sexy feelings? So inappropriate. They were supposed to be talking about the important stuff now. And judging from his watchful expression, whatever he wanted from her was probably something she would be reluctant to give.

She gulped. "I'm listening."

He braced one arm on the wheel and the other across the back of her seat. "We need to get to know each other, you and me. We need to start developing a relationship—and please don't give me that look."

"What look?"

"The *no way am I doing that* look. Think about it," he coaxed. "This is not about just you and me anymore."

"Frankly, for the next few months, it *is* about you and me."

"But we need to consider how it's going to work when we finally have to tell my family and your friends and colleagues at the library that you're having a baby and I'm the baby's father."

"It's not rocket science, Jason. We can just, you know, be discreet and play it by ear."

"Be discreet? Piper, I'm going to be there when the baby's born. I'm going to be there for both of you from now on. I'm going to be a hands-on dad. My kid is never going wonder if his dad wanted him—or her."

"I get it, I do. And I think it's admirable of you to step right up like this. I agree that we'll work together. As co-parents. But honestly, we can figure that out as we go. It's not something we have to get overly concerned with right this minute."

"Maybe not when it comes to your mom."

"What does my mom have to do with it?"

"Your mom already knows about the baby. She and I get along great. As of now, she's the only one who isn't going to get a big shock when we finally let everyone else know what's going on." Suddenly, his gaze slid away. "And that reminds me. You should know that I told my cousin Ty about the baby."

It took effort, but she managed to ask quietly, "You told Ty Bravo that I'm pregnant with your baby?"

"I did, yeah. I needed a little advice, okay? And you don't have to worry. Ty's not going to go spreading the news all over town. He'll keep his mouth shut."

"Well, I hope so—and honestly, I just don't get it. Why would you tell your cousin?"

A muscle twitched in his sculpted jaw. "Come on, Piper. *You* told your mom."

"Okay, whatever." She blew out a hard breath. "So... you're saying you've changed your mind and you want to tell everybody about the baby right away?"

"No, that's not what I'm saying."

"Then, what?"

"I'm thinking, wouldn't it be better if it doesn't come out of the blue? Wouldn't it be better if it was more than a one-night stand and a broken condom?"

"Jason, it is what it is."

"I know, but it *could* be more. And why shouldn't it be more? If you and I were to start spending more time together, people would get used to seeing us as a couple. We might even find we like being together, that it's something we want to do more of."

She felt like Alice, lost in Wonderland. She'd dropped through a rabbit hole and suddenly down was up—and up was down. "But we're *not* a couple."

"I know. But we could be if you would only give us a chance. I'm asking for time with you, Piper. I want to see if we can have something good together, you and me. Maybe you'll find out we make a good team in every way."

"What are you saying?"

"Fine. I'll just lay it right out there."

"Yes! Please do."

"We need to date as parents-to-be."

Her head was spinning. "No."

"Yeah. We need to learn about each other, to come to trust each other. Because when it comes to the baby, we are going to be a team for the rest of our lives."

Well, now. That was pretty terrifying. And probably true, given how determined he was to be a real father to his child. But what good would their dating do? It seemed to her that there was a clear boundary between co-parenting and coupling up. She had no intention of crossing that line.

Did she?

No. No, of course not.

And yet, she felt so drawn to him. Even with her relationship phobia and their thirteen-year age gap that was bound to get tongues wagging, she did like him. A lot. How could she not?

He was thoughtful and kind. And way too attractive for her peace of mind. Since their night together, she couldn't stop thinking about all the sexy things they'd done, couldn't stop fantasizing about doing those things again. She remembered the sweetness and heat of his kisses, the feel of his strong body pressing close to hers...

"Well?" he asked.

She just stared at him. Because she had nothing. She needed a minute.

A whole bunch of minutes...

Chapter Five

Jason got the message. It was obvious from the look on her face that she wasn't buying what he was selling.

She asked, her tone carefully controlled, "You're serious. You want us to date because that will be best for the baby and will also get everyone in town accustomed to seeing us as a team?"

"Yeah—and don't forget that I just plain want to get closer to you."

"Jason, you've already asked me out. I turned you down, remember?" She said it so gently. Like she was trying really hard not to hurt his feelings.

He wanted to laugh and put his fist through the windshield, both at the same time. "Of course I remember. You shut me down every chance you get."

"That's not fair."

"Maybe not. But it's true."

She folded her arms under those beautiful breasts of hers. "Fine. I've shut you down. I said from the first that I wasn't interested in developing a relationship—with any guy. But now that there's a baby, you expect me to suddenly change my mind?"

Oh, hell, yes, he thought. But he said, "I just want you to think about it. I want you to give us a chance. We need

time to know each other better and the people we care
about need to see us together, to see that we *like* each
other, that we get along, that we understand each other.
That way, in a couple of months when we share our big
news, they'll already know that we're good together, that
we can work together."

She stared at him like she could see right through
him—and she probably could. "Your logic is skewed. This
isn't about other people. This is about you and me and the
baby. Forget this dating idea," she said flatly.

Was he giving up? Not a chance. "Look at it this way.
I want to spend time with you. We don't have to call it
dating. Think of it as starting to learn how to be parents
together. Consider it a chance to get everyone used to
us being a couple before they find out there's a baby on
the way. Call it becoming friends if that works for you.
Two weeks ago, at Henry's, you did say that we could be
friends."

"And you got up and walked out."

Busted. "So shoot me. I wanted more. I still want more."

"Jason…"

"Just hear me out. I'm not expecting you to be my girl.
I'm only asking you to give us a chance to get to know each
other better by being together—getting dinner, hanging out
at your house or mine, taking long walks, sharing a picnic.
I want us to find out where a little time together takes us."

She had a grim look, like she was lining up fresh arguments, finding a slew of new ways to tell him no. But
before she could come back with more reasons why his
plan didn't work for her, a curly-haired woman strolled
by the truck on Piper's side.

It was Marilee Lewis, who ran a pet grooming and

boarding business out of her cute Victorian house several blocks away. Marilee had two perky Pomeranians on the leash. She spotted Piper through the passenger window and waved. Piper waved back.

It was after seven by then. And Jason was getting nowhere. They were having a baby together and the chemistry between them was palpable.

And yet Piper wouldn't give an inch.

He wanted to ask what had happened to her that had made her so completely unwilling to give a man even the ghost of a chance.

But he knew damn well that he wouldn't be getting an answer to that question tonight. "Listen, just think about what I said, will you?"

Her slim fingers were already gripping the door handle. "I will."

"I'll walk you to the door."

"No. It's fine. Good night."

It took effort, but he stayed in his seat. "Don't be a stranger. Give me a call."

She pushed the door open. "Good night, Jason." She swung her feet to the ground.

He watched her go up her front walk and let herself inside.

Only then did he start up the truck and head for home.

Friday, Piper had an afternoon coffee date with Starr Tisdale at the Perfect Bean, a cute little place two blocks off Main on Pine Street. Starr owned the local newspaper, the *Medicine Creek Clarion*. Piper got together with her at least once a month. Not only did Piper enjoy hanging out with Starr, but the regular coffee dates allowed her to run down the list of upcoming events at the library. Starr always put out the word on library events ahead of time and then wrote articles about them afterward.

That day, Starr brought her toddler, Cara Grace, a quiet baby who was usually happy to sit in her stroller and play with whatever toys Starr had brought along for her.

This time, Cara seemed to recognize Piper. She held out her plump baby arms and cried, "Hi, hi!"

Piper glanced at Starr for permission. As soon as she got the nod, she turned her chair sideways and took that sweetheart in her lap.

"You are so gorgeous," Piper whispered to the little one—and she was. Cara took after her mom. She had thick black hair and stunning violet eyes.

The baby giggled and offered Piper her stuffed turtle. Once Piper had kissed the toy, she handed it back.

"Stay right there," Starr instructed. "Masala chai as usual?"

"Yes, please."

Starr went to the counter and came back with their drinks and a muffin for each of them. When Cara spotted the treats, she cried gleefully, "Yum-yum!" So they took turns feeding her bites, which she ate surprisingly neatly, sitting there on Piper's lap.

"It's so satisfying eating muffins with a hometown hero," teased Starr.

Piper groaned. "Stop it."

Starr smirked and rubbed it in. "Everyone loved the way you came to Bobby Trueblood's rescue at the Lego event."

Piper sipped her chai. "And *you* know you really didn't need to put that in the *Clarion*."

"Oh, yes I did."

"Anyone could have done that."

"Piper. *You* did that. We all take first aid, but how many of us leap into action when the moment comes? Very few. The citizens of Medicine Creek salute you." Starr raised her coffee cup.

Piper groaned. "Enough with that."

Starr shrugged—and finally let it be.

As they chatted, Piper kept thinking that Starr could always be trusted to keep a secret. She would be the perfect person to confide in. And Piper really did need to talk to someone about her unexpected pregnancy and Jason's out-there idea that they should date for the sake of the baby.

But she kept her mouth shut. After all, she and Jason had an agreement. Plus, Starr just happened to be yet another of Jason's cousins. Her dad was Zach Bravo, who ran the Bravo family ranch, the Rising Sun.

Small-town life. Everybody knew everybody—and half the time they were related.

A little later, when Starr went up to the counter to get Piper another chai and more coffee for herself, Piper looked down and saw that Cara had fallen asleep right there in her lap. The little girl had her arm around her stuffie and her chin on her chest. Her thick, black eyelashes made perfect fans against her plump cheeks.

It felt good, to cradle her warm little body, to imagine how, sometime next January, Piper would have her own baby to hold. The idea both thrilled and terrified her. She would follow in her grandmother's footsteps, having her first—and no doubt only—baby at forty-one.

Starr returned with their drinks. Piper sipped her chai leaning sideways over the table, taking extra care that none of it dripped on the sleeping child.

"You look great with a baby in your lap," Starr observed in a half whisper.

"I *feel* great with a baby in my lap." She glanced down at Cara's shining black curls. "She's just a bundle of wonderful, this little girl."

When she looked up again, her friend asked, "Ever think about having one of your own?"

She answered quietly—and honestly. "I do, yes."

"It could still happen."

Piper didn't want to lie—but she didn't want to break her agreement with Jason, either. "Wouldn't that be something?"

"You would make a terrific mom."

Piper didn't know what to say. Starr fell silent, too.

Piper tried not to ask, but somehow the words escaped anyway. "Okay, what's on your mind?"

"I probably shouldn't bring this up..."

"Just say it," Piper commanded.

Starr sipped her coffee. "So." She set the cup carefully back in its saucer. "You and my cousin Jason at Arlington's together on a recent Friday night..."

Piper went ahead and rolled her eyes. "Does everyone in town know about that?"

Starr thought the question over. "Well. Not *everyone*."

Piper brushed a featherlight kiss on the crown of Cara's head as she once again considered how much to say. "Jason's a great guy."

"That's right. He is. A hard worker. A magician with a chain saw. And solid, you know? The kind of guy you can count on. You two could be good together."

Piper glanced up from the sleeping Cara and into Starr's eyes. For several seconds, neither of them said a word.

Starr broke the silence. "Anytime you need to talk, I'm here. You know that, right?"

Piper nodded. "Thank you."

"As I said, anytime."

The weekend crawled by. Piper kept worrying that her period might start. She imagined she felt that familiar heaviness in her lower belly. More than once she checked for spotting. When there was none, a wave of relief washed through her.

A baby would change her life dramatically—and in a lot of challenging ways. But not being pregnant, after all?

For her, that would be harder. Like the death of hope, somehow.

Already, in a matter of days since she'd taken those three home tests, she'd accepted her baby as part of her future, as a major component of what made her life worthwhile.

She got the call from Dr. Hayes's nurse on Monday at three. As it happened, Piper was alone in her office at the time. The nurse said the test was positive.

Piper replied, "Great. Can you hold on just a moment?"

"Of course."

Piper put the phone on mute, dropped it on her desk and then ran around the room fist-pumping and silently screaming, *Yes! Yes! Yes! Yes!*

Because it was happening. It was on! She really was pregnant. The dream she'd never had the guts to actively pursue was coming true anyway.

As soon as she hung up, she called Jason.

He answered with, "Well?"

"The blood test was positive. We're still having a baby."

He said nothing. Had he hung up?

"Uh, Jason?"

"Right here. Sorry. Piper…" He sounded tense—had he suddenly decided that he didn't want to be a dad right now, after all?

"What?" she demanded, her heart sinking at the same time as she reminded herself that he had every right to change his mind and she would have no problem doing this all on her own. "What is it?" She kept her voice level with effort. "Just say it."

He made a rough sound, low in his throat. "It's only that I'm so glad, I don't know what the hell to say."

Relief rolled through her. It made her knees feel weak— and not for any silly romantic reason. No. It was because she'd already gotten used to thinking of him as her partner in this. In a strictly co-parenting capacity, of course. And because it was better for the baby to have a dad who wanted her.

Piper laughed. It was a strange, strangled sort of sound that made her feel way too vulnerable. "I hear you," she said firmly. "I completely understand."

"Good." And then he asked, "When can I see you again?"

She didn't even hesitate. "Tonight. My house. Six thirty?"

"I'll bring takeout. Italian?"

"That sounds great."

"Flowers?" Piper smiled at him as she greeted him at the door.

Jason imagined pulling her close and kissing her for a very long time. But that probably wouldn't go over well. Plus, he had his hands full. "I saw them as I was driving by that new flower shop on Gartner Street." He held out the big bouquet. "I thought of you."

She tried to look stern. "You shouldn't have done that."

"What?" He played it clueless for all he was worth. "You don't like flowers?"

She took them. He stepped back and admired the view. Damn, she looked fine in a calf-length skirt and a silky knit top. Her feet were bare, slim and pale, her toes painted red.

When he looked up, she was smiling. "I love flowers," she said. "Thank you."

"You're welcome. I also brought dinner, as promised." He flashed the two bags of takeout in his left hand.

"I appreciate that." She stepped back. "Come on in." He followed her across the living room and on to the kitchen area. "Just put the food on the counter," she said. He set the take-out bags next to the cooktop and she stuck the bouquet under his nose. "Would you hold this just for a minute?"

"Sure." He took the flowers again, and she went on tiptoe to bring down a vase from the cupboard.

She turned to the sink and filled the vase with water. Her red hair flowed down her back past her shoulders, so shiny, so sleek. "Here..." Reclaiming the flowers, she removed the cellophane wrapping and stuck them in the vase. "Lilies, tulips, hyacinth and carnations. All my favorites." She set the arrangement on one end of the central island.

And to hell with restraint. He made his move. "Hey." Catching her hand, he reeled her in slowly, giving her time to pull away.

But she didn't pull away. Those green eyes went wide, and her mouth went so soft.

"So. It's official," he said. "We are having a baby."

"Yes. Yes, we are."

"You'll be an amazing mom."

"I hope so…"

"I know so." He lowered his lips to hers.

Her sigh was all he needed to hear. He gathered her closer and she slid her hands up over his chest and onto his shoulders. When he deepened the kiss, she let him, her mouth opening beneath his, her fingers straying to brush the back of his neck and thread up into his hair. She tasted so good, sweet and fresh and way too tempting.

He nipped at her lower lip, testing the soft, giving flesh. She let out the cutest little moan. So he pulled her even closer, wrapped his arms around her even tighter.

The scent of her filled his head. She surged up onto her toes, pressing against him, her body curving into him, making him hard for her, making him burn for more of her…

With a low, regretful sound, she broke the kiss. He loosened his hold but didn't let go. "Co-parents," she reminded him in a husky whisper, her face still tipped up.

He pressed his forehead to hers. "Right…" He tried to sound regretful for stepping over the line. But he regretted nothing—except that he probably wouldn't get to kiss her again tonight. The tilt of her pretty chin and the resolve in her eyes told him he'd better keep his hands to himself from now on.

"I got Caesar salads and veal piccata," he said. "I hope that's okay."

"Perfect."

She dished up the food and they sat at the table near the French doors leading out to a back deck and a small, fenced yard. The bit of sky beyond the fence was clear blue. For a few minutes, they ate in silence.

Then he said, "So what's next, baby-wise?"

"Well, Dr. Hayes says I'm in excellent health." She spoke briskly, and she seemed so young right then, like a very good student, repeating what she'd learned in class that day. "He said what all doctors say to pregnant ladies— that I should get plenty of rest, try to keep my stress levels low, eat lots of fruits and vegetables and take the prenatal vitamins he recommended."

He wished he'd known her when she was a kid. He would bet she'd been curious and determined—and earnest, too, like right now. Earnest and a little bit awkward. No doubt adorably so.

She added, "Oh! I almost forgot. The first ultrasound— the early one I need because I'm over thirty-five—is four weeks from today, June 10, at eight in the morning, up in Sheridan at the hospital."

"I'll go with you."

"Okay." She cut a bite of veal and chewed it slowly. When she swallowed, she shot him a quick glance—not nervous, really. But maybe unsure.

He set down his fork and had a sip of the beer she'd poured for him. "Whatever's on your mind, just say it. I can take it."

She wrinkled her nose. "I'm that obvious?"

"Just tell me."

She drew a slow breath. "So your cousin Starr and I are friends. We get together for coffee often. We met up this afternoon. She'd heard about you and me meeting up at Arlington's that night in April."

"That surprises you?"

"No. I just find it ironic."

"What?"

"I was people-watching myself that night, remember?"

"I do, yeah."

"But I wasn't paying any attention to who might be watching me, though I suppose I should have been."

He reached across the table and put his hand over hers. "Do you think you did something wrong?"

She pulled her hand away and sat up a little straighter. "Absolutely not."

"Good. Because you didn't. *We* didn't. You should know, though, that Ty mentioned the same thing."

"That people saw us at Arlington's?"

"I'm not sure of his exact words, but yeah. Ty already knew that we'd been together at Arlington's that night. And I wasn't surprised that he knew. People talk. They always have."

"And now we've probably been seen at the Grill, too."

"That's true."

"*And* sitting out in your pickup afterward."

"Come on, Piper. We're single adults. Where's the problem?"

"Me," she said. "The problem is me."

He didn't get it. "Okay, you lost me there."

"Think about it, Jason. My mother never met a rule she wouldn't break. But as for me, I've never done anything in this town that anyone would ever gossip about—until recently, with you."

He studied her face. "I can't tell. Are you proud of yourself for being so good for so long? Or disappointed that you didn't get out and have more fun?"

She took a moment to consider his question. "I'm not

sure. Maybe a little of both. This whole thing with you has made me want to be braver."

"Braver? I like that."

"Well, good. But the age difference is a big deal to some people—especially if it's the woman who's older."

"It's not a big deal to me, Piper."

"But we're not talking about you. We're talking about everyone else in town. I mean, last Thursday you said we should date."

"And you said no way."

"Wrong. I said I would think about it."

"You only said you'd think about it so you could get away from me after Marilee Lewis spotted you in my truck."

"Okay, that's true," she conceded reluctantly. "But as it happens, I *have* given the idea some thought, and I've changed my mind."

"You have?"

"Yes. And I think you're right."

It was exactly what he'd been hoping for. "Did you just say that you think *I'm* right?"

"Don't be smug, Jason."

He suppressed a chuckle. "Sorry."

"No, you're not." The look on her face made him want to grab her and kiss her again. But somehow he managed to keep his hands to himself. She went on, "The thing is, eventually there will be talk about us anyway. We might as well take control of the narrative. And that's why I've come around to your point of view. I think we *should* date."

"Take control of the narrative." He nodded. "Yeah. I like that. A lot. Let's start with this weekend. Saturday night I want you to come to dinner with my family at the Double-K."

She blinked. "Wait. Jason. Isn't it kind of early for dinner with the parents?"

"Considering that you're already having my baby, no. Think about it. We'll be telling them about the baby in a matter of weeks. I want my family to start getting to know you *now*."

She set down her fork. "I don't know. It could be really awkward. I think it's better just to hold off on dinner with your parents until we're ready to tell them what's really going on."

"No. It's better that they be around you right now, that they start getting to know you. Look, *I* already know *your* mom. She and I get along great. I want you to know my folks, too. I really do. I want you to know them *before* it gets to be all about the baby."

"Yeesh."

"Hey." He took her hand and wove their fingers together. "It's just dinner." She looked away, but then she met his eyes again. He coaxed, "I know you'll like them."

She made a soft, thoughtful sound. "I've met your mom once or twice. And I did like her. She comes into the library now and then. She seems friendly and outgoing."

"She's great, I promise you." He brought her hand to his lips and kissed it. "Say you'll come out to the ranch with me Saturday."

Beneath the light dusting of freckles, her cheeks had flushed the prettiest shade of pink. She grumbled, "You know, you really are far too charming for my peace of mind."

"Was that a yes?"

Her gaze slid away. "Oh, all right."

He kissed her hand again. "All right, what?"

She glared at him—but then she sighed. "All right, Jason. Saturday night, I'll meet your parents."

Chapter Six

That night, Jason had trouble sleeping. He'd convinced Piper to come to dinner Saturday and now he needed to make sure the whole thing went off smoothly. He wanted to guarantee that everyone got along, that Piper liked his mom and dad, and that they welcomed her with open arms.

In hindsight, maybe he should have approached his parents first, made sure that Saturday dinner would work for them, though he couldn't see why it wouldn't. They ate at home most nights.

But what if Saturday just happened to be one of those times when they went to visit Sonny and Farrah down in Buffalo? Or maybe his dad was taking his mom out. That didn't happen too often, but now and then the two of them drove up to Sheridan to a quiet little Mexican place they liked there.

In the morning, he felt grouchy and tired from stewing all night—and also pissed off at himself for getting all tied in knots about this. He was acting like some silly kid, wanting to introduce his special girl to the family and not having a clue how to go about it.

He dragged through morning chores. Then he ate breakfast in the main house with his mom and dad sitting right there at the table with him—and failed to make a peep about Piper joining them on Saturday night.

His mom gave him funny looks. She knew he had something on his mind. But she also understood him, which meant she probably figured he would talk about it when he was ready.

After the meal, Joe and their mom rode out to check on the stock. Jason helped his dad repair one of the tractors. Around noon, he clicked his tongue for Kenzo, who got up from snoozing on the dirt floor of the tractor shed and followed him to his cabin and on through to the workshop in back.

Jason threw up the big door to let the sun in and got to work on a new carving of an Arabian rearing up from the tall, thick stump of a black walnut tree. It calmed him to concentrate on coaxing the horse from the dense wood. He found the muffled scream of the saw through his earmuffs downright soothing.

Yeah, he needed to go talk to his mom about dinner on Saturday. And he would. Very soon.

All that day, Piper felt anxious.

She never had trouble keeping her cool with library patrons. It was part of the job, after all.

That day, though, she wanted to say rude things to every single person who dared to ask her even the simplest, most innocent question. It got worse as the hours crawled by and Jason had yet to reach out, to let her know what Meggie and Nate Bravo had said when he proposed that he bring Piper to meet them on Saturday night.

Piper hadn't even wanted to go. But he'd kept after her

till she caved and said yes. Now, the more she stewed over it, the more it seemed like a bad, bad idea.

It wasn't as though she and Jason were really a couple. They were future co-parents.

Co-parents. She kept repeating the word in her head—*co-parents*, reminding herself that, though he was an amazing man, and she couldn't stop thinking about him, they weren't a couple—this wasn't that.

Co-parents. It was what they were and what they would remain.

At a little after three, Helen Linwood demanded to speak with "that new director." As if Helen didn't know Piper's name.

Today of all days, the feisty octogenarian was the last person Piper wanted to talk to. She almost instructed Libby at the circulation desk to tell Mrs. Linwood that the director was unavailable. After all, Helen would only be complaining about the same thing she always grumbled about.

But then Piper reminded herself that Helen Linwood was entitled to the respect and understanding every person who used the library deserved. The library and everyone who worked there provided an important public service paid for by the people of the community. When a patron wanted to speak with the library director, the director said yes if at all possible.

"Send her to my office, please," Piper instructed.

Libby sighed. "She's already on her way."

Helen Linwood, who wore a red straw hat on her curly silver head, a faded jean jacket over khaki pants and a pair of enormous wire-rimmed glasses, pushed open Piper's door without knocking. "Piper. There you are."

Piper rose. "Hello, Helen." She gestured at the guest chairs on the far side of her desk. "Have a seat." Helen marched over and took one of the chairs. "How are you?"

Helen adjusted her hat and smoothed nonexistent wrinkles from her khakis. "Well, I've been better."

"I'm sorry to hear that. What can I do to help you?"

Helen scoffed and crossed her arms. "I've been on the wait list for a hardcover copy of Marjorie Wade's *The Other Lover* for months, but somehow I never get my copy." The truth was, Helen wanted to borrow hardcover copies of all the major bestsellers the minute they hit the bookstores—as did a lot of other people in Medicine Creek and the surrounding areas.

Piper said, "As I might have explained to you last week when *The Secret of Samothrace* wasn't available—"

"I don't have that one yet, either," Helen huffed. "It's just not right. I get on the list good and early and yet it takes forever and a day to get my copy."

"If you would just give reading an ebook a chance, you might—"

"Good God, no. I want a *real* book—and that's not to say that current ebook bestsellers are any easier to come by than the hardcover editions. My friend Jeannetta Rossi explained to me that the library doesn't pay for enough ebook copies, either, so everyone's waiting for them, too."

It went on like that. Piper tried again gently to explain that the Medicine Creek Library did not have unlimited funds, that donations were much appreciated and would help a lot toward making sure more copies of bestsellers were available timely to avid readers.

When Helen got going on how if she had unlimited

funds, she would certainly be buying her own copies of the books she craved, Piper gave up and tuned her out.

It was that or say something she would later regret.

Because she just didn't have the patience to deal with the usual issues today. Today, all she could think about was that Jason hadn't called and what was *wrong* with her that she hadn't stuck to her guns and said absolutely not, she wouldn't be going to dinner at his mother's—and especially not as his girlfriend?

Helen trotted out her parting shot as she finally allowed Piper to usher her toward the door. "When June was director, I got my books sooner," she announced angrily—but then her silver eyebrows crunched together and she insisted, "I'm sure of it." By then, she sounded anything but sure. "I mean, I had to wait much too long even back then, but not as long as I am waiting now."

Piper apologized some more and promised that Helen would be called immediately when the books she was waiting for were ready for her to check out.

"Thank you," replied Helen, her tone softer now. "And that was rather mean of me, Piper, to imply that June was a better director than you are."

Even with all those grim thoughts about Jason and why he hadn't called yet gnawing away at the back of her mind, Piper wanted to hug Helen right then. "June was and is the best of the best. I'm lucky to have her to look up to."

Helen patted Piper's cheek. "You always were a sweet girl."

"Thank you, Helen."

"Have Libby call me the minute my books are available…"

"Of course I will."

When Helen finally went out the door, Piper checked her cell for news from Jason.

Nothing.

Oh, she should have nixed the idea of dinner with his family—nixed it and refused to budge on it no matter how long he kept after her to change her mind.

But she hadn't. She'd weakened and let him charm her into saying yes to his bad, bad idea. And now she was absolutely certain something upsetting had happened when he'd told his parents that he and Piper Wallace were a thing.

By the time he'd showered and headed back to the main house for dinner with Kenzo trotting along behind him, Jason felt good. He felt ready to tell his parents there was someone special he wanted them to meet on Saturday evening.

It was kind of funny, really. He'd been so confident, even downright cocky, while convincing Piper that she should get to know his family a little. But now that he had to propose the idea to his folks, he was having a hell of a time trying to decide what to say.

It was ridiculous and he knew it, to be all tied in knots about something so simple. It was dinner with the family. His parents always welcomed guests.

But no matter how he imagined getting the words out, they sounded abrupt and awkward when he tried to put them together inside his head.

Still, it had to be done.

In the kitchen of his mom's house, the food was on the table. His parents and his brother sat in their usual chairs. He'd just showered at his place, so he had no need to wash up.

"There you are, Jay," said his mom with a smile.

Kenzo flopped down in his favorite spot on the scuffed floor as Jason took his customary place at the table. He waited until they all had full plates in front of them before he said, "Mom, Dad. I've been seeing someone special, and I would like to bring her to dinner here Saturday night."

"Someone special?" His mom was smiling. Definitely a good sign.

Before he could tell them about Piper, Joe swallowed the big hunk of pot roast he'd just stuck in his mouth and said, "Piper Wallace, right? I heard you took her out to dinner at the Grill last week and she came by your place in the evening a couple weeks ago, didn't she?"

Jason had a very strong urge to punch his brother in the face—not because there was anything wrong with what Joe had just said. It was the interruption that got on Jason's last nerve. He'd hoped to handle this conversation himself. Smoothly, if possible.

But hey. Life didn't always go as planned. He nodded at his brother. "That's right. I took Piper to the Stagecoach Grill, and before that she came to see my workshop. I'm donating a carving for auction at the library fundraiser this summer."

"Piper Wallace," said his mother. She was frowning now—but a frown didn't necessarily mean anything bad. Maybe she didn't remember exactly who Piper was. "The librarian?"

"That's right. Piper and I have been seeing each other

for a while now. I really like her. And I want you and Dad to get to know her, too."

That frown on his mom's face? It wasn't going away. She asked, "Wasn't she married to that nice history teacher?"

"Piper's a widow," he said flatly. "Mr. Wallace died four years ago."

His mom replied, "I remember. And you were in Mr. Wallace's class in high school." It sounded like an accusation.

And the stern look on her face? Not good.

Now, he didn't know where to go with this. Should he have expected this kind of reaction? He hadn't—though maybe his own nervousness about approaching the subject should have clued him in that he wasn't as confident about this situation as he kept telling Piper he was.

"What are you getting at, Mom?"

Meggie looked away, but then she faced him again and drew herself up. "Honey, I'm just going to remind you of the obvious. She's so much older than you."

"Thirteen years, yeah. So what? Piper and I are both adults. You act like I'm still in high school."

"I didn't say that."

"Good. Because I'm not in high school anymore and I haven't been for almost ten years. I'm a grown-ass man. I can't see how my wanting to be with Piper is a problem for you."

"Well, if it's serious—"

"It is serious." Okay, maybe that was more than he'd meant to say at this point. And maybe Piper wouldn't say the same. Not yet. But it was the truth—*his* truth. And his mother might as well get used to it.

"But, Jay—"

"Meggie." His dad interrupted her this time.

She shot him a look. "What?"

"Let's not get ahead of ourselves."

"But, Nate, I just think we should—"

"—not get ahead of ourselves?" his dad suggested gently. Again.

Joe shifted in his chair. Jason glanced in his brother's direction. Joe's eyes were so wide they seemed to take over his face.

"It's fact," Meggie protested, her eyebrows pinched together, and her mouth all scrunched up. "Piper Wallace is—"

"—smart and helpful," his dad finished her sentence for her. "And did you read that great bit Starr put in the *Clarion*, about how that four-year-old boy almost choked on a plastic astronaut in the middle of some library event?"

"Yes, I did, but—"

"Piper Wallace saved that boy's life, Meggie. I'm really looking forward to getting to know her a little."

"But—"

"Oh, now, Meggie May," Nate said in a voice smooth as warm honey. "Jay and Piper are both grown adults and their choices are their own. Let it be."

Meggie bit her lip. Then she and Jason's dad did that thing they always did, staring at each other, saying things to each other without using words.

Finally, his mom nodded. "Yes," she said in a slow, considered tone. "I get it. And I know Piper Wallace is a good person."

"Yes, she is," said his dad.

Jason didn't know what to think. If he'd worried a little

that one of his parents might not be all in on Piper from the first, he would have guessed that would be his dad.

Which just proved that even people you'd known since birth could surprise you now and then. Sometimes in a good way. But sometimes not.

His mom turned her big brown eyes on him. "I apologize for trying to tell you how to live your life. I'm proud of you, Jay, and I do respect your right to make your own choices."

"It's okay, Mom." It wasn't, but right now, he just wanted to keep the peace and bring Piper to dinner.

"Piper is a fine person," she said. "And we would love to have her over for dinner on Saturday."

"Thanks, Mom." He had zero desire to stir up more trouble, but there was something he did need to say. "Look, Mom, if you're really opposed to my being with Piper, I don't want to bring her here, not until I know you're good with it."

"I…" Meggie took a moment before she answered. "I want you to be happy, Jay. Yes, I'm all right with it. Please tell Piper that we look forward to spending some time with her."

It was not the enthusiastic invitation he'd hoped for. But she'd as good as promised to treat Piper as a welcome guest. And he did want his mom and dad to know Piper before they found out there was a baby on the way.

He nodded at his mom and put on a smile. "Great. I'll ask her to Saturday dinner. Six o'clock?"

"That'll work," said his mom and the matter was settled.

Back at his place a little later, he sat on the front deck throwing a chewed-up red Frisbee for Kenzo, ruffling the dog's thick black coat and calling him a "Good boy" every time he returned with the drool-covered plastic disc.

Kenzo never tired of catching a Frisbee. Jason indulged him for more than an hour, though he knew he should have called Piper by now. It was just that he was trying to decide how much to say about the conversation he'd just had with his parents.

Jason believed that honesty was always the best policy. He made sure to live by that belief. But right now, the way his mom had reacted when he said that Piper was special to him…

He didn't want to tell Piper that. He'd worked hard to convince her that she would be welcomed at the Double-K. And she would be welcomed…

Just with reservations on his mother's part.

Really, it would be all right. He just didn't see the need to get into his mom's initial reaction to the news that he was bringing Piper to dinner.

Because why upset Piper when it was all worked out? Why scare her off?

Didn't he have enough of a challenge with her already? Here he was trying his damnedest to get closer to her while she kept pushing him away. For weeks, he'd gotten nothing but an endless chain of noes from her. And lately her favorite word was *co-parents*.

He hated that word already. It was a word that said they were connected, but only by the child they were raising. Not by their hearts, not by the life they might build together.

He damn well would be a father to his child, but he also planned to do anything and everything he had to do to see that he didn't end up a *co-parent* kind of dad. He wanted a family with Piper. He wanted his child to have what he'd had growing up—a mom and a dad who loved, trusted and counted on each other, a mom and a dad who could talk to each other without using words.

In the end, it really didn't matter that she was older than he was, or that they were going at it backward, starting with a one-night stand instead of taking a while to get to know each other first.

They could work it out. He knew they could. He would take it slow, show her day by day that she could count on him, that they could make a beautiful life together.

And right now, he wasn't going to say anything to freak her out. They would have a nice dinner here at the ranch on Saturday. His mom and dad would welcome her. By the end of the evening he would be one small step closer to earning her trust.

Kenzo came trotting back to him across the grass. The sweet mutt dropped the Frisbee on the ground at Jason's feet. It was covered in drool.

Jason chuckled. "Later for that, big guy. Let's go inside. I really need to make a call."

It was after seven when Piper's phone finally chimed with the call she'd been waiting for all day. She stared at the ringing phone there on the coffee table in front of her.

Voice mail would take it before the fourth ring. She waited till it rang three times before she picked it up. "Hello, Jason." She ladled on a little uncalled-for attitude. "What a surprise."

A silence on the other end, then, "You're pissed."

"Me? No, not at all," she lied through her teeth.

"You at home?"

"Why?"

"I'll come over there."

Now she just felt foolish. "No. Sorry. I was...well, a little nervous about what your parents might say when you told them you wanted to bring me to dinner." She gathered her legs up onto the sofa and snuggled her bare feet under a throw pillow. "When you didn't call, I just knew it must have gone badly."

"It didn't go badly." His voice was low, soothing. She felt instantly reassured. "I waited till dinnertime to talk to them, that's all."

She drew a slow breath and just went ahead and asked him, "So, then. How *did* it go?"

"It was fine, Piper." He sounded so sure of that. "It went great."

She breathed a slow sigh of relief. "Yeah?"

"Yeah. I told them we were going out together—dating, like you and I agreed. My dad said he's looking forward to getting to know you and my mom said they would love for you to come to dinner Saturday night."

Dating. He'd told his parents they were dating. Yes, it was what they'd agreed. But now that it was too late to take the words back, it seemed like a bad idea, after all, to tell lies to the people he loved the most.

"Don't." Jason's voice was firm and confident—like he was the mature, experienced one. And she was some shy youngster who had no idea what in the world she was doing. "Stop second-guessing. You're coming to dinner and it's going to be great. Saturday. I'll pick you up at five thirty."

She still had her doubts about this. But eventually, she would be getting to know Nate and Meggie Bravo anyway. Might as well get started on that. "I'll be ready. See you then."

* * *

When Saturday evening came, *ready* was the last word she would have used to describe herself.

But she pulled it together. She put on a pretty yellow cotton dress and the cute cowboy boots she kept in the back of her closet. She'd even made a quick trip to Betty's Blooms on State Street for a sweet little bouquet of pale pink tulips for Jason's mom.

"You look gorgeous," Jason said when she answered the door. That gleam in his eye said he wanted to kiss her. She would have let him if he'd tried.

But he didn't—which was good. Yes, they were "dating" for the world to see. But in private, they needed to remember that it was all about the baby. Sharing kisses right now would only confuse the issue for her—and for him, too.

"Ready?" he asked.

Was she? Not really. She felt on edge about this whole thing. "I have to tell you, meeting the parents? It makes me nervous. I never met Walter's parents. His father had died back when he was twenty. And his mom passed on five years later. And as for my college boyfriend..." She was babbling, she knew it. And talking about Brandon? No good could come from that. She finished lamely, "I, uh, did meet his parents..." It had been an absolute disaster.

He was frowning. "Are you okay?"

"Yes. Of course. I'm fine."

She locked her door and led the way down the front walk. At the curb, his pickup was sparkling clean, the chrome shiny bright. "You washed your truck," she said as he pulled open the door for her.

"Waxed it, too." His grin was slow and way too tempting. "I wanted everything just so for my special girl."

"You're such a romantic," she teased as she stepped up into the cab.

"You don't know the half of it—watch that pretty skirt, now."

She pulled it out of the way so that he could shut the door.

As they left the streets of town behind and headed west toward the mountains, she realized her nervousness had eased. She felt good. Happy to be with Jason on a warm, clear Saturday evening, on the way to spend a little time with his family.

At the ranch, Jason stopped his pickup in front of the main house, a sweet old Victorian-style two-story farmhouse painted white with a gray shingle roof and old-fashioned sash windows.

His mom and dad came out as Piper and Jason mounted the porch steps. Jason made the introductions. His parents seemed friendly and welcoming. His younger brother had gone into town to play pool with friends, so it was just the four of them.

Piper offered Meggie the bouquet she'd brought.

"I love tulips, thank you," Jason's mom replied.

They went in and straight through the great room into the kitchen, which smelled so good, of a juicy-looking rib roast that had just come out of the oven. Meggie put the tulips in a pretty crystal vase, and they took seats near the fireplace in the great room.

Nate offered drinks. "Piper, what'll you have?"

Was it a dead giveaway that she wanted club soda? Nobody looked at her funny when she asked for it, so she decided it was fine. Nate and Jason had whiskey with soda and Meggie had a glass of red wine.

They chatted, the getting-to-know-you kind of talk, most of it focused on Piper, which upped her nervousness a notch or two. But she was the newcomer, Jason's "special" girl, so of course his parents wanted to know all about her. Nate, tall and broad like his son, but with the same thick, dark hair, but with gray at his temples, said he'd read in the *Clarion* about the incident with little Bobby Trueblood.

Piper reassured Jason's dad that Bobby was fine, completely recovered. They asked after her mom.

"She never stops," Piper said. "She's running her art center and she's also painting and making jewelry. In addition to all that, she takes surveys and gets paid to watch videos."

Nate said, "She's one of a kind, your mother."

"Oh, yes she is."

Eventually, they moved into the formal dining room for the meal.

Meggie sipped her wine. "Until last week, I had no idea the two of you were dating." She asked Piper, "How did you get together?"

Piper realized she should have expected that question. Her mouth felt kind of dry. She grabbed her glass of club soda and knocked back a big gulp.

Jason answered his mother's question. "We ran into each other at Arlington's one night."

"It was back in April," Piper said. "The scare with Bobby Trueblood had happened that day, as a matter of fact."

Jason was nodding. "I bought her a drink. We talked. It was so easy, talking with Piper. Fun. I could have stayed there all night. Didn't matter what we talked about, I never wanted to leave." His hand brushed hers under the table.

She caught his fingers, gave them a grateful squeeze. "I tried to get her number. No luck. She turned me down more than once." One side of his mouth quirked up. "But I didn't give up. Eventually I convinced her to give me a chance."

Piper pulled it together and played her part. "I was hesitant. I've been on my own for four years now and I never planned to...get serious with anyone again."

"So, it really is serious, then, between you two?" Meggie asked.

"Well." Piper cleared her throat. "Maybe *serious* is a little too strong a word."

"No, it's not," Jason contradicted her. Piper shot him a warning look. He ignored that look and went right on. "It's not too strong a word at all—and, Mom, I already mentioned that I was serious about Piper."

Meggie nodded as she turned to Piper again. "I was sorry to hear that you'd lost your husband, Piper."

"Thank you. But, as I said, it's been four years. I've adjusted to being single."

"And yet here you are, dating my son." Meggie's voice was soft, her tone friendly. But there was something unnerving—and disapproving—about the look in her eye.

Piper got the message then. Meggie didn't want Piper getting close to her son. A glance at the man who'd brought her here confirmed it. Jason was glaring at his mother, his mouth a flat line.

Nate said, "Meggie May." It was a warning.

And apparently, Meggie knew she'd gone too far. "Yes," she replied and then murmured, "I hear you. I'm sorry..."

Piper had had enough. "I don't know quite how to ask this, but..."

Jason caught her hand again.

She turned and looked straight at him. "What?"

"It's okay," he said. "Really, it's fine."

"No, it's not. Jason, I'm not blind." Meggie didn't want her here and that was very far from fine. As for Piper, she felt a tightness in her throat and feared she might actually burst into tears right there at Meggie Bravo's dining room table.

Instead, she drew back her shoulders and met Meggie's dark eyes squarely. "Just answer me truthfully. Do you have a problem with Jason and me as a couple?"

"Piper," insisted Jason. "Come on. Let it go. It's okay."

She jerked her hand from his. "No. No, it's not. It's not in the least okay— Meggie?"

Meggie's lips trembled. For a moment, Piper was certain she would backpedal frantically and insist that she had no problem at all with the idea of Piper and Jason together.

But then Meggie shut her eyes and drew a slow breath. When she looked at Piper again, she nodded. "The truth is I think very highly of you, Piper. I honestly do. But you're not a good fit for Jason. I mean, he's so much younger. He should be with someone his own age, don't you think?"

"That's enough." Jason shoved back his chair and threw his napkin on the table. "We are done here."

"Jason, wait." Piper needed to hear the rest. She put her hand on his rock-hard forearm. "Let your mom finish. Please?"

He gave her a long, hard look. "Have it your way," he muttered as he dropped back into his chair.

"I have something to say first." Nate's voice was measured, calm. "I just want to make it clear that *I* think our son should be with the one who's right for him. And only he can decide who that woman is."

Piper's gaze slid to Meggie, whose eyes shone with un-shed tears.

"I'm sorry, Nate," Meggie said. "And, Jason, I know I promised you that I would welcome Piper—and I do, except... Well, I just don't see you two being right for each other. When you turn fifty, Piper will already be in her sixties. Plus, what about children?"

Jason stared at Meggie as though he wondered who she was and what she'd done with his real mom. "What about them?" he sneered.

"Well, Jay. It's a hard, sad fact that a woman's fertility declines sharply after forty."

Jason shot Piper a questioning glance. She just knew he was going to blurt out the news of the baby. She gave a small, negative shake of her head. Her fertility was only part of the main issue here and she refused to let Jason use the new life inside her to one-up his mom.

Jason shifted his angry gaze back to Meggie. Piper held her breath, certain he was going to break the agreement they'd made and bring up the baby, after all.

But he didn't. "This isn't like you," he said to his mother. "It's narrow-minded, Mom. Piper and I have every right to be together and I think you know that."

Meggie looked miserable. Piper actually felt kind of sorry for her. "You're right on every count," Meggie said. "And I'm sorry. I feel awful about this. I'm not proud that I can't get past the age difference between you two, I'm truly not. But, Jay, it's honestly how I feel. And I couldn't just sit here and pretend that it's all okay when I have so many doubts."

"Well, I don't have doubts, Mom. I have none. Zero.

And it's what *I* think and what Piper thinks that matters here."

Piper couldn't take it anymore. "What I think is that this, tonight, was a bad idea." She felt sick to her stomach from sheer embarrassment. Life was too short. She had no desire to sit here in this charming old dining room and be judged as not good enough for Meggie Bravo's precious son—no. Uh-uh. She refused to stay in this house one minute longer. "Jason, please take me home now."

At least he didn't argue. He only asked, "Are you sure?"

She nodded. "Take me home."

Chapter Seven

Five minutes later, they were back in Jason's shiny-clean
pickup driving away from the ranch house.

Neither of them spoke. Piper watched the drift fences
flying past and the evening shadows growing longer.

When they finally got to her place, he said, "Let me come
in."

"Jason, please. No. I'm tired."

"When can we talk?"

"I don't know right now. That was horrible. I'm going
to need some time."

"Time for what?" he demanded.

His curt tone flat out pissed her off. "You set me up."

He flinched. "No. Piper, I—"

"You knew that your mom wasn't on board with the idea
of you and me together."

"She promised she would welcome you. She said she
wouldn't make any trouble."

"And that would have been *after* she said that she
thought I was too old for you, am I right?"

He had no viable comeback for that, and both of them
knew it. "Listen. I'm sorry, okay? I wanted you to get to
know them. I was sure my mom would change her mind
about us as a couple as soon as she saw us together. I knew

she would only need to spend a little time with you to realize how wrong she was."

"Seems to me like you're the one who got it wrong."

"Yeah. I pushed too fast. But it will be all right, you'll see. It's just going to take her a little longer than I thought it would to see how great you and I are together."

Piper longed to start shrieking at him in sheer frustration. But she was a mature adult, after all—*too* mature if you asked Meggie Bravo. "There are so many ways you are off base here." It took effort, but she managed to speak in a level, reasonable tone. "First, we are not a couple."

"But we agreed—"

"I'm not finished." She gathered her thoughts again. "Second, I don't care what you assumed about how your mom would react when she saw us together, you had a responsibility to clue me in that she was against the idea of you and me as a couple. You needed to tell me how she felt. Instead, I ended up blindsided. It was awful and I had no idea that any of that would happen because you didn't warn me."

He swiped off his hat and sank back against the seat. "You're right. And I am truly sorry. I know I blew it. I just wanted it so bad—for them to get to know you and admire you, for you to like them and want to be around them. I was afraid if you knew my mom had doubts, you would refuse to meet them tonight."

"And how is what just happened better than your being honest with me about Meggie's reservations and my deciding I wasn't ready to go there now?"

He tipped his head up and stared at the headliner as though seeking answers from above. "I see your point," he answered wearily. "It was a major screw up on my part.

I was way too eager and all I've got now is how damn sorry I am."

She studied his profile—the strong, proud nose, the sculpted jaw. He was one handsome specimen of a man.

And at least he'd admitted that he'd messed up. Unlike Brandon, who flat out never owned up to being in the wrong about anything—and Walter, who always had some long-winded explanation of how he might have made a mistake, but it wasn't really his fault.

"You're forgiven," she said.

He looked at her then. "Just like that?"

"Yeah. As long as you promise not to pull that kind of crap again."

He put his hand over heart. "Swear to God, Piper. Never again."

"Okay, then. We're good. But I'm still going to need some time. This is all moving way too fast and I'm putting the brakes on as of now."

His beautiful smile faded to a watchful frown. "Putting the brakes on, how?"

"I need a little space, that's all."

"For how long?"

"Please. Now you want to put me on a schedule for getting over what happened tonight?"

"I didn't say that."

"Good. Because I don't know how long it will take me to get past this. A few weeks, at least."

"A few weeks…" He draped his arm on the steering wheel and stared out the windshield as though bad stuff was going on out there. "A few weeks is too long."

Something tightened in her chest. It felt like yearning,

the deep-down kind that aches so bad and won't go away. Or maybe it was just desire, pure and simple.

Because even after the disaster of this evening, she still felt so powerfully drawn to him. Her good sense kept saying no. But the rest of her just wanted more of him.

He turned his head to meet her eyes. "I mean it, Piper. I don't want to go weeks without seeing you."

"You'll see me at the first ultrasound. It's not that far away, the second Monday in June."

"That's more than three weeks."

She held his gaze without wavering. "I'll say it again. Time, Jason. I do need some time."

"We agreed we were supposed to be dating, remember?"

She couldn't help but chuckle. "It's unnecessary. I think you know that. We spent a night together, the contraception failed and now we're having a baby. That's the truth and I'm comfortable with it. It's our business how we handle this, and after tonight, I'm kind of over trying to get ahead of people's judgments."

He slid her a glance. "You're saying you're bowing out of fake dating me?"

"Yes, I am."

He laughed then, though the sound had very little humor in it. "The truth is, I was just trying to get more time with you."

Her heart did that foolish yearning thing again. He was such a good guy and there was all that sizzling-hot chemistry between them...

But no. She couldn't afford to get swept up into an affair with him. She could so easily lose her head over him—not to mention, her heart.

The baby. The baby was what mattered.

She anchored her purse more firmly on her shoulder. "I'll see you at the ultrasound up in Sheridan."

"Piper..."

She pulled on the handle and the door swung open. "Good night, Jason." She jumped out before he could say something to make her stay.

"I'll go with you if that's what it will take," Emmaline said. It was Friday night, almost a week since she'd told Jason she needed some space.

Piper missed him.

A lot.

And she spent way too much time trying not to think about him and his beautiful smile and the look in his eyes that said he only wanted to be with her, that she was someone special to him.

"Think about it seriously, please," Emmaline said.

They sat at the table in the kitchen of the house where both of them had grown up, Emmaline from birth, the only child of middle-aged parents—and Piper starting at the age of nine when they moved home to take care of her grandma after her grandfather died. It was a simple two-story clapboard house built back in the 1920s.

Piper pushed the vegan stir-fry around on her plate. "I've got a lot going on now, Mom. I can't just head off to Southern California to meet my long-lost father and his family."

Emmaline wasn't buying her excuses. "You've always got a lot going on. And it will only get worse once you're past the first trimester. That baby's going to take up every spare second in your day and a lot of time you can't spare, just you wait—and don't try to tell me you can't get away from the library. You've mentioned more than once that you can't roll over your vacation time. You didn't even get a vacation last year, did you?"

"No, but I—"

"Just take some time off, my love. Go meet your father and his family."

"Look. I'll think about it."

"Less thinking, more action."

"Let it be, Mom."

Emmaline dropped her chopsticks and put up both hands. "Okay, okay."

They left it at that.

When Piper checked her email later that night, she had another note from the father she'd yet to meet. Simon Walsh was married with three children, two daughters and a son. His wife's name was Nia. Piper's half siblings were in their late twenties and early thirties. Her two half sisters had husbands and kids.

Simon seemed like a very nice man. Again, he invited her to come for a visit.

Just say when, he wrote. We can make it happen. Or if you would rather we came up there to Wyoming, we can do that instead. Just tell me what works for you, and we'll see what we can do.

She wrote back that she would love to come visit him, and she would let him know as soon as she could get the time away from work. It was a dodge. She could get the time if she really wanted it.

A week later, on Friday, the last day of May, Simon sent her another long, chatty email. At the end he wrote that he and her stepmom could come up to Wyoming to see her anytime over the summer, whatever worked for her.

Piper felt awful when she read that. Because Simon Walsh really did seem like a sweetheart, a sweetheart who very much wanted to meet her. Piper knew she had to quit jerking him around.

That Monday morning was the third of June. First thing that day, she checked in with Libby, who had the thankless job of managing the schedule this year. Libby took half an hour to juggle things around and then offered Piper two weeks of vacation at the end of the month.

Piper sat right down at her desk and composed an email to her father letting him know that she would love to come to visit him and the family—a short visit, for this first time.

I was thinking I would fly in for a weekend, if that works for you, she wrote, and named the dates.

He got back to her that same night. Piper, this is wonderful news. I'm so glad. And so is Nia. We will see you soon. I will be counting the days till then. There was more, about how he'd already made some calls and her half siblings would be there to meet her, too. She should stay as long as she possibly could, he wrote. And bring a friend if you'd like, he added. We have plenty of room...

Bring a friend. She would love to bring Starr. But the usual issues applied. Starr had a husband, a toddler and a business to take care of. Piper just didn't want to ask her to drop everything and hold Piper's hand while she met her father for the first time.

And she felt uncomfortable about bringing her mom along with her. At least not for this first visit.

It could end up feeling awkward with Emmaline there.

After all, Emmaline and Simon had spent a wild weekend of sex, drugs and rock and roll at the US Music Festival in the San Bernardino Mountains a little over forty years ago. Nia might be fine with all that. But Piper wanted to know her dad's wife better before springing Emmaline on her.

The week crawled by. She thought of Jason way too often, wondered what he was doing, wanted to reach out to him. But she didn't. Because they had their separate lives and they both needed to remember that.

Friday morning, she texted him a reminder that the ultrasound was set for 8:00 a.m. on Monday up in Sheridan, adding, Meet you at the front entrance at 7:45.

Four hours later, he still hadn't replied. She tried not to wonder why he hadn't gotten back. Up till now in their... whatever this thing was between them. Relationship? Friendship? Future co-parents-ship? Whatever they had going on together here, he'd always been right there, ready and waiting whenever she'd reached out to him.

Not this time.

Okay, true, she'd asked him not to contact her, so the fact that he hadn't gotten in touch the past few weeks was on her. But if being there for the ultrasound was so important to him, couldn't he hurry up and confirm that he was coming?

She promised herself she wouldn't think about him or worry about why he wasn't getting back. If he showed up, fine.

Two hours later, he did get back. Sorry. Moving cattle. Out of cell range until just now. Will be there Monday morning. Hospital front entrance. 7:45.

And that was all.

Not that she expected anything more—what else was

there to expect? He'd done what she'd asked and waited for her to contact him. As for the ultrasound, he would be there, no problem.

She tried, as she'd tried for the past three weeks, to put him from her mind. She failed. Completely. Because he was there, in her head, in her heart. In all the secret, private parts of her.

She missed him. Way too much.

Monday, he was waiting for her at the main hospital entrance looking like everybody's fantasy of a hot cowboy in clean jeans, rawhide boots, a Western shirt and a jean jacket. He swiped off his hat with a big smile as she came walking across the parking lot toward him. His hair shone black as a crow's wing in the morning sun.

Her heart just… Well, it lifted at the sight of him. There was no other word for it. Her heart went airborne the moment she saw his handsome face again. Her feet seemed to float right up off the ground.

She wanted to run to him, to throw her arms around him, show him how glad she was to see him again.

But she didn't. She walked at a steady pace and when she reached him she kept her arms to her sides. "Ready?"

"Oh, yeah. Let's get after it. I'm excited."

That just made her smile like a fool. "Me, too—and nervous. Very nervous."

His expression grew more serious. "Any problems? You feeling okay?"

"No problems, none. I feel great. It's just…a big moment. And I hope everything's okay."

He took her hand then, his rough fingers sliding between hers, grounding her somehow, easing her fears. "It's going to be fine."

"Thanks." The word came out in a breathless whisper. "That's what I needed to hear."

They went in.

After check-in, they waited until a woman in scrubs came for them. She introduced herself as the sonographer's assistant and led them into a regular exam room. Jason took a chair in the corner and Piper sat on the exam table. The woman took Piper's vitals and explained that the procedure would be transvaginal. At six weeks, the baby was so small that a traditional abdominal ultrasound might not pick up the necessary information.

The woman left long enough for Piper to take off her jeans, sneakers and panties, and cover herself with a sheet. When the assistant returned, the sonographer came, too. Piper settled her feet in the stirrups.

"This may be a little uncomfortable," said the sonographer, as she eased the long, wand-like device up under the sheet. "But there shouldn't be any pain."

Piper drew a slow, careful breath. "Jason?" She glanced his way and he rose from the chair.

When she held out her hand, he took it. It helped, the warmth of him right there beside her, the press of his palm to hers.

The wand went in. On the monitor beside her, a flickering gray image filled the screen.

"There's the sac," said the sonographer, indicating a curving black space within the flickering gray. "And... We have a heartbeat." The image zoomed in and there in the black space was a pulsing speck of...something. The sonographer fiddled with the controls and the speck became more defined. The pulsing was in the center of it.

"Is that the baby?" Jason asked.

"Oh, yes it is," replied the sonographer. "The heart is what's pulsing. It's very early days, but everything looks good at this point."

"Just one, right?" Piper asked.

"One baby, yes," the sonographer replied.

Fifteen minutes later, Piper had a flash drive of pictures in her purse and Jason at her side as they walked out into the morning sunlight.

He asked, "Do you have to get to work?"

"Not till afternoon. I took the morning off."

"Did you get breakfast?"

"I couldn't."

"Me neither. Let's get some food. It's a nice day. How about takeout? Maybe a picnic. I know a great spot by Crystal Creek."

"The same spot you mentioned when you were trying to get me to go out with you?"

He nodded. "That's the one. What do you say?"

She felt…drugged, somehow. High on his presence. Happier than she'd been in weeks. "Yes, all right. Food would be good."

He called ahead to Henry's. She followed him back down to Medicine Creek. Jason went in to pick up the food. Piper left her car around the corner from the diner and climbed up into his pickup with him.

A few miles out of town, he turned off onto a gravel side road. They rumbled along for a couple of hundred yards and then he pulled over and parked.

She took one bag. He took the other, along with a blanket from the storage box in the pickup bed. He led the way along a winding path to the creek's edge and a nice grassy spot beneath a willow tree. Five feet down the bank, the clear water raced by, glittering in the sun as it tumbled over the rocks below.

It really was a pretty spot. And right now, they had it all to themselves.

He spread the blanket and they ate breakfast—egg-and-ham sandwiches on English muffins and the best hash browns ever. She drank her orange juice and enjoyed her once-daily cup of coffee.

"I missed you," he said, his eyes on the far bank.

"You didn't call," she replied, which she knew very well was totally unfair given that she'd asked him not to.

"Come on, Piper." He stared straight ahead, toward the opposite bank. "You said you needed time."

"Yes, I did. Let me rephrase my last remark. Thank you for respecting my request."

"You're welcome." He slid her a glance then.

She gave him a smile and bumped his shoulder with hers. It felt so good that he was here, beside her, on this sunny almost-summer morning. It filled her with happiness that he'd been there to see that tiny, pulsing speck of a heart on the ultrasound monitor. The sight had made it all the more real to her that she just might become a mother, after all—so real that her throat clutched and her view of the pretty creek burbling along below them grew misty.

"Hey," he said. "What's wrong?"

She swiped away a tear as it slid down her cheek and sniffed back the next one before it could fall. "Just hormones."

"Piper..."

She swayed against him. He wrapped an arm around her. His lips touched her hair. "Is this about what happened with my mother? Please don't worry," he whispered.

"She'll come around. Plus, when she finds out about the baby, the news really will be less of a..." He seemed to have trouble choosing the right word.

She couldn't hold back a chuckle. "I think *shock* is what you're going for here."

"Hmm. More like *surprise*."

"Yeah, right." She settled her head on his shoulder. A breeze ruffled the leaves of the willow overhead. "Think of it," she said dreamily. "You're going to be a dad."

"I do think of it." She felt his lips in her hair again, and the warmth of his breath on her skin. "I think of it all the time."

It felt really good to lean on him, so she kept doing it as she continued to marvel that she was having a baby and he would be her baby's dad, a dad who insisted he would be there to see their baby grow up. She thought of her own dad and how much he seemed to want to get to get to know her. "Did you know I've never met my own dad?"

He rubbed her arm with his big hand, slowly, soothingly. "No. I noticed you never mentioned him, but sometimes people's dads just kind of drift away."

"Yeah. That's sad, but also true. I think most people assume that he must have been a deadbeat—or that my mom never even knew who he was, which is a little bit closer to the truth. We *didn't* know much about him until recently. I found him through 23andMe."

"Wow. I had no idea."

"I've been thinking it over, working my way toward the big step of meeting him in person."

Jason just went on holding her. Across the creek, a pair of bobolinks chirped at each other from the branches of a hackberry tree.

"My mom never knew his last name," she said. "She met him at a rock festival in the San Bernardino Mountains. They smoked a lot of weed, had a great time together and said goodbye when the festival was over without exchanging any information that would have helped her track him down when she found out that I was on the way. I grew up knowing virtually nothing about him, wanting desperately to find him, having no way to do that."

"That would be hard. A lifetime of wondering if you would ever get to meet him."

"I did wonder. As a little girl I used to dream of meeting him. When we lived in my mom's Volkswagen bus, I just knew that any day, he would find us somehow. He'd appear at our campsite or show up at some outdoor art show where Mom had her paintings for sale. He would stop at our booth, and I would look up. Our eyes would meet. I would know instantly that he was my dad. I would run to his arms, and he'd scoop me up and twirl me around and whisper, *There you are, Piper. I've been looking for you.*"

Jason stroked her hair with a slow hand. "Didn't happen, though, huh?"

She shook her head. "He never appeared. Then we moved to Medicine Creek to live with my grandmother. He never knocked on our door. By the time I was fourteen or so, it started to seem pointless to keep waiting, keep hoping."

"You gave up?"

"I did, yeah. My mom knew I was losing faith that I would ever meet him. She hired a private investigator to search for him. It cost money she didn't have, and the so-called investigation went nowhere. I was seventeen or so when I finally admitted to myself that I was never going to know him. From then on, I put him behind me. I honestly wouldn't even have tried 23andMe if Mom hadn't nagged at me until I finally signed up and sent in my DNA sample."

"And now?"

"I've agreed to go meet him and his family. They live in San Diego. It'll be a short visit, just for a weekend. But I did get some time off. Two weeks starting on the fifteenth. I'll fly down there for two or three days then."

"Alone?"

"Looks like it, yes. My friends are all busy with their own lives. My mom would go, but my father is married with grown children and, well, it probably wouldn't be awkward, but you never know. For this first visit, I don't want to take any chances."

"I'll go with you."

She pulled away, but only so that she could meet his eyes. It surprised her how much his offer meant. "You would? Really?"

"I will, yeah."

She gulped down the lump in her throat. "Just as... friends, right? And as co-parents. I mean, it would be good, don't you think? For us to spend some time together before the baby's born, see how we do as a team?"

"However you want it, Piper. Two weeks starting on the fifteenth, you said?"

"No. The trip to San Diego will only be one weekend, Friday or Saturday through Sunday—or Monday at the latest. We'll fly down there and back."

"But you said you have two weeks of vacation time."

"Yes." She could see by the look on his gorgeous face that he was planning something more than just a weekend in San Diego. Whatever it was, she should put the brakes on.

Except that she did have two whole weeks of freedom coming and wouldn't it be fun to have a real vacation for once? Her mom was right. The baby would change everything. Her schedule would only get tighter. Soon enough, any getaway she managed to find the time for would include an infant and an endless array of baby gear.

"Why not make it a road trip?" he suggested. "We'll take a few days driving down there, and then map out a different route coming back. We could stop in Las Vegas on the way south and drive up the Coast Highway coming home. Remember I mentioned that my grandmother Sharilyn lives in Los Angeles?"

"I do, yes."

"If you're willing, we can stop for a visit with her and her husband, Hector. The two of them came up to the ranch for a week during the summer a few years back, but I haven't seen them since then and they are not getting any younger."

A road trip, just the two of us? She started to run a mental inventory of all the reasons she couldn't say yes.

But her mind simply refused to cooperate.

Because his suggestion sounded great. Aside from a couple of work-related conferences, she hadn't been anywhere but down to Buffalo or up to Sheridan for the past two years. This was her chance to get away for a while. And all her very good reasons not to do that just made her feel sad. For once, she wanted to do the fun thing rather than the practical one.

"Think about it, Piper. It'll be good, just you and me

on our own schedule, taking life as it comes. It'll be an adventure."

She waffled. "Are you sure you can get away?"

"Yes. Let's do it."

"I don't know…"

"Sure you do. It's a great idea. We're having a baby together. It'll be good for us, two weeks on the road, just us, alone."

When he put it like that, she should definitely say no. Shouldn't she?

But she'd missed him so much since she'd asked him to stay away. It was starting to seem nothing short of foolish to keep rejecting him.

For once, she wanted to forget what she *should* do. She wanted to be with him far away from their everyday lives. She wanted to know him better. Because he was right. Whatever went on between the two of them personally, their baby would connect them for the rest of their lives.

"Okay, Jason. Let's do it."

He leaned closer. "What was that? I didn't quite hear what you said."

She laughed. "You heard me. The road trip. Let's do it."

"You sure?"

"Yes, I am."

"That's what I wanted to hear." And then he caught her hand, jumped to his feet and pulled her up with him.

"What is it? What's going on? I don't trust that evil gleam in your eye."

Turned out she was right to be suspicious. Because with no warning whatsoever, he dipped and then scooped her high against his broad chest. "How about a swim?"

She manacled her arms around his neck. "Don't you dare."

He threw back his head with a deep, happy laugh and his hat fell off.

"Your hat!" She tried to catch it as it tumbled to the blanket.

"Don't worry about my hat. It's not going anywhere. It'll be right there when we get back."

"I have no idea what you're talking about. Back from where?"

"Our swim." He started walking down the bank.

And she almost demanded he set her down this minute. But the light in his eyes—it was beautiful. And a swim?

Not a bad idea at all.

He walked right into the icy stream. Not far from the bank, he bent at the knees and lowered them both into the freezing current. Wet from her sneakers to her butt, she laughed as he plopped down to sit on the rocky streambed.

The water reached her shoulders. It wasn't very deep, but it was cold, and it was swift. "Oh, you are going to pay for this!" she vowed gleefully. And then she took her hands from around his neck and stacked them on top of his head.

"What do you think you're doing?" He laughed at her.

"Dunking you." She pushed.

"Good luck with that." He hardly budged.

So she settled for splashing him—and herself at the same time as he just sat there in the knee-deep water, laughing at her efforts to push him under.

But then his eyes narrowed. "You're shivering," he said. He wasn't laughing anymore.

"I'm fine," she replied.

"This was a bad idea."

"Uh-uh. It was a great idea." She splashed him some more. But he just got his boots under him again and rose to his height. Water streamed off them as he carried her to the shore and up the bank to the waiting blanket.

Carefully, he set her on her feet. "There you go."

"That was so refreshing," she said brightly as her teeth knocked together.

"Yeah?"

"Oh, yeah."

"It seemed like a good idea at the time—but look at you. You're dripping wet and shaking like a leaf."

"I'm fine, Jason."

Stooping, he grabbed the blanket and shook it out, scattering the remains of their breakfast and sending his hat tumbling a few feet away in the process. He wrapped the blanket around her shoulders.

"Thank you," she said between shivers. "I might be just a tad chilly, after all."

Using the sides of the blanket, he pulled her close to him. "You sure you're okay?"

She beamed up at him. "I am, definitely."

Those blue eyes glittered down at her. "You look like a drowned rat. A really cute redheaded rat."

"You are just asking for trouble," she sneered, thinking that she was having a whole lot of fun and maybe there hadn't been enough of that in her life—not that she planned to admit it to him.

He stared down at her.

She grinned right back at him.

And everything changed. Suddenly, her heart was beating hard and deep, and her breath had gotten all snarled up inside her chest.

He said in a growl, "Tell me no. Say it now."

She blinked up at him. "Or what?"

"You know what."

She swallowed hard and tried to make that *no* take form. It didn't. And now she was biting her lip, whispering, "Jason…?" It came out like a question, like she was asking him for something.

Because she was. How could she help it?

She hadn't kissed him in four weeks. Not since the day Dr. Hayes confirmed her pregnancy.

Yes, she ought to be ashamed of herself for not stopping him now.

But all she could think about was the press of his lips to hers, the longing for him that would not go away no matter how many times she told herself to get over him—*and* their one unforgettable night together.

"Jason…"

"Piper." He said her name in the sweetest, roughest whisper.

And then that wonderful mouth came down to cover hers.

Chapter Eight

Jason just might have been the happiest man on the planet at that moment—and with very good reason. He had Piper in his arms and his mouth on hers, and so far she hadn't pushed him away.

On the contrary, she let go of the blanket. It plopped down around their feet. Her hands slid up his chest to encircle his neck. The move brought her right where he wanted her—even closer. Her soft breasts pressed against him. As for that perfect, plump, supple mouth of hers, it was *his* right now.

He took shameless advantage of her sudden willingness. Dipping his tongue into the heat beyond her parted lips, he stroked it slowly over hers.

She moaned. The sound echoed in his head and in an instant, he was hard. It was almost painful, how much he wanted her. How much he longed to rip off that soaking-wet camp shirt she was wearing, to shove down her dripping jeans and her panties along with them. He burned to strip her bare right there at the side of the creek.

But even if she let him, the chances were far too high that she would regret that choice later. She could too easily come down with a serious case of buyer's remorse for allowing herself to get carried away with him. If he didn't keep a rein on his eagerness to get up close and personal with her again, she just might change her mind about letting him go with her to meet her father.

That couldn't happen. He needed the time with her on the road, just the two of them. Time to be together, to grow closer, with none of their usual everyday concerns to drive a wedge between them. He couldn't wait to be on the way.

And he wasn't going to mess this up, not even for the chance to hold her sweet, naked body in his arms again after so damn long.

With a last, slow brush of his lips across hers, he lifted his head. She opened those leaf-green eyes and stared up at him, dazed.

He gave her a smile. "You're still shivering."

She blinked and instantly she was her usual, brisk, commanding self. "Probably because somebody dunked me in the creek."

He rubbed his hands up and down her chilled, wet arms. "Some people are just plain rude."

"Humph. Tell me about it—I can't believe I just kissed you. We can't be letting that happen again."

Oh, yes they could. If things went the way he wanted them to, she'd be doing a lot more than just kissing him. But right now, she wasn't ready for any of that, and he needed to respect her wishes. "I should get you home, huh?"

Did he see the shadow of disappointment in her eyes because she wasn't ready to go home yet? He sure hoped so. She drew a deep breath and aimed her pretty chin high. "Yes, I suppose you should. I need to clean up for work this afternoon." She was maybe five foot three in her soaking-wet Vans, yet somehow she had the ability to seem tall and commanding even when she was looking up.

"All right, then." He bent, picked up his hat and plunked it on his head. Then he gathered the scattered remains of their breakfast and stuffed it all back in the to-go bags. "Hold these." He held out the bags. When she took them, he grabbed the blanket, shook it once more and quickly folded it so he could drape it over his shoulder. "Ready?"

She nodded and started to turn.

"Wait a minute." He caught her free hand.

She glanced back at him. "What?" In response, he guided her captured hand around his neck and lifted her high into his arms again. "Well," she said, clearly trying not to grin. "Now you've got hold of me again, what next?"

He let his feet do the talking. His waterlogged boots made squishy noises as he carried her up to the truck, where he set her down in order to open her door. "I'll get water all over the seat," she warned.

"No problem. Up you go…"

Too soon, he was parking his pickup around the corner from Henry's in the empty space behind her SUV.

Turning in his seat to face her, he asked, "What day are we leaving?"

"My vacation starts this Saturday. I'm expected at my father's house the following weekend."

"So we can take our time getting there. I used to drive back and forth to Los Angeles when I was going to school. If we take the route down through Utah and Nevada, it's about twenty hours driving time from here to San Diego. You want to leave on Saturday? We can stop at Yellowstone, Palm Springs, Bryce Canyon, Las Vegas—and there's more. Think about it. We should get going now on the hotel reservations along the way—unless you're in the mood for camping."

"Maybe a little of both?"

That she didn't balk at the idea of camping pleased him. He liked sleeping outside. "A little of both, that works."

"And I would like to leave Monday, give myself a day to pack and get ready."

"Monday, it is."

She took hold of the door handle. "I need to get moving—to clean up and go to work. But I keep thinking that two weeks is a long time. Are you sure you can get away for that long?"

"Yeah, I'm sure." There was always too much to do on the Double-K during the summer. But too bad. He more than carried his weight as a rule. They would have to manage without him for a little while. And he had a project to carve on-site—a farmer in Clear Creek wanted a bald eagle from a lodgepole pine stump that was still in the ground not far from his back door. Jason felt confident he could get that finished before the time to go.

Piper gave him a look from under her eyelashes. It was a sweet look, almost shy, and it made his chest ache in a good way. He had that feeling that finally they were getting somewhere, the two of them. That her considerable defenses against him were weakening at last.

"You could come to my house for dinner, say on Wednesday?" she suggested. "Bring your ideas, places you want to visit. I'll think about where I'd like to go. We'll put our heads together." She sounded excited, to be planning her road trip adventure—with him.

He kind of wanted to let out a whoop of triumph, that she really must have missed him after she sent him away, that by some minor miracle, they were running off together for two weeks on the road. "Wednesday," he repeated. "I'll be there."

"All right, then—and thank you," she said, her face flushing the prettiest pink. "For today at the hospital. It was good, having you there."

He kept his butt in his seat and his hands to himself, though doing so required considerable effort. "I wanted to be there."

With a quick nod, she grabbed the door handle again.

Too soon, she was gone. He watched her get into her car and waved as she drove off.

At home, he changed into dry work clothes. With Kenzo in the front seat beside him, he headed for the corrals and the pastures farther out, to help with whatever needed doing.

That night, he skipped dinner with the family. Instead, he made himself a couple of roast beef sandwiches, sat at his kitchen table with the food and his laptop, and began planning his dream route to and from San Diego. He'd finished the food and was checking into the lodging options in and near Yellowstone when there was a knock on the front door.

It was his mother, her hands in the pockets of her faded jeans. "Jay." She smiled kind of nervously. "We missed you at dinner."

Now was as good a time as any to let her in on his plans. "I'm glad you came over. I need to talk to you." Now she looked worried. He asked, "Want some coffee?"

She managed a smile. "I would love some."

In the kitchen, he put a pod in the machine. "Have a seat."

She sat at the table. Neither of them spoke until he

set her coffee in front of her. She sipped it. "It's good. Thanks."

He took his own chair again. shut his laptop and pushed it aside. "What I wanted to talk to you about is that I'm going away for a couple of weeks starting next Monday, so if there's anything you really need me for, we should try to get on it this week. Also. I'll be staying at a lot of different places while I'm gone. Some of them likely won't take pets, so I'm hoping you'll look after Kenzo for me?" At his feet, the dog let out a whine. He leaned down to give the guy a reassuring scratch between the ears. "It's okay, boy…"

"Of course we'll look after Kenzo," she said. "But you're going away where…?" Her voice was too soft, too careful—because she knew damn well he was having trouble getting over the way she'd disrespected Piper. He loved his mother, and he didn't want to give himself any opportunities to say things he would later regret, so he'd been avoiding her lately.

"Piper and I are driving to San Diego to visit her father and his family. We're also stopping to see Grandma and Hector. The rest of the trip is kind of open-ended. We'll be taking our time, driving down through Las Vegas, then coming back up along the Coast Highway—at least that's the plan as of now. We just started figuring out the route."

"Ah. So, then you *are* still seeing her?"

"Not exactly. She wanted some time away from me after you ambushed her during dinner last month." Was that too harsh? Probably. But he felt zero desire to take the words back.

"You're *not exactly* seeing her, but you're leaving on a two-week trip with her?"

"That's right."

Meggie's eyes filled with tears. She blinked the wetness away and set her cup down with great care. "I understand that you're angry with me. But I honestly only want the best for you."

"I think I'm the one who gets to decide what's best for me, Mom."

She met his eyes squarely. "You're in love with her."

Love. That was between him and Piper, and they hadn't come anywhere near saying that word to each other. Damned if he would be discussing it with his mother first. "If I want to talk about Piper with you, Mom, I'll let you know."

Her mouth twisted. "I'm sorry, Jay." It came out in a ragged little whisper. "Your father says I've really put my foot in it. And I suppose I have. I never thought of myself as a person with prejudices."

"Oh, come on, Mom. We all have them. Face it."

"I'm sitting here looking at you and I see in your eyes that you are disappointed in me. And that breaks my heart. At the same time, I still feel that you would be happier with someone your own age."

"I'll say it again. It's up to me to decide who I'll be happy with. It's your job to back me up."

"Not if you're making a big mistake."

"A big mistake according to you, Mom. Think about it. Piper is a good person. She's smart and beautiful, with a big heart. She's also a lot of fun. She's someone you can count on to always hold up her end—and she works for a living at a job that really matters. I will never do better than Piper. I have a hard time believing that you can't see that. Piper and I are both adults. At this point in our lives, the years between us don't matter all that much, not the way I see it."

"But—"

He put up a hand. "But nothing. I could get hit by a truck tomorrow, or thrown from a horse. I could slip up with a chain saw, cut my femoral artery and bleed out before anyone knew I was dying. And then Piper could live on for fifty more years. Because we don't get to know how it's all going to shake out, how much time we'll be given. The best we can do is to choose someone extraordinary to stand up beside us and pray that our chosen one chooses us right back."

His mother looked down at her folded hands. When she lifted her head again, she gulped. "I know I already said this and that it offended you horribly, but what if you can never have children with her?"

He thought of the pulsing heart on the monitor that morning. That tiny life mattered to him. A lot. But that life was not the reason that he wanted Piper. "There are children in the world who need parents. That would be an option. And some couples never have kids, Mom—they never have kids and yet they have a great life together anyway."

Meggie picked up her empty cup and went to the counter. She rinsed it out and set it on the rack to dry. Finally, she turned and folded her arms across her middle. "I'll go to her. I'll apologize."

He shook his head. "Mom."

"What?"

"Just leave it alone for now."

"But I want to—"

"Don't. Leave it be."

She let out a frustrated sound. "Are you going to for-give me?"

"Of course."

She studied his face. "But…?"

"Please don't mess things up any more than you already have."

"I have a question," Piper said.

"Shoot."

"Would you consider just climbing in your pickup and winging it?"

It was almost nine on Wednesday night. After the ter-rific slow-cooker chicken cacciatore dinner she'd served him, they'd cleared off the table, opened their laptops and started planning their route to and from San Diego. So far, they'd discussed Yellowstone and Grand Teton, Salt Lake City and Las Vegas.

But campsites in Yellowstone were booked up months—even years—ahead. The hotels near the park were mostly booked, too. In Grand Teton, you couldn't book a camp-site in advance. They would need to get there early in the morning or after four at night to have a chance at a spot. There was always a hotel room available in Vegas, but by the time they moved on to planning that part of the trip, Piper seemed pretty tense.

He put his hand over hers. "If you want to wing it, we'll wing it."

"You mean that?"

"Sure. But you know, if we don't book ahead, there might be nights when we can't get a room or a campsite. We could end up sleeping in the truck."

"One night in a truck isn't going to kill me—especially if it's that roomy GMC Sierra Denali of yours."

He wanted to kiss her. But then, he always wanted to kiss her. "Piper, we have to face facts."

"What facts, exactly?"

"You're pregnant. You sure that you want to sleep in the back of my truck?"

"Please. I'm perfectly healthy and not even showing yet. A night on a blow-up mattress or one of those foam pads is not going to kill me. My mom slept in the back of a VW bus through all but the last two months she was pregnant with me with no ill effects whatsoever."

"You're sure about this?"

"I am positive."

"Alrighty, then. We'll wing it."

She pushed her laptop away with a sigh. "Can you guess I have issues around planning trips? I really thought I was over that. But apparently not."

He still had hold of her other hand, so he gave it a squeeze. "What kind of issues?"

There was more sighing. She flipped a long swatch of that cinnamon-red hair back over her shoulder. "I really hate to criticize a man who can't defend himself."

This was getting more interesting by the minute. "You must mean Walter, am I right?"

"I do, yes. He planned every vacation we took together. He planned them meticulously, getting the best deals, locking us into a schedule we weren't allowed to vary from. He planned what time we would get up and what time we had to be in bed to get eight hours of sleep every night. He planned what restaurants we would go to. And he invariably tried to find a hotel with a free breakfast that we would eat in the hour he had reserved for breakfast on any given day.

"Every moment of every day was on the schedule. If anything ever messed up the schedule, he was a nervous wreck. He was driven to get things back to the plan. He meant well, you know? He really did. He wanted things to go smoothly. But by the last vacation we took together the year before he died, I didn't want to go. We had one of our few serious arguments that year. I laid it on the line that I wasn't going on a trip with him again until he could get a handle on his obsession with scheduling. He very gently suggested that I was making a big deal out of nothing. We left it at that. He died eight months later."

"Hey…"

She made a pouty face at him. "Now I feel terrible, saying bad things about Walter. He was a good man."

"Yes, he was."

"We had a good life, overall." What was it in her voice? Sadness? Yearning?

"Come here." He wrapped his arm around her and felt a surge of satisfaction when she didn't duck away.

And then she rested her head on his shoulder. Suddenly, life was nothing short of perfect. "Walter's been gone for four years," she said. "I really thought I could plan a trip without having a flashback over his obsession with scheduling…"

He stroked her arm and breathed in the apple scent of her shampoo. "So, then. What you're saying is that you need to get in the truck and hit the road. As for planning, you want to start looking for a place to eat whenever we get hungry. You want to find a motel when we need one and if one's not available, we'll camp out or sleep in the truck."

"That sounds so good."

"All right. I'll put on the camper shell. It's going to be downright cozy."

She laughed. The husky sound made him smile. "Yes. Please. I don't want a damn plan. I want to spend a weekend at my dad's place and then go see your grandmother from there. The rest can take care of itself."

"You're just lucky I've got a decent tent and sleeping bags. Bring hiking boots."

"I will, don't worry. Oh, Jason, a camper shell, a nice, big comfy truck, a tent and two sleeping bags. That's all the planning we need."

They left Medicine Creek behind at 8:00 a.m. on Monday morning. The sun was up, the sky a wide, baby blue bowl overhead with a few clouds snagged on the crests of the Bighorns to the west.

Jason felt like a million bucks, heading off for two weeks with Piper. Did it get any better than this?

Doubtful.

"What about Kenzo?" she asked, as the Welcome to Medicine Creek sign got smaller in the rearview. "I just assumed that you would bring him."

"He's a big guy and he needs space to roam. Plus, having him along would make it even harder to get a room at the last minute."

"Will he be all right without you there?"

"Oh, yeah. My mom loves him. He follows my dad around. And Kenzo loves his Frisbee. Joe is always willing to throw it for him."

They stopped at the Henry's Diner in Buffalo for breakfast and got right back on the road. The rolling land was still green, the prairie grasses waving in the wind, stretching out forever to the east, meeting the mountains in the west.

Piper said, "We could spend a little time in Red Lodge or Sweetwater, visit the county museums."

"I can't believe we're skipping both Yellowstone and Grand Teton."

"It's okay. I like this route better. And right now, I'm just not in the mood for driving around trying to get a good shot of a bear or maybe a buffalo so I can post it to Instagram. But I do love that we're taking our time getting there. It feels less pressured than jumping on a plane and showing up at my long-lost father's house that same day."

He stole another look at her. She had her head tipped back, her eyes closed, and she'd opened her window a crack. Her hair was gathered up in a fat knot, but bits of it had escaped. The wind blew the shiny strands against her cheek. She kept brushing them away from those soft lips of hers.

"This is wonderful," she said kind of drowsily. "You know, the open road? Just you and me heading on toward the far horizon."

"I like it, too." A lot. "Are you nervous about meeting your dad?"

She slid him a look then. "I am, yes. But that won't be till next weekend. I'm going to try not to get too worked up about it ahead of time."

"Good idea. Are we telling him that he's going to be a grandfather?"

She made a little humming sound. It was soft and husky at the same time. It reminded him of their one night together, of her lips on his skin, of all the things he'd done to her, and also the ones he hadn't done. Yet. "I haven't decided if I'm ready to tell him," she said. "I don't even know him, Jason. And I'm still in the first trimester. We had kind of decided to wait until the twelve-week mark, hadn't we?"

"Yeah. You'll be nine weeks along on the day we arrive at your dad's."

"I am aware." She pressed a palm to her flat belly. "The day I meet my father, our baby will be the size of a Hershey's Kiss."

Our baby. He loved the sound of that even more than he had hearing her say she liked being out on the open road with him.

The rest of the morning went by mostly in silence. He drove. She read one of the books she'd brought and snoozed on and off. He played country and soft rock, nothing too exciting, the kind of music that didn't interfere with conversation—or with her dropping off to sleep now and then.

They stopped in Rawlins for a quick lunch.

Back in the car, she rolled up her window. He heard her soft sigh as she tucked her small pillow against the glass and rested her head on it.

They rode in silence for a while. It didn't take long for her to fall asleep again. She looked peaceful, he thought, as he turned his gaze back to the road.

Piper woke with a groan. Her belly churned. "Oh, no! Not now..."

"What is it? What's wrong?" Jason shot her a worried glance from behind the wheel. "Are you sick?"

"I'm about to throw up. Pull over, please."

The road went on forever, the land stretching out end-lessly to either side, mesas and buttes rising in the distance, red and gold against the endless sky. Charming, wispy clouds drifted in the giant bowl of the sky. There was an 18-wheeler in front of them and another big rig coming up fast in her side-view mirror.

Again, her stomach lurched. "I'm sorry, Jason. I'm about to…"

"It's okay, we're stopping." He was already pulling to the shoulder. The semitruck behind them blew on by.

Not that she cared about anything but getting out of that vehicle before she ejected the contents of her stomach all over the dashboard.

She yanked the handle and the door swung open as she more or less fell out onto the graveled shoulder, getting her feet under her just in time to keep from ending up flat on her face. Vaguely, she heard the sound of the driver's door slamming shut.

A dry, narrow ditch waited about ten inches from her Nikes. All she had to do was lean over it and let nature take its course.

It was convenient, but not pretty. By then, Jason had rounded the front of the crew cab. He skidded to a halt beside her as the remains of the burger and fries she'd gobbled back in Rawlins made a truly unattractive reap-pearance.

She coughed and sputtered.

Hey, at least she had her hair anchored in a bun and out of the way.

"Oh, sweetheart…" *Sweetheart.* He'd never called her that before. It sounded way too wonderful in that deep, serious voice of his. He rubbed her back, his big, warm hand stroking between her shoulder blades. His touch felt so right, so soothing and good.

Or it did until she started heaving again. Every last thing in her stomach came up. There was nothing left in there but a weird, gurgling sound.

"Oh, my dear Lord," she moaned.

"That's right," he said, his voice so calm and in control, reminding her sharply of the night in April when she'd been bold and free and naked in his big arms. "That's right," he soothed again. "Better...?"

"Ugh. Well, it seems to be over, so that's something."

"Here." He took her hand and put a bottled water in her palm. He must have grabbed it from the cooler in the back seat before racing to her side.

"You read my mind." Screwing off the cap, she took a big sip and used it to rinse the awful taste from her mouth by gargling and spitting right there in front of him. Once that was done, she took a long, much-needed drink. "Oh, Jason. Thank you."

He kept rubbing her back. It felt really good. "Be honest with me. Are you okay?"

She sipped more water and then took a few slow, deep breaths. "I am now."

"Should we find a doctor?" Beneath the shadow of his hat, his face was drawn with concern.

"A doctor? It's just morning sickness."

He blinked at her. "You never said you had morning sickness."

"You're right. I didn't. It never, uh, came up." She stuck out her tongue and pretended to gag.

He groaned. "Oh, now you're a comedian." Another

semitruck flew past, loud and fast. The pickup behind them swayed in its wake.

"We should get back on the road," she said, "before one of those big rigs mows us down."

He didn't reply, just backed up and held the door wide as she climbed into her seat. Two minutes later, they were on their way again.

She drank the last of her water and slipped the empty bottle down by her feet to deal with later. The cab seemed too quiet. At some point, he'd turned the music off.

"How about if we stop in Green River?" he asked. "We can look around there for a place to spend the night."

"It's early," she said. "It hasn't even been seven hours since we left home."

"It's not a race," he offered quietly. "We have days to get there."

She glanced his way, saw how serious he looked and dropped the teasing attitude. "You're worried about me."

"Well, Piper. You're pregnant. You just threw up everything you've eaten today."

"I'm okay, I promise you. Throwing up is what pregnant ladies do—at least during the first few months." She kept her voice light and teasing.

He still looked grim. "Are you sick every morning?"

"No."

"How often?"

She thought about that. "Two or three times a week. And not always in the morning. Sometimes, like today, it happens in the afternoon. Sometimes in the evening."

"Have you lost weight?"

"Stop worrying. This is normal. Just ask Dr. Hayes. All the pregnancy and childbirth books say so, too."

"But have you lost weight?"

"A few pounds, which is also normal. Don't worry. I'll put it back on and a lot more before this baby makes her appearance in the big, wide world."

"You think it's a girl?" Was he almost smiling now? Definitely.

"Not sure," she said. "Sometimes I do. Sometimes I'm a hundred percent positive it's a strong, handsome boy. Then a day or two later, I'm absolutely certain it's a beautiful little girl all over again."

"It's just that I had no idea." He was so solemn, so serious again. "You should have told me."

"I'm lost. I should have told you what?"

"The morning sickness. Has it been bad?"

"No. I mean, it's no fun, but I really am healthy and feeling great overall. Plus, I read that some experts believe that women who have morning sickness during the first trimester have a lower risk of miscarriage than women who don't."

"You think that's true?"

"I have no idea, but every time I run to the bathroom to lose my lunch, I remind myself that hugging the toilet is a good thing because it's proof that the baby is doing just fine."

"Well, all right, then." He took off his hat and plunked it on her head.

Grinning, she flipped down the visor to admire her look in the mirror there. "I've always loved this hat. Unfortunately, it's too big for me." She had to push it back off her forehead or it covered her eyes. "Here you go." Plucking it off, she reached across the console and put it back on his head. "And stop worrying about the morning sickness. I'm the expert and I'm telling you it's perfectly natural."

He tipped the brim to his liking. "Got it all figured out, huh?"

"No. But I'm faking it for all I'm worth."

At the Green River Hampton Inn and Suites, they could have had adjoining rooms. But they agreed that one room with two queen beds would do just fine. Sharing a room saved money. Plus, Piper didn't want to be apart from him—and no, she would not be sharing his queen bed with him. But it was so great, just the two of them, off on their big adventure, future co-parents getting to know each other better. It seemed so natural to stay in the same room.

The room was inviting and comfortable. It even had a view of the Green River Buttes, a beautiful, layered shale formation rising up out of the desert hills behind the hotel.

"Maybe an early dinner?" he asked as soon as they'd each claimed a bed and put their toiletries in the bathroom.

"Absolutely. I need to eat. And soon."

They went to the Hitching Post, a rustic place on the main drag a few miles from the hotel. Their server was friendly and fast. Piper ate all of her salad and then gobbled down her chicken fried steak and fries—and some of Jason's, too.

He sipped his beer and watched her eat. "So, then, I guess you're feeling better?"

"Pass the hot sauce. Yes, I am."

After dinner, they returned to the hotel. Jason toed off his boots, grabbed the remote and dropped to the end of his bed.

Piper removed her shoes, too, and stretched out on her

bed. Her stomach was full, and she felt good—tired, but satisfied. And completely relaxed, too. She'd left all her everyday concerns back home in Medicine Creek. She stared up at the ceiling as she slowly wound a swatch of her hair around her index finger.

"Deep thoughts?" Jason asked.

She glanced his way and saw he'd hitched a knee up on his bed and turned to watch her. "Not really," she said. "Just thinking that until I was nine years old, all I wanted in the world was to get out of my mom's Volkswagen bus and go live in Medicine Creek like a regular girl. And yet, here I am, finally back on the road thirty-one years later, headed off to meet my bio-dad for the first time. And so far, I'm loving every minute of it."

"You are, huh?"

"Yeah."

"Well, good." His eyes still locked with hers, he pointed the remote at the TV, muting the sound.

They shared a smile that went on for a long time. Finally, she covered her mouth with the back of her hand as she yawned. "I'm just going to close my eyes for a minute."

"Go for it. Sleep as long as you want."

She yawned again and let her eyes drift shut. "Not sleeping, only...resting."

For a while, Jason just sat there at the end of his bed watching her sleep. She was really out. He could see her eyes moving behind the delicate screens of her eyelids. She must be dreaming.

He looked down at his stocking feet and grinned. Because hey, it was just him and Piper and life was good.

Couldn't get any better—unless at some point they only needed one bed.

That would be about as perfect as it gets.

He crawled up the mattress, tucked a pillow under his head and pointed the remote at the TV one more time to turn it off. And then he shut his eyes.

Might as well nap while she was napping.

The next thing he knew, Piper was standing over him, wearing a red swimsuit that clung to every beautiful curve. "Wake up, sleepyhead."

"Huh?" he asked stupidly, enraptured by the view. She had a happy gleam in her eyes and constellations of freckles on her shoulders and down her pale arms. He hadn't seen most of those freckles since that night in April.

"They have an indoor pool here," she said. "I want to try it. Come with me. Put on your swim trunks and let's go."

How could he say no to Piper in a red swimsuit?

He dug his board shorts from his duffel and changed in the bathroom like the future co-parent and good friend he'd agreed to be.

The pool was pretty basic. The only people there were kids and enough parents to keep an eye on them. Still, he and Piper got in and swam around a bit. They acted like kids themselves, dunking each other and splashing around.

Eventually, they got out, toweled off and went back to the room, where they took turns in the shower. At her urging, he went first. Took him fifteen minutes to shower, brush his teeth and get dressed for bed in an old pair of gray sweatpants. He flopped down on his bed.

"My turn," she said, and disappeared into the bathroom, where she took her time. When she came out into the main room again, she had on a big T-shirt printed with an image of a flying female superhero holding a thick book high beneath the caption *Librarian. The original search engine.*

"Lookin' good," he remarked.

"Why, thank you." She gave him a game little grin and moved in between their two beds. As she climbed into her bed, he got a whiff of apple-scented shampoo and minty toothpaste.

"Want to try a movie?" he asked.

She turned to lie on her side facing him. Plumping her pillow, she tucked it under her cheek. "Go for it. Choose whatever you like." Her eyes were already drifting closed.

"Never mind," he said. "We can watch a movie some other time."

"Okay, then…" She smiled but didn't open her eyes.

He got up to get his sketch pad from his duffel bag. Back in bed, he fiddled around drawing the buttes that rose up behind the hotel. The curtains were shut and he couldn't actually see them, so he faked it from memory. When that got old, he put the sketch pad aside and turned off the lamp between their beds.

His eyes adjusted to the gloom. There was just enough light bleeding through from outside that he could he indulge himself watching Piper sleep. She didn't move at all. Her breath came shallow and even. The pale curve of her cheek enthralled him.

"Jason?" she asked sleepily.

"Yeah?"

"You're staring at me."

He laughed. "Call me a creeper. I thought you were out for the night."

"Actually, I *was* asleep. For a few minutes anyway." She rolled to her back and put her hands behind her head.

"You know, you've listened to me blather on about Walter and my childhood. I think you should tell me about you."

"What? So we can be better co-parents?" He said the dreaded word and waited for the irritation to rise. But strangely enough, right now, with her nice and close in the other bed, saying *co-parent* out loud didn't piss him off as much as usual.

"No," she replied. "You should tell me more about you so that we can be better friends."

Friends. Another word he didn't like all that much since she started using it to define the distance between them. But fair enough. She wanted him to talk about himself. He would talk. "Relationships with women, you mean?"

"Sure."

"I told you about Jenny Rosario."

"You did. Now tell me more."

"What, specifically?"

"You said that you told her you loved her."

"I did, yes."

"So, then, what happened? How did it end with her?"

"We found out we wanted different things."

"Like…?"

"I realized I wanted to go away to college for a couple of years. She didn't want me to go."

"When did you decide to go away to college?"

"The summer after junior year. I went off to California to visit my grandma Sharilyn. My grandmother saw that I'd started carrying a sketchbook around with me. I would draw all the time, doodles mostly, but also sketches of things I saw or imagined. Grandma Sharilyn took me to art shows, and I loved it."

"And you decided you wanted to go away to college?"

"That's right. I came back to Wyoming excited over the idea of spending a couple of years in California, studying art. I told Jenny all about it, reassuring her that it wouldn't be forever, that I would come home to live, help run the ranch as I'd grown up knowing I would. We would get married in a few years, as we'd planned. But I wanted more, too. I wanted to find a way to get lost in making something beautiful, something special. I said I would love it if she wanted to come with me. Or that if she chose to stay home, we would make it work long-distance. After all, I would be home in the summers and back at the ranch for good within two years."

"How did she react?"

"She asked me why I couldn't just draw my pictures right here in Wyoming, maybe go to Wyoming State if I just *had* to go to college. Her idea was that I could take a few art classes and study ranch management, too. She pretty much had our future mapped out. But I wasn't on board with her plan anymore, and it just kind of fell apart between us. We broke up before Christmas that year." It still hurt to remember how it had ended with Jenny. She'd cried and said he'd ruined everything, that he'd changed, and she hardly knew him anymore.

And he *had* changed. He'd flown to California to see his grandmother and returned wanting something he hadn't realized he needed.

Piper lifted up on an elbow. "Are you okay? You seem kind of down all of a sudden." She turned on the light.

He blinked against the sudden brightness. And then he shook his head. "When I look back on that time, I'm disappointed. In myself, mostly. I hurt Jenny. When we broke up, she said that I'd lied to her, that I'd said I wanted our life together just the way she had it all planned—and then suddenly I decided I needed to move halfway across the country for two years."

"But Jason, you were in high school. You were just learning what you wanted from life. It turned out that what you wanted didn't mesh with Jenny's goals. That seems like a natural progression to me. And by that I mean, people do fall in love in high school all the time—and then most of them change. They grow apart. It doesn't last."

"Yeah, that is exactly what happened. But I'd had it in my head that Jenny and I were going to be the rare exception. We were going to be forever—and we didn't even make it till graduation. I'd believed we had everything in common. I'd considered her my everything and then all of a sudden she was walking away. And I let her go. I wanted those two years at college in LA more than I wanted a lifetime with Jenny."

"Look on the bright side. You didn't let what happened with Jenny make you cynical about love. You said you did try again…"

"Right. I wasn't giving up. I met Eloise Delaney at Santa Monica College. She was studying graphic design. Eloise and I lasted until I was ready to come home. She made it crystal clear that she had no interest in moving to Wyoming. And I realized I wasn't willing to stay in California for her. I came home alone. For a while, I tried just being single, hooking up now and then, keeping it casual. But then, two years after Eloise and I called it quits, I started going out with Caroline Frost."

"I think I've met her. She's a teacher, right?"

"Yep. Caroline teaches first grade at Medicine Creek Elementary. I was settled at the ranch by then, building my house, planning to add my workshop in back. Caroline's a good woman. She's sweet and she's giving. She was willing to move in with me, but..."

"What?"

"It just wasn't right between us. There was something missing. I don't even know what to call it. I mean, I did love her, but the word *love* covers a whole lot of ground. What I've been looking for is more specific."

"Specific, how?"

He leveled his best tough-guy glare at her. "Don't laugh."

"I won't. I swear it," she vowed. His heart ached at the fierce determination on her face. She looked so young right then. He could almost picture what she must have been like as a child. Quiet. Curious. Observant. Passionate about the things that mattered to her. No doubt an avid reader with a big vocabulary.

He wanted to get up, join her in her bed, take her in his arms. But he doubted she would go for that—not right now anyway—so he stayed where he was and said, "It's my parents."

"What do you mean, what about them?"

"It's...what they have together. Who they are to each other. My dad can be too tough for his own good and my mom can be infuriatingly overprotective of me and my brother and sister. But together, they have what I'm talking about. They have that...connection. I grew up seeing that every day. Feeling the strength in it, the power of knowing you're with someone who thrills you, someone who's with you in the deepest ways. Someone you can count on who knows she can depend on you right back."

Those green eyes were enormous now. "Jason, what you just said..."

"What about it?"

"It's beautiful."

"You think so?" He didn't know what he felt now. Embarrassed to have said so much? Thrilled that she seemed to get it?

"Yes, I do think so," she answered him in a near whisper. And then she sighed. It wasn't a happy sound.

He tried to lighten the mood by teasing, "I didn't talk your ear off just to make you feel sad."

"Sometimes life is sad, that's all."

He should let it go. He knew it. Enough had been said for one night—and way too much of it by him. But he wanted to know about her life, about the events and choices that made her who she was. "Why did you marry Walter Wallace? I mean, you told me you shouldn't have married him, but that he made you feel safe. So is that it? You married him because you needed to feel safe?"

She said nothing.

He had no idea what was happening in that sharp mind of hers. And after several painful seconds ticked by in silence, he knew he'd pushed her further than she was willing to go. "You're not going to tell me, are you?"

She shook her head. "Not tonight."

"Fair enough." He tamped down his impatience with her and kept his voice neutral. Yeah, he wanted her to let him in on her secrets. He wanted that a lot. But only when she was ready to share them with him. "Good night, Piper." He turned out the light.

Chapter Nine

Piper didn't sleep well that night.

And not because she was in a strange bed.

She felt guilty that she hadn't made herself answer Jason when he'd asked her why she'd married Walter. After all, the man had answered every question she'd thrown at him about Jenny and Eloise and Caroline. About his take on love in general and how his parents' relationship had shaped his beliefs about life. Whatever she'd asked, he'd answered frankly and directly. And before that, in the afternoon, he'd rubbed her back while she chucked up her lunch on the side of the road.

Jason Bravo was a good man with an honest heart. And yet, she couldn't bring herself to explain to him why she'd said yes when Walter Wallace asked her to be his wife. To explain that she would have to talk about Brandon McAdams.

Piper hated to get into the catastrophe of Brandon. It was an ugly story. One best left unshared.

In the morning, she expected Jason to be unhappy with her—either curt and sarcastic or distant and reproachful. In her intimate experience with the male of the species, she'd found that neither Brandon nor Walter could just let an issue go. If they didn't get their way, they seemed driven to make their displeasure painfully clear, Brandon aggressively and Walter with silence and wounded looks.

But not Jason.

He woke with a smile. "Mornin'. Are you starving or is it just me?" Sitting up, he stretched and yawned, his strong arms flexing, those beautiful back muscles bunching in the most tempting way under all that smooth, tanned skin—and then he caught her watching him. He winked.

She laughed and threw her pillow at him.

He caught it. "So, then. Breakfast here at the hotel?"

"Yes. And let's get going on that. I'm starving."

After they left the hotel, they paid a visit to the Sweetwater County Historical Museum right there in Green River. It was a quick tour. They viewed several fine examples of Native American art and learned about coal mining in Sweetwater County.

By ten, they were back on the road. She used a little of the drive time to book them a nice room at the Hyatt in Lehi for that night.

"Separate rooms?" she asked. "We can get them adjoining…"

He shot her a look—half amused, half watchful—and then dumped the question right back in her lap. "What do *you* think?"

"Well, there's a separate sitting area in each room anyway. Why waste our money? I'll just get us one room with two queens. Last night, it worked out fine, I thought."

"Sounds great to me."

Three hours after leaving Green River, they reached the Great Salt Lake at Saltair, a former resort area where they could walk out across the endless hard, white sand to the edge of what was left of the lake.

It was beautiful and somewhat haunting, the whiteness of all that sand, the diminishing lake gray in the shallows, cool blue farther out. The wind tossed her hair and Jason took her hand.

She was glad just to be there, to have his fingers twined with hers.

And she didn't throw up until they were headed east toward the junction of I-80 and I-15. Once again, he rubbed her back as she lost the contents of her stomach on the side of the road. At least she'd had the good sense to pull her hair back again, so he didn't have to choose between holding it out of the way and giving her that gentle, soothing back rub that made puking a lot easier to bear.

Afterward, he gave her a bottle of water just like the day before. She took it gratefully.

When they got back in the car, she burst into tears for no real reason that she could come up with. He popped open the glove box and handed her a packet of tissues.

After she blew her nose and dabbed at her eyes, she sniffled and admitted, "I honestly have no idea why I'm crying."

"You're allowed." He reached out an arm and wrapped his fingers around the back of her neck.

She sagged across the console to rest her head on his shoulder. "My life as I have known it is gone."

He stroked her pulled-back hair. "A lot of things will stay the same."

"Uh-uh. Everything's changing. I love it."

He kissed the top of her head and she liked it too much to remind him that they were friends and future co-parents and that was all. Then he asked, "You love that everything's changing and that makes you cry?"

She glanced up at his granite-firm jaw and those lips she thought way too often about kissing again. "Actually, it's the terror that makes me cry."

"The terror of...?"

"Childbirth, stretch marks, not being any good at nursing, doing everything wrong and traumatizing an innocent child. Being torn between my work and my baby. Never getting a single night of decent sleep for... I don't know, two or three years, at least."

"It's not going to be that bad."

"Easy for you to say."

"Yeah, because I intend to hold up my end. You won't be doing this alone."

She dabbed at her eyes again. "Thank you. I needed to hear that."

"Well, it's true. As for the rest of your concerns, you're going to be a wonderful mother and our kid will be a happy kid. You're amazing at your job and you'll work out a good balance. They have drugs to help you through labor if you need them. And I'm happy to look after the baby whenever you're short on sleep."

"Hmph. I notice you failed to address stretch marks or nursing."

He gave her that irresistible half grin of his. "Keeping track, were you?"

"Well, they are my worries. Of course I was keeping track—and we should probably get off the shoulder before a state trooper stops to ask us what's going on."

"Good idea."

She peeled herself off him and he started up the truck.

At the Hyatt Place in Lehi, their sleek, modern room had a view of Traverse Mountain.

"See?" she said only half-jokingly. "We always get the terrific mountain views in our hotels—and okay, the butte in Green River isn't quite a mountain. But close…"

"The mountain looks great," he agreed.

"And there's an outside pool. The weather's good. We can swim."

"But first…"

"Food," she finished for him. "Absolutely."

They left their suitcases in the middle of the floor and went to search out a good place to eat.

It was late afternoon when they returned to the Hyatt. She had a nap. When she woke, Jason was drawing something in his sketchbook, and it was still daylight.

"Swim?" she asked.

He tossed his sketchbook aside. "Sure."

In the pool, they acted like a couple of rowdy fools. She made him let her get up on his shoulders and then had him walk around in the water with her that way while she laughed and waved her arms and then had to grab his head with both hands so she wouldn't fall off. He ended up dunking her. She squealed like a six-year-old as she went under. It was so much fun.

How long had it been, really, since she'd laughed with a man and acted silly and young? Forever, it felt like—and just possibly never. Walter was always so serious. As for Brandon, well, she'd been head over heels for him, but he'd never been the type to goof around. Far from it. Brandon approached every activity as an opportunity to win.

When it started to get dark, they went back to the room. She had a shower, put on her sleep shirt and sat on her bed with her iPad to check messages. There was an email from Starr asking where she'd run off to.

I stopped in at the library today. Libby at the circulation desk says you're away on a two-week vacation. Good for you—and where to? I will need details.

Piper started to compose a fluffy response about driving to San Diego just for the fun of it, implying that she was all on her own. But no way Starr would buy that story. And why keep the truth about the trip a secret anyway? Starr was her friend and friends deserved the truth—no, not about the baby. Yet. But everything else, definitely.

She wrote a long, chatty email explaining that she was on the road with Jason to meet her bio-dad and visit his grandmother in LA.

Starr zipped back a short response. You're on a road trip with my cousin to meet your long-lost father? I am smiling ear to ear. Send my love to Jason and have a fabulous time. I will want to know all on our next coffee date.

On the other bed, Jason looked up from his sketchbook. "Good news?"

She realized she'd chuckled over Starr's note. "Just an email from Starr. She sends you her love."

"So Starr knows…?"

"…that we're on our way to meet my dad and see your grandmother."

He gave her a slow nod and a smile to match. Then he tossed his sketchbook aside. "How about a movie?"

They chose one together. She fell asleep before the end without getting under the covers.

When she woke at four the next morning, she had the extra blanket from the closet tucked in close around her. In the other bed, Jason was fast asleep. With a happy sigh, she closed her eyes and drifted off again.

* * *

Jason woke suddenly. The sun was up, light bleeding into the room around the edges of the still-shut blinds. He stretched out a hand for his phone to check the time.

"It's a little after eight," Piper informed him from the other bed. "I brought you coffee. It's right there on the nightstand, next to your phone."

"Uh, thanks." Blinking away the last remnants of sleep, he dragged himself to a sitting position and grabbed the coffee. It was perfect, hot and black. "So good," he said.

Piper was sitting up against the headboard with her iPad. She still wore her big shirt, but she'd pulled on a pair of jeans, too. "I have a plan." She slid him a grin.

He took another sip of coffee. "Tell me."

"We haven't camped. You brought a tent and sleeping bags. I say we skip Vegas and camp at Zion National Park."

Gently, he reminded her, "We'll never get a campsite."

"Never say never. I was up and online at six. Somebody canceled. It's at Watchman Campground. I read a bunch of reviews. It's kind of crowded, not a lot of shade. But there's parking right there in the campground. No showers, but water and nice restrooms. It's a good place to hike from and the views are spectacular." She looked at him hopefully.

"Tell me you already booked it."

"Well, yeah. I did."

"Terrific. Otherwise it would be gone by now."

She grinned. "I kind of figured that, so I made my move."

"Smart girl."

She dropped her iPad to the mattress, jumped up and plopped down next to him on his bed. Her hair hung in a braid down her back and her face was scrubbed clean of makeup. She looked so young—young and carefree, ready for anything. "Is that a yes to camping at Zion National Park?"

He dared to reach out and tug on that red braid. "You bet."

"Yes!" And she threw those soft arms around him.

What could he do but wrap her up in a hug? He breathed in her sweetness and reveled in the feel of her soft cheek against his scruffy one.

Too soon, she was pulling away. Taking him by the shoulders, she announced, "It's a three-and-a-half-hour drive to the park. I booked tonight and tomorrow night. I was thinking we'd get up early Friday, drive to San Diego and get a room for that night. And then we can go on to my dad's house Saturday morning."

"Well, all right. We'll need to stop for food and a few supplies. Let's get some breakfast and get a move on."

The Watchman Campground was pretty much what he'd expected—endless loops of camping slots, lots of people, kind of noisy.

And gorgeous, with the giant sandstone bluffs known as monoliths all around. Deer that had no fear of noise or giant RVs wandered freely among the campsites, nipping at the grass.

Piper had reserved a spot midway between the creek and the road. Their camp was out of sight of the parking area, so that was pretty nice. They set up the tent and walked past the visitor center and right into the town of Springdale to eat.

That night, he built a campfire. They roasted marshmallows and laughed together at the stuff the people camping nearby said and did. There was trash talk and even a little yelling and at one point, someone played "Hey, Soul Sister" on the ukulele. It was noisy, no doubt about it.

Around ten thirty they crawled into the tent. They were lying close, their sleeping bags touching. He didn't mind that at all. A couple nearby argued over whether or not they were stopping in Palm Springs to visit her mother.

Piper whispered, "Don't you just love the wilderness?"

"I do," he agreed. "Or I would, if there was anything left of it around here."

Sometime after midnight, he finally fell asleep.

When he woke up later in the night, Piper was even closer than before. Much closer. She'd turned on her side with her back to him and scooted his way until they were smashed together, spoon-style, separated only by their sleeping bags. For about half a second, he felt guilty that he was in her space, cradling her round bottom on his thighs—but she was out cold, completely unbothered by the fact that she was essentially perched in his lap. He wrapped an arm around her, pulled her closer still, buried his face in her apple-scented hair and went back to sleep.

Near daylight, he woke again, smiling before he opened his eyes because he still held her in his arms, though she'd turned over at some point. Now they were face-to-face. Through the layers of their sleeping bags, he could feel the curve of her waist, the round softness of her breasts.

"Jason..."

He let his eyelids drift open and found himself looking directly into her green eyes. "Mornin'," he said. She brought her hands up between them and pressed them to his chest. He grumbled, "I suppose I'm going to have to let you go."

She nodded but made no move to escape. "I was thinking we could get up, grab a couple of protein bars and bottles of water and take the Watchman Trail. The trailhead is here, by the visitor center. From what I read about it, the hike is pretty easy, the trail smooth and clear, about three miles round trip, and the views are supposed to be spectacular."

"You want it, we'll do it."

Twenty minutes later, they were on their way.

As she'd predicted, the trail was easy and well marked, scattered with pretty patches of wildflowers. They weren't alone. Others walked ahead and behind them.

At the lookout, they got a panoramic view of Zion National Park, including more than one of the spectacular sandstone monoliths. As a bonus, they could see the town of Springdale tucked beneath the cliffs below.

Piper had her hair corralled in that big braid, but bits of it were loose, blowing against her cheeks. She would brush them away and they would blow right back again. He got out his phone and took some pictures of her gazing out over the town below.

The rest of the day went by too fast. They took the shuttle to the trailhead and hiked the West Bank of the Virgin River. Then they explored the Emerald Pools Trails, where there were waterfalls tumbling into small green pools and gorgeous views of stunning cliffs in all directions.

As dinnertime approached, they took the shuttle back to camp, washed up in the campground restroom and then went to Springdale for burgers. They turned in early with plans to get going before dawn for the long drive to San Diego.

"Today was amazing," she said, when they were bedded down in the tent, facing each other in their separate sleeping bags. "I'm glad you got pictures."

"Me, too." He'd taken a bunch of them, the majority with Piper in the foreground. It had been a great day and he hated to see it end. He was smiling to himself, feeling good about this trip, happy about his growing closeness with Piper. Everything seemed to be going so well.

And then, with zero warning, Piper said, "I feel kind of sick to my stomach."

Alarm skittered through him. Vomit in sleeping bags was never pretty. "Let's get you outside."

He was crawling out of his bag when she put her hand on his arm. "It's okay. I'm not actually going to throw up this time."

How could she know that? "You're sure?"

"Yeah. I'm not *that* kind of sick."

"Okay." He was all the way out of his sleeping bag and staying there in case quick action might still be called for. "What kind of sick are we talking about, then?" Sitting cross-legged in the fleece shorts he'd worn to sleep in, he turned on his lantern and waited for her to explain.

Meanwhile, from the next camp over, a woman started singing "Someone Like You." She sounded drunk.

Piper laughed. "I'm pretty sure that's not Adele."

"I'm pretty sure you're right—tell me what's wrong."

The woman kept on singing. Piper clutched her middle and laughed even harder. And then, in an instant, she was sobbing.

"Ah, sweetheart..." He reached for her.

With a little moan, she scrambled from her sleeping bag and crawled into his lap.

He held her close, rubbed her back and whispered soothing, meaningless things. It was heaven, the feel of her in his arms. He enjoyed the moment far too much, given that she was clearly miserable, and he had no real idea how to help. At least his duffel was in reach. He took a travel pack of tissues from the front pocket and handed them over.

She laughed through her tears. "At this rate, I'm going to use up all your Kleenex."

He stroked her hair. "It's not a problem. I know where they sell them."

She sniffled and blew her nose as the woman at the other campsite finished the song.

There was clapping from more than one direction.

The drunken singer shouted, "Thank you, thank you! I love you all!"

"No more, damn it!" a gruff voice bellowed from the opposite direction. "No more, I'm begging you!"

Not too far away, someone burst into laughter.

By then, Piper's tears had stopped. She looked up at him through misty eyes. Her nose was red. He wanted to kiss her so bad it hurt.

But right now, kissing was not what she needed. "Talk to me," he said.

She sniffed. "I'm meeting my father the day after tomorrow. It's really going to happen. And I can't stop thinking, what if I hate him? What if his wife resents me? And what about their kids—who aren't actually kids anymore? What if my half sisters and brother want nothing to do with me?"

"You liked him from his emails and texts, remember? You said you thought he was a very nice man."

"You're right, I did." She swiped at her eyes with the tissue again. "But what if I was wrong? What if…?" She stopped in midsentence and let out a long sigh. "I'm being ridiculous."

"Uh-uh. You're being human. You're going to meet your father for the first time. That's big. So big. It's only natural for you to have all kinds of questions that can't be answered until you get to know him a little. Of course you feel anxious and uneasy…"

"Is it only natural to crawl into your lap and cry like a baby?"

"What are you talking about? You didn't cry like a baby."

She scoffed. "Jason, we both know I did."

"No. You cried like a woman—for a totally understandable reason. It's a whole different thing."

That brought a sniffly laugh from her. "Well. I feel so much better about bawling all over you now." Biting that tender lower lip of hers, she patted his chest. "You're a rock. Thank you."

"You can bawl all over me anytime."

"Yeah, well…" Now her cheeks were as red as her nose. She chose that moment to retreat. Scrambling out of his lap, she wriggled back into her sleeping bag. "We should probably try to get some sleep."

"Good idea," he lied. He would rather she crawled back into his lap so that he could sit there, grinning like a fool, holding her all night long.

But that wasn't going to happen, so he turned off the lantern and climbed into his own bag.

It took him quite a while to get to sleep. When he did, it wasn't for all that long.

He woke again to the feel of Piper, sound asleep and plastered right up against him the way she'd done the night before. He eased onto his side. Pulling her closer still, he buried his face in her hair.

Piper woke to the gray light of dawn bleeding in through the tent flap, which was no longer zipped. She glanced over her shoulder to find Jason's sleeping bag neatly rolled and ready for their imminent departure.

Right then, she heard the crunch of boots outside. A moment later he ducked through the flaps, looking like a hot mountain-climbing cowboy in jeans, a blue plaid flannel shirt and black Timberlands.

"You're awake." He gave her that special smile, the one that made her feel everything was right with the world. "I was thinking of getting the fire going, making coffee…"

Her eyes felt puffy from all that crying. She must look half-dead. Gulping down a soggy mishmash of feelings, she shook her head. "Let's just pack up, have breakfast in Springdale and then get on the road."

"You got it."

After quickly cleaning up in the campground washrooms, they got breakfast burritos and really great coffee in a little place called the Deep Creek Coffee Company. The service was as good as the food. Smiling, with full bellies, they were on the road by seven.

The trip through the desert to Southern California took almost eight hours. There were lots of things to see on the way, but Piper wasn't paying a whole lot of attention. The endless, dry, rolling desert fled away beneath the wheels of Jason's crew cab. She kept thinking of the stranger and his family she was rushing to meet.

It all seemed unreal.

Never leaving the highway, they blew right past Vegas and kept going till Barstow, where they stopped at a roadside diner for lunch. She barely tasted her Reuben sandwich and Jason ate most of her fries.

He didn't ask her if she was okay. She could see in his eyes that he understood her anxiety. It wasn't something she wanted to talk about. She just needed to get there and get that first meeting over with.

Too bad she had to live through the rest of the day and the night to follow before she would see her father's face for the very first time and begin to find out if he was someone she could ever feel close to.

"You in the mood to take the wheel?" Jason asked when they left the diner. He'd driven the whole way up till now and they'd both been perfectly happy with that.

She knew his game. "You're trying to distract me from this latest bout of tortured anxiety and doubt, right?"

"Is it working?"

"No. But I appreciate the effort. And sure, I'll drive for a while."

She got behind the wheel. He took her spot on the passenger side and off they went.

"We need some good music," he announced and then got busy working up a playlist. He turned the sound up loud. Everything he played was upbeat—from "Walking on Sunshine" to "Get the Party Started" to "Boot Scootin' Boogie" and "Proud Mary."

After an hour of relentlessly happy songs, she groaned.

"Okay, okay. I'm starting to feel cheerful. I promise you I am. You can turn it down a little now."

He laughed. Really, he had the greatest laugh. Rich and happy, deep and real. "I *might* be willing to turn the volume down," he hedged. "But at the first sign of moping, it's getting loud in here again."

She couldn't hold back a laugh of her own then. "You're going to make a wonderful dad." The words were out of her mouth before she knew she would say them.

Time stopped—well, not really. But it sure felt like it. When she snuck a glance at him, he was looking straight at her. "I'm sure as hell going to give it my all," he replied.

"Yeah." Her voice was barely a whisper. "I get that. I believe that you will."

She drove the rest of the way to the Marriott Del Mar, which Jason had booked during the ride.

San Diego was gorgeous, beachy and bright. They checked into the Marriott, went to their room, stuck their bags in the corner and stared at each other.

"We made it," she said. "I want a shower so bad."

"Go ahead."

"No way. You go first. Make it fast. I'm going to be in there for a while."

He hoisted his duffel onto one of the beds, zipped it open and pulled out a fresh change of clothes.

When he vanished into the bathroom, she got out her phone to text her dad. But then she hesitated, her heart thumping against her breastbone, her face hot and her hands clammy.

Because how long was she going to avoid actually talking to him? He'd called her twice in the past couple of weeks. She'd listened to his voice mails and then texted her replies.

Somehow, being on the phone with him, hearing his voice in real time and letting him hear hers, had seemed too scary, too...real.

"Oh, just do it," she whispered to herself—because she was that nervous right now, nervous enough to give herself orders out loud.

She brought up her dad's number and hit the phone icon.

He picked up on the first ring. "Is this Piper?" He sounded excited, like he'd been waiting, phone in hand, to hear from her.

"Hi, uh, Simon. Just wanted you to know that we're here—me and my friend, Jason."

"You did bring a friend. Wonderful." Simon really did sound nice... "Piper? You still with me?"

"Yes. Yes, I am. And yes, I did bring a friend. Jason's a great guy."

"We can't wait to meet him—and you, Piper. You most of all." Now he sounded choked up. "Oh, listen to me. I'm almost blubbering all over you right here on the phone. Don't be afraid. I promise to pull myself together before you arrive. When will you be here?"

"Well, it's been a long trip so we're going to get some rest and see you in the morning."

"Oh, Piper. It's so good to hear your voice at last and to know that I'll be seeing you tomorrow. Nia is as excited as I am. And Maris, Shannon and Cameron will be here, too." Those were her half siblings. Maris and Shannon were married with kids. Cameron was still single.

"I...can't wait." She knew she sounded hesitant and nervous. Because she was. "What time should we be there?"

"The earlier the better. Where are you for tonight?"

"The Marriott Del Mar."

"That's nice and close. Hold on. Let me consult with my better half."

"Sure." She tried to regulate her breathing as she waited for him to come back on the phone. He did seem like a sweetheart. He really did.

"Piper? Do you think you could come at ten for a late breakfast?"

"Yes. Ten is great. We'll be there."

"And you'll stay over tomorrow night—Sunday night, too, if that works for you. But tomorrow night, definitely?"

She agreed that she would. "So we'll see you at ten in the morning, then."

"We'll be expecting you."

Piper hung up, tossed her phone on the nearest bed and then stood there staring at a vivid seascape above the headboard. She was shaking a little just from the un-reality of having an actual phone conversation with her father after she'd long stopped believing she would ever even know his name.

But aside from the trembling, she felt fine.

Good. Pleased, even.

Yes, she still worried a little that she might burst into tears, but in a happy way. He really had seemed welcom-ing, eager to meet her in person at last.

The bathroom door opened.

She glanced that way as Jason emerged wearing clean jeans that rode low on his lean hips. He truly was a beau-tiful man, strong and broad in all the right places, with just the right amount of silky dark hair trailing across his hard chest and down, leading the way to all the good stuff below.

He was rubbing his wet hair with a towel, but when he saw her staring, he stopped. "Piper?" The sound of his voice had her suddenly wanting to cry again. He asked, "Did something happen?"

She nodded. "I just called my dad. He sounds like a really nice person."

"Well, great." He still looked unsure. "So... You're okay, then?"

"Yeah. I just..." She turned and dropped to the end of the bed. "The truth is, I've been avoiding calling him, afraid of... Oh, I don't even know what I was afraid of. That I wouldn't like him, I guess. That he would seem like someone I didn't even want to know. So I've been texting and emailing him instead of calling."

"But just now, you did call?"

"Yeah. Yeah, I did. I called him. And he sounds like a lovely man. And... I just never thought I would meet him. I gave up on ever knowing him so long ago. I walled him off in my mind, in my heart. And it makes no sense, but now that I've found him, I've been afraid to let down that wall."

"Hey." He came and sat on the bed beside her. When she leaned into him, he put his arm around her. She rested her head on his bare shoulder, breathed in his just-showered scent. "You were cautious," he said. "You were protecting your heart. That's completely understandable."

"Yeah, but it wasn't his fault, not ever. He had no idea I even existed—as my mother has told me repeatedly. But I wouldn't listen to her. I blamed him for not finding me."

"You were a kid."

"True. But I didn't stop blaming him, not really—not even after I grew up."

Jason said nothing. He just sat there with his arm around her, giving her time to let go of some of the old crap in her head.

Eventually, she drew a breath and straightened her shoulders. "Well. All of a sudden, I'm thinking this might be a very nice visit."

"That's the spirit."

She nudged him with her elbow. "I really need to stop having these meltdowns around you."

"Nah. I can take it."

"But you shouldn't have to."

"Piper. I don't *have* to. I'm here because I want to be here."

She met his eyes directly. "Thank you."

"Anytime."

She nudged him again. "Your mom thinks I'm too old for you—but sometimes I wonder if it's the other way around."

Chapter Ten

The minute Simon Walsh answered the door and she saw his face for the very first time, Piper knew that everything really was going to be all right.

Her father had ruddy skin, white hair and a short beard to match. His eyes were the same green as hers. He reached for a hug, and she didn't hesitate to hug him right back.

Inside, he introduced her to his pretty wife, Nia, and to Piper's adult half siblings. Everyone seemed welcoming. There were children, five of them, aged two through thirteen. Maris had three kids, Shannon had two. Maris's two-year-old regarded her warily, but the other four children smiled and called her Aunt Piper, which felt simultaneously wonderful and disorienting.

They had breakfast at a giant, round table in the sunroom, where the arched floor-to-ceiling windows looked out on lush, subtropical landscaping and a gleaming fenced-in pool. Clearly, Simon and Nia had done well for themselves. Simon seemed happy—with his children and grandchildren. And most of all, with his wife. It was Nia who encouraged him to talk about how he'd met Piper's mom.

Simon explained that he'd been on his way to USC from

the Kansas farm where he'd grown up. He'd stopped at a music festival in the San Bernardino Mountains.

"And I met your mom," he said to Piper. "We should have exchanged phone numbers, I know that now. But I was away from the farm and out on my own, feeling free for the first time in my life, everything wide-open. No boundaries, no morning chores, nobody reminding me what to do or when to do it. Your mom and I agreed it was first names only and that made perfect sense at the time. She was going north, and I was headed south. What can I tell you? We were young and it was the eighties…"

Nia leaned close enough to Simon to brush his shoulder with hers. She gave him a small, private smile and then she said to Piper, "When he found out he had a daughter he'd never met, he went in our bedroom and didn't come out for two days."

"It was a shock," said Simon, his voice a little unsteady. "To accept how much I had missed, all the years you were growing up, your first steps, your first high school dance…"

Piper blinked away the sudden tears. "I understand completely. Believe me, I do."

"I'm just glad that you're here now," said her father. "I hope that we can keep in touch, get to know each other better, make up for at least a little of all the time we've lost."

"I would love that."

A few minutes later, Maris asked, "So, Jason. How did you and Piper meet?"

He put his arm across the back of her chair. She leaned toward him a little, realizing that she felt comfortable in her father's house. Safe. And that whatever Jason said in response to her half sister's question was all right with her.

"We met at the public library years ago," Jason explained. "I thought she was beautiful. She helped me find whatever books I needed, and I had a giant crush on her. But I was too shy to make a move—plus, I knew I didn't have a chance."

Piper added, "But lately we've become very good friends."

"Oh, we can see that," said Shannon with a sly grin.

Piper only smiled.

By then, the kids were getting rowdy. Everyone helped clear the table and they all moved out to the backyard. The children went swimming. Later, there was a big family dinner on the patio, with everyone laughing and talking over each other. It was absolutely beautiful, Piper thought. Her fantasy of a big, close, happy family come miraculously to life.

After the meal, Nia took Piper aside. "I've put you and Jason in the same room. It's a nice size, with its own bath. Does that work?"

"Absolutely." She winked at her stepmother. "As I said, we are very good friends."

And as very good friends, they got to share a queen-size bed. Which was fine. By now, Piper was accustomed to being near him at night—more than accustomed, to be strictly honest.

She liked being near him as they slept, liked waking up spooned against him with his muscular arm holding her close. She even liked feeling how much he wanted her, which happened every morning—and sometimes during the night. Neither of them ever mentioned that. She always knew when he was awake because he would groan softly, carefully remove his arm from around her and roll over onto his other side.

That night at bedtime, they took turns in the bathroom. Piper emerged in both a T-shirt and pajama shorts. Jason came out in sleep pants and a soft, short-sleeved Henley. In bed, they were careful to respect each other's space, facing each other on their separate pillows, leaving the center of the bed empty. They whispered together about how well the day had gone. He said he liked her newfound family.

She whispered back, "I like them, too."

When she faded into sleep, she was still very much on her own side of the bed. But in the middle of the night, she woke plastered close to his big, hard body, with his arm wrapped around her.

"Sorry," he mumbled a few minutes later, and pulled away.

Her side of the bed felt empty without him.

But then, in the morning, she woke with him curled around her all over again. And she thought how good it felt to be with him this way.

Until he groaned, rolled off the far side of the bed and disappeared into the bathroom.

They spent Sunday there at her father's house. It was a good day, easy and relaxed. She got a little time with each of her sisters and she and Cameron played Ping-Pong. Her half brother was very competitive. But way back in college, Piper had learned how to play from Brandon, who always played to win. Brandon had coached her as fiercely and aggressively as he did everything else. Now, all these years later, she managed to hold her own against her newfound half brother.

They said goodbye to Cameron before dinner. He lived in Denver and had a flight to catch. Her half sisters and their families lived in the San Diego area. They stayed for the evening meal but left soon after.

That night, Piper decided she'd had enough of trying to stay on her side of the bed. She scooted right over to Jason. He reached out his arm and pulled her close.

She settled in with a happy sigh. "This is nice."

He made a sound. It might have been a laugh. Or possibly a groan.

Monday morning, it was just the four of them—Jason and Piper, Simon and Nia. Piper felt right at home. They made plans. Simon and Nia accepted Piper's invitation to visit Wyoming next year for the Fourth of July. Piper felt Jason's gaze on her when Nia said they would love to come. She looked his way and knew just what he was thinking.

Next July, their baby would be six months old. And by then, her dad and her stepmom would be well aware of their new grandbaby. Piper planned to call them and tell them as soon as she made the three-month mark.

After breakfast, Simon and Nia stood in the long, curving driveway with their arms wrapped around each other waving goodbye under the bright morning sun. Piper leaned out her window and waved right back at them until Jason turned the corner.

"I miss them already." She sat back in her seat, stared out the windshield and almost considered ordering Jason to turn around and go back. Maybe they could stay on for a few days. Or longer. She laughed at the thought.

Jason sent her a quick glance and focused his eyes on the road again. "You miss them and that's funny?"

"I was just thinking that I wish we could stay longer—

and yet a couple of days ago, I was a basket case at the prospect of seeing my father's face."

"Sometimes, you put one foot in front of the other and you keep moving forward and things work themselves out."

"I get that, I do."

He shifted his gaze her way again, those blue eyes sweeping over her, warm and thrilling as a physical caress. How did he do that? The man excited her with just a look. "But...?" he asked.

"Some things are just so...difficult, that's all. Sometimes the past makes it hard to give people a chance."

He was watching the road again. "You worked through it, though."

"I did—and all of a sudden, I have a dad and a stepmom, two sisters, a brother, a couple of brothers-in-law... Oh, and I'm an auntie several times over. Miracles can happen, they really can."

A little while later, she got out her iPad. "I'll find us a place to stay in Hollywood," she said.

"No need." He sent her a quick, warm glance. "I already booked us a room."

"What hotel?"

"You'll see..."

Two and a half hours after they left her father's house, they were cruising down Hollywood Boulevard. Jason turned in at the Hollywood Roosevelt Hotel.

A valet appeared. Jason leaned out the truck window. "Two nights. The reservation is under Jason Bravo."

The valet took their bags from the back. Piper sat in the truck, watching Jason and the valet in her side-view mirror. Jason tipped the valet, who hustled right over to open her door. "Enjoy your stay, miss."

"Thank you." A bellman had emerged from the hotel. He piled their bags on a cart and wheeled the cart back inside.

Piper felt more than a little out of the loop, but she followed Jason through the glass-and-ironwork entry doors to the lobby with its coffered ceiling and Spanish archways. He checked in and they went to their room, a cabana room complete with balcony overlooking the long blue pool in a central courtyard below. The room had light oak walls, an ebony floor and midcentury modern furniture. It was as cool and bright as the lobby had been.

She sat on the end of the platform bed and smoothed the skirt of her red sleeveless sundress, waiting as the bellman delivered their luggage. When it was finally just the two of them, she fell back across the bed, arms spread wide. "Well, this is all very glamorous."

He stood over her. "This hotel is a Hollywood landmark. They held the first Oscar awards here. Marilyn Monroe used to stay in one of these cabana rooms before she made it big—oh, and the inside of the blue pool down below was painted by David Hockney. He's—"

"I know who David Hockney is. I took a few art classes in college myself—and as I said, so glamorous. And I had no idea you would book us a room here. When did you do that?"

"I booked it yesterday while you were beating your brother at Ping-Pong."

"Sneaky. I like that. And by the way, excellent choice."

"I'm glad you approve." He sat on the end of the bed. She moved her arm so that he could lie back beside her.

They turned their heads to smile at each other and he said, "I've always wanted to stay here. For sentimental reasons."

Kicking off her red wedges, she rolled to her side facing him and rested her cheek on her hand. "Okay, now I'm intrigued. What sentimental reasons?"

"My mom stayed here before I was born—before she married my dad. She'd been in love with him since they were both fourteen years old. But he'd left Wyoming and come here to LA. He'd set up shop as a private investigator."

"And your mom came after him."

"That's right."

"I'm impressed. I mean, your mom and I may have our issues to work through, but props to her, going after her man like that."

He touched her cheek, a slow, featherlight caress. Her skin warmed at his touch. "You think so?"

"I do…"

"Too bad my dad turned her down."

She laughed, the sound low. Husky to her own ears. "But wait. Let me guess. Judging by the fact that they are very much together now and have been for years, I'm guessing that in the end, he couldn't resist her."

"That's right. He couldn't." He stroked a slow finger down her bare arm, raising a lovely chain of happy shivers. "I like this dress." It had a flipped-up red collar and little buttons down the front, very '50s retro. He undid the first button and then the one after that. Her body felt lazy now, lazy and warm and so relaxed. "I would really like to take this dress off you. Does that work for you?"

"Hmm." She scooted closer as she pretended to consider his request.

"Well?"

"Yes! That works. You should definitely take this dress off me." She was looking in his eyes, thinking that she'd never felt this good, this easy and open, with anyone before. There were maybe three inches between his mouth and hers now. He closed that distance. She sighed and opened for him. "Jason…"

"Right here…" His mouth covered hers again. He shared her breath as he drew her closer, his hand stroking down her arm and lower. Fireworks exploded, bright and so hot, rolling out along her limbs.

"The way I see it," she began on a breathy sigh, "why not make the most of this time we have together? Just for now, just until we get home…"

He laughed, low and soft and somehow rough all at the same time. "You want to have sex with me until we get home?"

"Oh, yes, I do. So much. I want to have *all* the sex…"

"Well, now that's a tall order." He pressed a perfect line of kisses along the edge of her jaw.

Did he want that, too? She needed to find out. "I mean, if *you* want that, too…"

"Is that a question?"

"Well, do you?"

He pulled back enough to look down at her. Now his eyes were watchful. "Yeah, Piper. I do. But you need to be sure about it."

She swallowed. Hard. "Okay, then. We can be together. *Really* together in every way for the rest of this trip. And then, when we get home, we can go back to being—"

He cut her off. "I don't need to hear it. I get it. It's just for now."

"Yes. Just for now. While we're on our way home."

"Seven days, six nights. Today through Sunday."

"Yes, please." She couldn't help grinning.

"And one more thing…" He hesitated.

"Just say it," she coaxed. "It's okay."

"Well, other than the morning sickness, you seem perfectly healthy."

"Because I am."

"So then, no danger to the baby if we—"

"Honestly, Jason. Dr. Hayes says I'm healthy and strong. There is no danger to the baby at all."

He smiled. Finally. It was a very wicked smile, which made it all the better. "I'm glad we're taking the long way," he added, the dark glint of sexual promise in his eyes. "We'll need to make the most of every moment."

Oh, that sounded so very good good. "Yes, Jason. Exactly. That. Let's do that."

He caught her lower lip between his teeth and worried it with care. She felt that gentle bite all the way through her body. Heat bloomed in her core, and she moaned.

"It's been way too long," he growled against her throat, kissing his way downward, unbuttoning her sundress as he went. "Two damn months since that one night in April…"

"It seems like forever," she agreed, breathless now, eager to have him, to be with him in every way.

He asked, "What about condoms?"

"Do you have them?"

"I do," he said. "I wanted to be ready. Just in case."

"What do you think…?"

"Piper, it's your call. There's been no one else, I promise you."

"Well, then, never mind about them."

"Works for me." He turned his attention to her dress again. It had buttons all the way down the front. He undid them to her waist. And then, with slow care, he peeled the dress wide. "So pretty." Bending close, he pressed a line of kisses where the tops of her breasts met the lace cups of her bra. Her skin burned with each kiss. Her breasts ached so sweetly, and her breath came ragged now.

He took hold of her hand. "Come on." Rising, he pulled her up with him. "All these clothes have to go."

That sounded so good to her. "Okay…" She stood before him, deliciously dazed, as he untied the sash belt at her waist and undid a few more buttons.

The dress collapsed around her feet. When she stepped out of it, he bent, scooped it up and tossed it toward the nearest chair.

"There we go— Damn, Piper. You are fine." He pulled her into those big, hard arms and kissed her long and thoroughly. She moaned shamelessly into his mouth.

But then he tried to step away.

"Wait…" She grabbed for him.

Grinning, he caught her hand and kissed it. "Have patience." His voice was slow and sweet as honey. He got to work unbuckling his belt, undoing his jeans. Sitting just long enough to tug off his boots and socks, he rose once more and shoved down his pants. He kicked them away as he whipped his black T-shirt over his head.

Ohmygoodness. She'd forgotten how good he looked minus all his clothes. Every inch of him broad and hard and strong, his legs muscled from all that time spent on horseback, his arms corded and powerful. Just looking at him made her melt into a hot puddle of longing.

"Turn around."

She sucked in a sharp breath and did as he instructed. He took away her bra, hooked his thumbs in at the sides of her panties and slid them down to her feet.

"Step out."

She did, and then she turned to face him again. They stared at each other. Her body ached with yearning.

"Come here..." He took her arm and pulled her close.

She lifted on tiptoe, offering her mouth. He claimed it. They kissed for an endless time. She pressed herself against him, felt his desire hot and hard, poking at her belly.

It was paradise, to be in his arms this way once more.

She'd told herself so many times that this couldn't happen ever again.

Well, she'd been wrong. This was perfect. And they had days together, just the two of them.

His big hands roamed her back, stroking her, *knowing* her, straying down her sides in long, caressing sweeps and sliding in between their bodies, cupping her breasts, rolling her nipples.

Making her groan and whisper, "Yes. Like that. More..." against his hot, ardent mouth.

His palms glided downward. He grasped her waist. She let out a sharp "Oh!" of surprise as he lifted her. But then she twined her legs around him, clutched her arms even tighter around his neck and kissed him all the harder as he climbed onto the bed carrying her wrapped around him like a vine on a tree.

As soon as they were prone on the white coverlet, he rolled her beneath him. For a long, sweet string of minutes, he kissed her, his mouth playing on hers, his hands on either side of her head, fingers threading through her hair.

But then his lips wandered. They burned a searing path down the side of her neck, out along the ridge of her collar-bone and back again. Detouring lower, he rained kisses across the top of her chest.

"Freckles," he whispered against her skin. She had them there, too, on her upper chest. "I love them."

She surfaced from the delicious haze of pleasure long enough to laugh. "It's good that somebody does."

"They're beautiful," he said. "*You're* beautiful."

She didn't reply, just caught his face between her hands and kissed him again, slow and deep and achingly sweet.

Until he took her wrists and pressed her hands back onto the pillow to either side of her head. "Open your eyes."

She blinked up at him, feeling like a dreamer roused from a deep and satisfying sleep. "What?"

"This."

And then he kissed her again. Endlessly. Perfectly.

She sank again beneath the sweet waves of pleasure, giving herself up to the moment, to his big hands on her tender skin. It was so good.

Better, even, than their one glorious night in April.

Because she knew him now. Knew his heart-deep good-ness. Knew his kindness and his honest, helpful ways. She trusted him to treat her with understanding, to respect her wishes even when he didn't agree with them.

He took her nipple in his mouth. She moaned in de-light as he swirled his tongue around it before settling in to suck slow and deep, making her lift herself eagerly up to him, making her beg him never to stop.

But he did stop—in order to kiss his way lower, his lips straying to the thin skin over her ribs. She cried out at the shiver that went through her when he scraped his teeth over her flesh, followed immediately by the warm, rough lapping of his clever tongue.

And then he was on the move again. Her belly jerked and a laugh escaped her when he stuck his tongue in her navel. "Don't!" she cried, laughing some more.

He did it again anyway.

And then he went lower, his big hands sliding under her thighs, lifting them so he could ease between them. She rested them on his shoulders, moaning as he began to kiss her in the most intimate way.

She clutched the sheets and begged him—a cascade of pleas completely at odds with each other. She demanded more, ordered him to hold it right there, then commanded him never, ever to stop...

He just went on pleasuring her until she was nothing but a hot, tightening spiral of purest sensation. She cried out at the thrilling agony of it as the scorching swirl of bliss broke wide open into the joyous pulse of completion.

She was still in the throes of that bone-melting climax when he crawled up her body, notched his thick erection at her entrance and pushed inside.

It felt so good, so right, to have him filling her, pressing her down, surrounding her completely.

"Piper..." His mouth claimed hers. He tasted of sex, of sheer, undiluted desire. He was everything carnal, all the sins of the flesh turned to something so good and true and pure.

She put her arms around him and her legs, too, hooking her ankles at the small of his back.

He lifted his mouth from hers on a guttural moan. And then he smiled. "Seven days, six nights, huh?"

"That's right," she managed on a breathless sigh.

His hips kept rolling, pressing her down, then pulling back so that she could feel him slipping away—until the very last possible second, when he thrust in to fill her again. "We need to make the most of the time we have."

"Yes," she said on a bare husk of breath. Because he was right—and also because *yes* was the only word she knew at that moment.

And then words deserted her completely. There was only Jason, inside her, above her, pressing her into the white bed—and then rolling them so they were on their sides, facing each other, moving together, pleasure pulsing between them, filling her with heat and yearning, over-whelming her with that desperate need for more.

He rolled again and now he was under her, taking her shoulders in those strong hands of his, pushing her up so she sat above him, looking down, feeling him so deep within her.

"Move," he commanded. "Take me."

And she did. She moved, rocking on him, lifting and sinking, stroking him with her body, taking him with her as her body rose toward climax again. His big hands slid down the front of her, clasping her breasts, squeezing them so that she moaned at the pleasure that skirted the sharp edge of pain.

His touch moved lower. He clasped her hips, holding on as she rode him. She stared down at him, and he held her gaze, never once looking away.

All thought deserted her. There was only the feel of him, under her, in her. Only the glide and lift of her body on his. Only his blue eyes holding her, owning her.

A second climax came rolling through her. She went

under, still rocking, moaning his name. His hands gripped her hips even tighter, his thumbs pressing into the tender, giving flesh beneath her hip bones. She felt him throbbing within her, his climax taking form as hers began to subside.

They went absolutely still at the same time, hips pressed hard into each other as the finish swept through them both.

He said her name so softly. "Piper."

"Jason," she responded on a faint thread of breath. "Oh, yes..."

The rest was wordless—just the two of them holding on as the endless, white-hot moment opened out into afterglow.

He laughed, a husky, knowing sound. Her body went boneless. She curved over him. He reached up and gently pulled her down. Sighing, she stretched out beside him and snuggled closer.

He was hers in every way—for now. They would be together all the way home.

Chapter Eleven

Jason's grandmother Sharilyn and her husband, Hector, lived in a Spanish Colonial one-bedroom bungalow on a street that dead-ended into Melrose Avenue and Paramount Studios.

"They moved here about five years ago to downsize a little," Jason explained as he led the way up terra-cotta-tiled steps to a long walkway with glass-fronted apartment doors on either side. Birds of paradise, yucca, elephant ears and miniature palm trees lined the walk. "Before that, they lived in a small Spanish-style cottage off of Wilshire. Like this place, it was straight out of the 1920s. That house had two bedrooms and I stayed with them there while I was going to SMC. They both like these old Spanish Revival places with stucco walls and red tile roofs."

"I can see why. This is magical. Like we've gone back in time."

Jason's grandmother, a thin woman with white hair, answered the door before they could knock. "There you are!" She held out her arms. Jason stepped right up and grabbed her in a hug. "Oh, Jason. It's so good to see you."

"Good to see you, too, Grandma. Really good."

The network of wrinkles on the woman's face deepened as she smiled at Piper over his shoulder. "Hello. Piper?"

"That's me."

"I'm so glad to meet you—come in, come in!"

They stepped right into the Leversons' living room, which was furnished with a couple of recliners, a coffee table and a green sofa. There was a small flat-screen mounted on one wall. By the windows to either side of the front door, houseplants grew in profusion, some hanging in macramé pots, others on side tables and tucked into the corners.

Sharilyn's husband, Hector, emerged from the archway that led to the apartment's tiny kitchen, where something that smelled delicious was cooking. "Welcome, you two." The old man, who was stooped and nearly bald, shuffled toward them.

There were more hugs. Piper hadn't known what to expect from Jason's grandmother and her husband. She'd felt a little on edge that Jason's mom might have said something negative about her. But whatever Meggie Bravo had told them, the Leversons welcomed her with open arms.

The old man had cooked for them. They all four sat packed close together at the small table in the nook of a kitchen, eating excellent carne asada. There were homemade tortillas, too.

Hector said he'd coaxed the recipe out of a former landlady who lived in West Hollywood. "Her name is Dolores," he said. "She's something of a real estate mogul. Dolores owned the building I lived in when I met this beautiful woman right here." He leaned close to his wife and Sharilyn gave him a peck on the cheek. Nodding at Jason, he said to Piper, "Before that one was born, his father lived in the building next door to me, which was also owned by Dolores."

The old man and Sharilyn shared a slow private smile. Then Hector spoke to Jason. "Your grandmother came looking for your father all those years and years ago. I was a widower. I never planned to love again. But I took one look at this woman right here and knew that love wasn't done with me yet."

"I remember that story," Jason said. He was smiling, glancing between his grandmother and her husband.

Sharilyn added, "Oh, by the way, Jason. Your mother called a couple of days ago."

Piper's stomach, which had given her zero trouble for almost a week, suddenly felt queasy.

Jason's hand brushed hers under the table. She pasted on a smile to let him know she was absolutely fine and not the least bothered by anything Meggie Bravo might have to say.

"Your mother said to give you her love." Sharilyn's dark eyes shifted to Piper. "And to wish you both a great trip."

Well. That didn't sound so bad. Piper's stomach relaxed a bit. She ate another bite of her dinner. The food really was terrific, the meat rich and tender, just spicy enough.

Sharilyn said, "I love your mother, Jason. I love her like I love your dad and you and your brother and sister—and this wonderful man sitting right here beside me. With all of my heart. But she's such a mama bear. The way she's always pushing and suggesting and making plans for us, you would think Hector and I were a pair of wayward children."

Jason was nodding. Apparently, he'd heard all this before, too. "I take it she's still after you to move to one of those retirement communities she found?"

Sharilyn scoffed. "That or pack up and head for Wyoming where she can help take care of us now that we're practically decrepit. We're not ready for either of those choices. Yes, we know that eventually we will have to move again. But right now, we are managing just fine. Life's too short as it is, Jason James. I screwed up a lot when I was younger. For years, I made one wrong choice after another." She gave her husband an adoring glance. "But I've finally got the life I've always dreamed of. I'm not changing things up until I'm damn good and ready to."

Jason caught Piper's hand under the table, weaving his fingers between hers. "You do you, Grandma."

"Oh, you bet I will."

Piper braced on an elbow in the big, white bed of their cabana balcony room. Jason reached up to press his hand to the side of her flushed face. She looked rumpled and happy. And damn, she smelled good, like apples and sex, which wasn't surprising as they'd just made love. Twice. Each time was better than the last. Thinking about it had him ready to go for round three.

"I like your grandmother," she said. "Sharilyn's strong-minded and sure of what she wants."

Jason lifted off his pillow enough to press a kiss to the side of her throat. Her skin was like silk. He nipped her chin lightly.

She gave a low chuckle. "You didn't hear a word I said."

Reaching out a finger, he stroked it over the cute little muscle of her biceps. "Yes, I did. And you're right. She is strong-minded. According to both my dad and my mom—and Sharilyn herself—she didn't used to be. My grandfather was a terrible person who made her life a living hell."

"You mentioned him before, that he was not a good guy."

"That's right. Bad Clint Bravo was very bad news. It took Grandma—and my dad, too—years to get over the things he put them through. But now my dad's happy and Grandma's got Hector. Her life suits her perfectly. She doesn't let anyone push her around—not even my mother."

"Well, your grandmother is wonderful. Hector, too."

The slider was open to the balcony. Faintly, they could hear splashing and laughter from down at the pool.

Piper sat up. The covers fell away from her bare breasts. He couldn't wait to get his hands on them again—on all of her. Every sweet, silky inch. "It's warm out," she said. "Let's go swimming."

He would rather take her in his arms and kiss her senseless. But those green eyes were shining and, hey, swimming with Piper was always fun.

Later, back in their room again, they dropped their wet swimsuits on the bathroom floor and shared a quick shower that led to fooling around. When they finally dried off, she pulled on a sleep shirt and laid their swim stuff on the balcony chairs to dry. Back in bed, she was as eager as he was, reaching for him, kissing him like she couldn't get enough of him. He knew the feeling. Because he felt the same.

He made himself slow down, though. He took his time with her, savoring every touch, every sweet, hungry sigh.

They had six more nights and as many days.

It wasn't enough. Not if she really did insist they go backward once they got home. He didn't get that. As though they could flip a switch and be happy relegated to

the friend zone again. He seriously doubted he was going
to handle that well.

But why get all tied in knots about it now? They had almost a week before they rolled into Medicine Creek again.
Anything could happen in that time. She might finally let
herself admit what he'd known for months now, that the
two of them were a whole lot more than just friends with
a baby on the way.

"So I've been thinking," he said in the morning before they went to pick up Sharilyn and Hector for breakfast. "We haven't really gone over the specifics of the trip
home."

She pulled on a sleeveless top. Unfortunately, that top
covered her satin bra and the sweet swells of her breasts.
On the plus side, it clung. As she tugged on the hem,
smoothing it, she slanted him a look. "What, you don't
like this shirt?"

"I love that shirt." *But I like what's under it a lot more.*

"Well, thank you—and why do I get the feeling you
have a plan for our trip?"

"Because I do. You should know right up front, though,
that the shortest way home is back the way we came."

"Hello. I can read a map, too—and short isn't the goal.
We're taking the *long* way back, remember?"

"All right, then. I'm thinking we go ahead and take
101 north to Monterey. It's beautiful along the coast. But
we have to be careful. We can't be stopping every time
the mood strikes or we'll still be in California when our
six days are up."

"I can be careful."

"That grin on your face tells me you left *careful* behind
back in Medicine Creek more than a week ago." She gave

a husky laugh at that. He said, "Okay. So it's seven-plus hours of drive time to Monterey. How about we aim for Monterey tonight?"

"Perfect."

They packed up and checked out of the hotel. When they got to the apartment, his grandmother and Hector were ready to go.

They found a cute café a few minutes away on Melrose and took their time over the meal. Jason kind of hated to leave them. In the bright morning light shining in the café windows, his grandma and her husband looked frail. Like a strong wind could sweep them up and carry them away. Right then, he could understand his mother's concern for their care and well-being.

But then Hector laughed. The sound was rich, full of life and happiness. His grandma bent close to the old man. They shared a quick kiss. Jason decided to forget what his grandmother and her husband *should* do. Their life choices were their own.

It was hard to say goodbye, though. They ended up hanging around for a couple of hours back at the apartment. They drank lemonade and looked at the pictures in some old photo albums his grandmother dug out of the closet. The albums had faded shots of his parents and of him as a baby and even some of Sharilyn when she was young, holding his dad when he was only a few months old. Bad Clint was in some of those pictures, too. In black jeans and a black hat, Clint Bravo looked like trouble just waiting to happen.

Piper seemed as reluctant to leave as Jason was. Twice, he had to remind her that they needed to get on the road.

When they finally said goodbye, it was past one in the afternoon.

An hour and a half later, they were approaching Santa Barbara.

"I've been thinking," Piper said.

He thought, *Uh-oh*, but he kept it to himself.

She went on, "I can't just drive by and not tour Mission Santa Barbara. I'm forty years old, Jason, and I've never been there." And then she frowned. "Or if I have been there, I don't remember it. My mother and I might have toured the mission way back in the day. We went a lot of places in that VW bus…"

"So call your mom," he teased her as he merged for the off-ramp.

She scoffed. "Why?"

"Ask her if you've been here. If she says you have, we can keep going."

She gave him a playful slap on the shoulder. "Not a chance. Mission Santa Barbara, here we come!"

They wandered the mission and the nearby rose garden for a couple of hours. He bought her a Celtic cross in the gift shop, and she loved the lifelike statues of Jesus and Mary Magdalene in an alcove off the sanctuary. She pouted a little when she learned that the library archive was only open Tuesday through Thursday, and then by advance appointment only.

"This is what happens when you don't plan ahead," he teased.

"It's okay." She took hold of his arm and tipped her face up to him with a radiant smile. "I'm so glad that we stopped. Thank you."

"For you, anything." They shared a quick kiss and moved on.

When they left the mission, it was after five. They climbed in his crew cab, and she leaned across the console. "Let's get a room."

An hour later, they found a motel surrounded by sand and palm trees. It wasn't glamorous, but they could walk to the beach. And they did. They took off their shoes and strolled along barefoot as the sunset painted the sky purple and pink out over the Pacific.

"Tomorrow we'll make it to Monterey," he said firmly.

"Yeah, good luck with that." She laughed, turning toward him. Going on tiptoe, she commanded, "Kiss me."

"Anytime." He let his boots fall to the sand and captured her sweet face between his hands. The kiss went on forever. It wasn't long enough.

When she dropped her heels into the sand again, she gazed up at him, beaming. He caught her around the waist, turning her, pulling her back against his chest. They stared out at the waves together as the colors of the sunset deepened.

"I'm having the best time. I haven't been out like this, taking life as it comes, since I was nine years old." She rested her head against his chest and sighed. "I hated life in that bus. But now, with you, I kind of love just winging it, going wherever the mood takes us."

He nuzzled her hair. "Yeah, the way the mood's taking you so far, we could end up driving all night to get you home in time for work next Monday."

"Relax," She tipped her face back to him and they shared another kiss. "We have plenty of time."

Not really. Time went by too fast when you had long

distances to cover. But then again, he wanted to give her the kind of trip she would remember. If that meant driving nonstop to get home on schedule, so be it.

The next day, he drove straight through to Monterey with only one stop for a bathroom break. She'd found and reserved them a room at a beachfront hotel. But they got there at noon and check-in wasn't till four. They made good use of the time, visiting Cannery Row and the Old Fisherman's Wharf.

As soon as they checked into their room, she admitted she'd booked it for two nights. "I'm thinking tomorrow, we'll take a quick trip down to Big Sur, you know?"

He shook his head, but he was grinning. "You are so sneaky."

She grabbed the collar of his shirt and got right up in his face. "It'll be fun. You'll see."

And it was. The friendly guy at the hotel desk warned that there was no cell service through most of Big Sur, so Jason bought a guidebook with a paper map of what to see along Highway 1.

Piper leaned close and whispered in his ear. "You're going to make a great dad—willing to be flexible about where to go and when to stop, but always ready with the maps and the planning."

"No kid of mine will get lost on my watch," he replied.

As the guidebook advised, they went straight through Carmel without stopping in order to get going on the drive through Big Sur, all of it along Highway 1 with its gorgeous views of the Pacific. They found a parking space at Point Lobos and hiked for a while, holding hands, following the easy trails through coastal scrub grasses and even a gorgeous, twisted stand of rare Monterey cypress.

At one point, they got lucky and spotted a group of sea lions basking on a big rock.

Back in the truck, they headed on down the highway another thirty miles or so, enjoying the breathtaking views, stopping at Castle Rock to take pictures with the rest of the tourists.

When they decided they should turn around, Piper joked that all they did was drive. Even when they took a break and stayed in one place for a couple of days, it was only to drive some more.

On the return trip to Monterey, they stopped in Carmel-by-the-Sea. In the colorful little beach town, almost everyone they passed on the steep streets seemed to be walking a friendly dog.

"I'm beat," Piper said during the short return trip to their hotel in Monterey. "I don't think I can drum up the energy to visit the famous aquarium."

"So we'll order takeout and turn in early."

They got sandwiches and chips from a nearby sub shop and returned to the hotel, where they sat at the little table by the window to eat.

She was too quiet—and had been since they got back to the hotel.

Finally, he went ahead and asked, "Something on your mind?"

She made a thoughtful sound. "Today was so beautiful. Thank you for indulging me."

They would have some serious miles to make up, but so what? "It was a great day for me, too."

She almost smiled then—but not quite. "So... Aren't you glad I tricked you into staying here another day?"

"*So* glad," he agreed.

After they ate, he coaxed her to walk with him along the beach that was just down a sandy slope from the hotel. Holding hands, they wandered along the water's edge. The wind blew her hair back and the cool waves foamed around their feet.

"How did it get to be Thursday already?" Brushing a few strands of bright hair away from her soft lips, she glanced his way.

"It happens. You turn around and suddenly…"

"…it's tomorrow," she finished for him. "And then it's Saturday. And suddenly it's Sunday and you're almost home." She was so right. And no matter how they split up the rest of the trip, they were going to be driving eight-to-ten-hour days from here on in, Sunday included, to make it back in time for her return to work on Monday.

But it wasn't the long hours of driving that concerned him. It was the somber tone of her voice and the faraway look in her eyes. Something really was bothering her.

He stopped in midstride. Tugging on her hand, he pulled her back.

"What?" She turned and faced him.

"Talk to me."

She gazed up at him for the longest time, her eyes full of shadows. Finally, she confessed, "I don't want to go home. I just want to go on like this, you and me, headed wherever the mood takes us, with nobody to judge us. Nobody to tell us that…"

He took her shoulders and pulled her close. "What?"

"Hmm?"

"*Nobody to tell us that…what?*"

She sagged against him. "Sorry. But you know what

I mean—that you're too young and I'm too old and what do we think we're doing anyway?"

"Who said that?" He kind of wanted to go a few rounds with whoever it was.

"Well, your mother for one."

Crap. He should have seen that coming. "Look. She's sorry. Honestly, she is. She wanted to tell you so, but I asked her to leave it alone for now."

"Thank you. I don't want to get into it with Meggie, I really don't."

"I know."

She drew herself up and looked directly into his eyes. "And I will be fine, I promise. I'm feeling absurdly emotional right now, that's all. It's hormones. It'll pass."

He didn't believe that—yeah, hormones might be part of it. But there was more, and they both knew it. "Hey, now…"

She looked up. "What?" Her eyes shone with unhappy tears.

He framed her sweet face with both hands. "Say it," he coaxed. "Just put it on out there."

"Something got broken in me, Jason. I was…young and brave once, I really was. I knew what I wanted, and I was determined to have a bold life with the right man, to have kids, to have it all." She was shivering suddenly. "But then I chose all wrong. That almost destroyed me. And after that, I wasn't brave anymore. Eventually, I met Walter and I…got it all wrong again." She shivered a little and put her hand on her belly. "Ugh. I probably shouldn't have eaten all those barbecue chips."

"Come on. Let's get back to the room." He wrapped an arm across her shoulders and turned her toward the hotel.

As soon as he ushered her inside, she bolted for the bathroom. He was right behind her when she dropped to the floor and threw back the toilet seat. Going to his knees at her side, he held her hair out of the way as she lost everything she'd eaten earlier.

Once that was over, she dropped to her butt and scooted back to lean against the tub. "Well, there goes dinner." She forced out a laugh.

He rose, went to the cooler he'd left near the door in the main room and came back with the usual bottle of water.

"Always right there with what I need," she said. "Thank you." She screwed off the top and drank half of it down. "Okay, then. That's a little better." She spoke cautiously, one hand on her stomach. "I, uh, really need a shower."

"You want help with that?"

"Oh, Jason. Thank you, but no."

He didn't want to leave her. But this wasn't about what he wanted. "So you're telling me that you'd like a little time alone?"

A slow nod this time. "Yes, please."

Reluctantly, he volunteered, "I'll take a walk."

"Thank you."

So he left their room and went down to the beach again. The sunset was every bit as gorgeous as the night before, lighting the sky in purple and orange, the vivid colors reflected in the shifting sea below.

He plopped to his butt in the sand and watched the colors change as night came on. Eventually, he got up again, brushed off the sand and headed back the way he'd come.

In their room, he found her lying on the bed in a big, white T-shirt, her hair in that cute single braid. She opened her eyes as he entered.

"Sorry," he said. "I didn't mean to wake you."

Sitting up, she scooted to the end of the bed and put her bare feet on the floor. "You didn't." She held up the remote in her hand. "I was thinking of turning on the TV, but then I ended up just lying here, waiting for you. Want to watch a movie?"

He didn't, not really. He wanted to know more about what was making her sad. But that was for her to share when and if she was damn good and ready. He slipped off his flip-flops right there by the door. "Sure."

"Come sit by me." She patted the space at her side. He went to her and sat down. With a sigh, she leaned her head on his shoulder. "I'm kind of a coward. I just want to relax and watch something fun and mindless."

"I get it." Catching the tail of her braid, he gave it a tug.

Smiling now, she took his free hand, turned it over and plunked the remote in it. "You pick."

He pointed the device at the screen and started scrolling through the options. "*Guardians of the Galaxy*?"

She nodded. "Those are good. Which one?"

"Might as well go for the best."

"Ah." She tipped her chin up. "The first one…" Her mouth was right there, softly parted. Irresistible.

As if he even wanted to resist. "On second thought…"

"Hmm?" She tipped that mouth higher, a clear invitation. He tossed the remote over his shoulder. It bounced on the bed behind them and then dropped to the rug. Not that he cared where it landed. "Later for Peter Quill," she said. "Kiss me."

"Good thinking…" He claimed her mouth, taking her under the arms, pulling her with him until they were stretched out on the mattress.

What was it about kissing her? How could a kiss make everything better? These were deep questions—and right now, all he wanted was to kiss her some more. He stroked his tongue along the seam where her lips met, and she opened for him.

The sadness in her eyes earlier, the troubling things she'd said that didn't really tell him what the matter was?

He put all that from his mind.

For now, it was just the two of them, Jason and Piper, alone on a big, comfortable bed. The three long days of driving ahead of them, followed by an iffy future at best for them as a couple, and in time a baby that would change his world completely?

He let all that go. It would still be there to stew over in the morning.

"Be right back," he said as he rolled off the bed and started tearing off his clothes.

"Hurry," she urged him.

And he did, pulling his shirt off over his head, shoving down his jeans and briefs and kicking them away.

A moment later, he was back on the bed with her, gathering her into his arms. "I like this shirt," he whispered against her parted lips.

"It's a plain white T-shirt. Extra-large. Nothing special about it," she chided as her fingers, cool and soft, brushed at his temples.

"Oh, it's special, all right." He eased his hand up under the hem of the shirt, letting his palm glide over her thigh, teasing her a little with his hand between her legs, rubbing at the sweetness beneath her silky panties, then tugging at her shirt again. "This shirt is special because you're in it."

She chuckled. "I know that look. I won't be in it for long."

"Smart girl."

"Yes, I am. And don't you forget it."

He pulled back to look at her.

"What?" she asked.

"Panties first, I think..." He slipped one finger under the elastic at her left hip.

"Here. Let me help you." She eased her hand between their bodies and took the other side. Together, they pushed them down.

When those panties reached her knees, she lifted both pale, shapely legs straight up toward the ceiling. He whipped them off and tossed them toward a chair—and after more careful consideration, he saw that he didn't need that big, white shirt off.

Not yet anyway.

Instead, he scooted down the bed. Before she could lower her legs back to the mattress, he was between them, guiding them to rest on his shoulders. That put his face right where he needed it—with one smooth, white thigh to either side.

He started kissing her again, light kisses at first, bringing his fingers into play, too. She moaned and called his name, tossing her head on the pillow, begging him, "Please, Jason. Yes, Jason. Oh, please, just like that..."

He followed her instructions to the letter, kissing her and stroking her until her moans grew more desperate. With his mouth and eager fingers right there, he could feel the moment her climax began, a flutter that quickly built to a pulse.

She moaned and tossed her head from side to side. He

went on kissing her, stroking her, as she soared over the edge of the world.

"Jason…" She reached down and tried to get hold of his shoulders. "Oh, please…"

He knew what she wanted. Still, he waited, letting her hit the peak and start to come down before sliding up her body, wrapping his arms around her and rolling them so he was on the bottom.

She blinked down at him, gasping. "Yeah?"

"Oh, yeah. No doubt." He eased a hand down the back of one perfect thigh.

She sighed as she swung that leg over him.

"Up you go." He took her by the waist and boosted her over him, until she straddled him on her knees.

She did the rest, reaching down between them, positioning his aching hardness just where they both wanted it. Her green eyes held his. "It's only fair that I torture you at least a little…"

As if he was going to make a peep of complaint. "Have at it, sweetheart."

And she did. Wearing the smile of a wayward angel, that braid hanging over her right shoulder, a rope of red silk against the cotton of her big white shirt, she took her sweet time, bending close, lowering that clever mouth onto him.

Time flew away as she tortured him so sweetly with that perfect mouth of hers.

And finally, when he hardly knew his own name anymore, she sat up again and reached down between them to position him just so.

Once she had him in place, she lowered her body by fractions of degrees. It took her forever to claim his full length. Until then, he existed in the sweetest, most perfect sort of agony, trying not to groan, not to toss all dignity to the wind and beg her outright to let him all the way inside.

When she finally had all of him, he took that white shirt by the hem on either side. "Arms up."

"Yes!" She shot her hands skyward.

He tugged that shirt up and over her head, balled it between his fists and then flung it in the general direction of the door.

She was laughing as he reached for her—but the laughter didn't last long. He pulled her down on top of him and took her mouth.

That kiss was endless. And all the while, she rocked on him.

The past, the future—all those days ahead with the question marks in them. Days when she might be his or might be lost to him. Days when he hoped to become a good father, a loving one, both protective and wise...

For right now, he let all that go. There was no future. No past. No questions. No doubts.

Just Piper all around him, taking him, owning him, riding him to the sweetest place where pleasure took over and there was only right now.

Chapter Twelve

When Jason woke, it was still dark. A glance at the blue numerals on the clock by the bed told him it was almost 3:00 a.m. Beside him, Piper stirred and tossed her head from side to side. She moaned, an unhappy sound.

"Piper?" he whispered.

He reached out to soothe her, but pulled his hand back when she spoke in a pained, pleading voice, "Don't… No… Stop it…"

"Hey…" Through the shadows, he could see that her eyes were shut. Her face seemed strained, her sweet mouth was twisted.

She struggled as though someone held her captive. "I don't want to do this, Brandon. It's too dangerous! Let me go!" Right then, she sat straight up in the bed. Her eyes popped open, wide and terrified. "No!"

He sat up beside her. "Hey…" She flinched when he touched her. Raising both hands, he showed her his palms. "It's okay. It's just me…"

For a moment, she stared at him, eyes blank. Then she crumpled. "Oh, Jason…" She swayed toward him. He took her in his arms and held her for a while, stroking her hair, rubbing her back.

"I'm okay," she said at last, and gently pulled away.

"I'll turn on the light…" He hesitated. But when she didn't object, he reached over and flipped the switch on the lamp by his side of the bed.

He sat up, propped his pillow behind him and adjusted the blankets. She did the same. For several awkward seconds, they sat there in silence. She was still breathing too fast. He didn't want to do anything to freak her out more than she already was.

Finally, she reached over and put her hand on his. He laced their fingers together and held on as her breathing slowed to a more normal rate.

"I guess I owe you an explanation," she said.

He lifted her hand and pressed his lips to the back of it. "No you don't. I want to hear whatever you have to tell me, but not because you feel you have to explain yourself."

She gave him the softest, sweetest smile then. "But I do have to explain. Because I care about you. Because we're having a baby. Because I need you to understand."

"Okay, then."

They pulled up the blankets, getting comfortable.

Finally, she leaned her head on his shoulder and said, "I dated now and then in high school and during my four years at Wyoming State, but nothing serious. Then I met Brandon McAdams at the University of Washington. I got my master's in library science there. Brandon was kind of a big deal, a high achiever, you know? Lettered in academics, baseball and football. All the girls were after him, but he was with me, the nerdy library science major. I was wildly in love with him…" Her voice faded to nothing.

He waited, wondering if she'd changed her mind about saying more.

But then she went on. "The thing about Brandon was

that he got a thrill out of taking things one step too far. Being with him was exciting. When we hiked, we always had to take the most challenging, dangerous trails. I went skiing with him once. He pushed me to try a run I wasn't ready for. I wiped out and ended up in a cast for six weeks. He loved a challenge, loved to take chances. I still have nightmares about him pressuring me to do stuff I wasn't ready for or comfortable with. The dream I just had is the worst one, the worst thing he ever did to me."

Jason wrapped an arm around her and pulled her closer.

"It happened here in California," she said.

That surprised him. "You mean here in Monterey?"

"No. Until this trip with you, I'd never been south of Sacramento. But Brandon's parents owned a cabin up in Placer County, on the American River. I had just finished my first year at UW the summer Brandon I and drove down to his parents' cabin from Seattle for Memorial Day weekend.

"We arrived on Friday afternoon. His parents weren't there yet. Brandon and I went down to the river for a swim. It was cold, deep and swift. We climbed up a rocky cliff until we came out on a promontory far above the racing water. He wanted to hold hands and jump. I could see boulders in the churning current below. I knew it wasn't safe. When I wouldn't take his dare, he pushed me in and then jumped in after me…"

It took considerable effort, but Jason kept his breathing slow and even. "The guy was a psychopath."

She made a low, humorless sound. "Yeah, you could say that. I didn't hit the rocks, but I got caught in the current. I almost drowned. He pulled me out, performed CPR…

And when I coughed and came to, he sat back on his heels, grinning. 'See? It all worked out just fine,' he said."

"Tell me you punched him in the face."

"No, I did not. And it wasn't because I took the high road. At the time, I was still coughing up water, barely able to breathe. When I could manage words again, I said I wanted to go back to the cabin. We went. Then his parents arrived. They'd always seemed kind of cold and distant, like I wasn't good enough for their precious, perfect son. I just wanted to get away from him and from them. But we were up in the mountains, almost eight hundred miles from Seattle, and I didn't have a car.

"Somehow, I got through the weekend, but I was miserable, scared of my own boyfriend and very pissed off. As for Brandon, he put on a good act for his parents, but as soon as we were in his car driving back to Seattle, he hit the roof, calling me rude and self-indulgent and other names I would rather not repeat. I just sat there, silent, waiting to get away from him. The drive took twelve endless hours. When he dropped me off in Seattle at my studio apartment, he pulled the latch on the trunk. I jumped out and got my suitcase. Then I leaned in the passenger side window—and broke up with him, right there on the street."

"Good for you."

"Yeah. I thought so, too. I thought I was home free."

He didn't like the sound of that. "But you weren't?"

She shook her head. "Brandon was furious. His eyes were…feral. He said, '*You* don't break up with me. *I* break up with you.' I said he could call it what he wanted. But he and I were done. I headed for my building…" She paused. Her breathing was agitated.

"Take your time," he whispered.

She nodded. "He, uh, he left his car right there in the middle of the street and followed me up to my apartment. I was really scared by then. I didn't know how far he would go, what he would do. I got to my door, and I told him to leave. He wouldn't go. He ripped my purse off my shoulder and dug around in it until he came up with my keys. Then he dangled them in front of my face. When I grabbed for them, he whipped them away.

"He said, 'I'm coming in and before I go, you're going to understand how things work around here.' By then, I was beyond scared. I didn't know what he'd do. I screamed."

"Tell me someone came."

She nodded on a ragged little breath. "The guy next door, a middle-aged guy, came out of his place and said, right to Brandon, 'What the hell's going on here? What do you think you're up to, mister?'"

"And…?"

"It was like my neighbor had flipped a switch. Brandon dropped my purse and keys and put up both hands. 'Not a thing,' he said. 'Not a thing.' And he took off without another word."

"Did he leave you alone after that?"

She nodded. "I think he actually realized that he'd gone too far. The summer went by, and I never saw or heard from him. I had a job there in Seattle and I was taking classes, too. When the fall semester came, I saw him on campus more than once. He looked away. So did I."

"I would say you got lucky."

"Oh, yes I did."

"But, Piper, what happened, what you just described—both the nightmare, and the reality. There was nothing lucky about what that guy did to you."

"Yeah. I know. I haven't had that dream in the longest time, though. I kind of thought I was done with it." She scooted down under the covers, pulling her pillow with her. He stretched out on his side, facing her.

They were quiet together. The story she'd just told him still had him wanting to punch a hole through a wall—or better yet, go looking for the guy who'd almost drowned her.

He should probably just let her go back to sleep. But he wanted to know more—everything about her. Whatever she was willing to share with him. "So... Walter?"

She gave him a strange, wry little smile. "Yeah. You're catching on about Walter, aren't you?"

"You've said that Walter made you feel safe—and I'm guessing you needed safety, after what happened with that douchebag in Seattle."

She tucked her hands under her pillow. "I didn't date anyone else while I was at UW. Then I got my first job as a librarian, in Billings. I was there for two years, and I made some friends. But if a guy asked me out, I tried to be nice about it, but I always said no. Then there was an opening in Medicine Creek. I took it and I met Walter."

"I get it. Walter was good, right? He was what you needed."

"Oh, Jason..." Her eyes were all shadows, bottomless.

He wanted to touch her—stroke her hair, caress her cheek. But he kept his hands to himself. "What? Say it."

"No. Walter was not what I needed, though at first I really believed it would work with him, that I *had* found what I needed in him. Back when we first started dating, I told Walter everything about the awfulness with Brandon.

Walter said he understood. He said that what I had with Brandon wasn't love. He said, 'I'll show you what love is.'"

"That's a little…"

"Smug?" she asked with a groan.

"Yeah. *Smug*'s a good word for it."

"Well, Walter was kind of smug. But he did show me what love could be—up to a point. He was a good, steady man who treated me with consideration and respect. But whatever that special connection is between two people, Walter and I didn't have it. He was kind and he was gentle, but I didn't know his heart at all. And I never really showed him mine. We just went through the motions. We got through the days together, not exactly miserable, but never really happy, either—I mean, we'd agreed we wanted kids, but I never got pregnant naturally. And neither of us pushed to find out why."

"Sweetheart…" He touched her cheek and smoothed her hair.

She gave him the saddest little smile then. "The last couple of years, we rarely had sex. We were old friends who shared the same house. And when he died, I felt sad, I really did. But then slowly I came to realize that I was so much happier on my own. I like my life. Just as it is. I really do."

He wanted to argue, to tell her that it could be better, richer, with the right person. But he doubted she'd believe it just because he told her so. "This—all that you just told me—it's what you meant last night, on the beach, when you said that you made two wrong choices…"

"Yes." She held his gaze, unblinking. "Two wrong choices—Brandon and then Walter. I didn't get it right with either of them. I don't think that I know how to get it right. I don't think I'm cut out for a real, deep, successful relationship. I just don't know what I'm doing when it comes to all that relationship stuff."

"Hey." He nuzzled her cheek. "Don't sell yourself short."

"Oh, I'm not. Honestly. I keep hoping to get you to see that I'm perfectly happy being single and I'm done with trying to understand all the coupling-up crap. Being half of a couple just doesn't work for me. I'll be a single mom like my mom before me and there's nothing wrong with that."

He really wanted to argue with her, to insist that she shouldn't give up on love. But he'd tried that already, back at the end of April, when he'd cornered her at the diner. Arguing with her about love hadn't worked then.

Why should it work now? And anyway, wouldn't that only make him more like Brandon and Walter? The last thing she needed was another guy mansplaining away all her valid concerns.

"You're right," he said, choosing his words carefully. "Your mom did a great job raising you and there is no reason you can't do the same with our child. You're going to be a terrific mom."

She gave him a sly smile. "You're refusing to argue with me."

"I am. Will you please let me get away with that?"

"Oh, Jason. I have to admit, there is no man quite like you."

"I'm thinking that's a good thing. Right?"

"It is, yeah." She scooted a little closer. "It's a very good thing."

Now her lips were right there, inches from his. He couldn't help but claim them.

With a sigh, she snuggled closer.

He wrapped her up in his arms and deepened the kiss.

* * *

Piper woke with a start. She was leaning against the passenger-side window as they sped along I-5. Her neck had a crick in it and there was drool down her chin. She swiped the drool away, brushed her hair out of her eyes and glanced at Jason over there behind the wheel. As usual, he looked like every woman's dream of a smoking-hot cowboy. A quick glance at the speedometer told her that they were sailing along at sixty-eight miles an hour.

"Hey there, sunshine." He grinned at her and tipped his hat.

"How long have I been asleep?"

"An hour or so."

Flatland spread out in all directions. Far off, she could see the gray humps of mountains. With a yawn, she asked, "Where are we?"

"In the Sacramento Valley five miles from Willows, California. Halfway to Grants Pass." They were staying in Grants Pass, Oregon, for the night. She'd booked them a room before she conked out against the window.

Her stomach growled. "How about stopping for lunch?" she asked hopefully.

"Sure. Check your phone for a good place?"

"Will do."

They ate fat roast beef sandwiches at a cute little deli in Willows. In no time, they were back on the endless, flat highway.

"I'm happy to drive," Piper offered.

"I'm good staying behind the wheel unless you really want to take over."

She didn't. He drove on.

She grabbed a pillow from the back seat and napped

some more. When she woke again they were still in California, just passing Red Bluff. She smoothed her sleep-tangled hair back over her shoulder and asked, "Whose idea was it to take the long way home?"

He glanced her way and then focused his eyes on the road again. "I see no upside to answering that question."

She faked a frown. "You're no fun. But at least there are a few more hills around here—and I really do have to pee."

They stopped at a gas station and then got right back on the road.

It was still afternoon when they checked in at the hotel she'd found in Grants Pass. Their room had a balcony and a gorgeous view of the Rogue River.

After dinner, they took a little stroll around the hotel grounds. And later, back in the room, she kissed him eagerly and pulled him down onto the soft sheets of the big, comfortable bed.

Their time together was flying by. They only had one more night on the road after this. And she wanted his arms around her far too desperately for this love affair they were having to be almost over.

The next day, they drove 595 miles from Grants Pass to Spokane, through the vineyards and farmlands of the Willamette Valley, past Portland, and then northeast through the Columbia Gorge.

Her stomach started churning before they crossed into Washington. She asked Jason to pull over.

On the side of the highway right there in the glorious Columbia River Gorge, she threw up. Cars went by fast enough to make the crew cab rock behind her. Didn't even faze her. She rinsed out her mouth with the water from the bottle Jason handed her.

"My turn to drive," she said.

She drove the rest of the way to the KOA campground just beyond Spokane where Jason had reserved them a spot for the night.

"Like old times," she teased as they got ready to bed down in the tent.

"Old times, only better," he added. "Because this time we're zipping the sleeping bags together."

She climbed in the double bag with him and spooned back against him wearing her big turquoise T-shirt with an open book and Just One More Chapter printed on the front. When he trailed a finger up her thigh, taking the hem of her big shirt along with him, she smiled. And when he pulled that shirt off over her head, she raised her arms high.

A sleeping bag on a thin foam pad didn't make a very comfortable bed, but she hardly noticed. She was far too busy enjoying every last minute with Jason. They tried to be quiet, but at one point, some guy at the next campsite over whistled and suggested that they get a room.

Snickering like a couple of naughty kids, they whispered, "Shh," to each other. And then snickered some more.

Sunday morning came much too soon. They had ten hours in the crew cab ahead of them. After breakfast at a coffee shop right off I-90, they headed for home.

She drove first, through the Idaho towns of Coeur d'Alene, Kellogg, Wallace and Mullan. They rolled on into Montana. She stayed behind the wheel through Haugan, Saint Regis and Superior. A few miles out of Missoula, she had to pull off in order to lose what was left of her breakfast.

Jason handed her the usual bottle of cold, delicious water and took over behind the wheel. They stopped in Missoula for gas and a bathroom break and then kept going to Butte, where they got off the highway long enough to find the Hanging Five Restaurant, a family-style establishment that served cinnamon rolls as big as Piper's head.

She wanted one so bad. But she was way too likely to gobble the whole thing. And with the morning sickness situation, she couldn't be sure all that buttery, sugary goodness would stay down the rest of the way home.

Jason pulled her close with an arm around her shoulders. "I support you, whatever your choice."

With a sigh, she passed on the cinnamon roll and settled on an excellent turkey club sandwich instead.

From Butte, it was a little over five more hours to Medicine Creek. Jason drove and Piper alternately napped, read, fiddled with the radio and kept him company.

They talked about safe things—his life on the ranch, her plans for the library. She got him talking about his chain saw art.

He said he used to whittle. "But I like the big statement of a chain saw carving. A ten-foot red cedar dragon isn't something you can set on a shelf and forget until you have to dust it again."

He mentioned the carvers he'd met over the years, often at competitions. "Several carvers I know live on the West Coast. One's in Santa Cruz, as a matter of fact."

"We should have stopped in to see him…"

"Her," he corrected. "Molly Taft is her name."

"Is she good?"

"Her work is exceptional—and as for stopping to see her, I thought about suggesting that." He glanced her way.

Her skin warmed at the look in his eyes. "I think you would like Molly."

"So why didn't you mention her?"

"I wanted you all to myself." His voice was rough in the best sort of way. He turned his gaze back to the road.

Her throat felt thick. She swallowed to push down the knot of emotion. Their two weeks had whizzed by so fast. It almost didn't seem possible that they were already almost home.

Too soon, they were leaving Billings behind, then Lockwood and Toluca. And suddenly, they were passing the Crow Agency and then Garryowen, a town with a population of two, where the Battle of the Little Bighorn began. It wasn't far from there to the Wyoming border. Sheridan went by in a blur.

Twenty minutes later, Jason pulled the pickup to a stop in front of her house. He turned off the engine.

Panic rose inside her, a hot ball of desperation—to get out of the truck and flee up the front walk, to make it into her house before she burst into a flood of ridiculous tears and begged the man behind the wheel for more time, at least a few days. Another week. And then another...

More time for the two of them, more time for this heat and joy and wonder between them to burn on.

But that was just foolish. They had an agreement. And she was determined to stick by it.

She grabbed the door handle in a death grip and stared across the console at his beautiful, beard-scruffy face. Those blue eyes regarded her so calmly, like he had a clear purpose, like he knew what to do next.

Too bad she didn't. "Thank you." She sounded downright frantic. That wouldn't do. Sucking in a slow breath, she let it all the way out before drawing in one more and giving him what she hoped was a warm smile. "It was such a great trip. And you know, I'll just grab my stuff from the back and—"

"I'll get the stuff and walk you to your door."

"Jason, it really isn't—"

"Yeah, Piper. It's necessary." He was out of the truck before she could think of a way to stop him. She jumped out, too, and met him at the back, where he grabbed her suitcase and the big duffel with her camping clothes and gear in it. "Lead the way," he said.

So she did, striding swiftly up the walk, fumbling to get her key out of her shoulder bag and then finally managing to stick it in the lock. She pushed the door inward onto her small entry hall. Home. It all looked so perfectly peaceful, spotless and neat.

When she stepped inside he was right behind her.

"Just put those down. Thank you again. I'll take it from here."

He set both bags on the floor. But instead of leaving, he shut the door.

She took a step back. "Jason, I…" All she had to do was say, *please go*, and he would. It shouldn't have been that difficult.

Oh, but it was. She needed him to go. But his leaving was the last thing she wanted. Already, she ached for him, for their time together these past two glorious weeks.

How had it flown by so fast? Two weeks gone in what felt like an instant, a kaleidoscope of sweet moments, spinning and glittering, then suddenly tunneling down to this…

The two of them at her door, saying goodbye—or trying to anyway.

"Give me your hand," he said.

Without the slightest hesitation, she did. His fingers closed over hers and it felt like a lifeline, like everything that really mattered was now held, warm and hopeful, between their joined hands.

He pulled her closer. She failed to object.

A moment later, she was captured in the perfect prison of his big arms. She looked up at him, whispered his name.

He took that as an invitation to lower those beautiful lips of his to hers.

She kissed him. How could she not? She kissed him and she wished they could stay like this forever holding each other so tight, her soft breasts to his hard chest, her mouth opening under his. She needed him to go, but this kiss…

She never, ever wanted it to end.

When he finally lifted his head, she stared up at him and tried to summon the gentle words that would send him on his way.

"You really want me to go?" he asked, his voice rough, low, thrilling. A hot shiver coursed through her. No, she didn't want him to go. What she wanted—what she needed—was to keep on feeling the way she felt whenever he touched her.

But that wasn't the deal. She opened her mouth to tell him to go.

And instead, she surged up on tiptoe, reaching for him. He met her halfway, kissing her wildly as she ran her hands up over his hard shoulders and strong neck. His hat was in her way. She took it by the brim and tossed it over her shoulder. There. Now she could thread her fingers into his dark, thick hair.

Her feet left the floor as he scooped her up against his broad chest. She wrapped her legs around his waist and felt him, hard and ready for her. That only made her clutch at him tighter and kiss him more deeply.

The stairs were right there, a few feet from the front door. He lifted his head and asked, "Your bedroom?" in a rough, low voice that promised unearthly delights.

And then he waited, giving her yet another opportunity to stop this madness now.

"Upstairs," she instructed breathlessly, "first door on your left."

And up they went.

A minute later, he was carrying her into her room and straight to the sleigh bed she'd found at a yard sale and painted snowy white. Gently, he set her on the turquoise-and-white duvet.

She stared up at him. His eyes were all pupil, his mouth fuller than ever, deep red from their kisses.

Without a word, by silent mutual agreement, they undressed. She kicked off her hiking sandals and dropped each piece of clothing to the floor by the bed. He followed her lead, toeing off his boots and tossing his clothes to the rug, too.

And then, when they were both naked, she reached out her arms again. He came down on the bed with her.

Their kisses grew more desperate, even hungrier than on the way up the stairs. The summer sunlight slanted in through the filmy white curtains. It was so good with him, always had been. Every time, starting with their first night back in April.

She reached down between them, wrapped her fingers around his hard, ready length and guided him into her, crying out as he filled her. He whispered her name as he covered her lips with his.

They moved together, arms wrapped around each other. Her mind was spinning. The world seemed full of golden light. She could go on like this forever—and oh, she wished she could. She wished that this moment might never end.

Too soon, she felt her body rising toward the peak. With another cry, she sailed out into fulfillment, finding that sweet spot where the tension tightened so perfectly, then burst wide in a shower of glorious sparks. For several sweet moments, he held her good and tight. Her breathing slowed and she sighed in completion.

He didn't leave her. Instead, he continued to hold her. He kissed her cheeks and her throat, and then covered her mouth again as he began to move inside her once more.

Her body responded. She wrapped both legs around him, hooked her feet at the small of his back and lost herself to everything but the flow of perfect sensation.

That time, he rode the crest with her. She went over into free fall, and he followed right behind. The pulsing within continued for the longest time.

But at last, the hurricane of pleasure mellowed, leaving her breathing like she'd run a hard race, still twined around him, holding him so tight, wishing that she didn't have to let him go.

Slowly, she came back to herself. He eased his weight off her. But he didn't leave her—not yet. He rested his head on her shoulder. As for her, she was still holding on to him, not quite able to take her hands off him, though she knew she needed to put a little space between them.

It would be so easy to freak out right now. This was not the way it was supposed to go, not what they'd agreed on. She should have said goodbye to him downstairs at the door.

He was stroking her arm, lazily letting his fingers drift down into the crook of her elbow and lower, to the tender, pale skin of her inner wrist. It felt so good, their bodies pressed warm and close. She had matched her breathing to his.

Peace. Yes. Peace was the essence of this moment. She didn't want to give this up.

And really, why should she?

"Jason?" She kissed him on his scruffy cheek, using her teeth a little, soothing the scrape with more brushing kisses.

"Piper..." He turned his head enough to meet her lips with his.

They opened at the same time, tongues coming out to play, tangling, wet. She loved kissing him. He made kissing an art—spontaneous, playful, delicious and fun.

It came to her then, the answer to this ongoing problem. So simple. And it could work. She knew that it could.

She clasped his big shoulders, pushing him away just enough to break the sweet, endless kiss. "Jason..."

He looked at her with a slow smile. "Yeah?"

She lost her train of thought as she gazed at him. He had the longest eyelashes. What was it about really good-looking men? Why did they always have lush, thick, beautiful eyelashes that any woman would envy?

And where was she? Right. "I've been thinking."

"Yeah?" He guided a swatch of hair off her forehead and back behind the shell of her ear. "About what?"

"I don't want to give this up—you and me, like this. Jason, it's so good. I don't want to go backward."

He made a lazy, happy sound. "Tell me about it."

"So, remember that day at the diner way back in April? You suggested that we could try being friends with benefits?"

His brow crinkled a little—in thought? Or was he actually frowning? "I remember."

"Well, I think you were right. I think that might work. I mean, I would have my life. And you would have yours. And, you know, later, when the time comes, we'll work things out to take care of our baby.

"Oh, but Jason, I do want the sex, too. I really do. It's so good with you. And it could be so simple. I'll keep my house and you'll have yours. We won't be a couple. We're not getting married or anything."

"Let me get this straight. You want me to be your friend—*and* your booty call?" He didn't sound all that excited at the idea.

"Well, yes, for as long as it works for both of us. I mean, whatever happens will just happen. You might…meet someone else eventually. If you do, well, I'll miss the sex. But we will still be friends and co-parents. And you know how it goes, it could be that this thing between us will just fade away in time, and we'll both be fine with that. Because, honestly, who knows what happens with this stuff? I certainly don't."

The way he looked at her then, as though he was the older one, wiser and more experienced in…everything. And she was the youngster, green and untested, struggling to figure out how life really works.

"There's only one problem with your plan," he said.

"Problem?" She blinked at him, confused. "But *you* were the one who suggested it first."

"That was then. Things have changed."

"Well, okay. How so?" she asked.

"Damn. Piper..." Instead of giving her an answer, he wrapped his hand around the back of her head and moved in close again for a quick, hard kiss.

When he pulled away, she stared at him, completely bewildered. "Jason. What are you getting at?"

"You're not going to like it."

"Just say it, already."

"Fine. You can lie to yourself all you want to, but the friends-with-benefits solution? That ship has sailed."

"What are you talking about?"

"You're in love with me, Piper. You're in love with me deeply, completely and forever."

She gasped. "That's not true."

"Yeah, it is. And if you think your college boyfriend broke you, then you ought to give some serious consideration to how you'll feel the day I show up at your door to let you know there's someone else."

Piper could not believe what he'd just said. "You don't know what you're talking about. How many times do I have to tell you that I'm not doing that? I'm not falling in love with you or with anyone. Not ever again."

He didn't argue. Instead, he sat up and asked gently, "You want me to go?"

Did she? "You have no right to start telling me what's in my own heart."

"True." He rose and started picking up his clothes.

She stared at him, furious—and yet also bereft. "And now you're leaving, just like that?"

He pulled on his jeans, then sat on the bed to put on his socks and boots. "Do you want me to stay?"

"I... No. No, really. This is not working. You should go."

"Okay, then." He yanked his T-shirt on over his head. Finally, he rose. "I'm out of here."

Stunned, she stared after him as he left her bedroom. The sound of his boots echoed on the wooden stairs.

She never heard the front door open or click shut. He must have gone out very quietly. But he really was gone. Because a minute later, she heard his truck start up and drive away.

Chapter Thirteen

"So, what's up with you and Medicine Creek's hottest librarian?" asked Ty.

Knocking back a big gulp of champagne, Jason tried to decide how to answer his rosy second cousin.

The two of them stood under a giant ash tree next to a pretty rail fence. Beyond the fence, cattle grazed peacefully on rolling, green Rising Sun Cattle Company land. Far off to the west, the Bighorn Mountains rose, gray and craggy, poking into the wide, blue Wyoming sky.

It was a perfect Saturday afternoon for an outdoor wedding, and two hours ago, Ty and Sadie McBride had tied the knot. Jason wore his best black Western suit coat, matching dress pants and a white shirt with a string tie. His black tooled boots were buffed to a fine shine.

Ty nudged him with an elbow. "I mean, I thought she might be here with you today, you know?"

Jason continued to consider his reply. *Mind your business* had kind of a nice ring to it.

Then again, hauling off and punching Ty in the mouth held a special kind of appeal—not because Ty's questions were in any way deserving of a fist to the face. More because Ty looked so happy, and Jason was envious as hell that his cousin had the woman he wanted and a lifetime ahead of him with Sadie at his side.

Ty clapped him on the back. "Sorry, cousin. Anything I can do—anything—you just say the word."

"Thanks," Jason replied through clenched teeth. Because it would be all kinds of wrong to beat the crap out of his well-meaning cousin on the man's wedding day.

"Isn't it spectacular?" June Copely, in a blue sequined cocktail dress that clung to her generous curves, wrapped a plump arm around Piper's waist. It was an hour before the doors opened on the Medicine Creek Library's Annual Gala and Silent Auction. They stood in the atrium-like space near reception just beyond the wide entry hallway. "Jason is so talented."

Piper stared at the life-size Tyrannosaurus rex carved of white pine. The dinosaur had its mouth open, displaying hundreds of sharp, powerful teeth.

"It's impressive," she agreed, and wanted to cry. She missed him so much. There was an ache in the center of her chest, a gaping hole through which all her happiness had somehow leaked out. She kept reminding herself that cutting it clean was for the best.

But it didn't feel like the best. It felt like she was missing what made life worthwhile.

June was still admiring the T. rex. "You think it'll give the little ones nightmares?"

"Are you kidding? They'll love it."

June laughed. "Oh, yes they will—and thank God for Hunter Bartley." A year ago, Hunter and his reality show, *Rebuilt by Bartley*, had raised the ceilings and pushed out the walls on the main entrance and the reception atrium.

Even after those renovations, it had still been necessary to do some fancy maneuvering to get the enormous carving into the building. But now it stood proudly in the center of the atrium. "If it weren't for Hunter we never could have gotten this big boy in the door."

Two hours later, the event was in full swing. They had an excellent turnout. It seemed like just about everyone in town had shown up this year.

Guests of all ages wandered among the stacks and along the rows of tables set up with donated goodies for auction. They sipped sparkling cider and placed their bids.

Starr was there with Cara in her arms and Beau at her side. Piper greeted them.

"We missed our morning at the Perfect Bean last month," Starr chided.

Piper made a sad face. "I hate when that happens. Next week? I can do Wednesday at ten."

"I'll meet you there," replied Starr as Cara held out her arms for a hug.

Piper took the little girl, kissed her velvety cheek and chatted with Starr and her husband for a few minutes. When they moved on to check out the auction tables, Bobby Trueblood appeared, his mom right behind him.

The little boy grinned up at Piper. "Hi, Mithuth Wallath." He had two teeth missing in front and he looked about three inches taller than he was back in April.

"Bobby! How are you?"

"Real good. I *like* that big dinothaur!" he exclaimed.

Behind him, Maxine laughed. "We checked out three books on dinosaurs last week. He can't get enough."

"There's a stack of good ones available on the auction table," Piper reminded her.

"I thaw them!" Bobby grinned wider. "We bidded on them."

"Excellent." Piper nodded. "Good luck." Right then, Bobby's little sister peeked out from behind Maxine. Piper greeted her. "Nice to see you, Reina." The wide-eyed child raised her hand in a shy wave.

A moment later, Maxine herded the kids toward the refreshment tables in the open area between the children's and teens sections.

Piper watched them go—and spotted Jason for the first time that evening. He stood at the table with the paper plates, plastic cutlery and beverages on it, a foam cup in his hand, talking to Carolyn Kipp. About Jason's age, Carolyn ran the front desk at Don Deal Insurance Agency right there in town. She was pretty and friendly. Piper liked her.

Or she had until right this minute.

Jason glanced up suddenly. It was like he had radar.

Their eyes locked. And that hollow space inside her? It ached harder with emptiness.

She turned away.

Somehow, she managed to avoid eye contact with him for the rest of the evening. He was the star of the event. His T. rex brought a final bid of $10,000. There was fierce competition for it. And in the end, it went to some big spender from San Francisco who'd moved to town five years ago and built himself a giant house on the banks of Crystal Creek—a house that would now have a T. rex in the backyard.

The weekend crawled by. On Monday, Jason called her. Like the big, fat coward she was, she let it go to voice mail. And then she put off playing his message back.

Tuesday, he texted her. She avoided looking at that text for a couple of hours. But she was three months pregnant. They were having a baby together. He'd made it clear from the beginning that he intended to be part of everything that had to do with their child.

She forced herself to read the text.

When is your next doctor's appointment? It should have been last week, right? And do you have a date for the thirteen-week ultrasound? That's coming up soon. Call me. I mean it.

Though it broke her heart all over again to have to see him or talk to him, she made herself call him back.

The first words out of his mouth were, "Did I miss one of your visits with Dr. Hayes?"

Her heart ached all the harder at the sound of his voice. The pain was made even worse because she'd broken her agreement with him that he would be in on everything involving the baby—and judging by the banked anger in his question, he knew that she had. "Yes. I went last Thursday."

Silence echoed for several seconds before he spoke again. "We had an agreement, Piper."

"I know we did. I'm sorry. It won't happen again."

He seemed to be thinking that over. Finally, he said, "So, then, I have your word on that?"

"Yes. I won't leave you out again."

"All right. The next ultrasound?"

He was going to be there for that. He was going to be there, and she would have to see him, to have him right there beside her through the procedure. That was going to be painful.

But what was the alternative? To shut him out? She could probably do that, insist that he stay in the waiting room. He might even accept her decision. But her baby had a father who wanted to be involved. She needed to put on her big-girl panties and be glad for that.

"Piper? You still there?"

"Uh, yes. The ultrasound is this Friday at eleven in the morning. Up in Sheridan, same as before."

"I'll drive you."

At least that much, she could fairly object to. "No. I'll meet you there."

"Fine."

She swallowed. Hard. "All right. I'll see you then."

"Wait. Anything new at your appointment with Dr. Hayes?"

"No. Really. Everything's fine. The baby is fine. I'm doing well."

"Can you send me the after-visit summary?"

She started to argue that there really was nothing he needed to know. But why? Arguing would only stretch out the agony of this phone call. "Sure. I can email it to you."

"That'll work." He rattled off an email address. She grabbed a pencil and pad from the kitchen junk drawer and wrote it down. "How's your morning sickness?"

"Actually, it's better. I'm finally through the first trimester, so that makes sense, right?"

"Yes, it does. And I'm so glad to hear that you're getting past feeling sick all the time." His voice was softer now. She didn't know if his sudden gentleness made her feel better—or all the worse. Really, when would she stop missing him? When would she stop hurting at the sight of him, the sound of his voice, the mere mention of his name? He said, "And that leads us to my next question…"

She pulled out a chair at her kitchen table and dropped into it. "There's another question?"

"Yeah, Piper, there is." His tone had cooled again. "You're at three months and it's time to tell my family that in January we're having a baby."

Oh, sweet Lord. This was her life now. She was not her mother, getting pregnant by a stranger at a rock festival, blithely walking away to raise her baby on her own.

Nope. She was having a baby with a responsible man who lived in her hometown. And he would damn well demand to be there for every step of this process—he and his large, loving extended family. He had a *right* to be involved. And it was good for their baby that he demanded that right.

But at this particular moment in time, she just wanted to stretch out on the sofa with her eyes closed and an ice pack on her forehead. "Listen, Jason?"

"Yeah?"

"I need to think that over."

"It has to happen. My family *will* know. There's no getting around it."

"I realize that. I promise you I do. I just, well, it's a lot all at one time."

"What's a lot?"

"Everything."

"Piper, are you all right?" His voice had gentled yet again. He really was worried about her.

"Yes!" It took everything she had in her not to burst into tears. "I'm fine, I'm just…adjusting, you know, to the way things are. And I'll see you for the ultrasound on Friday. We can decide then about how and when to tell your family."

He said nothing for several seconds. She braced for his objections.

But then he agreed, "All right. We'll talk about it then. Goodbye for now."

And that was it. He was gone. She shoved her phone halfway across the table and put her head in her hands.

The next day, she met Starr at the Perfect Bean. It was just the two of them. Beau was watching Cara at home with the help of old Daniel Hart, who was like a father to Beau and a grandfather to Starr and Beau's kids.

Piper sipped her masala chai, and they spent the first few minutes talking about what a success the auction had been and what was coming up next at the library.

Then Starr got around to the elephant in the room. "So, you and Jason…?"

Piper stared across the cute cast-iron café table at her friend and hardly knew where to begin. "There's something you probably should know."

"Omigod. What happened? Are you all right?"

Piper leaned across the table and lowered her voice to keep it just between the two of them. "He wants more. I can't handle more."

Starr slowly sipped her coffee. When she set the cup down, she suggested, "Don't sell yourself short."

Piper almost choked on her chai. "Jason said the same thing to me one of the times I tried to explain to him why I've got no idea how to have a real relationship with a man."

Starr leaned even closer. "Jason's a good man. You're

both adults. The age difference doesn't have to be a big deal if you don't let it. As for the past—meaning Walter and whatever happened before you met Walter. That's over. Let it go."

"Oh, Starr…" She reached out.

Starr was right there, taking her hand, holding on tight. "Piper. I get that you're afraid. But you should see the look in your eyes when his name is mentioned. I'm just going to say it. You're in love with him."

"I…"

"Hey. It's okay. I get it. Sometimes the words are hard to find. But I do know Jason. He's one of the good guys."

"You're right." Piper put her hand on her still-flat belly. When she glanced up again, Starr was watching her fondly. Right then, Piper wanted to tell her about the baby. And why shouldn't she? It really was time to start sharing the good news with people she cared about. "And listen, there's another thing. ."

"Let me guess…" Starr leaned that extra few inches so that she could whisper in Piper's ear. "You're having Jason's baby and you're just now getting around to telling me about it."

Piper's stomach lurched. She breathed through her nose and the queasy feeling faded. "How did you…?"

"You know your mother is not real big on keeping secrets, right?"

"My mother…" Piper slowly shook her head. "Right now, I don't know whether to laugh or cry—my mother." She groaned and leaned toward her friend so the conversation could remain just between the two of them. "I mean, she's always saying that secrets are destructive. I guess

I should have made her promise to keep quiet about the news until Jason and I were ready to let people know."

Starr whispered, "You're how far along?"

"Thirteen weeks on Friday—and yes, I will start showing soon. It's about time to begin letting people know that there's a baby on the way."

"You're going to be a wonderful mom."

"I will try my best."

"There is no doubt about it. You will be a great mom. And I'm hoping you'll think about maybe telling Jason how you really feel?"

Her stomach was suddenly swooshy again. She took another deep, slow breath. "I will. I'll think about it."

Starr beamed. "That's what I wanted to hear."

Emmaline answered the door in a paint-spattered smock, her acres of graying red hair gathered and twisted up in a giant pile with the aid of a tie-dye scarf. She had a dab of yellow paint on her nose. "There's my girl."

It was a little after six. Piper had come straight from the library. "Hey, Mom."

Emmaline pulled her in for a hug. "You came at the perfect time. I just finished a painting and I've made your favorite sticky tofu bowl."

Piper waited until they were sitting at the table to bring up what Starr had told her. "Mom. I saw Starr this morning. She knows I'm pregnant and when I asked her how she knew…"

Emmaline shrugged. "Yep. I told her. You didn't want me to?"

"Well, Mom. We were waiting until the three-month mark, just to be sure everything was okay."

"I'm sorry, my love. I didn't get the memo on that. I won't tell anyone else until I get your say-so. And if you ever have another baby, I won't say a word about it until you give me the go-ahead."

"Great. But… How many people did you tell?"

"Hmm. A few. Mostly my artist friends. They're thrilled—for you, for me. And for Jason, too."

"So that means just about anyone in town might know by now."

"Yes, it does—and the baby is fine, right?"

Piper nodded. "Last week, Dr. Hayes said that things are looking really good."

"Wonderful. And as far as my telling people, you do realize they're all going to find out one way or another anyway, right?"

Piper suppressed a giant sigh. "Yes, Mom. But it really was my news to share."

"You're absolutely right. It won't happen again. I won't tell anyone else until you give me the okay."

"Thanks." What more could she say? The damage, if there was any, had already been done.

"So. How is Jason? You should have brought him with you tonight. There's plenty of food." Emmaline ate a chunk of the perfectly seared and sauced tofu.

As for Piper, right now she just wanted to cry again. She ate some rice, taking her sweet time about it.

But stalling did her no good.

Her mom studied her face and just *knew*. "Oh, my baby." Emmaline set her napkin by her plate and pushed back her chair. "Come here." She pulled Piper from her seat.

Piper didn't even pretend to resist. She went gratefully

into her mom's open arms. "I sent him away," she confessed, breathing in her mom's familiar earthy scent.

Emmaline held her close and rubbed her back. "It's not the end of the world. Sometimes a woman just needs a little space."

"I don't know what I needed. I mean, the truth is I had all these doubts and fears and bad memories of what happened with Brandon, of how wrong Walter and I were together. I got scared that it couldn't work with Jason, either, that I wouldn't know how to try again, to really be with him. To love him the way he deserves to be loved. I didn't know how to take the next step, so I, um, insulted him and then broke it off with him."

Her mom asked gently, "Insulted, how?"

Piper pulled back enough to give her mother a scowl. "Look. I don't want to go into detail, okay?"

"I understand." Her mom spoke softly, soothingly. "And whatever happened before, now you will fix it. You will go to him and tell him how wrong you were and ask him to please give you another chance."

"Oh, Mom…"

Emmaline took her by the shoulders and looked her squarely in the eyes. "Nothing's unfixable—unless you give up and don't even try."

That night, Piper called her dad. He answered on the first ring. She had him put her on speaker so that Nia could join the conversation. And then she told them that they were going to be grandparents again.

Her dad got all choked up and Nia said maybe they would be showing up in Wyoming earlier than originally planned.

"I'm thinking that we'll try early spring, if that works for you?" suggested Nia.

Piper said, "Yes. It'll be so great to see you. Just come whenever you can."

When she hung up, she almost called Jason to tell him that she'd called her dad about the baby.

But then she thought how he was still waiting for her okay before he told Meggie and Nate. He might be put out with her, that she hadn't even given him a heads-up before sharing the news with her dad.

She dropped the phone on the counter and promised herself she would reach out to him tomorrow.

That night, very late, Jason woke to the sound of heavy rain drumming on the roof. In his bed by the window, Kenzo stirred, his tags jingling as he gave his neck a scratch.

Jason rolled over and tried to go back to sleep, but the drumming overhead seemed to get louder, waking him every time he started to drop off. He thought of Piper—no big surprise. The beautiful, frustrating redhead who was having his baby was never far from his thoughts.

Was the rain invading her dreams tonight, too?

He would see her Friday, the day after tomorrow, for the ultrasound. And he'd get to see his baby again, too— his baby who was now, according to Google, as big as a Meyer lemon.

Thoughts of the baby always made him smile.

The rain kept coming down. Now he was starting to feel kind of antsy. He turned on the lamp, swung his feet to the floor and headed for the john.

When he returned to the bedroom, Kenzo was out of

his bed. The dog stretched and yawned, then dropped to his haunches and stared up at Jason hopefully.

"You're kidding me, man. It's pouring down rain out there."

Kenzo whined again. He needed to go out.

"Just don't say I didn't warn you. I'll let you out, but I'm not going out in that frog strangler with you."

He followed the eager dog into the two-story great room and was almost at the front door when his bare foot landed in a puddle of water. "What the...?"

Kenzo whined again.

"All right, you got it." He let the dog out, turned on the wagon wheel chandelier hanging from the rafters above and spotted the leak right away, way up there at the peak.

Last winter during a blizzard, they'd lost a couple of big branches off the Douglas fir ten feet from the house. Those branches had sounded like boulders when they hit the roof and then loudly tumbled the two stories to the ground. Apparently, they'd done some damage.

He mopped up the water, then got a bucket from under the kitchen sink and stuck it below the drip.

By morning, the rain had cleared off. He got busy gathering eggs and feeding horses. After stopping for breakfast, he and Joe went to work burning ditches. In the process, Jason told his baby brother about the leak. They'd put on that roof together, he and Joe and their dad.

"I want to get up there," he said. "Locate the leak, diagnose the problem. I'm thinking the flashing at the roofline was damaged when those big branches hit last winter."

Joe nodded. "I'll spot you."

It was almost one when Jason got back to his place. He made himself a sandwich and ate it standing at the sink.

Figuring now was as good a time as any to get a look at the roof, he gave Joe a call. His brother said he'd be over in twenty minutes.

That gave Jason time to hop in his crew cab and drive to the storage shed where they kept the ladders. He loaded up a lightweight aluminum nineteen-footer and headed back to the cabin. Kenzo was right there with him, panting contentedly in the passenger seat.

Jason thought of Piper. Because every damn thing in the world reminded him of Piper lately. Right now, it was his panting dog sitting in *her* seat.

Sometimes a man got lucky. He found a woman and the two of them were just right for each other. They had that special combination of commonality and disparities. They took pleasure in a lot of the same things, but they also helped each other. Where one lacked, the other had more than enough to pull them through any difficulty.

He and Piper were like that. Together, they could have the best kind of life—if only she'd get out of her own way long enough to see the truth of who they were to each other.

Joe was waiting on the deck. Jason parked as close as he could to the steps. He hauled the ladder out of the back and Joe helped him get it in place, fully extended, with the base effectively braced in position at the far end of the deck, so that the ladder could lie flat against the steep slant of the roof on the two-story central section of the house.

Jason put on his Rockport work shoes and his grip gloves and up the ladder he went. Just as he'd suspected, the flashing was damaged along the ridgeline.

Mentally ticking off what he'd need for the repair, he started back down. He was off the roof and on the second-to-last rung a few feet from the deck floor when Joe said, "Here comes Mom. Looks like she's headed for the barn."

He heard the sound of her pickup's engine and glanced that way at the same time as he took the next step down and missed the last rung. Tipping over backward, he hit the deck, his head bouncing hard against the wide-plank boards.

Everything went black.

Chapter Fourteen

Piper was reviewing her report for the upcoming board meeting when the phone on the desk rang. "This is Piper."

"You have a call from Meggie Bravo," said Marnie Fox, who was out in front, stationed at the circulation desk today.

Piper's heart was suddenly racing. She couldn't think of anything good that Jason's mom might want to say to her.

But whatever it was, Piper would deal with it. If she was ever going to have a chance with Jason again, getting along with his mother would be part of her job. "Put her through."

A moment later, Jason's mom said, "Hello, Piper?"

"Hi, Meggie," she cautiously replied. "What can I do for you?"

Meggie made a nervous sound. "Hmm. Well, first of all, I would like to apologize for my behavior that night you came for dinner. I have no excuse for myself. I'm overprotective sometimes, though my grown children are very capable of taking care of themselves and of making their own adult decisions."

An apology? Meggie Bravo had called to say she was sorry? Warmth bloomed in Piper's chest. "Well, I..." She struggled to come up with the right words. *Any* words. "Thank you."

Meggie jumped right in. "Oh, don't thank me. I'm the one in the wrong. I need to apologize. And I *am* apologizing. I hope that eventually, you can forgive me."

"Of course I can forgive you..." Right then, Piper guessed what must be going on here. Meggie knew about the baby. She'd heard it from one of Emmaline's artist friends—which was fine. Piper said sincerely, "I completely understand that you only wanted what's best for Jason."

"That's true. But I was hasty and judgmental and—"

"Meggie." Piper decided to just lay the cards right out on the table. "It's okay. I get it. With the baby coming, you're worried I'll try to keep you from being involved in your grandchild's life, and I want to reassure you right here and now that I would never..."

Meggie's gasp cut her off. "There's a baby? You and Jay are having a baby?"

Piper groaned. "You didn't know?"

"No! I had no clue."

"Oh, Meggie. Now I'm the one who's sorry—for laying the big news on you so badly. My mom has been telling her friends that Jason and I are having a baby. I assumed that one of them must have told you."

Meggie laughed. "Oh, Piper..." And then a sob escaped her. "This is wonderful news. I can hardly believe it..."

"Well. Um, now you know."

"Oh, yes I do. I can hardly believe it. I really can't. This news does make me so happy."

"I'm glad."

"But, Piper, I want to make it very clear that I called because my son loves you and because I was wrong and I want to make it right with you—not because I'm getting a grandchild, after all."

Piper was smiling now. "Yes. I understand. And I am so happy to hear from you."

"When are you due?"

"Mid-January."

"Is everything going well?"

"It is. No issues so far—except quite a bit of morning sickness, which seems to be tapering off now that I'm moving into the second trimester."

"Excellent. I simply... Well, I'm downright thunderstruck over your news."

"Thunderstruck. I hope that's a good thing."

"Oh, Piper. Yes it is. It is very, very good. Now I'm doubly glad I called. I've been concerned about Jay, I really have."

"Concerned...how?"

"Well, he's been more and more distant the past couple of weeks since you two came back from your trip. I've worried that something might have gone wrong between you, and if it has, I know I'm at least partly to blame. I've promised him I would stay out of it, and I tried. Piper, I really tried."

"I believe you. And it's okay. I'm *glad* that you called."

"That's such a relief. Thank you."

"The truth is, Meggie, I broke it off with him."

Meggie sighed. "I'm sorry to hear that."

"I, uh... Well, I got a little overwhelmed and messed everything up. I'm planning to reach out to him, to see if we can..." Where to go with this? How to even begin?

"Hey. Piper, it's okay. I realize I'm not the one you need to talk to about this—which brings me to the main reason I called."

The main reason? "What do you mean? What reason?"

"Let me just start by saying that Jason is okay."

Her heart was suddenly throwing itself at the cage of her ribs. "What happened?"

"He's all right now. But a couple of hours ago, he fell off a ladder."

She let out a cry. "No!"

"Yes. I'm happy to say that he didn't crack his skull, but the fall knocked him out. He was unconscious for several minutes."

Piper jumped up so fast, her chair flew back and hit the bookcase behind her desk. "Where is he? I need to—"

"Hey, now…" Meggie said in the voice she probably used to soothe agitated ranch animals. "It's okay, honestly. He has a mild concussion and a nasty bump on the back of his head. But he's all right. He's here, with me and Joe, up at the hospital in Sheridan. I mainly called because I was thinking that if you wanted to be here, too—"

"I do, Meggie." Her whole heart and soul were in those words. "Very much."

"Well, all right. That's great. Come on up. I'll wait for you out in front."

At the hospital, Piper parked a bit crooked and ran for the main entrance. Meggie was right there in front of the glass doors as she'd promised she would be, wearing old jeans, a faded long-sleeved shirt and dusty rawhide boots, her gray-streaked dark hair pulled back in a low ponytail. She held out her arms and Piper went into them.

"I'm so glad you called," Piper whispered as Jason's mom held her tight.

Meggie pulled back smiling. "Me, too." She took Piper's

hand. "Come on. I know a certain cranky cowboy who will be so happy to see you."

They waited at Reception until a nurse came. "I can take you back," the nurse said. "But Jason's brother is with him. We don't usually let three visitors into our small exam rooms all at the same time."

"Just give us a minute with Jason, please?" Meggie coaxed. "I'll make sure that two of us clear out quickly."

The nurse led them through a door and into a narrower hallway and a smaller door labeled Exam Room Three.

In the cramped room, Jason's brother sat in a guest chair fiddling with something on his phone. Jason himself, in a floral-patterned hospital gown and thick socks, was stretched out on the exam table. Even fully extended, the table was too short for him. His stocking feet hung off the end. He seemed to be sleeping. His head was turned away from the door and he'd thrown an arm over his eyes.

Peering closer, Piper could make out the bump on the back of his head. She longed to launch herself at him, grab him close, promise him he would be all right—and beg him to give her just one more chance.

Joe looked up. "Hey, Piper," he whispered so quietly, she understood his words more by the movement of his lips than by the sound. His mouth stretched wide in a giant smile. "Good to see you." He nodded in Jason's direction. "He's conked out. It's so boring in here and he's not supposed to read or strain his eyes."

Jason stirred and mumbled, "Not now, Joe. Let me sleep…" But he didn't turn his head. His big arm remained covering the top half of his face.

Joe kept right on whispering. "Don't worry. The doctor

said napping is fine. Just ask him a simple question when he wakes up. If he answers clearly, he's okay."

With a pointed look at her younger son, Meggie shot a thumb over her shoulder.

"Yes, ma'am." Joe got up and followed Meggie out, pulling the door silently shut behind him.

Now it was just the two of them. Piper stared down at the man she loved, the father of her baby, the man she'd honestly believed she would never find.

Jason slept on, his big chest rising and falling with each breath.

Quietly, Piper moved the chair Joe had been sitting in closer to the exam table. Then she sat down and waited for the man on the table to open his eyes.

Apples.

Still half-asleep, Jason drew in a slow breath through his nose.

The concussion must have made him delusional. He could swear he smelled Piper's shampoo. He drew another slow breath and let it out with care. Yep. The scent of apples, clean and sweet and delicious.

Definitely delusional. No doubt about it.

And how damn long would it be before someone came and said he could go? He'd been cooped up in this tiny room for too long now. They'd poked and prodded and asked him a million questions, all of which he'd answered clearly and correctly. Yeah, his head hurt. But there was nothing more they could do for him here. He wanted to go home and stretch out in his own bed.

He rolled fully onto his side toward where Joe sat, drew his legs up onto the dinky exam table and opened his eyes.

He was fully expecting to see his brother sitting there, fooling around on his phone.

But it was Piper in the chair instead—Piper, in a green skirt and a white silk shirt, right next to him, up close and personal.

He groaned. Maybe he was worse off than he'd thought.

"Hey," the vision said with a slow, sweet smile. "How're you feeling?"

He blinked. Twice. But each time he looked again, she was still there. "Uh, Piper?"

"Yes?"

"Are you really here?" He reached out.

She took his hand. Real. Her touch was real. And then she brushed her soft lips against his skin. "I am here, yes. Your mom called me. We made peace. I told her about the baby. She said you'd been hurt and asked me if I wanted to be here with you. I couldn't say yes fast enough."

He closed his eyes at the wonder of all that. "If you're not real, don't tell me, okay?"

"Oh, Jason." She bent close. He felt her breath on his cheek. "I am real, I promise you." And then her lips were there, pressed to his cheek, so soft, so absolutely perfect.

He turned his aching head just enough to capture those lips with his own.

That kiss lasted a long time. When he opened his eyes again, he said, "Ask me a simple question."

She gave a soft laugh. "I love you. I was wrong. I don't want to be without you. And here's the question—will you give me another chance?"

"Oh, hell yes."

She laughed. "You are so easy."

"Hey. Cut me some slack. I have a head injury."

"Oh, Jason…" She looked at him like he was the answer to all the questions in her heart. He'd fall off a ladder every day for a chance to see her like this, with nothing but love and hope in those green eyes of hers.

"I love you, Piper. You're it for me. You're everything."

"Well," she said in a sweet, breathless whisper. "I'm really glad to hear that. Because I feel the same way about you—but then you already knew that. You said as much two and a half weeks ago. Right before you walked out my door."

"I was hurt," he said gruffly.

"I'm so sorry. Please forgive me."

"You know I do."

There was a tap on the exam room. A nurse came in. "Jason, how are you feeling?"

Wincing as his injury pressed against the exam table, he turned his head toward the woman at the door. "My head hurts some. But overall, I feel good." He gave Piper's hand a squeeze. "Real good."

"What day is it?" asked the nurse.

"Thursday, July 18."

"Excellent. You ready to go home?"

"Yes, I am."

"Go ahead and get dressed and we can let you out of here."

Piper didn't want to be apart from him—which was just as well because Jason said he wasn't letting her out of his sight.

Joe took the crew cab back to the ranch. Jason rode with Piper to her house, but only long enough for her to pack a bag. At the Double-K, Nate and Meggie's cousin Sonny had fixed the leak in Jason's roof and put the ladder away.

They had dinner at the main house that night. The mood was festive. Meggie broke out the bubbly in celebration of the news that she and Nate were going to be grandparents. Piper opted for ginger ale because of the baby—and Jason did, too.

They all raised their glasses high when Nate offered the toast. "To Jason and Piper and the little one we can't wait to meet."

Piper spent the night in Jason's bed spooned up nice and close. And early the next day, they returned to the hospital together for her thirteen-week ultrasound.

It was a revelation. Piper cried happy tears. Their lemon-size baby girl waved her arms and kicked her feet. They could see her brain and her heart. She looked healthy and so active.

That night, in bed, she said, "I don't think it's possible to be happier than I am right now."

Oh, but it was.

Two weeks later, Piper moved in with Jason at the Double-K. She put her house in town up for sale. It sold in mid-August to a young couple from Houston.

On Labor Day, she and Jason shared a picnic at that special spot where he'd taken her once before, under a willow tree by Crystal Creek. He knelt on their picnic blanket and asked her to marry him. As soon as she said yes, he slipped a vintage-style ring on her finger. It was just what she would have chosen for herself, with an oval diamond flanked by two gleaming emeralds. When she threw her arms around his neck, he scooped her up, carried her out into the creek and dunked her good and proper.

They were married on Thanksgiving Day in a simple ceremony at the Rising Sun Ranch, with Jason's big extended family all around them. Piper's filmy pearl-white dress had an empire waist that flowed out and down over her giant belly. Her mom, an ordained minister of the Unity Church, officiated.

And when Jason took her in his arms to kiss her, he whispered, "I love you."

"And I love you," she answered. "Deeply, completely and…"

"Forever," he finished for her as his lips met hers.

Piper wasn't feeling quite so romantic on that brutal day in January when their daughter decided to be born. In fact, she was scared to death.

Outside a blizzard had descended. The world was a frozen landscape of wind-driven white, making a trip to the hospital impossible. Piper tried her best to put a brave face on the situation, but she really had planned to cap off her advanced-age pregnancy by having her baby in the hospital, where the professionals would know what to do if anything went wrong.

She labored for hours, with Jason and Meggie taking turns coaching her. Piper cried. She moaned. She screamed at the ceiling—and at Jason and Meggie, too. At one point, when she was feeling completely exhausted, she even called Dr. Hayes. He offered suggestions and encouragements. Piper screamed at him a few times, too. As the hours went by, she doubted her ability to do this, to make it through.

But then finally, at 1:10 a.m. on the twenty-fifth of

January, her little girl let out that first furious wail. Jason caught her and laid her on Piper's chest.

Meggie bustled out into the great room, giving the three of them a little time alone together as a new family.

When Jason's mom returned, she tied off the cord with two sterilized shoelaces, and then cut the space between. A bit later, as the baby nursed for the first time, Jason and Meggie discussed names.

Piper said, "You two can talk it over all you want. I already know her name. It's Megan Emmaline. What else could it be?"

Meggie started crying then. "It's only from sheer happiness," she reassured the new parents.

"Come here, Mom." Jason grabbed her in a hug.

Later, during a break in the storm, Nate and Joe came over. They each got to hold little Meg. And then they took the exhausted new grandma back to the main house.

"You did it," said Jason reverently, as he climbed into bed with Piper and their newborn daughter.

"*We* did it," she replied.

On the floor, Kenzo whined.

"Fine," Jason muttered. "But only this once."

Kenzo jumped up on the mattress and settled, like the gentleman he was, down at the foot of the bed.

Jason nuzzled Piper's nose and pressed a kiss at her temple. "I keep thinking of that first night back in April. That was a great night. My dream come true."

She gave a tired little chuckle. "I made it very clear that it was one night and one night only."

His grin was smug. "And look at us now."

She touched his beard-scruffy cheek. "Together. With our little girl…"

"You didn't make it easy, though."

She laughed then, but softly so as not to wake the baby. And then she said sincerely, "I should have trusted you sooner."

He shook his head. "You needed the time."

"I did, yes. And that's why we took the long way getting here."

"The long way is the best way," he said. And then he kissed her, a slow kiss, but light as a breath.

* * * * *

Snowed In With A Stranger

Brenda Harlen

MILLS & BOON

Brenda Harlen is a former attorney who once had the privilege of appearing before the Supreme Court of Canada. The practice of law taught her a lot about the world and reinforced her determination to become a writer—because in fiction, she could promise a happy ending! Now she is an award-winning, RITA® Award—nominated, nationally bestselling author of more than fifty titles for Harlequin. You can keep up-to-date with Brenda on Facebook and Twitter, or through her website, brendaharlen.com.

Dear Reader,

Event planner Finley Gilmore was ten years old when her parents divorced, proving that not every walk down the aisle leads to happily-ever-after. Weddings might be the heart of her business, but she has no interest in romance. Then a blizzard strands her in Haven, Nevada, with a sexy stranger, and Finley finds herself with time—and temptation!—on her hands.

College professor Lachlan Kellett isn't in the market for a relationship, either. A short-lived marriage followed by a painful divorce taught him some hard lessons about love, and being snowed in at the Dusty Boots Motel—even with a stunningly beautiful woman—isn't likely to change his perspective.

Morning brings clear skies again, and Finley and Lachlan intend to go their separate ways. Until they realise they are both heading for Northern California and agree to share a ride. The road trip only continues to fan the sparks that ignited during the storm.

But will their return to the real world mean an end to the connection they forged in Haven? Or will they find a way to overcome the obstacles keeping them apart?

I hope you have as much fun reading about these wary lovers as I did writing their story—and that you'll look for more Match Made in Haven titles coming soon.

Enjoy!

Brenda

xo

DEDICATION

In memory of a treasured stepmum and "gramma"—
Marjorie Anne Stickles.

02 March 1939–27 May 2023

Chapter One

I should have listened to my sister.

From the backseat of the Subaru Forrester in which she was riding, Finley Gilmore couldn't see anything but snow. Whether she was peering through the front or back or side windows, there was only white.

And the way Ozzie was gripping the steering wheel and squinting through the windshield, she doubted that his view was much better.

Apparently ignoring the weather warnings had been a bad idea.

But honestly, how could she have known that today would be the one day the forecasters finally got it right?

"They say it could be the biggest storm this area has seen in a decade," Haylee had cautioned when Finley set her carry-on suitcase by the door.

"They say a lot of things," Finley noted. "And they're usually wrong."

"It's snowing already," her sister pointed out.

And it had been.

But that snow was big, fluffy flakes that seemed to float on the air—nothing at all like the whiteout conditions that her driver was dealing with now.

"I've got a four o'clock flight to Oakland," she'd reminded her sister. "And a busy weekend ahead of me."

Haylee had sighed before turning to her husband. "Tell her to stay."

"You should stay," Trevor Blake had dutifully intoned.

"I appreciate your concern," Finley said. "But I really need to get home."

A horn had sounded from the driveway then, so she'd exchanged hugs and kisses with Aidan and Ellie—her three-year-old nephew and niece—and Haylee and Trevor, then picked up her suitcase (with a Tupperware container of leftover birthday cake nestled safely inside) and headed out to meet her ride-share driver.

The snow had been falling noticeably thicker and faster before they reached the end of Main Street.

"You check with the airport to see if your flight is on time?" Ozzie asked.

"I did and it is," she confirmed.

Then her phone buzzed.

She glanced at the screen, exhaled a weary sigh.

"It *was*," she corrected. "Now it's listed as delayed."

"Delayed often leads to canceled," he warned. "You want me to turn around and take you back?"

"No," she said. "I need to get to the airport."

Ozzie shrugged. "Your call."

Ten minutes later, the driver wasn't shrugging but cursing.

Her phone buzzed again.

Now her flight was canceled.

Damn.

I definitely should have listened to my sister.

"Canceled?" Ozzie guessed.

"Yeah." Finley looked out the window again. "How far are we from the airport now?"

"Too far."

"What does that mean?"

"It means there's no way we're going to make it there before they close the highway."

"Can we go back?"

"I wouldn't," he said.

"What would you do?" she asked, trying to ignore the knots of apprehension forming in her stomach.

Ozzie looked out at the swirling storm for a minute as his vehicle crawled along the road. "We're not far from the Dusty Boots Motel," he noted. "You could call to see if they've got a room available."

It was a good idea, she decided. "Do you need a room, too?" she asked.

"Nah. I've got a lady friend who lives nearby," he said. "She'll let me hang with her until the storm passes."

Finley called the number on the card that Ozzie handed to her. Luckily, there was one room available. She booked it for one night, hoping it was all she'd need.

But staring out at what was nothing less than a full-fledged blizzard, she had to wonder just how long she'd be trapped.

I should have changed my plans.

Unfortunately, the realization came to Lachlan Kellett a little too late, after he'd already started his journey.

But after three weeks in northern Nevada, he was eager to get home to Aislynn.

He'd disregarded the blizzard warning, confident that an early start would put him well out of range when the snow started to fall. His confidence had obviously been misplaced.

He might have been okay if he hadn't detoured into Haven to pick up a pizza to fuel him on his drive. But Jo's Pizza was the stuff of legends, and since his first taste of her pie, more than a decade earlier, he'd never managed to pass by the town without stopping to pick one up.

But the box sat on the passenger seat, its contents untouched, because driving in this storm required every bit of his concentration and skill. And still, there were moments when he wondered if he'd ever make it out of Nevada. Or even out of Haven.

After another twenty minutes of white-knuckle driving, he acknowledged that there was no way he was going to get home tonight. The all-weather tires that were more than adequate for his purposes in California weren't faring so well on roads covered in snow and ice. And of course they did absolutely nothing to improve visibility, which was somewhere in the vicinity of zero. Thankfully he remembered that there was a motel on the lonely stretch of highway he was traveling. The Rusty Spurs or Battered Hat or something like that.

He glanced quickly at the map displayed on the screen of his phone. There it was—the Dusty Boots Motel—half a mile ahead.

When he finally reached the driveway, he gently tapped the brake, slowing his vehicle to a crawl to navigate the turn, and still his SUV skidded on the slick surface. He tightened his hands on the wheel and steered into the skid, fervently praying that he wouldn't end up nose first in a snowbank or a drift. Thankfully, he didn't, but that brief (and scary) moment of uncertainty assured him that seeking shelter from the storm was the right course of action.

There were several other vehicles in the lot, most of them parked in front of numbered units and already buried beneath several inches of the snow that showed no signs of abating anytime soon. Since he didn't yet have a room, he parked beside a pickup truck near the main entrance and stepped out of his vehicle. It was a short trek to the door, but long enough that he could understand how people got thrown off course in snowstorms as he battled against buffeting winds and blowing snow the whole way.

By the time his hand closed around the handle, he suspected

that he bore more than a passing resemblance to the abominable snowman, covered head to toe as he was.

Once inside, he stomped his feet to knock some of the white stuff off his boots and pulled off his leather gloves to dig his wallet out of his pocket. He fished out his driver's license and credit card, then took a few steps further into the reception area to drop them on the counter for the middle-aged desk clerk with platinum-blonde hair piled on top of her head and bright pink lipstick smeared over her mouth.

Shirla—according to the name badge pinned on her thick wool sweater—reluctantly tore her gaze away from the online casino game she was playing on her phone to glance up.

The way her heavily mascaraed eyes immediately grew wide confirmed his suspicion that he looked like the mythical Yeti.

"It's snowing out there," he said, hoping the humorous understatement would put her at ease.

Her gaze shifted to the window, and her initial surprise gave way to amusement, as evidenced by the curve of her bright pink lips.

"Checking in?" she asked, in a raspy tone that suggested she'd been a pack-a-day smoker for a lot of her fifty-plus years.

"I hope so," he responded to her question.

She reached for the mouse beside the computer on the desk, sliding it over the pad to wake up the screen.

"Your name?" she prompted.

"Lachlan Kellett."

A pleat formed between her brows as she scanned her computer screen. "Do you have a reservation?"

"No," he admitted. "I'd planned to be back in California and sleeping in my own bed tonight, but that's obviously not going to happen."

"I'm sorry, Mr. Kellett, but we don't have any rooms available."

He sighed wearily and glanced out at the storm again. "So what am I supposed to do now?"

"Depending on which way you're headed, you could try your luck in Haven or Battle Mountain," Shirla said.

He immediately shook his head. "There's no way I'm driving any further tonight."

"Well, there are several sofas in the lounge," she allowed, gesturing vaguely to the far side of the room.

That was when he noticed the row of hooks on the wall behind her. The hangers had numbers above them to indicate the room to which the keys belonged. Had all the hooks been empty, he would have assumed that the motel had upgraded to keycards, but the single key attached to a plastic tag hanging under one of the numbers suggested otherwise.

"I know it's not ideal, but you're welcome to crash there," Shirla continued.

"What about Number Six?" Lachlan asked now, pointing to the lone key on the wall.

"It's reserved."

"Reserved for who?"

Big silver hoops swayed in her ears as she shook her head. "I can't give you that information."

"I understand," he assured her. "What I should have asked is—how late do you hold the room? Because if your guest isn't here now, I doubt very much that he's going to make it."

"A confirmed reservation holds a room until six o'clock," Shirla said.

"So if your guest isn't here by six o'clock, maybe I could buy out the room?" he suggested.

"I guess that would be okay," she agreed.

He glanced at his watch to check the current time and felt a gust of cold air blow through the doors as they opened behind him.

Glancing over his shoulder, he saw a woman—young, blond,

gorgeous—brushing snow off the shoulders of her cardinal red coat.

She caught his eye and offered a smile that he suspected could have melted the three-foot drift outside the door, then she shifted her attention to the clerk as she moved toward the counter.

"My name's Finley Gilmore," she said. "I have a reservation."

"Welcome to the Dusty Boots Motel, Ms. Gilmore." The clerk glanced apologetically in the direction of the man lounging against the counter, then asked her newly-arrived guest for her ID and credit card.

Finley went through the motions of checking in to her room, conscious of the man's gaze on her. As an event planner, she'd dealt with all kinds of people in various situations—from shy quinceañeras and bubbly brides to demanding mothers and implacable fathers—and she handled them all. Julia, one of her business partners, had teasingly nicknamed Finley "the wallet-whisperer," claiming that she had a gift for ensuring that whatever expectations potential clients had when they walked into her office for a consult, every one of them left feeling confident that Gilmore Galas would give them the event they wanted, right down to the tiniest detail.

Finley certainly endeavored to do her best, though there were inevitably snags that occurred—a misspelled name on a cake or the wrong shade of roses in a bouquet or a tardy beer delivery—but Finley made sure that she was the one to deal with those snags, so that the birthday celebrant or anxious bride or happy retiree never had to know there'd been a problem. And that was the real reason Gilmore Galas had an overall five-star rating on Yelp and was fully booked for the next eighteen months.

Yet, despite her purported skill at reading people, she

couldn't quite get a handle on the stranger with the mouth-wateringly broad shoulders, longish dark—almost black—hair, scruffy beard and piercing blue eyes. But something about the way he was looking at her made her insides quiver—not with nervousness so much as awareness.

Which was ridiculous, because brooding, bearded men were not at all her type.

But those shoulders.

And those eyes.

Perhaps it wasn't a wonder that all her female body parts were suddenly humming.

"You'll be in Room Six." The desk clerk swiveled on her chair and reached for the lone remaining key hanging on a hook on the wall.

An actual key.

As if she was checking into a roadside motel in an old movie. Or Schitt's Creek.

Still, she was grateful to have a room. And hopeful that the beds had been replaced more recently than the door locks. Though all she really cared about was that it was clean.

"The room has two double beds and a shower-tub combo," Shirla continued, setting the key on the counter. "There's also cable TV and free Wi-Fi, a mini-fridge, coffee maker and microwave."

"Thank you," Finley said, struggling to slide the oversized plastic tag attached to the key into the pocket of her coat.

"Continental breakfast is served in the lounge—" Shirla gestured to an adjacent seating area with a couple of sofas and several mismatched armchairs in groupings around scarred tables "—starting at seven a.m. and ending when the coffee and pastries run out. Assuming we get our usual bakery delivery in the morning."

"What if I'm hungry now?" Finley asked, suddenly realizing that she was.

"There's a diner down the street."

The automatic response made Finley wonder if the woman had looked outside in the past few hours.

"And what are my options if I don't want to venture out in the storm?" she clarified.

Shirla lifted an arm to point again, this time to a vending machine against the wall.

A vending machine containing only a few bags of chips, a single chocolate bar and two full rows of chewing gum.

Apparently her dinner was going to be the leftover birthday cake in the Tupperware container inside her suitcase.

"Or pizza," the bearded stranger spoke up to say.

Finley's stomach rumbled.

"Pizza would be great," she said. "But I don't think anyone's going to be out delivering in this weather."

"I've got a large cheese and pepperoni in my SUV," he said, jingling his keys as he pulled them out of his pocket.

"Are you offering to share?" she asked hopefully.

"I'd be willing to consider a trade," he said, making his way to the door.

Shirla's gaze followed him as he walked out, then she sighed, a little wistfully. "Did you see those shoulders?"

"Hard to miss," Finley admitted.

"Do you think he got them working out in a prison gym?" the clerk wondered aloud.

"I would have guessed football."

"You could be right," Shirla acknowledged. "But a prison story would be much more interesting."

"Perhaps," Finley agreed dubiously.

The clerk chuckled. "I've always had a thing for bad boys," she confided. "Just the rumble of a Harley's engine gets my juices flowing. Add a leather jacket and some tatts, and I'm a puddle on the floor."

Which was a lot more information than Finley needed to know about the woman working the desk.

"I bet you go for the corporate type," Shirla guessed, assessing Finley. "A guy who wears a shirt and tie to the office every day and golfs with his buddies on Friday afternoons."

It was admittedly close to the mark, and perhaps the reason that Finley felt compelled to respond.

"I couldn't actually tell you the last time I was on a date," she confided. "My job keeps me so busy, I don't have time for much else."

Shirla tsked. "You've gotta make time for the things that matter."

"What matters is keeping a roof over my head." And it was true, even if Finley wasn't really worried about being kicked out of the carriage house she'd been renting from her dad and stepmom for the past half a dozen years.

"Youth is, indeed, wasted on the young," Shirla lamented.

The door opened again, and the man with the mouth-watering shoulders and mesmerizing eyes returned with a blast of icy wind and a flat square box.

At first glance, the stranger's appearance was somewhat intimidating, and Finley could understand why the clerk had pegged him as a bad boy. But nothing about him set off Finley's internal radar. Her hormones, perhaps, but not her radar—though perhaps the tingles in her womanly parts should be heeded as a warning.

Over the years, Finley had learned to be a pretty good judge of character, at least when it came to professional interactions. Unfortunately, her romantic history told a very different story about her personal life.

He stomped the snow off his boots before carrying his pizza through to the lounge.

There was a pot of coffee on the table where Shirla had indicated continental breakfast would be found in the morning. Finley left her suitcase by the desk and ventured over to pour a cup.

She took a tentative sip, shuddered, then emptied a couple of packets of sugar and three creamers into the cup and tried again. It was marginally less horrible now, so she poured a second cup and carried both into the lounge.

"You said something about a possible trade," Finley reminded the stranger, who was already halfway through his first slice of pizza. "So how about I trade you a cup of coffee for a slice?"

He finished chewing and swallowed before responding. "You mean a cup of free, really bad coffee?"

She shrugged. "Desperate times."

"Hardly seems like a fair trade to me," he said conversationally. "Because this is really good pizza."

"Jo's?" she guessed, her stomach rumbling again as the tantalizing scent of the pie teased her nostrils.

"How'd you know?"

"My sister and brother-in-law live in Haven," she told him. "Every time I visit, we have Jo's."

"So you know how good it is." He took another bite of the slice he was holding.

She nodded.

"And you know I'd be a fool to swap a slice of superior pizza for a cup of stale coffee."

"So let me buy a slice." Her stomach rumbled again. "Or two."

His lips twitched. "I probably wasn't going to eat the whole thing in one sitting," he acknowledged. "So you can have a slice."

She set the two cups of coffee on the table and reached into the box before he could rescind his offer.

She lifted a slice to her mouth, not quite managing to hold

back the moan of pleasure that sounded low in her throat as she bit into it.

His lips twitched again.

She was too grateful for the pizza to care that he was silently laughing at her.

She chewed slowly, savoring the combination of flavors and textures: tangy sauce, gooey cheese, spicy pepperoni.

"So where were you headed when the storm brought you here?" he asked, reaching into the box again.

"Airport." She licked a spot of sauce off her thumb. "I had a four o'clock flight to Oakland that was canceled."

"Yours wasn't the only one," he told her. "The whole airport shut down."

"Hopefully the storm will pass quickly so it can reopen in the morning, because I have an engagement party tomorrow night that I cannot miss."

His gaze automatically went to her left hand, bare of rings.

"Not mine," she said, shaking her head for emphasis. "I'm an event planner. Gilmore Galas."

"So what'll happen if you miss the party?"

"I'll have a couple of very unhappy clients on my hands—or former clients."

Dark brows winged up. "Would they really fire you for something completely out of your control?"

"Maybe not," she allowed. "Especially as we're already deep into planning their November wedding. But they'd be disappointed and, truthfully, so would I."

She finished off her slice, her gaze shifting to the remaining slices of pizza in the box.

"Did that take the edge off your hunger?" the stranger asked.

"Only the very tip," she told him.

"So let's talk trade," he suggested.

"I don't know what I have that you might want," she said warily.

"The last vacant room in this motel."

"And I'm not giving it up."

"Do you plan on sleeping in both of the beds?" he asked.

"No. And no."

His brows lifted again. "What was the second no?"

"I'm not going to let you sleep in the other one," she said firmly.

"Why not?" he challenged.

"Because I've seen too many crime dramas on TV to willingly put myself in the middle of a real-life one."

"What if I offered to pay for the room?"

She shook her head. "Then I'd be about seventy-five dollars richer but no less dead."

His lips quirked at the corners. "Do you really think I'm a dangerous criminal?"

"I don't know you, do I?" she pointed out reasonably.

"What do you want to know?"

"A lot more than a quick session of twenty questions is going to tell me."

"So go ahead and Google me," he suggested, pulling his driver's license out of his wallet and offering it to her. "My name is Lachlan Kellett, and I'm a professor of anthropology at Merivale College."

She knew of Merivale College, of course. Not only as a private school in San Francisco but also as a gorgeous venue for both indoor and outdoor events.

"So you're from California, too?" She wasn't sure why that little bit of information seemed reassuring, but it was.

"Born and raised," he told her.

Since he'd invited her to do so, she opened a search engine and punched in the name on his license, along with the name of the school.

"Apparently there is a Lachlan Kellett who teaches anthropology at Merivale College," she acknowledged. "But the thumbnail-sized black-and-white photo on the website doesn't look anything like you."

"The photo's at least ten years old and the beard—" he rubbed the dark hair covering the lower half of his face "—is much more recent."

She wondered if the beard was prickly or smooth, and found herself wanting to find out.

"Pizza's getting cold," he said, reaching for another slice.

Finley felt herself wavering.

"I promise I'm not after anything more than a place to sleep that's a little less public than this," he said, gesturing to the sofa on which he was seated. "I've spent the last three weeks in a falling-down cabin in the mountains and I was really looking forward to sleeping in my own bed at home tonight. Since that obviously isn't going to happen, I'd like to catch a few decent hours of shut-eye before my long drive tomorrow." He glanced out the window. "At least, I hope I have a long drive tomorrow."

She wasn't completely unsympathetic to his plight, but she was still wary. "How about two more slices of pizza for a two-hour nap in my room, after which time I'll wake you up and you'll leave?"

"Two more slices for six hours," he countered.

She shook her head. "I need to get some sleep tonight, too."

"And you're afraid to sleep in the same room as me," he acknowledged.

"I don't know you," she reminded him.

"I don't know you, either," he noted. "But I'm willing to trust that you won't accost me or rob me blind while I'm sleeping."

"Because it's unlikely that I'd get the upper hand on a man who's at least six inches taller and probably fifty pounds heavier than me," she pointed out.

"Would you feel better if I said you could handcuff me to the bed?"

That mental image sparked her hormones again.

"Do you have handcuffs?" she asked.

"No." He winked. "But I was hoping you might."

Her gaze narrowed. "Are you *flirting* with me?"

Now he smiled.

A real smile this time.

The kind of smile that tempted a woman to say "yes" to almost anything.

A different woman, Finley reminded herself firmly.

Perhaps not unlike the woman she used to be, but she was smarter now.

Or at least trying to be.

"And what if I said that I was flirting with you?" he asked her.

"I'd tell you that I appreciate the effort, Professor Kellett, but—"

"Lachlan," he interrupted. "If we're going to be sharing a room, you should call me Lachlan."

"We're *not* going to be sharing a room. I'm offering you two hours in my bed—the spare bed," she hastily amended.

He smiled again, and her heart actually skipped a beat.

Damn. He really was cute in a rough-around-the-edges sort of way.

But now that she was looking at him more closely, she could see the fatigue in his eyes. A bone-deep weariness that tugged at her.

"So what compelled you to spend three weeks in the mountains of northern Nevada in the middle of winter?" she asked him now.

All traces of humor disappeared from his eyes. "The last request of a dying friend."

Her heart squeezed. "I'm sorry."

"Me, too."

She cursed herself for being a fool even as she opened her

phone again to compose a text message to her sister. Since his driver's license was still on the table, she snapped a photo of it to attach to the message.

"You can have the spare bed," she decided. "But I just sent your contact information to my sister, so if housekeeping finds my lifeless body in the morning, the police will be coming for you."

"Good thing I know where there's a cabin in the mountains to hide out," he said, and winked at her again.

She reached into the box for another slice of pizza, because she was almost one hundred percent certain that he was joking.

Chapter Two

Lachlan closed the lid of the empty pizza box.

His soon-to-be roommate had not been kidding when she said she was hungry, as she'd quickly polished off another two slices. He'd devoured four himself and then offered the last slice to Shirla. The desk clerk had gratefully accepted, because even though she'd brought her own dinner, there was nothing better than Jo's pizza.

"We should probably head to our room," he said to Finley.

"It's *my* room," she noted, with a glance at the fancy watch on her wrist. "And it's barely six o'clock."

"And there's a major blizzard raging outside," he reminded her. "If we don't go now, we might not get out the door. Or the wind might knock out the power, and then we'll be bumping around in the dark."

A furrow formed between her perfectly arched brows—a sign of worry that he wished he could soothe.

But the facts were irrefutable, and he had no business wanting anything from this woman—or at least nothing more than the bed that she'd already agreed (with obvious reluctance) to let him have.

"Do you really think we might lose power?" she asked, retrieving her discarded coat from the arm of the sofa and donning it over the snug-fitting dark jeans and cropped pale blue sweater she wore.

Following her lead, he shoved his arms into his down-filled parka and settled his fleece-lined trapper hat on his head. "In a storm like this, we have to at least consider the possibility."

She buttoned up her coat, knotted her scarf around her throat and pulled on a pair of matching mittens.

Cashmere, he guessed. Or some other equally expensive and completely impractical material that was more fashionable than warm. Just like the boots on her feet that barely qualified as such, with chunky little heels and shiny zipper pulls with tassels.

Or maybe he was judging her too harshly.

After all, she was a California girl, possibly unaccustomed to northern Nevada winters and obviously unprepared for the storm that was currently raging.

To be fair, he hadn't been prepared for the intensity of the storm, either. If he had, he would have had chains on his tires and might have been able to continue on his way rather than having to take shelter.

A minor inconvenience, he'd decided, when he'd turned off the highway.

A frustration, he'd amended, upon discovering that the motel didn't have any rooms available.

But now that he'd met the lovely Finley Gilmore, he had to wonder if his lack of preparedness hadn't actually been a stroke of good luck rather than bad.

Shirla managed to tear her attention away from the weather report on the television when they approached the desk to retrieve their bags. "I see you're both heading out."

Finley flushed in response to the clerk's sly smile.

"Ms. Gilmore has graciously agreed to let me crash in her spare bed," Lachlan said, coming to her rescue.

"Not any of my business," Shirla assured them, though her exaggerated wink confirmed that she was speculating nonetheless. "Though I've always said a smart girl makes a man buy her dinner first before she invites him to spend the night."

Finley's cheeks turned an even deeper shade of red.

"Good night, Shirla," Lachlan said firmly.

"I'll probably see you in the morning," the clerk told them. "The girl who usually covers the night shift just called to let me know she can't make it in, so I guess the weather forecasters were right about this one."

"How lucky for us," Finley said dryly.

Lachlan wasn't sure if she was responding to Shirla's comment that she'd see them in the morning or her remark about the forecast, because it seemed equally applicable to both.

"Stay close to the building so you don't get disoriented in the storm," Shirla cautioned, as he reached for the handle of the door.

"Will do," Finley promised.

"I'll lead the way," Lachlan said, as she moved past him.

"I'm not going to get lost." Finley's tone was indignant.

"I wasn't questioning your sense of direction," he assured her. "Just suggesting that you walk behind me, so that you're shielded from the wind."

"I don't need—"

Whatever else she'd intended to say was lost as a blast of wind hit her full on, stealing the words along with her breath.

She took a step back, blinking long, dark lashes dusted with snowflakes. "You can go ahead."

With a shake of his head, he stepped around her and began trudging through the knee-deep snow, creating a path for her to follow. He thought he'd gotten used to the cold over the past few weeks, but the temperature had plummeted even more since he'd set out earlier in the day. With every step he took, he was assaulted by icy pellets of snow, and every breath he drew stabbed like icy needles in his lungs.

He heard Finley mutter a couple of times as she struggled

to maneuver her suitcase through the snow. So he slung his duffel bag over his shoulder and reached back to take her case.

"I can manage," she protested, though not very vehemently.

"I'd like to get to the room before we both get frostbite," he said.

She relinquished her grip on the handle and he lifted the case off the ground before forging ahead, conscious of her scrambling to stay close.

So close that she didn't realize he'd stopped in front of their door until she slammed into him.

The contact made her stumble back, and those silly heels failed to find purchase on the snow-covered walk. She wobbled, her arms pinwheeling as she started to fall. He dropped the case and reached for her, hauling her upright again and holding her steady.

She exhaled a shuddery sigh of relief before tipping her head back to look at him.

Despite the snow that continued to swirl, the air between them suddenly crackled with heated awareness.

"Are you okay?" he asked gruffly.

She nodded. "Th-thanks."

"What kind of boots are those anyway?"

"Oh. Um. They're Cynthia Bane. She's an up-and-coming West Coast designer."

"It was a rhetorical question," he told her. "But the right answer would have been 'useless.' Those boots are useless in northern Nevada winter."

"But stylish in California, which is where I bought them."

He suddenly realized he was still holding her and let his arms drop away. "Key?"

She shoved a mittened hand into the pocket of her coat and pulled out the oversized plastic tag stamped with the number 6.

He opened the door and gestured for her to precede him.

Then he picked up her suitcase again and followed.

Finley halted in the middle of the room, her gaze moving from one bed to the other, that already familiar furrow forming between her brows.

To him, it looked like a typical roadside motel room, with cheap floral spreads covering the beds, flimsy curtains on the window and threadbare carpet on the floor. But perhaps Finley was frowning not over the décor but the close confines of the room, suddenly aware that she would be sleeping only feet away from a virtual stranger.

His gaze shifted back to her face just in time to see the tip of her tongue sweep along her bottom lip, moistening it.

His attention was riveted by the action, his interest piqued by the lushness of her mouth.

He wondered if it could possibly feel as soft as it looked. Not that he had any intention of finding out. Because he suspected that making a move would be a good way to get himself kicked out of her room and onto his ass in the snow.

But it was fun to think about.

And that in and of itself was a surprise, because he hadn't felt the urge to kiss a woman in a very long time. Especially not a woman about whom he knew little more than her name.

Of course, they were going to be spending the night in the same room, which would provide him with the opportunity to learn more.

Or maybe he should forget about making conversation with his reluctant roommate and focus on getting some much-needed sleep before he embarked on the long journey home the next day—providing the inclement weather didn't continue to thwart his plans.

"I'm sure the desk clerk said two double beds," Finley remarked now.

"That's what I heard," he confirmed.

"Do they look like doubles to you?"

He shrugged. "We could push them together to make one big bed, if you want."

"I don't think so."

"You don't think we can?" he asked, deliberately misunderstanding her response.

"We're not going to," she said firmly, as she unwound her scarf and draped it over a hook by the door. Then she slipped off her coat and hung it up, too.

"It's not too warm in here, is it?" she noted, rubbing her hands up and down her arms.

"I'll crank up the heat," Lachlan said, turning away from her to adjust the temperature control on the wall.

"Thanks."

He shrugged out of his coat and placed it on a hook beside hers.

She turned in a slow circle, surveying the room.

"It's not very big," she noted. "But at least it looks clean."

"That's always a plus," he agreed, setting her suitcase on the dresser.

She wandered into the bathroom to continue her cursory inspection.

"There are extra towels, but only one tiny bottle each of shampoo and conditioner," she told him, when she wandered back out again.

"I guess the first one in the shower gets to wash their hair."

"Knock yourself out," she said. "I don't travel anywhere without my own products."

He nodded toward the beds. "Which one do you want?"

"Doesn't matter."

He tossed his duffel onto the mattress of the one closest to the door, then picked up the remote on the nightstand.

"I thought you were desperate to get some sleep."

"I am," he said. "But I sleep better with the TV on. Or maybe I should say that I fall asleep better with the TV on."

"TV stimulates the brain, and they say that a stimulated brain prevents you from getting the deep sleep you really need."

"Who says?" he challenged, selecting a favorite movie.

"Experts," she responded vaguely. "And why does it matter what's on if you're going to be sleeping?"

"Because the experts also say that falling asleep to the sounds of something familiar can reduce stress so that you get a more restful sleep."

"You just made that up."

"Did I?" he challenged.

She dug around in her suitcase, looking for her toiletry bag, he guessed.

"I forgot I had this," she said.

He glanced over as she pulled a Tupperware container out of the case.

"What is it?" he asked.

"Cake."

"Do you always pack cake when you travel?"

"Hardly," she said. "It's leftover from my niece and nephew's birthday party."

"Your niece and nephew have the same birthday?"

"They're twins."

"So yes," he noted, then asked, "How old?"

"Three."

"What kind of cake is it?"

"Probably broken cake after you dropped my suitcase in the snow."

"It was your suitcase or you," he reminded her.

She pried open the lid to inspect the contents. "Well, it doesn't look as if any damage was done."

"What kind of cake?" he asked again.

"Funfetti cake with cherry filling and Italian meringue buttercream icing."

"So you were holding out on me," he mused. "Begging to

share my dinner when, all along, you had cake in your suitcase."

"I didn't beg," she said indignantly.

"Your eyes were begging."

"My eyes were *not* begging."

"Believe me, honey, I know when a woman is begging for
something—though it isn't usually to share my dinner."

"My name isn't *honey.*"

"Are you going to offer to share that cake, *Finley*?" he
asked.

"Maybe I'll wait for you to beg for it," she said.

He grinned, appreciating that she could give as good as
she got.

"If it's from Sweet Caroline's, I would beg," he told her.

"Since you obviously have an appreciation for the finer
things in life, I won't make you," she decided.

"You consider pizza and cake to be some of the finer things?"

"Pizza from Jo's and cake from Sweet Caroline's are definitely at the top of the list."

"A woman of simple pleasures," he mused.

"I also like good champagne and a grilled filet on occasion."

"Who doesn't?"

"Haylee—my sister and the mother of the twins—actually
gave me two slices of cake, so we don't have to worry about
cutting it," she said. "But the coffee tray only has stir sticks
not spoons, so we'll have to eat with our hands."

"Works for me," he said easily.

She set one of the slices on the lid of the Tupperware container and passed it to him.

"Thanks." He broke off a piece and popped it in his mouth.

He wasn't a big fan of sweets—he'd take chips over cookies any day of the week—but the cake was moist and the tart-
ness of the filling a nice contrast to the sweetness of the icing.

"This is really good," he said, savoring the vanilla flavor of the cake.

"Enjoy it while you can," she advised. "There's a rumor going around Haven that the owner of Sweet Caroline's is planning to sell."

"Maybe the buyer will get her recipes along with the shop."

"That's assuming the buyer continues to operate the space as a bakery. He might want to open an appliance repair shop instead."

"That would be a definite shame," Lachlan noted.

"Bliss in Oakland is the only bakery I've discovered that could give Sweet Caroline's a run for its money."

"Never heard of it," he said.

"They offer eight different cake flavors and twelve unique fillings, and I've probably sampled every single combination."

"How is that possible?" he wondered.

"I'm an event planner," she reminded him. "Clients often invite me to accompany them to menu samplings and cake tastings."

"That sounds like a pretty good job perk to me."

"Except that I pay fifty dollars a month for a gym membership to work off all that free cake."

"There are cheaper—and more satisfying—workouts than going to the gym," he said with a wink, as he popped the last bite of cake in his mouth.

"I think I'll stick with my fifty-dollar-a-month plan," Finley said, just a little primly.

He shrugged. "Your call."

"That *was* good," she said. licking icing off her thumb. "But now I'm thirsty."

"There might be drinks in the fridge."

"And the motel probably charges four dollars for a can of Coke."

He returned the Tupperware lid to her and reached toward the mini-fridge beside the desk.

"I'll pay for the drinks," he said, offering her a bottle of water with a label that read 'Complimentary for Guests.'

Except "guests" was spelled "geusts."

"Your generosity is overwhelming," she noted dryly.

"I did offer to pay for the room," he reminded her.

"You did," she acknowledged, as she uncapped the bottle.

Lachlan did the same with his, then guzzled down half the contents, his Adam's apple bobbing as he swallowed.

Her gaze followed the column of his throat to the line of his jaw. Or what she imagined was the line of his jaw if she could see through the dark hair that covered it. She suspected it was strong and square, and his lips temptingly shaped and surprisingly soft.

And what was wrong with her that she was thinking about such things? Looking at him as if he was a man she might be interested in?

Because he wasn't and she wasn't.

Still, it required more effort than she wanted to admit to tear her gaze away from him and focus it on the bottle in her hand.

"In the age of spell check and autocorrect, how do you make a mistake like that?" Finley wondered, tracing the word "geusts" on her label.

"Laziness," Lachlan suggested. "You should see some of the egregious errors on the papers that my students turn in."

"Egregious, huh?" She smiled. "Now you sound like a professor. You still don't look like one, though."

He reached into the end pocket of his duffel bag and pulled out a pair of dark-rimmed glasses.

"How about now?" he asked, when he'd settled them on his face.

The glasses didn't completely change his look, but they

did add a bit of a scholarly air. Which, on Lachlan Kellett, was incredibly sexy.

"A little bit," she allowed. "Though I still would have guessed that you were a football coach before college professor."

"I never coached, but I did play some football in high school," he told her.

"Ever been to prison?"

To her surprise, he smiled. "Isn't that a question you should have asked before you invited me into your room?"

"You invited yourself," she reminded him.

"I guess I did. And no, I've never been to prison."

"Anyway, it was Shirla who speculated that you'd done time."

"Shirla? The desk clerk?"

She nodded. "She told me she has a thing for bad boys."

He chuckled. "And she pegged me as a bad boy?"

"She was certainly hoping."

"When did you and Shirla have this conversation?" he wondered.

"When you went out to get your pizza."

"Well, I'm sorry if you're disappointed."

"I'm not disappointed. Harleys and tattoos don't do anything for me. Not that I was looking at you in that way," she hastened to assure him.

"What way were you looking at me?"

"Hungrily," she said. "Because you had the pizza."

He chuckled again, the low rumble sliding over her skin like a caress, raising goosebumps on her flesh.

"So what is your type—since it's apparently not bad boys?" he asked.

She rubbed her hands over her arms. "How did we get on this topic?"

"You asked if I'd ever been to prison."

"So I did," she acknowledged. "As for my type, I don't know that I have one. Or maybe it's been so long since I've been on a date that I can't remember."

"Any particular reason you haven't been dating?" he asked.

"Not really. I've just been focused on other priorities."

"Meaning Gilmore Galas?" he guessed.

"Yeah."

"You're too busy planning celebrations for the events in other people's lives that you don't have time to live your own?"

"I'm happy with my life as it is," she assured him.

"Which is what people say when they're really *not* happy with their lives," he remarked.

"I don't know what people you've been talking to," she said. "But in my case, it happens to be true."

"I'm a professor of anthropology," he reminded her. "I talk to all kinds of people."

He finished his drink, recapped the bottle and tossed it into the recycle bin under the desk.

"Okay if I take a shower?"

"The deal was for a bed," she reminded him. "If you want bathroom privileges, too, you'll have to buy me breakfast in the morning."

"Not a problem." He winked. "I always buy a woman breakfast after spending the night in her bed."

"You have your own bed," she reminded him, that prim note sneaking into her tone again.

"But the room is in your name," he pointed out. "So technically they're both your beds."

The chime of her cell phone was a timely interruption, giving her an excuse to turn her back on him so he couldn't see that he'd flustered her. *Again*.

But the soft chuckle she heard as he made his way into the bathroom told her that he knew it anyway.

Just got the kids into bed and saw your message—now tell me more about this hunky guy you're sleeping with tonight!

Finley immediately replied to her sister's message:

I'm not sleeping with anyone! He's just a fellow stranded traveler.

A HOT stranded traveler.

How can you tell from a DMV photo?

You can't. I Googled him.

WHAT? Why?!

Lots of pics online from Merivale College events. VERY. HOT.

How's the weather there?

Don't you dare change the subject!

I just wondered if the storm was starting to let up, because I can't see anything at all outside the tiny window in this room.

So ask the hunky college professor for this thoughts on the weather.

He's in the shower right now.

Which means naked!

Which definitely wasn't something Finley wanted to be thinking about.

Good night, Haylee. Love you.

Are you going to join him in the shower?

No. I'm going to get into my pjs and crawl under the covers of my own bed—on the opposite side of the room.

Hard to believe you're the same sister who told me to stop worrying about finding Mr. Right and be open to finding Mr. Right Now.

Not really hard to believe, considering I'm your only sister. And look what happened—you ended up pregnant.

I have absolutely no regrets.

Finley knew it was true.

But she also knew that there had been weeks—even months—of worry and uncertainty for her sister as Haylee figured out what her future was going to look like. Before she realized that Trevor Blake was as much in love with her as she was with him and finally agreed to let Finley plan their wedding.

She replied to her sister:

I'm glad, because nobody is more deserving of a happy ending than you.

You deserve to be happy, too.

I am happy.

How can you be happy when you haven't had sex in almost a year and a half?

Finley flushed reading the message, quickly typing a response.

Why did I ever tell you that?

Because I'm your sister and your best friend.

I think it's more likely because of the wine.

There was wine, Haylee confirmed.

A lot of wine, if Finley remembered correctly.

But maybe she didn't, as her memories of that night were admittedly a little fuzzy.

The sound of water running in the bathroom suddenly stopped, making Finley realize that Lachlan was finished in the shower. That he was probably, right now, reaching for a towel to rub over his wet, naked body.

Which meant that she needed to hurry if she was going to get changed before he came back.

Good night, she said again.

You'll check in with me in the morning?

As long as I'm still alive, she promised.

xoxoxo

She was rifling through the contents of her suitcase, in search of her pajamas, when the lights flickered.

She hastily exchanged her clothes for her sleepwear just as the room was plunged into darkness.

Chapter Three

Finley heard a crash, followed by a string of inventive curses. She ventured a few steps toward the bathroom—or at least in the direction she thought she remembered the bathroom being located before everything had gone black. "Are you alright?"

"Fine," Lachlan muttered in a tone that sounded anything but fine.

"Do you need ice? I can scrape some up from outside—if I can find the door."

"I don't need ice."

She heard the bathroom door open—the only warning she got that Lachlan was coming out before he barreled into her.

She stumbled back from the impact, and he instinctively reached out to catch her.

"This is getting to be a habit," he remarked, sounding more amused than annoyed now.

"You bumped into me this time," she pointed out to him.

"I guess I did," he acknowledged.

But he didn't immediately let go of her, and she didn't attempt to step away from him.

Instead, she stood there, unable to see anything in the pitch darkness but nevertheless achingly aware of the heat emanating from his body, the tantalizing scent of clean male that teased her nostrils and stirred her blood, the heat of his hands scorching her arms through the flannel sleeves of her pajama top.

"Finley." Her name was barely a whisper from his lips.

"Lachlan," she whispered in response.

Another few seconds passed.

He cleared his throat. "I should, um, find some clothes."

He was naked?

She swallowed. "You're not dressed?"

"I'm wearing a towel."

Lucky towel.

"I forgot to take a change of clothes into the bathroom with me," he explained.

"You should definitely find some clothes."

Still, neither of them moved.

"This probably isn't a good idea," he warned.

"What—" She had to swallow because her throat had gone dry again. "What isn't a good idea?"

"Using the darkness as an excuse to give in to whatever is going on between us."

"Maybe you're only imagining that there's something going on," she suggested.

"I'm not imagining your hand on my chest."

"Ohmygod." She immediately yanked it away, mortified by the brazenness of her own—completely subconscious—action. "I'm so sorry."

"No need to apologize," he told her. "But if you want me to behave like a gentleman, you have to try not to tempt me."

"I'm certainly not trying to tempt you," she assured him, ignoring the fact that her actions told a different story even if she wasn't able to ignore the tingling in her palm where it had been in contact with the warm, taut skin of his hard chest.

"Honey, even in flannel, you're the personification of temptation."

"You wouldn't say that if you could see that my pajamas are covered with cartoon pigs with wings."

"I don't need to see, because I have a very good imagination and I'm a lot less interested in what's on your pajamas than what's underneath them."

She had a pretty good imagination, too. But she didn't want to imagine his naked body, she wanted to explore it.

She wanted *him*.

So much so that she ached.

And though she barely knew the man, she knew it would be foolish to act on the attraction she felt.

There had been a time when she would have thrown caution to the wind and seized the moment—and the man—not caring, as her sister had reminded her, if he was "Mr. Right" so long as he was "Mr. Right Now." What she'd never admitted to anyone was that every time she'd jumped into a relationship (or bed!) with "'Mr. Right Now," she'd secretly been hoping that he would turn out to be "Mr. Right."

After too many disappointments, she'd decided that she needed to be more discerning so as not to set herself up for disappointment again. Remembering that, she took a deliberate step back now, away from Lachlan, away from temptation.

He didn't try to stop her.

"I need to, um, brush my teeth."

She stumbled back to the dresser, where she'd left her suitcase open, and pulled out her toiletry bag.

"The plumbing in the bathroom is backwards," he told her. "Turn the tap left for cold, right for hot."

"Thanks."

It was eerily quiet in the room now, the only audible sound that of the wind howling outside and rattling the panes of glass in the window. It was so quiet, in fact, that Finley heard his towel drop to the floor when he released it.

Now he was completely naked, and every female part of her quivered with awareness of that fact.

There was some rustling then, as he searched in his duffel bag for whatever items of clothing he planned to sleep in.

"Aren't hotels supposed to have backup generators?" she asked now.

"The Rusty Spurs isn't a Ritz Carlton."

"Dusty Boots," she corrected.

"Still not a Ritz Carlton."

She heard him pull back the covers on the bed and took it as a sign that he was no longer naked.

"Then I guess it's a good thing my phone has a torch light," she said, turning it on.

"Which will drain your battery pretty quickly," he pointed out. "And, without power, you won't be able to recharge it."

"You're not helping my efforts to hold back panic. Besides, I'm sure the two minutes I need it to brush my teeth won't kill the battery," she said, using the light to illuminate her path to the bathroom.

Of course, she had to use the toilet and then wash her hands, too, so it was probably closer to three minutes before she exited the bathroom again.

When she did, she discovered that the bedroom was no longer in pitch darkness but was, instead, softly illuminated by a greenish light.

"You had a glow stick?" She was surprised—and relieved.

"I've got a couple of them," he said. "But this one should see us through the night."

"I guess you weren't kidding about being out in the wilderness."

"Why would I kid about something like that?" he asked, his tone puzzled.

She shrugged.

"So much for your plan to fall asleep with the TV on," she remarked.

"I'm so tired, it probably won't matter tonight—so long as your snoring doesn't keep me awake."

"I don't snore," she said indignantly.

"How would you know?"

"No one I've ever shared a bed with has ever complained."

She caught a quick flash of white teeth as he grinned. "Which doesn't mean you don't snore."

She deliberately turned her back on him, tucked the covers under her chin and closed her eyes, though she suspected it would be a long time before sleep came with the sexy professor only a few feet away from her.

Lachlan could tell by the even rhythm of her breathing when Finley's fake sleep gave way to the real thing.

Unfortunately, slumber continued to elude him.

He'd thought he was clever, bartering for the spare bed in her room. But he realized now that it had been a mistake. He'd told himself that he only wanted a quiet place to crash— and it was true—but now that they were alone together, he couldn't seem to stop thinking about the fact that they were alone together. And that Finley Gilmore was the most intriguing woman he'd encountered in a long time.

He'd met her less than five hours earlier, but he couldn't close his eyes without seeing her in his mind. The way her eyes, as blue as a summer sky, shone when she was happy; the way her lips, as perfectly shaped as a Cupid's bow, curved when she smiled; the way she tilted her head, just a fraction, when she was thinking; the way her brow furrowed when she was unhappy with those thoughts.

That stunning face was surrounded by a fall of silky hair that tempted a man to slide his hands into it, tip her head back and cover her mouth with his own.

Yeah, he wished he'd never asked her to let him crash in the extra bed.

But mostly he wished that he'd ignored his conscience when she'd been in his arms. That instead of warning her that it wasn't a good idea to give in to the attraction between them, he'd kept his mouth shut and kissed her.

Because he felt confident that if he'd given in to the urge, she would have kissed him back. One kiss would have led to another, and then his towel and her flannel pj's would have both ended up on the floor.

So maybe it was a good thing that his conscience had kicked in, because the one thing he didn't have in his duffel bag was protection, and he was no longer a twenty-year-old college kid who didn't know not to take chances with birth control.

Which was almost too bad, because he had no doubt that he'd already be fast asleep if he'd found his release with her.

Seize every opportunity.

That was some of the advice his dying friend had given him when they were saying goodbye and pretending it wasn't for the last time.

"Don't be more afraid of life than death," Ben said.

"Dying seems to have made you philosophical," Lachlan responded lightly.

"Dying has made me realize what's important in life," his friend countered.

"And now you're going to tell me?"

Ben shook his head. *"You need to discover that for yourself."*

"And how do I do that?" he asked, more to humor his friend than because he expected an answer.

"Appreciate every moment, seize every opportunity and find joy in every day."

And while Lachlan might have been tempted to invoke his friend's advice, he couldn't take advantage of Finley's hospitality by making a move. Not even if he felt certain that she was as attracted to him as he was to her.

But damn, it was hard to do the right thing.

Achingly hard.

* * *

Finley woke up a few hours later. She slid out from under the covers and quickly made her way to the bathroom. The temperature in the room had dropped significantly while she slept, and the bathroom tiles were like ice beneath her feet.

She quickly did what she needed to do, washed and dried her hands and hurried back to her bed.

But the cotton sheet and thin blanket provided little comfort in the chilly room. She rubbed her feet together beneath the covers, hoping the friction would help warm them.

A weary sigh emanated from the other side of the room before Lachlan said, "What are you doing?"

"N-nothing."

"I can hear you fidgeting," he said.

"S-sorry." She crossed her feet at the ankles and tried to think warm thoughts: a steaming bath…a crackling fire…hot chocolate…a tropical beach…sweaty sex.

She immediately reined in her wayward thoughts.

Or tried to.

But apparently her mind was enjoying this mental exercise a little too much, because her next thought was: sweaty sex with a hot man on a tropical beach.

And then: sweaty sex with a hot man in a roadside motel.

"I have a long drive tomorrow." Lachlan's reminder interrupted her prurient fantasies. "So I'd really like to get some sleep tonight."

"I'm n-not s-stopping you."

"I can hear your teeth chattering."

"Well, I c-can't help it if I'm c-cold."

"It's not that cold in here," he told her. "Just close your eyes and when you wake up in the morning, the storm will have passed and the power will be back on."

She ignored his advice to push back the covers.

"What are you doing now?"

"I n-need s-socks," she said. "My f-feet are f-freezing."

Though the glow stick continued to provide faint light, he turned on the torch on his phone to better illuminate her search through her suitcase.

Not because he wanted to be helpful, she suspected, but because he wanted her to go back to sleep so that he could do the same.

"Got 'em," she said triumphantly.

He turned off the light and she unfolded the thick socks and pulled them onto her feet.

"Are you going to be able to sleep now?" he asked.

"I h-hope so."

He sighed again and, after a moment of internal debate, finally asked, "Do you want me to sleep with you?"

"What? N-no!"

"I only meant for the purpose of sharing body heat," he clarified.

"Oh." She was silent for a moment, considering his offer. "Would we have to be…n-naked?"

"Naked would make things more interesting," he mused.

"I'll p-pass, thanks," she said, a little primly.

He chuckled softly. "I was only teasing. Of course, we don't have to be naked."

She was silent for a minute, considering. "Can you explain to m-me how it works?"

"You want me to give you a lesson on thermodynamics?"

"Is that w-what it is?"

"That's what it is," he confirmed.

"And how d-does a professor of anthropology know a-about thermodynamics?" she wondered.

"I took several elective courses in physics."

"You took physics *for f-fun*?"

"Physics *is* fun."

"I think we're going to have to agree to d-disagree on that," she said. "But right n-now, I just want to know if the sharing body heat thing really does w-work."

"It really does."

"Okay, then," she finally relented.

He yanked the blanket and sheet off his bed and carried them to hers.

She scooched over on the mattress, making room for him.

He laid the extra covers on top of the bed before sliding beneath them.

Though she was pretty much hugging the edge of the mattress, as soon as he settled beside her, Finley felt the warmth radiating from his body.

"Heat conduction between two bodies occurs at the surface interface between them," he told her.

"C-can you translate that into English, p-please?"

"If you want to share my body heat, your body needs to be in contact with mine."

"Oh."

"Or I can go back to the other bed, if you've changed your mind."

"I haven't changed m-my m-mind." She released her grip on the edge of the mattress and slowly inched toward the middle of the bed.

"I'm not going to jump you, Finley." His tone wasn't just quiet but also sincere.

"I d-didn't think you were."

Hoped, maybe.

But only for a very brief minute.

He snaked an arm around her waist and pulled her closer.

"You really are cold," he noted, sounding surprised.

She nodded.

He held her wrapped in his arms for several minutes, until she stopped shivering and her teeth stopped chattering.

"Think you can sleep now?" he asked then.

She nodded again.

But the truth was, she wasn't sure.

Yes, she was feeling a lot warmer now.

And achingly aware of the man whose arms were around her.

She closed her eyes and drew in a slow, deep breath, inhaling his clean masculine scent.

Well, that wasn't helping.

She held her breath, but of course, that was only a very short-term solution.

"Relax, Finley."

"I'm trying," she admitted. "But I haven't shared a bed with a man in…a very long time."

"Why's that?"

She shrugged. "I've been too busy with work to even think about starting a relationship, and I don't do one-night stands. Not anymore."

"Me, neither," he confided.

"Really?" she asked, surprised and a little skeptical.

"When you get to a certain age, sex for the sake of sex, without any kind of connection, isn't fun anymore."

"And what age is that?"

"Are you asking how old I am?"

"Maybe."

"Then maybe I'm thirty-six."

"I might be twenty-eight," she told him.

"Kind of young to have given up on relationships," he mused.

"I haven't given up," she denied. "I'm just focusing on my career right now."

"And sleeping alone."

"Except for Simon, of course."

"Simon is…a cat?" he surmised

She frowned into the darkness. "How did you guess?"

"All the single people I know often give their pets human names."

"Well, I didn't name Simon," she told him.

"Who did?"

"My sister."

"The one with the twins?"

"She's the only sister I've got."

"She got the cat for you?"

"No, she adopted Simon from a local shelter. And then she moved to Nevada, so I offered to keep him."

"None of which disproves my point," he noted.

"Speaking of names," she said, eager to change the topic. "I don't think I've ever known a Lachlan before. Is it an Irish name?"

"It is," he confirmed.

"Does anyone ever call you Lach?"

"Only my ex-wife."

"You're divorced?"

"Yep."

"Another question I probably should have asked before I let you share my room," she admitted.

"Or at least before you invited me into your bed," he teased.

"Cuddling was your idea," she reminded him.

"We're not cuddling," he said, making the word sound distasteful.

"Snuggling?" she suggested as an alternative.

"We're sharing body heat."

"For which I'm extremely grateful," she told him.

"And I'm grateful your teeth have stopped chattering," he noted.

"Apparently this thermodynamics thing really does work." She shifted a little, pressing her back against him to absorb more of his body heat.

"Even without you wriggling around," he said through gritted teeth.

"I'm trying to find a comfortable position to sleep, but your body is hard."

"And it's going to get even harder, if you don't stop squirming," he warned.

She immediately stilled. "Oh. I didn't realize... Sorry."

"Don't be sorry," he told her. "Just go to sleep."

If only it was that easy.

"How do you expect me to sleep now that I know you're... um..."

"Semi-aroused?" he finished for her.

"Yeah," she admitted, grateful that it was too dark for him to see the flush of heat that filled her cheeks.

"Don't worry," he told her. "It isn't personal—just a physiological response to your body rubbing against mine."

"I'm not sure if I should be relieved or insulted."

"You should be asleep," he told her. "We both should be asleep."

Finley couldn't imagine being able to sleep now.

But being wrapped in his embrace made her feel warm and safe.

And finally, she slept.

Chapter Four

When she awakened again, Finley's first thought was that it was morning, as evidenced by the sun filtering through the sides of the curtains. Her second thought was that she was alone, not only in her bed but in the room.

Lachlan was gone.

She should have been relieved to be spared any awkward morning-after conversation with the man. Not that anything had happened between them. Nothing except that he'd shared his body heat so that she could sleep.

So why, in the light of day, did that act almost seem more intimate than sex?

Maybe because she understood that sex didn't always require intimacy. That sometimes sex was just a physical act no more significant (though hopefully more pleasurable) than a walk in the park.

To Finley, sharing a bed with a man required a greater level of trust than sharing her body. And she realized now that she'd never just *slept* with a man.

Until last night.

The quiet hum of the heating unit confirmed that Lachlan's assertion that the storm would pass and power would be restored by morning had turned out to be true. She pushed back the covers and slid out of bed, eager to hit the shower, when her phone chimed with a text.

Power meant she could charge her phone before heading to the airport, and she plugged it in before opening the message—an update from the airline notifying her that her rescheduled flight to Oakland was canceled.

"No." Finley shook her head as she scanned the words again. *"No, no, no."*

She first checked the weather report, then the airport status, then she called the customer service number provided in the message.

"I don't understand why my flight's been canceled," she said, after waiting nearly fifteen minutes and dialing through an endless series of voice prompts just to get to a human. "Again."

"Unfortunately, the incoming flight from Denver was grounded by the storm, so we don't have a plane to send to Oakland," the perky customer service rep who introduced herself as Peg informed her.

"What happened to the plane that couldn't take off for Oakland at four o'clock yesterday?"

Peg tapped some keys. "It's boarding passengers now and is scheduled to takeoff for Oakland at 9:20."

"Why was I booked on a twelve thirty flight if there was one leaving more than three hours earlier?"

"Likely because there were no available seats on the morning flight."

She closed her eyes and silently counted to ten before asking, "So what am I supposed to do now?"

"There are seats available on the twelve thirty flight tomorrow."

"But I need to get back to Oakland *today*."

More key tapping sounded over the line.

"If you can make your way to Salt Lake City, there's a direct flight from there at three-o-five."

"If I was going to drive to Salt Lake City—" which was a

four-hour trip in the wrong direction "—I might as well drive to Oakland."

"Would you like me to book you a seat on that twelve thirty flight tomorrow?"

"Unless it's a DeLorean leaving at twelve thirty tomorrow, it's not going to get me back to Oakland today, is it?"

"I'm sorry?"

She sighed. "Never mind."

"Is there anything else I can help you with today?" Perky Peg asked.

"No, thank you," she said, and disconnected the call.

Her problems weren't his problems, Lachlan assured himself.

So why, when he saw Finley toss her phone aside with obvious frustration, did he hear himself say, "I could give you a ride."

She whirled around, obviously startled to see him. "I thought you'd already gone. Your duffel bag was gone."

"I tossed it in my truck on the way to get the breakfast I promised you," he said, setting the cardboard tray holding two cups and a paper bag on the table between the two beds. "I didn't know how you take your coffee, so I got cream and sugar on the side."

"I'd take it intravenously if I could," she told him, prying the lid off one of the cups. "And usually black, but having sampled the motel's interpretation of coffee yesterday afternoon, I'm pretty sure it's going to need lots of cream and sugar to make it palatable."

She added both to her cup, stirred with a flimsy plastic stick, then lifted it to her lips for a cautious sip.

"There's a couple of Danishes in the bag," Lachlan said. "One lemon, one blueberry."

"Thanks, but I don't eat breakfast."

"Never?"

"Only the morning af—" She abruptly cut off her own response.

"The morning after what?" he prompted, a smile tugging the corners of his mouth.

She sipped her coffee again. "Clearly I need caffeine to kick in my conversational filter."

"After sex?" he guessed.

"After racquetball."

"I enjoy a spirited game of racquetball every now and then myself. It certainly does work up an appetite."

She reached for the bag of pastries.

"I thought you didn't eat breakfast?"

"Clearly I need to shove something in my mouth to stop talking."

He didn't try to hold back his smile this time.

"Do you want the lemon or blueberry?" she asked.

"You choose."

She chose the lemon.

She didn't speak again until all that was left of the pastry was crumbs. "Did you really offer to drive me to Oakland?"

"It's not exactly out of my way," he pointed out.

"But it's a long time in a car with someone you don't really know."

"Maybe we didn't spend a lot of time talking last night, but we did sleep together."

"We didn't sleep together," she said indignantly.

"I'm pretty sure we did."

"Okay, yes, we did," she confirmed. "But all we did was sleep."

"And you're regretting that this morning?"

"Of course not," she denied.

But the color that filled her cheeks suggested that she wasn't being entirely truthful.

"Can we maybe talk about something else?"

"You didn't have any trouble telling me about your dry spell last night," he mused.

"I simply mentioned that I was on a dating hiatus," she clarified.

"To-may-to, to-mah-to."

"And anyway, it was dark."

"I'm not sure how that's relevant," he said. "Unless you're one of those women who only ever makes love with the lights off."

"*That* isn't any of your business," she retorted.

"Which can be kind of annoying, because most guys want to see the woman they're with—to fully appreciate her attributes."

"I didn't ask."

"I'd definitely want to see you."

"That's *so* not going to happen."

"I'd be lying if I said I wasn't disappointed," he told her.

"Life's full of disappointments, isn't it?"

"Too true." He finished his coffee as she took another tentative sip from her cup.

"Anyway…" Finley hesitated a moment before continuing, "if you were serious about letting me hitch a ride to California, then I accept. Thank you."

"No worries. And there's a lot more room in my vehicle than in a DeLorean."

She grimaced. "You heard that, did you?"

"The neighbors on either side probably heard you," he said.

"I guess I was a little frustrated by that point in the conversation," she acknowledged.

"Travel delays can have that effect."

"Yeah."

"Speaking of travel," he prompted.

"Right." She set her unfinished coffee aside. "Do I have time for a shower?"

"If you can make it quick. We don't know what condition the roads are in or how long it will take us to get out of Nevada."

"I can be quick," she promised.

She found the clothes she wanted in her suitcase and carried them into the bathroom.

Lachlan settled back on the bed he hadn't slept in and turned on the TV, hoping the chatter of the morning show news anchors would drown out the sound of the water in the bathroom.

Because listening to the spray of the water, it was almost impossible not to think about Finley standing under that spray. Naked. Impossible not to picture the water sluicing over her body, washing soapy lather from the curve of her breasts, suds gliding over the indent of her waist, the flare of her hips.

Because after spending the night in her bed, he was achingly aware of every delectable curve of her body. He wouldn't have intentionally copped a feel, but he'd nevertheless awakened with Finley's back snug against his front, one of his knees between her thighs, an arm around her middle, his hand cupping her breast and a rock-hard erection pressing against her tailbone.

Thankfully she'd still been fast asleep when he'd carefully lifted his hand away, dislodged his knee, and gritted his teeth against the ache in his shorts.

A sharp ping from his cell snapped him back to the present. He reached for the device to check the message on the screen.

R u ever coming home? Miss you!

He smiled as the message from Aislynn effectively banished the naked Finley fantasy from his mind.

I should be home later today. And I miss you, too.

Do u miss me more?

Always.

* * *

Finley was in and out of the shower in record time. Not only because Lachlan had told her to be quick, but because she knew it was a long drive to Oakland (the reason she usually preferred to fly!) and she wanted to get on the road so that she would be back in time for Kelly and Paul's event that evening.

Officially it was on her calendar as the "Metler-Grzeszczak Engagement Party," but over the past few months, she'd gotten to know the couple quite well—as usually happened when she was planning an event—and had started to think of them by their given names. (Also, it was a lot easier to say "Kelly and Paul" than "Metler-Grzeszczak.")

She finished drying her hair, twisted it into a loose knot on top of her head, swiped mascara over her lashes, dabbed gloss on her lips and decided that was all the primping she needed to do to spend the next several hours in a car.

She opened the maps app on her phone to check the route from the Dusty Boots Motel to her home in Oakland.

Six hours and forty-three minutes?

Definitely time to get a move on.

She started to tuck her phone away again when it chimed with a message.

Did you survive the night?

She smiled as she tapped out a reply to her sister's query.

It seems I did.

The college professor didn't have any nefarious intentions?

None aside from stealing half my cake.

You shared?!? (The question was followed by a string of shocked-face emojis.)

It seemed like the right thing to do last night. This morning, I'm not so sure.

"Something put a smile on your face," Lachlan remarked, as Finley came out of the bathroom with her pajamas and toiletry bag in one hand and her cell phone in the other. "Was it the handheld showerhead?"

She rolled her eyes. "There was no handheld showerhead."

"Hmm…must have only been in my imagination then."

"For your information, it was my sister."

He shook his head. "Not even my imagination can conjure a woman I've never met."

She tucked her belongings into her suitcase. "I would have expected the mind of a college professor to be occupied by deeper thoughts."

"I'm still a man," he reminded her. "And most of the men I know think about naked women."

"Are you trying to make me change my mind about spending the next six-and-a-half hours in a vehicle with you?"

"It's probably going to be closer to eight hours, factoring in the snow and breaks for food and fuel."

"Eight hours?" She looked worried as she glanced at the time displayed on her phone.

"Give or take."

She zipped up her case.

"And anyway, you're not going to change your mind about riding with me to California, as I'm pretty much the only hope you have of making it home today."

"You're right about that," she confirmed.

"So…was your sister checking in to make sure I didn't kill you in your sleep?"

"Or while I was awake."

"She's not very trusting, is she?"

"She doesn't know you," Finley pointed out. "And neither do I."

"I imagine you'll know me a lot better after an almost five-hundred-mile drive."

"Let's get started."

"So tell me about this engagement party that you can't miss tonight," Lachlan said, when they were finally en route.

"You don't have to feign an interest in my work," Finley told him.

"Maybe my interest isn't feigned."

"What do you want to know? The menu options? The music selections?"

"I guess I'm mostly curious to know why you made the trip to Nevada when you had such an important event coming up in California?"

"Because there was an even more important event happening here."

"Your niece and nephew's birthday party?"

"Of course."

"They're three. They're not going to remember anything about the party, least of all whether or not you were there."

"But I'll remember," she said. "And I would have hated to miss it."

"You mean you would have hated to miss the Funfetti cake."

She grinned. "That, too."

"Do you see your sister and her family very often?"

"Not nearly as often as I'd like since she moved to Haven." She sighed. "And it's kind of my fault."

"Why would you say that?"

"When our cousin Caleb was getting married a few years

back, I nudged Haylee into attending. It was at the wedding that she fell for Trevor Blake."

And into his bed, though that wasn't a detail she intended to share with Lachlan.

"Wait a minute," he said. "Is your cousin Caleb Gilmore?"

"Do you know him?"

"I know the name. And I know that he's part of the family that operates the Circle G—one of the biggest cattle ranches in northern Nevada."

She nodded. "My dad grew up on the Circle G, but ranching wasn't in his blood the way it was his brothers', so when he was eighteen, he made his way to the West Coast and got a job on the docks. He learned the ropes, then started his own company."

"Gilmore Logistics," Lachlan realized.

"You've heard of it?"

"It's an international shipping conglomerate."

"I guess it is," she acknowledged.

"You've got an impressive family," he mused.

She couldn't disagree.

Nor could she deny that she'd traded on her family's reputation, to a certain extent, by using her surname in her company's name.

She'd never anticipated that doing so might make her a target of charming men who wanted her for all the wrong reasons. And she'd dated Gabriel Landon for almost six months before she figured out that her boyfriend's lifestyle was being financed not by his numerous business ventures but his wealthy girlfriends—of which she was only one.

"And I spend my days helping brides decide between cream and blush roses or debating the merits of chiffon versus organza," she said lightly, wanting to make it clear to him that her family's business success—and their wealth—had nothing to do with her.

"Which I'm sure is much more important to them than overseas shipping routes or the market price of cattle," he pointed out.

She was surprised—and pleased—that he could appreciate the value of her work, despite the fact that he likely had less than zero interest in bouquets or fabrics.

"Anyway," she said, attempting to steer the conversation back on track. "Six months after Caleb and Brielle's wedding, Haylee and Trevor were married."

"Did you plan the wedding?"

"Of course."

"So you must like this guy she hooked up with?"

"Trevor's great," she confirmed. "And he makes her happy, which makes me happy."

"Not envious?"

She frowned. "Why would I be envious of my sister's happiness?"

"Because you want what she has?" he suggested.

"I love my brother-in-law, but not in that way," she assured him.

"I was referring to a husband and kids generally rather than specifically."

"Oh." She considered. "Sure, I'd like to get married and have a family someday, but right now, my career takes all of my time and attention."

"Your career—and Simon."

"Right."

The funny thing was, everyone in the family had assumed that Finley would be the first to fall in love, get married and have a family—if only because Haylee had always been so notoriously shy, especially around members of the opposite sex. Now, in addition to being a career woman, Haylee was a wife and a mother, while Finley—previously of the active social life—was so busy planning events for other people that she didn't have time to date or even hang out with friends.

So it probably wasn't surprising that her last relationship (if a handful of dates could even be called a relationship) had fizzled out close to a year ago. Or maybe it had been even longer than that.

Fifteen months?

Eighteen?

She frowned.

She could remember specific details from the Lynch-Sandoval wedding the previous summer (number of guests at the event—192; color of the bridesmaids' dresses—violet fog; flavor of the cake—red velvet with chocolate mousse filling), but she couldn't remember the last time she'd been on a real date.

She missed dating.

And she missed sex.

At least when she thought about it.

Thankfully, she didn't think about it very often.

But sitting in close proximity to Lachlan for hours after having spent the night sleeping in his arms, she was thinking about it now.

Not so much the physical release (which she could take care of herself, thank you very much) as the intimate connection of being with another person.

She missed having someone to hang out with and talk to. Someone to chat with over dinner or snuggle up with on the sofa to watch a game on TV. Someone to tangle up the sheets with and wake up next to in the morning.

Instead, she had Simon and sole control of the TV remote.

And for now that was…perfectly fine.

Chapter Five

On more than one occasion, his ex-wife had accused Lachlan of having a white knight complex. Of course, Deirdre had said it as if it was a bad thing, but he didn't think there was anything wrong with wanting to help a damsel in distress. And his short-term roommate had obviously been in distress.

Or at least stuck.

Either way, it had been apparent that she was in a hurry to get back to California and, as he was headed in that direction, it seemed logical to invite her to go with him.

Now he was going to be riding in a vehicle with her for most of the day, and he had yet to decide if that was a good or bad thing.

He was accustomed to solo journeys. He'd been making the trip from San Francisco to Haven at least once every summer for the past twelve years. He never minded the solitude. In fact, he preferred listening to his favorite tunes over the forced conversation that sometimes took place on long drives.

But throughout the journey to Haven, all he'd been able to think about was his friend dying, alternating between optimism—hoping that the prognosis wasn't as bad as he suspected—and realism—knowing that Mara wouldn't have reached out to him if her husband wasn't in dire straits. Now, after spending the past three weeks with Ben, he could no longer pretend that his longtime friend wasn't very close to the end of his days.

It was a harsh reality that he didn't want to dwell on, so he was grateful to have company for the drive. And he knew Finley Gilmore would be a very pleasant distraction.

Thank goodness he had a maps app on his phone to illustrate his route, because all he could think about this morning was the glory of her curvy body tucked against his all through the night.

Even in sleep, she'd looked like a fairytale princess slumbering under the spell of an evil witch. Not that he'd stayed awake watching her sleep. Or not for very long, anyway.

It had taken several interminable—and uncomfortable—minutes for his body to accept that her nearness was simply a fact and not cause for celebration, but sheer physical exhaustion had eventually won out and he'd dropped off to sleep.

"Why anthropology?"

Finley's question intruded on his thoughts, drawing him back to the present.

"Where did that come from?" he asked her.

She shrugged. "You said we'd have hours to get to know one another. I'm trying to get to know you. So why anthropology?"

"I was in a computer science program and needed a social science course and anthropology fit into my timetable," he confided. "It wasn't ever supposed to be anything more than a required credit, but the professor was passionate about the subject and inspired in me the same desire to learn about other peoples and their cultures."

"Is there a particular branch of anthropology that's your focus?"

"Ethnology."

"I don't know what that is," she admitted.

"The study of cultures from the point of view of the subject of the study."

"And what was your thesis topic?"

"The influence of the Basque peoples on the ranching culture of the American West."

"I'm guessing you researched this by living in the mountains of northern Nevada?"

"Yeah."

"The friend you were visiting...he's a descendant of the Basques?"

"Yeah," he said again. "I met him when I was doing research for my thesis. In fact, I lived with his family for six months fourteen years ago."

"And you've stayed in contact with him since then?"

"I was the best man at his wedding, and he and his wife named their second son after me, though they anglicized the spelling."

"He's really dying?"

He nodded. "Stage four pancreatic cancer."

Finley grimaced. "That sucks."

"It does," he agreed.

"Want to change the subject?"

"To absolutely anything else," he told her.

She managed a smile. "Your choice."

"Why don't you tell me why you became a party planner?"

"Officially, I'm an event planner, because Gilmore Galas does more than just parties. We also organize company events and corporate retreats and we've even done a few memorials."

"I'm going to take a wild guess here and say that weddings are more fun than funerals."

"Obviously," she said. "But celebrating a life well lived can be enjoyable, too.

"Anyway, I was introduced to the business when I worked part-time for a company called Weddings, Etc. in college. To be honest, I was surprised to discover how lucrative the event planning business was—and how much in demand good planners are."

"And how did your former employer feel about you starting your own business in competition with hers?"

"Actually, Lola encouraged me—"

"Lola?" he interrupted, with a quizzical lift of his brows. "Was she a showgirl?"

"No, she was—and is—a wedding planner."

"Not a Barry Manilow fan, I see."

"Who?"

"He was a little before my time, too," Lachlan noted. "But my mom's a big fan. Anyway, Lola encouraged you to start your own business?"

"She had more work than she could handle, and she wanted to be able to focus on bigger events—society weddings and that sort of thing."

"Why does everything always have to be bigger and better?" he wondered aloud.

"Is that a rhetorical question or a social commentary?"

"It just seems as if weddings today are about excess. Formalwear with designer labels. Dresses with bling. Flowers overflowing from urns. Cocktail hour with a jazz quartet playing while guests sip fancy drinks specifically crafted for the bride and groom's happy day. And then a seven-course meal to precede the cutting of the seven-tier cake decorated with edible gold leaf.

"And, of course, you know the whole affair is costing the bride and groom—or their parents—a fortune, so you, as a guest, feel compelled to buy a bigger, more expensive gift or toss a couple extra C-notes in the card."

"I don't know what kind of weddings you've been attending," she remarked. "But I'm impressed by your attention to detail.

"And I can assure you that I work closely with each and

every couple to set a budget they're comfortable with and then stay within the constraints of that budget to give them a day that they'll remember forever."

"I didn't mean to be critical of what you do. I just think that if couples focused more on their marriages and less on their weddings, maybe more of those marriages would last."

"How many times have you been married?" she challenged.

"Once was enough for me," he said.

Lachlan drove in silence for the next several minutes before he said, "Are you hungry? Or do you not eat lunch either?"

"I eat lunch," she told him. "And yes, I'm hungry."

"How's a burger sound?"

"I don't think it makes any sound—though it might sizzle on a grill."

"I'm going to ignore your sarcasm because I'm starving," he said, taking the next exit off the highway.

Finley had seen the billboard advertising an In-N-Out Burger "half a mile ahead" and assumed that was where he was headed, so she was surprised when he pulled into a vacant parking spot in front of a small square building with neon letters that spelled out "Gigi's Diner."

"Best burgers in town," he said, shifting into Park and turning off the engine.

"But what town?" she wondered aloud.

He grinned. "Clipper Gap."

"How do you find these places?"

"Are you asking about the town or the diner?"

"Both."

"I like traveling off the beaten path," he admitted. "And I'd rather support a local eatery than a multi-million-dollar corporation."

"I can respect that," she said. "Although sometimes, especially when the clock is ticking, the convenience of a drive-through cheeseburger and fries can't be beat."

"This stop won't put us too far behind schedule," he said. "And I promise, you won't be sorry."

They'd spent almost five hours together in his SUV already and more than a dozen hours in the same motel room—the majority of those in the same bed. During that time, Finley had mostly managed to ignore the undercurrents of awareness between them. (The obvious exception being those few minutes right after the power had gone out.)

But that was a task more easily accomplished in the dark of night. Or even seated side-by-side in a moving vehicle.

Sitting across from him in the brightly lit diner, she couldn't help but be aware of his gaze upon her. Nor could she seem to pull her gaze away from him.

There was something compelling about Lachlan Kellett.

It didn't seem to matter that she wasn't looking for any romantic entanglements at this point in her life. Or that she'd never been a fan of bearded men. (Probably because her mom's first boyfriend—following the separation from her husband, of course—had been a guy with a beard. And long hair. And a skull earring. As if Sandra had gone out looking for a man as different from her husband as she could find.)

But Finley was a fan of his eyes. She didn't know that she'd ever seen eyes so blue.

And when he smiled, her body actually tingled.

Which only proved that it had been far too long since she'd been with a man.

She'd been lucky in the friend department, starting with her sister who'd been her BFF from the day Finley was born until they chose different paths after high school graduation. Not that anyone could ever replace Haylee as her best friend, but not seeing her sister every day had required Finley to make new friends in college, and she'd done so, many with whom she still maintained regular contact. Then there were

Julia and Rachel—not just her partners in Gilmore Galas but women she knew she could always count on to have her back, as she had theirs.

When it came to romantic relationships, however, her experience had been very different. She'd had a few boyfriends when she was in high school and had fallen in love for the first time when she was sixteen. Dylan had been on the rowing team and the student council—a sweet and earnest boy who'd aspired to study political science and work in local government someday. But like most young love, theirs had fizzled out during the summer between their junior and senior years.

She'd cried when they broke up, because the end of a relationship, even if inevitable, was sad. But she'd never imagined that she would spend the rest of her life with him. She was far too practical to believe they would love one another forever—and honestly, she had no desire to marry the first boy she loved—but she was still sad to say goodbye to him.

She'd dated casually in college, because she had plans for her life and wasn't ready to get serious. For the most part, the boys she'd dated (and they had been boys, compared to the men she would meet later) had been grateful that she wasn't looking for a long-term commitment.

It wasn't until she was twenty-four and she met Mark Nickel that she actually believed he might be "the one." He was gorgeous and fun, smart and charming, and he'd swept her off her feet without Finley even being aware it was happening. Unfortunately, while she'd been all in with respect to their relationship, Mark had only been going through the motions, because he was still in love with his ex.

Gabriel was her rebound relationship, and she often thought that if she hadn't been so distraught over her breakup with Mark, it wouldn't have taken her so long to see him for the lying, cheating schemer that he was.

That experience had been a wake-up call. That was when

she'd vowed to forget about men for a while to focus exclusively on Gilmore Galas. And her decision had paid off in spades. Not only had the business grown exponentially, but she was now too busy planning events for other people to even think about the fact that she didn't have a social life of her own.

And in any event, she hadn't met anyone who tempted her to break her self-imposed dating hiatus. Although the more time that she spent with Lachlan, the more she found herself wondering if he could be the one.

Thankfully, before her mind could wander too far down that path, a server appeared with two menus. "Nancy" wore a stereotypical waitress uniform consisting of a light blue dress with white collar and cuffs, a white apron tied around her waist and a plastic name tag.

"Coffee, please," Lachlan said to her.

"Same for you?" Nancy asked Finley.

"Yes, please."

The server returned shortly with two mugs.

Noting Lachlan's closed menu, she asked, "Are you ready to order?"

"We are," he said, ignoring the fact that Finley was still perusing her options.

"What can I get for you?"

"Two barbecue bacon cheeseburger platters."

Finley lifted a brow. "Are you really hungry or are you ordering for me, too?"

"I was ordering for you, too, because you were studying that menu as if the contents were going to be the subject of a final exam."

"There's a lot of stuff on this menu."

"And the barbecue bacon cheeseburger platter is the best thing on it," he told her.

"It's true," Nancy said, when Finley looked to her for confirmation. "We have customers who come regular from Sacramento for it."

Finley didn't have a clue how close they might be to Sacramento but assumed the comment was intended to be a recommendation.

"And for our Sunday waffles," the server added.

She handed her laminated menu back. "Apparently I'm having a barbecue bacon cheeseburger platter."

"You won't regret it," Nancy promised.

There was a good amount of food on the platter. In addition to the loaded burger, there was a mound of steak cut fries, a handful of onion rings, a scoop of creamy coleslaw and half a cob of seasoned corn.

Apparently Finley had meant it when she said she was hungry, because when she finally pushed her platter away, only a few random fries and a bare cob remained.

"Should I apologize for recommending a meal you obviously didn't enjoy?" Lachlan asked.

"Is that your way of saying 'I told you so'?"

"Well, I did tell you so."

"You did," she confirmed. "And you were right." She wiped her fingers on a paper napkin. "I considered skipping the onion rings, because I have an event tonight, but I figured onion rings are probably why Altoids were invented."

"Actually, Altoids date back to the late 1780s and the first known recipe for onion rings was published in 1802."

Amusement crinkled the corners of her eyes. "Why would you know something like that?" she asked, sounding baffled—and maybe a little bit impressed.

He shrugged. "I have a good memory for useless trivia. And you have barbecue sauce—" he touched a fingertip to the side of his own mouth to illustrate "—here."

"Oh." She tugged another napkin out of the dispenser on the table and scrubbed the side of her mouth.

"Other side."

She scrubbed the other side. "Did I get it?"

"Yeah."

But he couldn't seem to prevent his gaze from lingering on her mouth. Especially when her tongue swept along her lower lip, as if to moisten it.

He lifted his eyes then, and they locked with hers.

There was a definite zing in the air—a sizzle of attraction that ratcheted up the temperature about ten degrees whenever he was with her. As they'd proven when they'd huddled together during the power outage at the motel last night.

He'd been divorced for nearly a dozen years and, during that time, he'd gone out with any number of undeniably attractive women. He'd even taken a few of them to bed. But none of them had lingered in his mind for very long after they'd parted ways.

And even though he hadn't slept with Finley Gilmore except in the most literal sense, he knew that she wouldn't be so easy to forget. Because being with her, even just sitting across the table from her at a greasy spoon, made his heart feel lighter. And he knew that if he wasn't careful, she might make him forget all the reasons he wasn't looking for a romantic relationship.

"More coffee?"

Lachlan shifted his attention to the server.

"Yes, please," he said, and nudged his mug forward.

Finley managed to release the breath that had stalled in her lungs and tried not to resent Nancy's untimely interruption.

After all, it wasn't as if he was going to lean across the table and kiss her.

Even if she'd wanted him to.

And she had.

In that moment, she'd wanted nothing so much as she'd wanted to feel the press of his mouth against hers, the sweep of his tongue over the seam of her lips—

"Miss?"

Finley blinked. "Sorry?"

Nancy gestured with the pot she was holding.

"Oh, yes. Please."

The server topped up her cup.

"Thank you."

Lachlan settled back in his seat and sipped his coffee, amusement sparkling in those blue eyes. "Taking a little side trip, were you?"

"Actually, I was thinking about work," she told him.

His smirk told her more effectively than any words that he knew she was lying, but he played along.

"So what's the life of an event planner like?" he asked.

"Just an endless string of parties," she said lightly.

"I guess that means you work a lot of Fridays and Saturdays."

"Almost every Friday and Saturday," she confided. "Last weekend was the first weekend I've had off since…probably last March, when I made the trip to Haven for Aidan and Ellie's second birthday party."

"You're obviously close to your sister and her family."

"Except geographically."

"Do you have any other siblings?"

"A brother, Logan, in Oakland, who's an architect. And another, Sebastian, in Palm Beach. He's a high school senior."

"Are you close to them?"

"Logan more than Sebastian, because of the geography thing again, but also because we're closer in age. We get together for lunch every few weeks, though less often during the summer months, because my schedule is so packed."

"So when do you go out?" he asked.

"It seems as if I'm always out."

"I meant, like dating," he clarified.

"I already told you that I don't date. I can't remember the last time I was out with anyone, actually. When I started Gilmore Galas, I didn't let myself imagine that it could be so successful. I certainly never imagined that I'd be booking events two years ahead."

"I'm sure you don't have events every night of the week."

"No," she agreed. "And after an exhausting 2022, I had a meeting with my partners in which we all agreed that we needed to set limits, to ensure our own work-life balance. Which was much more important to Julia, who had a new—and very frustrated—boyfriend at the time, and Rachel, who had a husband and two little ones at home.

"Now we don't schedule more than five events a week and not more than four of those on a weekend, to ensure that we have at least a couple of nights off every week."

"So you *could* date, if you wanted to?"

"Sure," she said. "But there aren't a lot of guys who want to go dancing on a Monday night. Or plan dinner and a movie for a Tuesday."

"Those are your usual nights off? Mondays and Tuesdays?"

She nodded. "Usual but not guaranteed. And our Sunday events are most often daytime events—birthday parties, bridal or baby showers, baptisms or christenings, that sort of thing."

"Good to know."

She wasn't entirely sure what that was supposed to mean.

But the way he was looking at her made her want to consider the possibility that he might be thinking about asking her out.

And to say *yes* if he did.

Then he lifted a hand for the server to bring their check, and the moment was gone.

The last couple hours of their journey passed uneventfully and mostly quietly. Lachlan focused on the drive while Finley kept busy on her phone—responding to emails and exchanging text messages with Julia and Rachel about the evening event.

But she tucked her phone away when he exited the 580, only minutes from her home. She was glad to be back, looking forward to seeing Simon and her dad and Colleen, but she was also a little disappointed that her road trip with the sexy Lachlan Kellett was coming to an end.

He looked from the address she'd punched into his map to the number on the house and then at her.

"This is where you live?" His brows rose. "Apparently the party planning business is indeed lucrative."

"I grew up in the big house, but I live there," she said, pointing to the carriage house (really a renovated detached double garage) set a little further back.

"Still not too shabby," he noted.

"When Haylee and I first started making plans to move out, we were discouraged to realize that there was a significant gap between what we wanted and what we could afford. Or if we could afford a nice apartment, it was because it wasn't in a nice neighborhood.

"My dad thought—probably hoped—we'd give up and stay at home. But who wants to live with their parents forever? It was actually our brother Logan—the architect—who suggested building a second story above the garage.

"And he designed it, too. Kitchen, dining room, living room, three bedrooms, two bathrooms and a rooftop patio and garden."

She was rambling now, sharing details he hadn't asked for and likely had no interest in. But it occurred to her that, so long as they were talking about something else, it wasn't time to say goodbye. Because she wasn't ready to say goodbye.

Except *they* weren't talking.

She was the only one talking.

So she clamped her lips together to give him a chance to respond.

"All that for just you and your sister?" he said.

She nodded.

"So why three bedrooms?"

"Because Logan knew I'd use one as a home office."

"And now that your sister moved out, all that space is yours?"

"Mine and Simon's," she confirmed.

"I hope he took good care of the place while you were away."

"He usually does."

The hint of a smile played at the corners of his mouth as he opened the driver's side door and stepped out of the vehicle, going around the back to retrieve her suitcase.

She exited the passenger side and followed.

"Well, thank you again," she said. "For the ride."

"Thank you again—for the bed."

She lifted a shoulder. "As you pointed out, I wasn't going to be using it, anyway."

"And then I didn't, either."

"The power going out changed both our plans."

"In any event, I appreciated not having to sleep in the lounge." He set her suitcase on the ground. "And your snoring didn't keep me awake *all* night."

"I *don't* snore," she said again.

"How would you know? Only one of us was awake while you were sleeping," he pointed out with unerring logic—and a wink.

She extended the handle of her rolling case. "Are you sure I can't give you any money for gas?"

"I'm sure."

"I kind of feel as if I owe you dinner."

"You bought lunch," he reminded her.

"Because you wouldn't let me pay for gas."

"And now we've come full circle."

She nodded. "Well, maybe I'll see you around."

"I think you probably will."

And since there wasn't anything else to say—and he obviously didn't intend to ask for her number—she turned away.

Lachlan watched Finley make her way to the carriage house at the end of the lane, then retract the handle again so that she could pick up the case and carry it up the long flight of stairs to the side door at the top of the landing.

He should have offered to carry her bag.

He'd been raised to be a gentleman—to open doors for a lady, pull back her chair, stand when she did—and his mother would be appalled if she knew he'd stood there watching instead of helping. His grandmother would cuff the back of his head—after she'd made him bend down so that she could reach it.

But he knew that if he walked Finley to the door, he'd be tempted to kiss her, and he didn't trust himself to be able to resist the temptation.

It was easier—and much smarter, he decided—to let her walk away.

She hadn't seemed to be in a hurry, though. Despite repeated reminders throughout the journey about her urgency to get home and get ready for the evening's Gilmore Gala, she'd stalled when it actually came time to say goodbye.

He knew she'd been waiting for him to ask for her number. No doubt, men were always asking for Finley Gilmore's number. So he decided that, rather than following the expected pattern, it might be fun to keep her a little off-balance and not ask.

In any event, he didn't really need her number.

Because he'd be seeing her again very soon.

Chapter Six

Simon must have heard her key in the lock, because he was waiting by the door when Finley crossed the threshold.

"There's my handsome guy." She set down her suitcase and purse and picked up the cat to cuddle him close to her chest. "Did you miss me?" She nuzzled his fur. "Because I missed you. Haylee misses you, too. But she's got Trevor and Aidan and Ellie now. And if Trevor has his way, they might be adding a dog to the family."

Simon looked at her through narrowed eyes.

"Don't give me that look," she told him. "I'm not getting a dog. I've got everything I want right here."

Apparently Simon believed her, or maybe it was the stroking of his fur that soothed him, because he closed his eyes all the way and purred contentedly.

"I have a great apartment, a wonderful family, terrific friends, a job I love, and the world's most amazing cat. I don't want the complications of a relationship, and I definitely don't need a man who flirted with me every chance he got but then couldn't be bothered to ask for my number."

She continued her rhythmic stroking of the cat.

"But why didn't he ask for my number?"

Of course, Lachlan wouldn't have too much trouble getting in touch with her if he wanted to see her again. He knew her name, the name of her business, and now where she lived.

But he'd given no indication that he might want to see her again, and that was disappointing.

"Why doesn't he want to see me again?"

Simon opened one eye.

"I just don't understand what happened between the time we were in the diner, when he seemed to be on the verge of asking me out, and our arrival here."

She nuzzled the cat again, listening to the comforting purr in his response.

"There was a connection between us. I *know* there was.

"And anyway, he's the one who started the flirting, hinting that he'd let me handcuff him to the bed."

Finley sighed then and set Simon down on the sofa before making her way into the kitchen. "But maybe I did snore in the night.

"Or maybe he's involved with someone—although that's something I'd think he would have mentioned before offering to give me an up-close-and-personal lesson on thermodynamics." She opened the refrigerator and reached for a can of diet Coke. "He did mention that he was divorced, but that doesn't mean he isn't involved with someone else."

She pulled the tab to open her drink and lifted the can to her lips. "Because we know from experience, don't we, that guys aren't always forthcoming about those kind of details?

"Of course, another possibility is that he simply isn't interested," she acknowledged. "Maybe I misinterpreted his flirtation because I'm ready to end this dating hiatus and get out there again. But there are plenty of other guys if I need to scratch an itch.

"In fact, just last weekend when I was in Haven, I got a text message from Calvin Hines. You don't know Calvin," she said to Simon. "He was before your time. But we dated for a few months, had some good times together. And every once in a while, he reaches out and we get together again.

"And if I'd been home when he texted, I might have decided to scratch that itch."

"Oh, sweetie, you can do so much better than Calvin Hines."

Finley let out a startled gasp and spun around to face her stepmother.

"I didn't hear you come in," she confessed, as heat swept up her neck.

"You were pretty deep into your monologue," Colleen noted, sounding amused.

Finley set down her diet Coke to hug her mom.

"How much did you hear?"

"I came in when you were talking about an up-close-and-personal lesson on thermodynamics."

"So almost all of it."

Though, thankfully, not the part about the handcuffs.

"I meant what I said about Calvin—you can do a lot better."

"Calvin's not so bad."

"He's not bad at all," Colleen agreed. "But he's not right for you, which is why you ended your relationship with him—booty calls aside—a long time ago."

"But I know him," Finley pointed out. "Which means I know what I'm getting when I'm with him."

"There can be comfort in the familiar—but the familiar can also lead into a rut."

"Well, my schedule of late hasn't exactly made it easy for me to meet new people."

"Sounds as if you met someone last night."

"A stranded fellow traveler."

"Speaking of stranded, you were going to text your flight details, so that we could pick you up at the airport. The last I heard, your flight had been canceled—again. Which is why I came over to feed Simon."

"My flight *was* canceled again. So I hitched a ride."

Her stepmother frowned.

"I didn't actually stand on the side of the road with my thumb sticking out," Finley assured her. "I got a ride with someone I met at the motel."

"Your stranded fellow traveler?" her mom guessed.

"How do you *do* that?"

"Do what?" Colleen asked innocently.

"Know things I don't tell you."

"A mother's intuition."

"That must be it," she agreed. Because even though Colleen hadn't given birth to Finley—or Haylee or Logan—from the day she'd exchanged vows with Robert Gilmore, she'd been a mother to all of his kids in every way that counted.

"So tell me about him," her mom urged.

Finley didn't know where to begin. With the pizza they'd shared in the reception area of the motel? With the bargain they'd struck to share her motel room? With the storm knocking out the power? She didn't need to mention that he'd wrapped his hard body around her to keep her warm when the temperature plummeted, because Colleen had already heard that part of the story.

"I don't know what to tell you, other than that he's a professor at Merivale College who overheard me on the phone, trying—unsuccessfully—to rebook my canceled flight, and offered to let me ride back with him."

"The flush in your cheeks contradicts your words," her mother noted. "But I'm not going to press for details you're not ready to share."

Finley's already warm cheeks grew warmer.

"Instead, I'm going to invite you to come for dinner."

"So you can grill me after you're done with whatever's on the menu tonight?"

"Pasta carbonara," Colleen said. "No grilling required."

And one of Finley's favorites.

"I wish I could say yes, but I have to be at Harcourt House

for the Metler-Grzeszczak engagement party in less than an hour."

"You also need to eat, and I know you won't eat there."

"Because I don't get paid to eat. And anyway, I had a late—and really big—lunch."

"I'll bring over a plate that you can heat up when you get back."

"Thanks, Mom."

Colleen gave her another hug. "Don't forget to feed Simon before you go."

Going home felt strange.

Driving through the familiar streets of his neighborhood, it was almost as if the past three weeks hadn't happened. Or maybe it was just that Finley's *Back to the Future* reference had stuck in his head. Too much about the woman he'd met twenty-four hours earlier seemed to be stuck in his head.

Anyway, as much as Lachlan was glad that he'd taken the time to be with his friend, he was even more glad to be home.

Three weeks was a long time to be gone. To be away from Aislynn.

He decided that he'd give her a call as soon as he got in, to confirm plans for their weekend get-together. Then he'd tackle laundry and whatever other chores needed to be done around the house. He had a housekeeper who came in once a week to dust and vacuum the common areas, but he took care of his bedroom and home office himself.

He should reach out to Laurel Strickland, too, to thank her again for covering his classes while he was out of town and find out if there were any issues he needed to know about. He'd responded to email queries from his students as much as possible—cell phone service was surprisingly good in the mountains—but mostly he'd redirected his students to Dr. Strickland and promised to follow up when he returned.

After all of that, it might be time to think about ordering dinner. Because he had no idea what might be in his fridge after three weeks away, but he was sure none of it would be edible.

He should have stopped at a grocery store en route but he hadn't, and he had no desire to turn around now. And anyway, now that he was thinking about it, it had been a long time since he'd had Szechuan beef and Shanghai noodles.

As soon as he turned onto his street, he spotted Deirdre's car parked in front of his house and found it was oddly comforting to know there was someone at home to greet him after a long and difficult journey.

"This is a surprise," he said, when he walked in and found both his ex-wife and his daughter in the kitchen. "What are you guys doing here?"

"We wanted to see you." Aislynn threw herself into his arms. "We missed you."

"Aislynn missed you," Deirdre clarified.

"You were gone a really long time." Lachlan didn't have any trouble hearing the accusation in his daughter's tone, even with her face buried in his sweater.

"Longer than I expected to be," he acknowledged.

She drew back a little and tipped her head to look at him with eyes the exact same color as those he saw in the mirror every day. "You missed *three* Wednesday night dinners, a *whole* weekend *and* my spring music concert."

"I'll make it up to you," he promised.

"I don't know that you can," she said peevishly. "But a trip to Disneyland would be a good effort."

He managed a weary smile. "I'll keep that in mind."

"Bonus points if I get to bring a friend."

"That's enough, Aislynn," his ex-wife admonished their daughter.

"I'm just saying."

"And I said that's enough," Deirdre told her. "Your dad just got home from one trip—let him at least unpack before you start nagging him to plan another."

"Too late," Lachlan said, softening his words with a wink for his daughter.

"Why don't you go on upstairs and look for that sweater you've been moaning about not being able to find all week?" Deirdre suggested.

"Because I know it's not here," Aislynn said. "Because I specifically remember packing it to take to your house so I could wear it when me and Harmony went to see *Dirty Dancing.*"

"Go look anyway," her mom told her.

With an exaggerated sigh, Aislynn turned and clomped toward the stairs.

"I was sorry to hear that Ben's condition took such a bad turn so quickly," Deirdre said to Lachlan, speaking in a gentler tone now.

"Me, too."

"How's Mara doing?"

"She's putting on a brave face—for Ben and the kids."

"Will you go back…for the funeral?"

He shook his head. "His family will have lots of support then. I'll make a trip in the summer."

"You could take Aislynn with you."

"Yeah, because our daughter likes roughing it almost as much as you do," he noted dryly.

"She might not be a fan of outdoor bathing," Deirdre acknowledged. "But she does like hanging out with her dad."

"At Disneyland."

"Well, who wouldn't?" his ex agreed, with a small smile. "Anyway," she said, ready to move on to another topic. "I picked up a few groceries for you. The basics—bread, milk, eggs. And a bottle of Jack."

"Thanks."

She nodded.

After a beat, she said, "Now would be an appropriate time for you to invite me to stay for a drink."

"I'm not in the mood for company tonight."

Deirdre looked worried. "Which is exactly why you shouldn't be alone."

"I'll be fine."

"Okay," she relented. "But call me if you change your mind."

"I'm not going to change my mind," he told her.

She lifted a hand and laid it on his cheek, rubbing her palm gently against his scruffy beard. "You're going to get rid of this before the party next Saturday, aren't you?"

"You don't like it?"

She tilted her head, considering. "Actually, I think it's kind of sexy," she said. "But I guarantee your mother won't like it."

Deirdre was right about that. After eighteen years in his family—and notwithstanding the fact that they'd been divorced for a dozen years, she was still a member of his family—she knew his parents almost as well as he did.

"I'll get rid of it before the party," he confirmed, just as Aislynn returned with her missing sweater in hand. "In fact, probably before I go back to school on Monday."

"Grandma said she'd take me shopping for a new dress for the party," Aislynn chimed in.

"Lucky you," Deirdre said.

"You could come with us," Aislynn said to her mom. "You probably want a new dress for the party, too."

"I don't know if I'm going to the party," she hedged.

"Why not?"

"Because Philip might be out of town that weekend."

"You don't need to bring a date. Dad's not bringing a date," Aislynn said, before looking to him for confirmation. "You're not, are you, Dad?"

He thought fleetingly of Finley but gave a brief shake of his head. "No, I'm not taking a date."

"See?" Aislynn said.

"Well, that's a decision for another day," Deirdre said. "Right now, we need to be on our way."

"Why?"

"Because your dad's practically asleep on his feet."

"I didn't get a lot of sleep last night," he admitted.

Aislynn sighed. "Okay."

"But I'll see you tomorrow," Lachlan reminded her. "Because it's our weekend this weekend, right?"

"Actually, I didn't know if you were going to be back, so I made plans with Harmony for after school tomorrow."

"I can pick you up at Harmony's."

"Sleepover plans," she clarified.

"Oh."

"But I could come on Saturday."

"Then I'll see you Saturday," he confirmed.

"I'm glad you're back."

"Me, too."

She hugged him again and whispered in his ear. "And don't forget to think about Disneyland."

Finley had planned to be at the venue before the happy couple arrived, so that she could double- (and triple-) check that everything was as it should be. But she fussed a little too long with her hair and changed her shoes three times before she finally made her way out of the house—and then, when she got in her SUV, she saw that her fuel gauge was hovering perilously close to E.

Silently cursing her brother, because she had no doubt it was Logan who'd been zipping around town in her SUV while she was out of town, she detoured from her route to the nearest gas station. While she was fueling up—and continuing to curse her brother—she considered that having to make an unplanned stop wasn't necessarily a bad thing.

Though she trusted both of her partners implicitly, she was admittedly a bit of a control freak when it came to Gilmore Galas. (And justifiably so, in her opinion, as it was her name on the door.) But the truth was, she couldn't run the business without Julia and Rachel, and she knew that showing up a little bit late at an event for which she'd given them the reins weeks ago said far more than any words could about her faith in them.

So after she filled her tank with gas, she took a circuitous route to Harcourt House, ensuring that the party was well under way by the time she arrived.

"I was starting to think that you weren't going to make it," Julia said, when their paths crossed near the coat check.

"I told you I'd be here."

"And that's what I told Kelly and Paul, when they asked for you."

Customer service was key to the event planning business, and Finley prided herself on giving her clients whatever they needed, whenever they needed it. So while the general business line automatically went to voicemail after regular hours, clients who signed with Gilmore Galas were given her direct email and cell phone number so they could feel confident that she was always available to them.

The realization that she hadn't been on-site when the soon-lyweds (the moniker she assigned to brides-to-be and their grooms) were looking for her made her cringe inside, but she had no doubt that Julia had taken care of them.

"Was there a problem?"

"No," Julia said. "They just wanted to thank you personally—as they thanked me and Rachel—for ensuring that this party was everything they wanted it to be."

"I'll be sure to speak to them," Finley said. "But you and Rachel are the ones who put in all the work on this."

"We worked our butts off," Rachel confirmed, joining the conversation when her colleagues made their way into the ballroom. "But it didn't seem like it, because Kelly and Paul are both so much fun to work with."

Which was a good thing, Finley mused. Because this little party was going to seem like a walk in the park compared to the wedding that was being planned for November.

But she kept that thought to herself, unwilling to tarnish their shiny moment. Instead, she said, "I want to thank you both, too. Not just for planning this fabulous party, but for being the best partners any woman could ever ask for."

"Someone's in a reflective mood tonight," Rachel noted.

"I just want you to know how much I appreciate you. Because there's no way I could have taken a whole week off to spend with my sister and her family in Nevada if I didn't trust the business in your very capable and talented hands."

"You were Gilmore Galas before we came along," Julia pointed out. "But we're honored to help carry the banner."

Rachel nodded her agreement.

Finley surveyed the room, noting that there were a few guests examining the hot and cold hors d'oeuvres on the buffet table and several more hanging around the bar, but most were on the dance floor, shaking and shimmying to the music. Kelly and Paul were at the center of the group, showing off their moves.

The happy couple were planning a traditional wedding, because it was what their families expected, and they wanted to make them happy—especially as the respective parents were sharing the costs of the affair. So they'd requested an engagement party that would give them a chance to let loose with their friends. They'd assured Finley that they didn't care about themes or menus or flowers and were happy to leave all those decisions up to the professionals. They just wanted to have fun.

"What do you think?" Julia asked.

"It looks like fun is definitely being had," Rachel replied to her question.

Finley had to smile. "And that's why this is the best job in the world."

"One of the reasons," Rachel agreed.

"Another is the number of cute guys who cross our paths," Julia added.

"Says the woman who got engaged a few weeks ago."

"I'm scoping out the prospects for you—not me," her friend said.

"I appreciate your efforts, but I'm really not looking for a man right now."

"And isn't that when they usually come along?" Rachel mused.

"Speaking of—" Julia nudged Finley with her elbow "—check out Mr. Tall, Blond and Tanned checking *you* out."

"Even if I was looking," Finley said. "I wouldn't be looking at the guests at our events."

"Why not?"

"Because they're inevitably friends or relatives of our clients, which would make any…personal interactions…inherently more complicated."

"His name is Craig," Rachel said. "He's a cousin of the bride and also a groomsman in the wedding party. He went to college at UC Davis with Paul and introduced him to Kelly when their paths crossed at a music festival in Long Beach."

"And he's coming this way. Which is why we—" Julia took Rachel's arm "—need to go that way."

As her partners abandoned her, Finley continued to work on her tablet.

"Great event tonight," Craig said.

She glanced up then, as if she hadn't been aware of his approach, and was surprised to discover that he *was* cute, in a stereotypical California boy-next-door kind of way. Tall and lean with sun-bleached dark blond hair, warm brown eyes and an easy smile.

Unfortunately, nothing about Craig gave her tingles.

"Everyone seems to be having a good time," she agreed.

"Kelly and Paul definitely are," he said. "But now you have a problem."

"What's that?"

"They're going to expect something even bigger and better for the wedding."

"That's not a problem," she said. "Plans are already in the works and their wedding will be bigger and better."

"Then I guess I'm the one with the problem," he said.

"What's that?"

"I don't have a plus-one for the wedding."

"Sorry, that's not one of the services we provide."

"I'm not asking you to find me a date—I'm asking you to be my date." He smiled again. "So what do you say?"

"No."

"Ouch. Are you sure you don't want to take at least three seconds to think about it?"

"It's nothing personal," she hastened to assure him. "It's just a really bad idea to mix business with pleasure."

"Then how about being my plus-one for dinner tomorrow night?"

"I can't."

"Because I'm a friend of Kelly and Paul?"

"Because I've got an event tomorrow night."

"Would your answer be different if you didn't have an event?"

"I don't know."

"So tell me when you don't have an event."

"Three weeks from Tuesday… I think. I'll have to check my calendar to be sure."

"You're brushing me off."

"I can see why you'd think that, but my schedule is really crazy right now."

"Uh-huh."

She really didn't have time to date.

And she definitely wasn't looking for romance.

But he was good-looking.

Smart. Charming. Funny.

Not to mention that the bride and groom—both people that she liked—clearly adored him.

Which was why she *should* brush him off, because that connection added another level of complication.

But if she was being perfectly honest with herself, the biggest factor in her decision to *not* brush off boy-next-door Craig was that she was still stinging from the brush-off she'd been given by Lachlan Kellett earlier in the day.

"Are you free Tuesday night?" she asked, before she could talk herself out of it.

"If I'm not, I'll clear my schedule."

"There's a new restaurant—The Wine Cellar—in Bayside Village. The manager invited me to come in for a menu tasting in the hope that we'll add it to our list of recommended venues."

"What time should I pick you up?"

"I've got an appointment in the afternoon, so I'll be heading to the restaurant directly from there."

"Okay. What time should I meet you?"

"The reservation is for seven."

"I'll see you then."

She nodded, surprised to realize that she was looking forward to it.

Chapter Seven

Lachlan had one thing on his mind when he walked into his kitchen Monday morning: coffee.

"Jesus, Dee. It's not even seven thirty in the morning— what the hell are you doing here?"

"It's Monday," she reminded him.

"And?"

"And I often stop by for coffee after dropping Aislynn at band practice Monday mornings so we can talk."

"Weren't you here when I got home on Thursday? Didn't we talk then? Or was that a dream?"

"Aww, you still dream about me?" Deirdre batted her eyelashes playfully. "How sweet."

"Maybe it was a nightmare," he decided.

She poured a mug of coffee for him.

He accepted with a muttered, "Thanks."

"And one of the things Aislynn mentioned on Thursday is what I wanted to talk to you about."

He sipped his coffee, waiting for her to explain.

"I haven't RSVP'd to the invitation to your grandparents' anniversary party yet."

"Why not?" he wondered aloud.

"Because I haven't decided if I should go," she admitted.

He opened the loaf of bread on the counter and dropped two slices into the toaster. "Do you have other plans that day?"

"No."

"Then why wouldn't you want to go?"

"I didn't say I didn't *want* to go. I said I didn't know if I *should* go."

He swallowed another mouthful of coffee. "I'm going to need another minute for the caffeine to kick in to follow this conversation."

Deirdre huffed out a breath. "You know I love your grandparents. Your whole family."

"And they love you." He retrieved a knife from the cutlery drawer, then reached into the cupboard for the jar of peanut butter.

"But we're divorced."

"You're still Aislynn's mother," he pointed out reasonably.

She sipped her coffee. "Will it be weird for you if I bring Philip?"

"Why would it be weird for me?"

"Because we used to be together, and now, I'm with him."

"It might be weird for Philip," he acknowledged with a shrug. "It won't be weird for me."

"You should consider taking a date, too."

When the toast popped up, he slathered peanut butter on both slices, then transferred them to a plate. "You think that will make it less weird for Philip?"

"I think it will make it less…ambiguous…for our daughter."

"Well, now I'm confused," he said, carrying his plate and his mug to one of the stools at the island. "Didn't we agree, way back when, that it would be best not to introduce her to people who might only be a temporary presence in her life?"

"She's not six years old, anymore. She's almost sixteen. Which is something else we're going to have to talk about very soon."

He chewed a bite of toast, swallowed. "Her birthday's not until August."

"August might seem far away right now, but it's her Sweet Sixteen and plans need to be made. However, the anniversary party is a lot closer, and I really think you should take a date."

"As much as I value your insights into my personal life—and I really don't—I'm not dating anyone right now." He bit into his toast again. "And if I *was* dating someone, introducing her to my family for the first time at an event like that would likely lead to her status changing from girlfriend to *ex*-girlfriend."

"So invite a friend. Or even a colleague from work."

"Why is this so important to you?"

Deirdre stole the second slice of toast from his plate and took a bite.

"I figured that if you'd wanted breakfast, you would have made your own."

"I only wanted a bite," she said, returning the toast to his plate.

He didn't bother to sigh; instead he asked again, "Why is this so important to you?"

"Because I overheard Aislynn and Kendra talking one day while you were gone." She licked peanut butter off her thumb. "Kendra was upset because she'd just found out that her dad had asked his girlfriend to be wife number three, and she asked Aislynn if you ever dated girls who were barely out of college."

"Jesus." He lifted his mug to his lips and swallowed another mouthful of coffee. "Is Frank's new fiancée really that young?"

"Twenty-two," his ex-wife told him.

"That's just...wrong."

"Says the man who spends his days hanging out at the local college," she said, tongue in cheek.

He gave her a stern look. "Because it's where I work."

"Anyway, getting back to the girls' conversation..."

He nodded and resumed eating his breakfast, waiting for her to continue.

"Aislynn told Kendra that you don't date very much. Kendra then asked, why not? And Aislynn said it was because you're still in love with me."

"She can't honestly believe that," he protested.

"She's a child of divorce," she reminded him unnecessarily. "Most children of divorce harbor fantasies about their parents getting back together."

"As you pointed out, she's almost sixteen. Isn't she a little old to be fantasizing about a family reunion?"

His ex-wife shrugged. "How am I supposed to know?"

"Well, we can be sure of one thing at least."

"What's that?"

"She clearly has no memories from when we were married, because if she did, she'd have no desire to repeat that experience."

"We're much better as friends than we ever were as husband and wife," she agreed.

"Which doesn't mean I want you butting into my personal life."

Deirdre nodded. "Then find yourself a girlfriend so I don't have to."

Finley loved Mondays.

Most people with traditional jobs looked forward to Friday, because it was the end of the work week and the start of the weekend. And when they wanted to celebrate a special occasion with friends, they generally planned those celebrations for the weekend. Which was why, when everyone else was having fun, Finley was working. And also why, when they all returned to their Monday-to-Friday jobs, she got a reprieve.

Of course, a reprieve didn't necessarily mean a day off. And when Finley's phone rang early Monday morning, she immediately connected the call.

"Good morning, Mrs. Edwards."

Catherine and Douglas Edwards were going to be celebrating their milestone sixtieth anniversary the following Saturday with a party in the Sapphire Ballroom of the Courtland Hotel, San Francisco. From the very first meeting, the octogenarians had been an absolute joy to work with.

They'd come in for a preliminary consult already knowing exactly what they wanted and in sync with respect to every detail. But it wasn't just their complete synchronicity that Finley admired—it was that they were obviously still in love after six decades of marriage. And after every meeting with them, she found herself wondering what it would be like to have that history and connection with another person—and if she'd ever be lucky enough to find it for herself.

"How many times have I told you to call me Catherine?" the client asked Finley now.

"I'm not sure I can give you an actual number, but probably every time we've talked," she admitted. And while she was comfortable on a first-name basis with most of her clients, she'd been brought up to show a certain level of deference to her elders—and Catherine Edwards was certainly that.

"And now you can add this one to the tally."

"How can I help you… Catherine?"

The old woman chuckled. "I can tell that was hard for you, but it will get easier with practice," she promised. "And I'm calling to tell you that I found it."

Finley mentally sifted through the details of their previous conversations for a hint of what "it" might be.

"I knew it was in the attic somewhere," Catherine continued, her voice filled with childlike glee. "And I spent three days in that horrible stuffy space going through boxes and cases and chests, but I finally found it."

"Your original wedding cake topper?" Finley guessed, recalling one of their earliest discussions about the event.

"Our original wedding cake topper," Catherine confirmed.

"That's wonderful."

"Actually, it's hideous."

"I'm sorry?"

"I remembered it being beautiful—but obviously my memory was faulty, because it's not beautiful at all. It's old and ugly. The groom looks like he's wearing the same shade of bright red lipstick as the bride and her eyelashes practically touch her eyebrows. And while the figures are made out of some kind of ceramic, the skirt of the bride's dress is fabric, yellowed with age and fraying at the hem."

"We work with a wonderful company that restores and renews vintage items," Finley said, always glad to be able to provide a solution to a problem. "If you want to bring it in, we can have Mr. Ritchey take a look at it."

"Goodness, no," Catherine said, laughing. "I don't want anyone else looking at this thing. To be honest, I kind of wish I'd never found it. But my Douglas always says I'm like a dog with a bone—which is hardly a flattering analogy but true nonetheless—and I knew it was in that attic somewhere and simply couldn't rest until I'd found it."

"It's your decision, of course," Finley told her. "And if you change your mind, we can add it to the cake later."

"I'm not going to change my mind," Catherine assured her. "Some things from the past are better left there, and this is definitely one of them."

It was good advice, Finley mused, and vowed to do exactly that with her memories of Lachlan Kellett.

Finley had barely walked through the door Tuesday night before her sister initiated a FaceTime call. She connected as she kicked off her shoes and made her way into the kitchen to pour a glass of wine.

"How was your date?" Haylee wanted to know.

"It was good."

"Are you sure? Because it's just after ten o'clock and you're already home—and obviously alone."

"I'm sure." She carried her wine into the living room and settled onto the sofa with her feet tucked beneath her. "The food was fabulous. Squash ravioli with sage brown butter sauce, slow-roasted brined chicken with herbed risotto, seared scallops with grits and sweet corn, grilled tomahawk pork chop with cheesy scalloped potatoes, pan-fried sea bass with watercress salad, and prime rib with horseradish cream and roasted Brussels sprouts."

"You hate Brussels sprouts."

"Apparently I don't hate roasted Brussels sprouts."

"Well, it sounds like you tried everything on the menu."

"It was a tasting menu, so not full portions. But yes, it was a pretty good sampling of the restaurant's offerings."

"And a different wine with every entrée?"

"Of which I only had a couple sips," Finley assured her sister. "Oh, and there was dessert. You would've *loved* all the desserts. My favorite was the apple crisp with vanilla bean ice cream, but there was also a flourless chocolate cake, New York–style cheesecake, a lemon meringue tart, traditional tiramisu and homemade raspberry and lime sorbet."

"And Craig?" Haylee prompted.

"He said the sorbet was the best he'd ever had."

"That's not what I was asking," her sister chided.

"Craig was…great," Finley said.

Because it was true.

In fact, he'd been the perfect date—punctual, attentive and charming. He chewed with his mouth closed, hadn't balked at sharing from his plate and didn't drink too much.

"And the goodnight kiss?"

Finley's mind flashed back to leaving the restaurant with Craig.

"It's not too late," he noted, after he'd walked her to her car. "Do you want to come over to my place? For coffee?"

"We just had coffee," she reminded him.

"I know, but it seemed a little bold to ask if you wanted to come over for sex."

She laughed. "A tempting offer, but one I'm going to have to decline. I've got an early morning and a busy day tomorrow."

"Maybe next time?"

"Maybe." She didn't want to mislead him, and she'd genuinely enjoyed the time she'd spent with him. But while he was an undeniably attractive man, she wasn't attracted to him. She wanted to be—and on the surface, he checked all the boxes—but for some inexplicable reason, she couldn't stop thinking about Lachlan. And getting any further involved with Craig under those circumstances wouldn't be fair to him.

But something in her voice must have given her away, because he said, "There's not going to be a next time, is there?"

"I had a great time tonight, and—"

"I think I'd prefer you to stop right there," he interjected. "It's obvious you're not into me, and while I'm admittedly disappointed, I will at least go home with fond memories of an exceptional meal and a sweet goodbye kiss—with your permission, of course."

She assented with a nod, and he lowered his head to brush his lips over hers.

It was a sweet kiss, and over almost before it had begun.

"The kiss was…nice," Finley said, finally responding to her sister's question.

Haylee sighed. "That bad?"

"I didn't say it was bad."

"You said nice. With a pause preceding the word."

"And nice with a pause is bad?" she asked dubiously.

"What do I know?" Haylee said. "I married the first guy I ever slept with. But I know *you*, and there wasn't any of the excitement in your voice when you talked about Craig that I heard when you talked about Lachlan."

Finley took a long s p—okay, gulp—of wine. "I don't want to talk about Lachlan."

"He hasn't called you?"

"He never even asked for my number," she reminded her sister.

"But he knows your name. And where you work."

"You're right. And any man with half a brain and internet access could find my number easily enough if he wanted to get in touch with me, so clearly he doesn't."

"You also know his name and where he works," Haylee pointed out.

It was true. And in a moment of weakness, she'd actually looked up the faculty directory for Merivale College, so she had the general campus number and the extension for Dr. Kellett in the anthropology department. She'd also found his email address, but she had no intention of using either method of communication to reach out to him.

"I'm not calling him," she said.

"Why not?" her sister wanted to know.

"Because I don't have time to chase after a man and even less desire to do so."

"But haven't you wondered about the odds of two strangers who live in the same general part of California crossing paths five hundred miles away from their respective homes?"

"Not really."

"Well, *I* have," Haylee said. "And I don't think it was chance—I think it was fate."

Finley wasn't sure she believed in fate, but to appease her sister she said, "And if it was fate, then I have to believe our paths will cross again. But no way am I chasing after him."

It had been one of those days.

Actually, it had been one of those weeks in which it seemed as if one crisis had followed directly on the heels of the previous one. It started with a shipment of bridesmaids dresses in the wrong shade of pink (the bride wanted pink tutu but the dresses that arrived were ballet slipper); then a recently engaged couple, both avid hikers, ventured into Muir Woods for an engagement shoot and ended up in the hospital being treated for exposure to poison oak; followed by the guest of honor at a retirement party being caught with his pants down and his secretary saying a very personal goodbye.

And on Friday, at the rehearsal for the following day's wedding ceremony, it was discovered that the ring bearer had chicken pox, leaving the bridal party short two members as both the boy and his mother, one of the bride's attendants, were in quarantine. The drama continued Saturday, with Finley having to send an SOS to a local seamstress for an emergency fix because the bride's dress wouldn't zip up.

She might have been able to anticipate the problem if Naomi had mentioned, at any of her previous fittings, that she would be almost four months pregnant at the time of her nuptials. But the bride had been determined to keep her condition a secret from everyone—specifically from her mother but also, and unfortunately, from the wedding planner. Thankfully, Bridget from "With This Thread" had rescued the day—or at least Naomi's gown.

By seven o'clock, Finley had been on her feet for the better part of twelve hours already and wanted nothing more than to collapse on her sofa with a nice big glass of wine.

Unfortunately, the prospect of both of those things remained elusive. But she'd learned to find moments of Zen during times of chaos, and right now, she was basking in the relative peacefulness of Catherine and Douglas Edwards's sixtieth anniversary celebration while Julia and Rachel were on guard at the wedding across the hall.

As she scanned the room, her gaze snagged that of the man she'd noticed earlier. He was the personification of tall, dark and handsome in a very nice suit, and she'd found herself distracted by him far more often than she wanted to admit.

"Finley."

She broke the connection and summoned a professional smile before turning around. Her expression immediately warmed when she found herself face-to-face with Catherine Edwards.

"What can I do for you, Mrs.—Catherine?" she automatically corrected herself before the other woman could.

"You've done so much, Finley, that I was hoping that you'd let me do something for you."

It wasn't unusual for happy clients to offer a bonus at the conclusion of an event—and Finley tried to ensure that all her clients were happy—but the twinkle in the old woman's eyes warned Finley that she had something different in mind.

"You don't need to do anything for me," she said. "It's been my pleasure to ensure you and your husband are enjoying your celebration."

"It's been absolutely perfect. Or almost perfect."

Finley knew she was being played—and by a champ—but if there was any way she could upgrade the guest of honor's experience from "almost" to "perfect," she had to try.

"Tell me how I can make it perfect," she suggested.

"Let me introduce you to my grandson."

Years of practice allowed Finley to keep her smile in place even during the most awkward moments, like this one.

But still, she struggled to reply. "Oh. Um… Is he single?" she finally asked.

Though it seemed like the answer to her question should be obvious, Catherine Edwards was hardly the first client to want to play matchmaker and, on a previous occasion, it turned out that the client wanted to set her up with a son who was, in fact, married, because he was married to a woman she didn't like.

"Divorced, actually," Catherine responded to her question.

"But I hope you won't hold that against him, because he really is a wonderful man and—" she dropped her voice to a whisper "—my favorite grandson. He's handsome, of course, well-educated, and gainfully employed. A lot of men can't hold a job these days—or don't want to—and a successful woman like yourself has to be careful not to be taken in."

"I'm sure he's every bit as wonderful as you say," Finley interrupted gently. "But I have to stop you there, because I'm already in a committed relationship."

The old woman's brow furrowed. "There's no ring on your finger."

"That's because I'm married to my job."

The furrow eased.

"Unless you're in the business of selling feminine massagers—and I know you're not—then you need a man." The furrow returned. "Or a woman, I guess. Anyway, I'm not one to judge. Except, of course, when I was on the bench and that was my job," she clarified.

Finley gestured to the Bluetooth in her ear, as if she was listening to a communication from one of her associates.

"We're going to have to finish this conversation later," she said apologetically. "I'm being summoned to the bar."

"Oh, dear. I do hope Nathan isn't causing a problem."

"Nathan?"

"Another grandson—not the one I want you to meet," Catherine clarified. "He's been known to overindulge on occasion—most notably any occasion when someone else is paying for the drinks—so I asked the bartenders to keep an eye on him and cut him off if necessary." She frowned again. "Perhaps I should go with you."

"Not necessary," Finley assured her. "Tonight, it's my job to do any worrying that needs to be done and yours to enjoy the party—and the company of the very handsome man who's coming this way right now."

Catherine turned her head, a smile curving her lips as her gaze settled on her husband of sixty years.

"I don't mean to interrupt," Douglas said. "But I need to steal this pretty lady away for a dance."

"A tempting invitation," Catherine said. "But I don't know that these creaky bones can keep up with Beyoncé."

"But they're playing our song," he told her.

"'Single Ladies' most definitely isn't our song," she told him. "It's what happens when you let your grandkids tinker with your playlist before submitting it to the DJ."

The words were barely out of her mouth before the last "oh, oh, oh" faded away and another song started.

"Oh." Catherine's eyes grew misty as she recognized the opening notes of Elvis Presley's "Can't Help Falling in Love." "*This* is our song."

Douglas smiled and led his wife to the dance floor.

Finley loved weddings—the celebration of a new beginning was inherently joyful (though not always without conflict). But if she was being perfectly honest, she loved these milestone anniversaries even more, because they proved to her that love, if it was shared with the right person, really could last a lifetime.

What would it be like, Finley wondered, to love one person for so long? To share a life and a family together?

Of course, there were plenty of couples who stayed married for all the wrong reasons. But looking at Catherine and Douglas, it was apparent that they weren't just bound together by the vows they'd exchanged but by their continued devotion to one another.

Finley indulged herself watching them on the dance floor for another half a minute before heading to the bar to deal with the phantom issue that had interrupted her awkward conversation with Catherine.

On her way, she got a real communication from Rachel.

"Bouquet toss in thirty."

"I'll be there," Finley promised.

But she stopped at the bar first, to grab a glass of soda water with lime from the bartender who'd been keeping her hydrated all night.

"You look like you could use something a little stronger than that."

Finley appreciated the remark even less than the interruption, because it confirmed her suspicion that the expensive concealer she'd bought to hide the dark circles under her eyes wasn't doing its job. Not to mention that she was already juggling two events and not at all in the mood to deflect a guest's attempts at flirtation—even if she'd found her attention inexplicably drawn to this particular guest several times throughout the evening.

But he was the type of man any woman would notice: tall with broad shoulders, short dark hair and deep blue eyes. The first time she'd seen him, she'd experienced an odd sense of recognition, but she'd immediately dismissed the feeling, confident that she'd never crossed paths with him before. And yet, her gaze had gone back to him again and again, as if of its own volition, and the odd sense of familiarity remained.

At another time, she might have been flattered that he'd noticed her, but she didn't have time to indulge in the exchange of flirtatious banter or covert glances tonight.

Her eyes barely flickered in his direction. "That isn't at all a compliment."

"Maybe not," he acknowledged, with a half smile and a small shrug. "I was trying to segue into offering to buy you one."

"Thanks, but I'm working," she said, focusing her attention on the tablet that was always in her hand.

Instead of wandering away, he stayed where he was, apparently unable to take a hint.

"Do I know you?" she finally asked.

"I'm trying to give you the opportunity to know me," he said.

This time, she got the full wattage of his smile, and her knees actually quivered.

"So when do you expect to be finished working?"

"Late," she said bluntly, determined not to let him see how his nearness affected her.

"I'm happy to wait."

"Please don't bother." Her tone was admittedly sharp, perhaps even dismissive. But she really didn't have time for a flirtation with a stranger.

But was he a stranger?

There was something about his shoulders.

And his eyes.

And his voice.

The fragments attempted to come together in her mind, making her think that maybe she did know him. Or maybe she only wanted to.

But that was crazy. She didn't have time for a relationship, and no man had tempted her to wish otherwise in a very long time. Well, no one aside from—

Her gaze narrowed on his face as those fragmented pieces finally clicked into place. "Lachlan?"

Chapter Eight

His lips curved into a smile. "So you do remember me."

"Of course, I remember you," Finley said. "I just didn't recognize you."

"Do I really look so different without the beard?" he asked her.

"Yes." Her instinctive response was followed by a shake of her head. "No," she realized. "It's more than just the absence of the beard. You got your hair cut, too. And you're wearing a suit."

"My grandmother insisted."

"Catherine is your grandmother?"

He nodded. "On my mother's side, obviously."

Shirla, the desk clerk at the Dusty Boots Motel, had guessed that Finley dated "office-type guys who are comfortable in suits," and it was generally true—or had been, way back when Finley had time to date. And as much as this Lachlan Kellett was very much her usual type, she really didn't have time to flirt with him right now—no matter how much she might want to.

"You're the grandson," she realized.

"That's generally how it works," he said. "Her being my grandmother means that I'm her grandson."

"No, I meant that you're *the* grandson."

"Actually, I'm one of six," he told her.

"How many are divorced?"

"Just me," he confessed. "Why?"

"Because your grandmother has been trying to finagle an introduction between me and you."

"Really?" He grinned.

"You're not bothered by her blatant matchmaking efforts?"

"Why would I be when she's chosen a beautiful and interesting woman for me to meet?"

"I see that you can be every bit as charming as your grandfather when you want to be."

"Does that mean I'll get a different answer if I offer again to buy you a drink?"

She shook her head. "Unfortunately, no."

"Because you're working?"

Now she nodded.

"The party seems to be winding down," he noted. "And I don't mind waiting."

"*This* party might be winding down, but the one across the hall is still going strong."

"You've got two events happening right now?"

"That's not unusual for a Saturday," she said, though she was suddenly wishing that it wasn't true for *this* Saturday, because she didn't want to walk away from Lachlan—again.

"Apparently you weren't kidding when you said that you worked weekends."

"I definitely wasn't," she confirmed. "And now, I really do need to be across the hall."

Finley's love of weddings and almost every detail associated with the happy event didn't extend to the tossing of the bridal bouquet. In her opinion, it wasn't just an archaic tradition but borderline insulting to those encouraged to vie for the prize. On the other hand, it was obviously preferable to guests attempting to tear off pieces of the bride's dress in the hope that some of her good fortune would transfer to them, as was apparently the origin of the tradition.

In any event, it wasn't her place to judge or to question, only to give her clients what they wanted. And since Naomi wanted it, the ceremonial bouquet toss had been included in the evening's schedule of events.

"I think I'd rather be in a mob of Black Friday shoppers at Best Buy than in a crowd of single women trying to get their hands on a bride's flowers," Lachlan remarked, as the emcee invited all members of that demographic to gather on the dance floor.

"Then it's lucky that you're not a single woman," she said lightly.

"The garter toss is sometimes even worse," he noted. "Because usually by the time it happens, all the single men are drunk, competitive and reckless."

"Stay tuned," she said. "Or, here's a better idea, go back to the Sapphire Ballroom."

"That party's pretty much over. Grandma and Grandpa are starting to say goodbye to their guests, after which the grand-kids will load up gifts and flowers and various memorabilia to take over to their place."

"So that's the real reason you're here—you're ducking out on the work?"

"I think you know the real reason I'm here," he told her.

"You're stalking me?"

"I was hoping to spend some more time with you."

"Then maybe you should have asked for my number two weeks ago, because tonight, I'm working."

"I didn't need your number, because as soon as you mentioned Gilmore Galas, I knew I'd be seeing you here tonight."

"Well, I didn't know I'd be seeing you."

"Are you saying that you wanted to see me again?"

She lifted a shoulder. "I wasn't entirely opposed to the idea."

"Not entirely, huh?" He grinned. "And even with the beard?"

"The beard made you a little more mysterious but not at all unattractive," she noted.

He rubbed his chin. "I could grow it again."

"Your choice," she said. "But the clean-shaven look works, too. It's very classically handsome."

"*It's* classically handsome? Or *I'm* classically handsome?"

"Are you fishing for a compliment, Professor Kellett?"

"A man never objects to being told that a woman finds him attractive," he said.

"*A* man? Or *you*?"

"Busted," he said, and gave her another one of those bone-melting smiles.

"I'm sure you know that I wouldn't be ignoring my responsibilities to stand around talking to you if I wasn't attracted to you."

"And I'm sure you know that I wouldn't have crashed this party if I wasn't attracted to you."

The words sent delicious tingles down her spine.

"This is really bad timing," she told him.

"Are you referring to tonight specifically or your life in general?"

"More the former than the latter, but possibly both."

"So what happens now?" he asked.

"Now the bride and groom will have their last dance, and most of their guests will exit the reception behind them."

"That's not what I was asking."

"I know," she acknowledged. "But it was an easier question to answer."

Right on cue, the emcee announced the newlyweds' last dance, and Finley slipped away to check with the hotel staff that the requested strawberries and (now nonalcoholic) champagne had been delivered to the honeymoon suite in advance of their arrival. From there, she confirmed the timing of last call with the bartenders, made arrangements for the leftover food to be packed up and delivered to a local soup kitchen and then spent several minutes with the weepy mother of the bride, listening to her recount all her favorite moments of the day, of which there were many (and apparently—luckily— no memory of the zipper crisis).

When she returned to the main reception area, Lachlan was still there, chatting with the bartender while he sipped a Coke.

"Is there anything I can help you with?" he asked.

"No. I'm mostly in waiting mode until the band finishes up in—" she glanced at the time displayed on the corner of her tablet "—twenty-two minutes. The last few guests usually trickle out after that and then we can start the breakdown and cleanup."

"Twenty-two minutes doesn't leave much time for me to steal a dance with you."

"I'm the event coordinator, not a guest. And you're not a guest, either."

"Do you really think anyone cares?"

She glanced around. The final headcount for the event had been one hundred and twenty, including the bride and groom, but less than a quarter of that number remained in the ballroom. About a dozen guests were on the dance floor, half that number were lingering at the bar, and the rest were scattered at various tables around the room, picking at the remnants of cake or coaxing the last drops out of bottles of wine.

"Probably not," she finally admitted.

"Then let's take advantage of the moment—and the fact that they're playing our song."

She felt her lips twitch. "We don't have a song."

"Well, this will become our song if you agree to dance with me."

"Apparently you *are* every bit as charming as your grandfather."

"If only that were true," he said, taking the tablet out of her hand and sliding it into the pocket of his suit jacket.

She lifted a brow.

"One dance," he said. "For three minutes, just let yourself forget that you're working."

Another quick glance around confirmed that no one was paying them the least bit of attention. The bride and groom had already said goodbye to their guests and headed upstairs to the honeymoon suite, and their respective parents had likewise called it a night.

"One dance," she relented, because "Wonderful Tonight" had always been one of her favorite songs.

He took her hand in his and drew her close, then set his other hand on her hip.

As soon as she was in his arms, Finley realized her mistake. Because being held by this man made all the unwanted feelings that had stirred to life when they were in close quarters at the Dusty Boots Motel stir again.

She'd had more than a few boyfriends in her twenty-eight years, and she'd even imagined herself to be in love with a few of them. But her heart had bounced back after each of those failed relationships, making her wonder if she might have been wrong about the depth of her feelings.

Despite the time she'd spent with Lachlan in Haven, she still didn't know much about him. But the immediacy and intensity of the attraction she felt seemed to be a warning—that he might be the man she could completely fall for. If she let herself.

And while she was flattered that Catherine Edwards thought she might be a suitable match for her favorite grandson, she hadn't got the impression that Lachlan was looking for a life partner. A flirtation or a fling, sure. But his brief and blunt comments about his marriage gone wrong suggested that he wasn't looking for a long-term relationship.

But maybe she could be satisfied with a flirtation or a fling. Because even a casual relationship with a man whose mere proximity made her body ache in all the right places had to be more satisfying than sitting at home every night with only Simon for company.

The last bars of the song faded away and Finley reluctantly pulled out of his arms. "Are you going to ask for my number now?"

"If I do, and then I call and ask you on a date, will you say *yes*?"

"I'll want to," she admitted. "But as you know, I'm rarely free on a Friday or Saturday night."

"My schedule's flexible," he said. "I'm only teaching three classes this term and none of them are at night."

"So maybe we can figure something out."

"I definitely think we can."

He offered his phone. She added her contact information and returned it to him.

He tapped out a quick message.

Her phone vibrated.

She pulled it out of her pocket.

Now you have my number, too.

She smiled and tucked her phone away again.

"And now I really have to get back to work."

"And I really have to kiss you."

The heat in his gaze combined with the intensity in his words made her knees quiver.

But as much as she wanted him to kiss her, there was no way she would risk damage to her professional reputation by letting it happen here and now.

"I'm working," she reminded him.

And herself.

But she did take a step forward, reach into the pocket of his jacket and retrieve her tablet.

He looked disappointed but not really surprised.

"I'll call you," he promised.

"I hope you do."

Two hours later, Finley, Julia and Rachel had completed a final walk-through of the Diamond Ballroom to pick up anything that might have been lost or left behind by the wedding guests.

"I've got a chandelier-style earring and one of the flower girl's shoes," Julia said.

"I've got a monogrammed cufflink, an abandoned boutonniere and a strapless bra—black satin, 32AA," Rachel announced.

"The boutonniere can be tossed," Finley said. "Everything else goes in the box."

The box was exactly that—a medium-sized cardboard container that served as a portable lost and found. Most event venues had their own policies and procedures for lost-and-found items, but Finley and her team were usually able to reunite misplaced items with their event guests more quickly themselves.

"Can we go now?" Rachel asked wearily.

"We're walking out the door," Finley said, heading toward the exit.

Because in addition to being coworkers, they were friends who looked out for one another. And they had a hard-and-fast rule that none of them was allowed to walk out of an event in the dark of night on her own.

A buzz from her jacket pocket had her shifting the box to check her phone.

Are you finished work yet?

She couldn't help but smile when she saw the message from Lachlan. She'd wondered how long he'd make her wait to hear from him again and was pleased to discover that it wasn't very long at all.

"Problem?" Julia asked, as the sliding glass doors whooshed open and they stepped outside.

"No."

"Man?" Rachel guessed.

"Yeah."

She tapped out a quick reply.

Just leaving the hotel now.

And looking every bit as fabulous as you did two hours ago.

Fabulous? At nearly two a.m. and the end of a very long day, she was more than a little skeptical that anyone would think so.

And anyway, how could he know how she looked unless…

She literally stopped in mid-stride, glancing up from the screen of her phone to see Lachlan standing beside one of the potted trees that flanked the stone columns of the porte cochere.

Her heartbeat quickened.

Her friends paused beside her.

"I'm guessing that's the man," Julia murmured, following the direction of Finley's gaze.

"You guys go ahead," she told them. "I'll meet you at the office in the morning to head over to the baby shower together."

"We have a rule," Rachel reminded her, at the same time Julia took her arm and steered her away.

Finley waited until her friends were out of earshot before approaching Lachlan.

"I can't believe you're still here," she said.

"Not still," he told her. "I helped transport the gifts and flowers and leftover cake to my grandparents' place, and then I came back."

"Did you have some of the cake?"

"I did."

"Was it good?"

"It was… Bliss."

She smiled. "So why did you come back?"

"Because ever since you walked away from me on the dance floor, I haven't stopped thinking about kissing you. Or maybe the truth is that I haven't stopped thinking about you since our road trip."

"I don't know whether to be flattered or scared," she confided.

"Considering that we've already slept together—"

"Only so we didn't freeze to death," she interjected to remind him.

"—and then traveled nearly five hundred miles in the same vehicle, I should hope you know that there's no reason to be afraid of me."

But he was wrong.

She had plenty of reasons to be afraid—for her heart.

Because the more time she spent with him—and the more she thought about him—the more she liked him.

And dancing with him earlier in the evening had reignited the attraction that had first sparked between them more than two weeks earlier, and she suspected that if she let him kiss her now, she wouldn't want him to stop.

Lachlan must have sensed her indecision, because instead of moving in, he said, "But tell me you don't want me to kiss you, and I'll say goodnight again and walk away."

He was letting it be her choice, giving her the space to take responsibility for her own desires.

Finley breached the short distance between them and lifted

her arms to link them behind his head. "I don't want you to kiss me."

Then she drew his mouth down so that *she* could kiss *him*.

It turned out that Finley's lips *were* as soft as they looked, and their flavor even more intoxicating than Lachlan had imagined. He'd only wanted a taste, but as soon as her mouth came into contact with his, he knew that one taste wouldn't be enough.

He held his hands clenched at his sides, because he suspected that if he touched her now, he wouldn't want to stop. But when the tip of her tongue glided over the seam of his lips, the fragile thread of control slipped through his fingers.

He uncurled his fists and lifted one hand to cup the back of her head. His fingers sifted through the silky strands of hair, scattering pins as he adjusted the angle of their kiss. His other hand found its way to her back, his splayed palm urging her closer until their bodies were pressed together from shoulder to thigh and all points in-between.

Their tongues danced a sensual rhythm that heated the blood that pulsed in his veins, and when Finley made a sound low in her throat—a hum of pleasure—it stoked the fire burning inside him.

After a minute—or maybe two or ten—she eased away from him, breathless and panting.

He took a moment to draw air into his own lungs before he said, "Definitely worth waiting for."

"Definitely," she agreed. "Still, it's probably a good idea to slow things down a little."

"It might be a good idea, but it's not what I want right now," he told her.

The confession made her knees quiver.

"Right now, it's not what I want, either," she admitted. "But

I think we should at least go out on a first date before I invite you to come home with me."

"Pizza and cake counts as a first date in my books," he said, in an obviously hopeful tone.

"Well, my standards are a little higher," she told him, fighting the urge to throw herself in his arms again.

"What did you have in mind?"

She decided there was no point in making it difficult to get them to where they both wanted to be. "Dinner in an actual restaurant."

"Tell me when," he said, his easy acquiescence proving that they were on the same page.

"I have a baby shower tomorrow, but I should be free after four o'clock."

He leaned down and brushed another quick kiss on her lips. "I'll pick you up at six."

Chapter Nine

"Are you sure you don't want to come with us to Napa?"

Aislynn didn't look up from the YouTube video she was watching on her phone when she responded to her mother's question. "And sit around with the five-year-olds and their coloring pages while you and Philip get drunk? No, thank you."

"Nobody's going to get drunk," Deirdre assured her. "And if you stay here, what are you going to do all day?"

"I've got math homework to finish." If she could get over to Harmony's to retrieve the textbook she'd left at her friend's house—or convince Harmony to bring it to her.

"To finish? Or start?"

"Have a good time, Mom."

Deirdre took the hint. "You can invite Harmony to come over, if you want."

"Yeah, I might do that," she said.

"But *after* you finish your assignment."

"Yes, Mom."

"And there's leftover roast beef in the fridge for dinner. Enough for both of you, if she wants to stay."

"Leftovers? Yay!"

Deirdre sighed at her daughter's sarcasm. "Or you can order something from UberEats, if you prefer."

"I prefer."

"So…what do you think?" her mom asked, brushing her

hands down the front of her floral chiffon Adrianna Papell dress. "Do I look okay?"

Aislynn was surprised by the question, because it wasn't one her mother usually asked. And why would she when she always looked like she walked off the cover of a fashion magazine?

Deirdre Waterford (she'd never used "Kellett," not even when she was married to Aislynn's dad) was a stunningly beautiful woman. On more than one occasion, Aislynn had heard her grandma say that Deirdre—tall and slender with great bone structure, flawless skin, honey-blonde hair and blue-green eyes—could have made a fortune as a model, if she'd been so inclined.

But Deirdre had been born into a wealthy family, so making another fortune was of little interest to her. Instead, she'd gone to school to learn about things that did. She'd studied history, sociology, anthropology, astrology, criminology and various other topics. She hadn't focused enough on any one subject to earn a degree, but it was in one of her anthropology classes that she'd met Lachlan Kellett. Fourteen months later, they were married, and six months after that, their daughter was born.

Unfortunately for Aislynn, most of her genes came from her dad's side. She had his dark hair, blue eyes and big feet. She hated her feet most of all, because her mom had the most amazing collection of shoes that Aislynn could never borrow because she couldn't squeeze into them.

"Aislynn?" her mom prompted.

"Yeah. You look fine."

"Fine?" Deirdre wrinkled her nose.

She looked up again. "Actually...you look nervous."

"I guess I am. A little."

"First date with a new man?"

Her mom rolled her eyes. "Hardly. In fact, today is the

three-year anniversary of my first date with Philip, and I think he might be planning to ask me to marry him."

"What?" Aislynn had not seen *that* coming. "Why?"

"Because we've been dating three years and a formal commitment is the next step in a relationship." Deirdre's brow furrowed. "You can't honestly be surprised—I've talked to you about the possibility of Philip and I marrying on several occasions."

"I didn't think you were serious."

"Of course, I was serious. I *am* serious." Her mom perched on the edge of the coffee table, facing the sofa where Aislynn was sprawled. "You like Philip, don't you?"

"He's okay, I guess."

"He's a good man," Deirdre said. "And he's known, from day one, that you and I are a package deal."

"Does that mean I get to vote *yes* or *no* on the proposal?"

"No. It means you get to vote on the style and color of the dress you'll wear for our wedding."

Despair enveloped her like a weighted blanket. "You're really going to say *yes*?"

"Why wouldn't I say *yes*?"

"Because…"

Because then there's no way you and Dad will ever get back together.

But of course she couldn't say that aloud to her mom.

Because Deirdre had told her, on more than one occasion, that she had to let go of her silly fantasies about her parents reconciling, because it wasn't going to happen.

But Aislynn didn't believe it. She was sure her mom was just saying that because she didn't want to admit that she was still in love with her ex-husband. And she was equally sure that her dad still loved Deirdre, too.

She didn't know why they'd divorced. She'd been too young to have any memories from way back then. But she did remember hearing her mom and grandma arguing after the fact. (Grandma Waterford did *not* approve of divorce!) Grandma had commented that maybe Deirdre and Lachlan didn't try hard enough to keep their family together and insisted that it was never too late to try again.

Maybe Aislynn could nudge them toward giving it another shot.

Lachlan was absolutely not counting the hours.

If, after a quick glance at the clock, he realized that he would be seeing Finley in a little less than five hours, well, that was just basic mental math.

And anyway, what was wrong with looking forward to spending time with a woman he liked? And who seemed to like him?

Especially considering that he hadn't dated much in recent years.

Not since Victoria.

His most recent ex hadn't broken his heart, but the end of their relationship—or maybe the relationship itself—had left him disillusioned.

Making space in his life for another person required both willingness and effort, but something about Finley made him want to do the work.

Okay, maybe he was jumping the gun a little. After all, it was a long road from a first date—or even a third date—to a relationship, but he was looking forward to taking the first step on that road with Finley tonight.

When his phone pinged, he immediately snatched it up, half-dreading that it might be a message from Finley—because the only reason he could think for her to reach out would be to cancel their plans.

So he was both relieved and surprised when he saw that the message was from Aislynn.

Need ride 2 H's. OK?

H meant Harmony Stevens, his daughter's best friend since kindergarten. The rest of the message seemed clear enough, if a little short on details.

Rather than text a response, he tapped the screen to initiate a call.

"Hi, honey."

She huffed out a breath. "You're supposed to text before you call, to make sure it's a good time for me to talk."

"Considering you just texted me, I didn't think you were busy with something else."

"You're still supposed to text first."

"But now that we're on the phone," he said, eager to move the conversation along, "why don't you tell me why you need a ride to Harmony's house?"

"Because I forgot my math textbook when I was there yesterday and Mom's out with Philip."

"Okay," he said. "I'll be there in ten minutes."

"I can't go right now," she protested.

"Why not?"

She huffed out another breath. "Because Harmony isn't home right now."

"Are her parents there?" he asked, thinking Aislynn just needed someone to let her in the door so she could grab her book.

"No. Her dad's out of town on business and her mom's at her boyfriend's house."

He frowned. "I didn't realize Harmony's parents were separated."

"They're not," Aislynn said matter-of-factly. "She just screws around on him when he's away."

"Or perhaps Harmony is misreading the situation," Lachlan said.

"She caught her mom in the pool house with the boyfriend. Naked."

Okay, not much room for misinterpretation there, he acknowledged, if only to himself.

"Even if she did, you shouldn't be repeating gossip about your friend's mother."

"You asked," she reminded him. "Anyway, Harmony went to Long Beach with her brother today, and they won't be back until five, so I can't pick up my textbook until then."

"And what if I have plans for tonight?"

"You mean, like a date?" The question fairly dripped with skepticism.

"Is that really so unlikely?" he challenged.

His daughter responded by laughing. "Have you had a date in this decade?"

"Tonight could be the first one," he told her.

"Well, even if you did have plans, you'd change them for me," she said confidently. "Because *I'm* the most important girl in your life."

It was what he always told her, because it was true.

Still, he couldn't help wishing that today wasn't the day she needed him to prove it to her.

"Okay," he said. "I'll pick you up at five."

After he hung up with his daughter, he sent a quick text message to Finley.

Something came up. OK if we bump our dinner from 6 to 7?

OK.

Thanks. I'll make it up to you. I promise.

Two desserts?

At the very least.

Lachlan was smiling as he tucked his phone back in his pocket, satisfied that he'd be able to take Aislynn where she needed to go and still make his date—and whatever might come after—with Finley.

Unfortunately, fate had other plans.

Finley sincerely loved her job, because she had the pleasure and privilege of working with couples at some of the happiest stages of their lives.

Of course, every Gilmore Gala was her absolute favorite at the time it was happening, but she had a particular fondness for baby showers. Today was a baby shower in honor of Emily Berringer-Thompson and her three-and-a-half-week-old daughter, Mia Margaret Thompson.

The celebration was taking place at the home of the infant's maternal grandparents—a stunning four-story Victorian in San Francisco's prestigious Pacific Heights neighborhood. The house had been lovingly restored and professionally decorated, so there wasn't a lot of dressing required—just some tasteful accents here and there and, per the hostess's request, lots of flowers.

The menu was similarly understated but elegant, an approximation of British low tea, including finger sandwiches, cream scones with lemon curd, assorted petit fours and miniature fruit tarts. All of it washed down by the guest's selection from a variety of teas—hot and cold—or champagne punch.

"Somebody's got plans tonight," Rachel surmised.

"Why would you say that?" Finley asked her friend.

"Because you've glanced at your watch three times in the past twenty minutes."

"Margaret Berringer wants all of the guests gone by two o'clock so that Emily can nurse the baby on schedule at two thirty."

"No way the new mom has that baby on a schedule at three-and-a-half weeks." Rachel said.

"You know more about babies than I do," Finley assured the mother of three. "But you were at home with your youngest when we did Emily and Ryan's wedding, so you wouldn't know that every single event occurred precisely on schedule that day—from the arrival of the crew to do the bridal party's hair and makeup all the way to the bride and groom's exit from the party."

"That doesn't surprise me," Rachel remarked. "You always have a detailed outline for events."

"And I always build in a buffer, to repair the bride's makeup if any pre-ceremony tears are shed or to accommodate candid photos of the flower girl and ring bearer skipping through the park or drunk Uncle Stanley's rambling toast to the happy couple."

"Because there's always something," Rachel noted.

"Always," Finley agreed. "Except at Emily and Ryan's wedding."

"I don't believe it."

"It's true," she insisted.

"No coffee run for a father-of-the-bride who started celebrating his daughter's impending nuptials with champagne a little too early in the day? No ring bearer playing hide-and-seek when it was time to walk down the aisle? No mother-of-the-groom bitch-slapping her ex-husband's trophy wife?"

"None of that."

"Then it must have been the most boring wedding in the history of Gilmore Galas," Rachel declared.

"It wasn't," Finley assured her. "It was absolutely picture perfect from beginning to end."

"Except for the panties," Julia chimed in.

"I almost forgot about the panties," she admitted, chuckling softly.

"What panties?" Rachel asked, intrigued.

"When we did our walk-through of the event venue after all the guests had gone, we found a pair of pink lace panties in the back corner of the cloakroom."

"The lace panties that all the bridesmaids were wearing," Julia added.

"How do you know what panties they were wearing?"

"I was delivering the bouquets when they were getting dressed—and posing for photos in their undergarments."

"I wonder if those photos made it into the bride's display album."

"Anyway, that's why I'm sure they belonged to one of the bridesmaids. And I have my suspicions as to which one snuck off for a private celebration with her groomsman."

"So there *was* some unplanned extracurricular activity."

"But none that impacted the bride and groom's schedule."

"So what are your plans tonight?" Julia asked, when she caught Finley sneaking another glance at her watch.

"Are they with the hunky guy who was waiting around for you at the hotel last night?" Rachel wondered.

Julia wiggled her brows suggestively. "And did you wake up with him this morning?"

"I have a date," she finally confided to her friends. "Yes, with the guy from last night, and no, I did not wake up with him this morning."

"But maybe you'll wake up with him tomorrow?" Rachel suggested.

Finley couldn't hold back the smile that curved her lips. "I'm not ruling anything out for tomorrow, but first, we need to focus on finishing this event today."

He was going to be late.

It was his own fault for assuming that when Aislynn said she needed to pick up her textbook after five o'clock, it meant that he'd be on his way back home by 5:15. Instead, it was—Lachlan twisted his wrist to glance at his watch again—5:25 and there was still no sign of his daughter's friend.

"Why don't you text Harmony again and ask for an updated ETA?" he suggested.

Aislynn swiped away from the game she was playing on her phone and dutifully sent another message to her friend.

"I'm starting to think you do have plans tonight," she said, her tone accusing.

"I do," he confirmed.

She scowled. "Who is she?"

"Who is who?"

"The woman you're dating."

"We're not really dating," he said, steeling himself for a confrontation. "We're just going for dinner."

"That's not a date?"

"I guess it's a first date," he acknowledged.

Aislynn's scowl deepened.

"Do you have a problem with me dating?"

"Why would I?" she countered.

"I don't know," he said. "That's why I'm asking."

"You can do whatever you want." She shrugged, as if to prove she didn't care. "Just like Mom does."

"Do you have a problem with Philip?" he asked now.

"No." She folded her arms over her chest and stared straight ahead out the window. "But I'm not gonna call him Dad."

"No one expects you to call him Dad," Lachlan assured her.

"Not now," she agreed. "But what about when they're married?"

"Are they getting married?"

She shrugged. "Mom seemed to think he was going to propose today."

Lachlan wasn't surprised by this announcement, considering that his ex-wife had been dating her current beau for close to three years now. And if she was happy with Philip Cohen, then he was happy for her.

His only concern was for his daughter, so he asked her now, "How do you feel about that?"

"It has nothing to do with me."

"We both know that's not true."

"What do you want me to say?"

"Whatever you're thinking," he told her.

She huffed out a breath. "Okay. I think it sucks! I don't want Mom to marry Philip. I want—"

Whatever else she'd intended to say was cut off by the chime of her cell phone.

She glanced at the message on the screen disinterestedly, then her eyes grew wide. "Ohmygod."

"What is it?"

"Harmony's at the hospital. Her brother crashed his car. She's okay, she says, but they're taking Jarrod into surgery."

Aislynn looked at him then, her eyes swimming with tears. "Can we go?"

Lachlan was already backing out of the driveway.

By the time they arrived, Jarrod was in surgery and Harmony was having her arm casted. Marcia Stevens rushed into the waiting room a few minutes later, her face streaked with mascara and tears. She threw herself into Lachlan's arms, obviously desperate for comfort and reassurance.

As a parent, he understood the helplessness and frustration of being unable to fix a child's illness or injury, to take away their pain. He offered her a tissue that he'd plucked from the box on the table and patted her back while they waited for the doctor to give them an update.

Aislynn texted her mom to let her know where she was, so that Deirdre wouldn't freak out when she got home and discovered her daughter wasn't there. Lachlan wasn't surprised when she and Philip came directly to the hospital, so that they could be there to offer support and prayers, too.

It was only when the doctor came out to give an update after Jarrod's surgery that Lachlan thought to look at his watch again.

It was almost eleven p.m.

And he'd completely forgotten about his date with Finley.

Chapter Ten

"**Y**ou look like hell."

Lachlan set a mug beneath the spout of the Keurig on the credenza in his friend's office and hit the button to dispense a much-needed hit of caffeine. "I feel like hell."

"Must have been quite the party your grandparents had on Saturday if you're still hungover today," Ethan Hayes remarked.

Had the party really only been two days ago?

So much had happened since then, Lachlan felt as if a week had passed.

"I'm not hungover. I'm sleep-deprived." He lifted the mug to his lips. "I was at the hospital with Aislynn until three a.m. this morning."

All signs of amusement vanished from Ethan's face. "What happened? Is she okay?"

"She's fine," Lachlan assured his friend, who had known Aislynn for the whole of her life. "But a friend of hers was in a car accident."

"Is her friend okay?"

"Yeah. The friend's brother, who was driving the car, got banged up pretty good, though."

"That's scary stuff for a kid to deal with," Ethan acknowledged.

He nodded.

"So why are you here? You don't have a class until three o'clock this afternoon."

"Because I need your advice."

"Woman trouble?" his friend guessed.

"I'm not sure."

"How can you not be sure?"

"I haven't actually spoken to her since I did the thing that she might be upset about."

"If you want my advice, you're going to have to be a little more specific about the details."

"I had plans to have dinner last night with a fascinating, smart, gorgeous woman and… I didn't show."

"You stood her up?"

"I was at the hospital with Aislynn," he reminded his friend.

"You called and told her that?"

"No. I, uh, lost track of time and then…it was too late."

"What date number was it?" Ethan asked. "Third? Fourth?"

"First," he admitted.

"You stood her up on what was supposed to be your first date?"

He nodded.

"Forget the apology and cut your losses," his friend advised. "Because there's no coming back from that."

Lachlan swore under his breath.

"Not the answer you were hoping for," Ethan guessed.

"There has to be something I can do."

"You could try finding a good set of kneepads on Amazon and requesting expedited delivery. Because you're going to have to do some serious groveling, my friend."

"I can grovel," he decided.

"And flowers might soften her up for the groveling," Ethan said.

He nodded. "I can do flowers, too."

"Try Oasis." His friend tapped some keys on his computer,

then turned the monitor to show Lachlan the florist's web-page. "Steph likes their arrangements."

"What kind of flowers am I supposed to send?"

"What does she like?"

"First date," he reminded his friend. "I have no idea."

Ethan vacated his seat and gestured for Lachlan to take it so that he could more easily peruse the website.

"Browse by occasion," his friend suggested.

Lachlan frowned at the options on the drop-down menu. "What's the occasion? Make Someone Smile? Love and Romance? Just Because?"

"Just Because," Ethan said. "It's florist code for 'Just Because I'm an Idiot.'"

"Ha-ha."

"You think I'm joking, but I'm not."

"What do you think of this one?" he asked, clicking on an image to enlarge it.

His friend shook his head. "No."

"What's wrong with it?"

"Roses."

"What's wrong with roses?"

"They have *meaning*."

"What are you talking about?"

"There's an actual list. Every color of rose means something different, and the last thing you want to do is give her an opportunity to interpret—or misinterpret—the meaning," Ethan explained. "Carnations, mini carnations, gerbera daisies, chrysanthemums—any of those are fine, but you want to avoid roses."

"Lilies?"

"Lilies are okay."

"This one has sunny lilies, purple asters, green cushion spray chrysanthemums, lavender daisy chrysanthemums and something called Limonium," he said, quoting from the on-line description.

Ethan looked over his shoulder at the picture on the screen. "Nice," he said approvingly. "Now make it bigger."

"Bigger?"

"There's always an option to upsize," his friend told him, gesturing to the "select size" option on the right side of the page.

He scowled at the prices. "That's a lot of money for flowers."

"Do you like this woman a little bit or a lot?"

He clicked on the "deluxe" button.

"Wow," Ethan mused. "Obviously you like her a lot. So why is this the first time I'm hearing about her?"

"Because unlike you, I like to keep my private life private."

"Until you need my advice, apparently."

"Fair point," Lachlan acknowledged.

"So who is she?"

"Her name is Finley Gilmore."

"Tell me more. And—on a scale of one to ten—how hot is she?"

"I met her when I was on my way home from Nevada. We both got caught in that snowstorm and ended up at the same motel. The next day, her flight was canceled again, so I offered her a ride. She has an event planning business and I am *not* going to insult her by rating her on your stupid scale."

"That means she's a three, maybe a four," Ethan said. "Because if she was a nine or a ten, you wouldn't hesitate to say so."

"Not rating her," Lachlan said again.

"Wait a minute—did you say her last name was Gilmore and she's an event planner?"

"Yeah."

"Gilmore Galas did Steph's sister's wedding last summer."

"The *Beauty and the Beast*–themed event you mocked in-cessantly?"

"Yeah. I thought it would be tacky—and insulting to the groom, because obviously the bride was the 'beauty,' relegating him to 'beast' status—but it was really well done. From the invitations that said 'Be Our Guest' to the three-armed gold-colored candelabras and pendulum clocks around the room and the 'enchanted rose' centerpieces on each of the tables."

"Sounds as if somebody took detailed notes," Lachlan remarked.

"Steph raved about everything, and I've learned to pay attention when she talks. Most of the time, anyway. And, by the way, Finley's a solid ten."

Lachlan frowned. "You don't get to rate my girlfriend."

"You stood her up on your first date—she's not your girlfriend."

"You're right. Maybe I should forget the flowers—and forget about her altogether." The problem, of course, was that he knew he wouldn't.

"Your call." Ethan shrugged. "But I never took you for a quitter."

"I'm not any good at this," Lachlan told him. "I haven't dated…in a long time."

"You've been focused on your daughter. No one can fault you for that."

"Tell that to Finley."

"You tell it to Finley," Ethan said. "I'm sure if you do, she'll forgive you." He tapped the screen. "But you could add on the teddy bear, for a little extra insurance."

Finley wasn't entirely sure what Lachlan was trying to accomplish with the flowers, but she had to give him an A for effort. The bouquet from Oasis Florists—"A Gilmore Galas Approved Vendor"—was absolutely stunning.

"Oh, wow," Julia said, moving closer to inspect the arrangement of flowers on her friend's desk.

"Nobody does flowers like Oasis."

"Are these from the guy you had dinner with last night?"

"Actually, they're from the guy who stood me up last night," Finley told her.

Julia's jaw dropped. "He was a no-show?"

"Not just a no-show, but no phone call, no text message. Nothing."

"Oh, Fin. I'm so sorry." Julia glanced at the stunning display of blooms again. "And obviously he is, too."

She shrugged.

"He really didn't call—or at least text—with an explanation?"

Now she shook her head. "Not last night. I did get a text message this morning."

"What did it say?"

"Only what the card says." She gestured to the florist card nestled in the flowers.

Julia plucked the note out of the blooms.

I'm so sorry.
-L

"Seriously?" Julia frowned. "That's all he had to say after standing you up?"

"That's it," she confirmed.

"Did you call him?"

"No."

"Why not?"

"Because I wanted to, and my instincts, when it comes to personal relationships, are usually all wrong."

"It's not a weakness to want a connection with another person," Julia said gently.

"I know."

But it was a weakness, at least from her perspective, to want a man more than he wanted her. And if Lachlan wasn't interested enough to show up for their first date, she wasn't going to waste another minute of her time wishing for something that obviously wasn't meant to be.

"You could call him now," her friend suggested.

"I could," she agreed. "Except that I'm working on our presentation for this afternoon, updating our package prices to reflect the latest increases at Bliss Bakery and Flora's."

"I was a little surprised by the price hikes at first," Julia told her. "Until I remembered that I'm surprised at the higher costs every week when I check out at the grocery store."

"We're going to have to consider adding some more budget-friendly vendors," Finley acknowledged. "But I want to be sure that a lower price point isn't indicative of lower quality."

"I actually prepared a list of vendors that I think it would be worth reaching out to." Julia passed the folder in her hand to Finley.

She opened the cover and quickly skimmed the page. "That's an extensive list."

"I thought it made sense to gather as much information as possible before narrowing the field and making any final decisions."

"It does," Finley agreed.

"I'll set up the front parlor for our meeting and then start making calls."

"If you're heading to the parlor, can you take the flowers with you? They'll provide a nice pop of color there."

Julia picked up the vase and Finley turned her attention back to her computer.

A few minutes later, Taylor buzzed from the reception desk.

"There's a Mr. Kellett here, asking to see you."

And Finley's foolish heart actually skipped a beat.

She debated her response for three seconds.

She could send him away.

She *should* send him away.

That would make it clear that she wasn't the type of woman willing to be jerked around by a man.

And really, it was what she should do, because she didn't have time for unscheduled visitors.

But if she sent him away, it was unlikely that she'd ever know why he'd made plans with her and then failed to show up.

And she wanted an explanation, dammit.

Something more than the lame "I'm so sorry" that he'd texted to her and then echoed on an electronically printed card.

"Ms. Gilmore?" Taylor prompted.

"You can send him in," she decided.

When Taylor escorted Lachlan to her office, Finley remained seated behind her desk.

"Hello, Finley."

"Lachlan."

"I considered wearing a hat," he said. "So that I could come in with my hat in hand."

She didn't crack a smile. "Or you could simply tell me why you're here."

"Maybe I should have brought a hat *and* gloves—it suddenly feels as cold as a Haven blizzard in here."

"I have less than thirty minutes before my next appointment and I need at least ten of those to review the client's file, so whatever you came here to say, just say it," she advised.

"Okay," he said. But first he took a minute to survey her office.

Was he looking for the flowers he'd sent? Wondering what she'd done with the obviously pricey arrangement?

"This is quite the place," he noted approvingly.

"We like it," she told him.

"Setting up shop in a renovated home rather than a traditional office building demonstrates a more personal touch for your business. And positioning yourself between a bridal dress boutique and a stationery shop was pretty genius."

"The credit for that belongs to my Realtor."

"Still, you've created a warm and welcoming space here."

"Thank you. Now are you here to schedule a consult?" she asked. "Or was there another reason for your visit?"

He shoved his hands into his pockets. "I'm here to apologize."

"I'm not sure why you felt the need to drop by after sending such a detailed text message and expressing the same sentiment on the card attached to the flowers that were delivered."

"Well, you didn't respond to my text message," he noted, looking around her office again. "And I don't see the flowers."

"I'm not so petty as to throw away a gorgeous arrangement," she assured him. "I had them put in another room for our clients and prospective clients to enjoy."

"But you're still mad."

"I'm not mad," she denied. "We made plans to get together, those plans didn't pan out. There's no point in making a big deal out of something that wasn't."

"It was a big deal to me."

"If it had been a big deal to you, you would have shown up."

"Will you let me explain?"

She glanced at her watch. "You've got three more minutes, then I need to get back to work."

He nodded, wanting to believe that she was a reasonable woman who would accept a reasonable explanation. All he had to do was explain to Finley that his daughter's best friend had been in a car accident. Surely, she wouldn't fault him for forgetting about everything else in order to focus on soothing his distraught child.

The problem, of course, was that he hadn't told Finley that he had a child.

When she'd asked about his marriage, he'd braced himself

for the usual follow-up question about kids—and breathed a sigh of relief when it hadn't materialized. He hadn't wanted to lie to her, but he also hadn't wanted to volunteer any additional details. Because his experience as a single dad in the dating world had shown him that there were a lot of women who didn't want to get involved with a man who shared a child with another woman, and still others who resented that his daughter was his number one priority.

Obviously now was the time to tell Finley about Aislynn, to explain that the only reason he'd stood her up was that his daughter needed him. And if she had a problem with the fact that he had a child, well, it would be better to know sooner rather than later.

But when he opened his mouth, what he heard himself say was, "I had to take a neighbor to the hospital."

And though he inwardly winced at the prevarication, it wasn't really a lie. When he and Deirdre decided to go their separate ways, they'd promised to always put their daughter's best interests ahead of their own wants and needs. Which meant that, in order to simplify the sharing of custody, when it was time for Aislynn to start school, Lachlan had looked for a home in the same neighborhood in which Deirdre was already settled with their daughter.

So? Neighbors.

But still, he felt like kicking himself.

"Ohmygod." Finley's expression immediately changed— her cool indifference giving way to real sympathy. "Is your neighbor okay?"

"Oh. Um Yeah. She's fine. But her friend was in an accident and she doesn't drive, so I took her to the hospital and stayed with her until she knew that her friend was alright.

"I should have called. I meant to call. But once we got to the hospital...it was just chaos and I completely lost track of time. I'm so sorry, Finley."

She finally pushed her chair away from the desk and rose to her feet. "I think you've apologized enough."

"I don't think that's true. I don't think I can express how truly sorry I am that I didn't get to see you last night. And kiss you last night."

"That's a little presumptuous, isn't it?" she asked, the hint of a smile tugging at the corners of her mouth. "Assuming that I'd let you kiss me on a first date."

"Our first date was pizza at the Dusty Boots Motel."

"That wasn't a date," she chided.

"We had dinner—and dessert—and then we slept together."

"We shared a bed because the power was out and the room was freezing cold."

Still, it had been an intimate experience, even if they'd kept their clothes on, and the memory of that night never failed to stir his blood.

"But even if you did count that as a date—and I don't— how do you get from a first date to a third?"

"Our second date was Saturday night."

"That wasn't a date, either."

"We danced to our song and you kissed me goodnight."

"'Wonderful Tonight' is our song now, is it?"

"It is," he confirmed.

"Good thing I like Eric Clapton."

"I like *you*," he said now. "And I'd really like to reschedule…if you'll give me another chance."

"It so happens that I'm a big believer in second chances," she told him.

He smiled, relieved. "I missed you."

"You saw me two days ago," she reminded him.

"But after last night, I wasn't sure if I'd ever see you again."

"I had no intention of forgiving you," she admitted. "But apparently I'm a sucker for the truth."

He cringed inwardly, because while he'd technically told her the truth, it hadn't been the whole truth.

He would tell her about Aislynn, of course. He just wanted to get to know her a little better first—and for her to know him.

"Pick a date," he said. "You let me know when you're available, and we'll make it happen."

She opened the calendar app on her phone, frowned. "I don't have any nights free this week."

"None?"

"I took five days off last week for my niece and nephew's birthday party," she reminded him. "In order to make up the time away, I have meetings or consults every night this week." She scrolled through her calendar. "Oh, wait. One of my October brides rescheduled her Wednesday night appointment, so I'm free after seven."

He shook his head. "I can do any day *except* Wednesday."

"I guess our rescheduled date will have to wait until next week then," she said.

"Well, I'm not waiting that long for another kiss," he said, drawing her toward him again.

The first touch of his lips against hers was all it took to completely fog her brain, clouding any thoughts of protest. As his mouth moved over hers, heat—like molten lava—spread through her veins. Their tongues touched, then retreated. Once. Twice. More. The rhythm, mimicking the sensual act of lovemaking, created a wave of lust that crashed through her already shaky defenses.

His hand slid up her back, and down again, a slow, sensual caress that melted her bones. She lifted her hands to his shoulders, clinging to him for support.

"Finley."

Her name was a whisper from his lips to her own.

"Yes."

He hadn't asked a question, but that didn't matter. Her answer was *yes*.

Yes to anything.

Everything.

He kissed her again. Like a man who knew what he wanted—and who wanted her.

And she wanted him.

She had just started to consider the possibility of canceling her next appointment so that she could give Lachlan a more complete tour of the building—including the bride's dressing room upstairs, where there was a surprisingly comfortable Victorian chesterfield sofa—when her office door opened again.

"Monica Greer and Peter Topham are—oh."

Finley quickly pulled out of Lachlan's arms.

"Ohmygod," Julia said. "I'm *so* sorry."

"It's okay," Finley told her, grateful that her voice was level despite the fact that her face was burning.

Her friend's gaze skittered to Lachlan, who didn't look the least bit bothered to have been caught in an embrace.

"Julia, this is Lachlan Kellett. Lachlan, meet the indispensable and irreplaceable Julia Morgan."

"Finley always goes heavy on the superlatives after a four-event weekend," Julia noted.

"It's nice to meet you," Lachlan said smoothly.

She accepted his proffered hand. "Lachlan… The sender of the flowers?"

He nodded.

"As you can see, there are no secrets in this office," Finley noted dryly.

"And no locks on the doors," Julia added with a grin.

"I was on my way out, anyway," Lachlan assured her. To Finley he said, "I'll call you to confirm our plans for next week."

"Sounds good."

Julia waited until he was gone before she spoke again.

"Can I just say that he's even hotter up close?" She fanned her face with her hand.

"He stood me up last night," Finley reminded her friend.

"For which he's obviously very sorry. And—considering that you were in his arms when I walked in and he made mention of a date next week—I'm guessing that you've already forgiven him."

Finley forced her attention back to the matter at hand. "You were saying something about the Greer-Topham consult?"

"Right." Julia immediately shifted gears, too. "They're here. They know they're early—Monica noted the wrong time in her calendar—so they're prepared to wait, but I said I'd check to see if we could accommodate their early arrival."

"Is the parlor set up?"

"It is," Julia confirmed. "And Rachel has a pot of fresh coffee on and was arranging a plate of cookies when I checked in with her."

Finley grabbed her tablet. "Then let's get started."

"Before we go…"

She paused.

"…you might want to dab on some lip gloss," Julia suggested, smirking a little. "Because your bare lips look very thoroughly kissed."

As Finley's face heated, her friend's smile widened. "The color in your cheeks looks completely natural though."

Chapter Eleven

As a result of Aislynn and Harmony having been friends since preschool and sharing countless playdates and sleepovers through the years, the parents of each had gotten to know the other child—and her family—quite well. Which meant that Lachlan had known Harmony's brother, Jarrod, since he'd needed five stitches in his chin after diving headfirst into second base playing Little League.

This time, the now eighteen-year-old's injuries were much more significant, including three cracked ribs, a punctured lung, broken collarbone, ruptured spleen and concussion. If he'd been driving his dad's car—a late model Audi A3 with seven airbags—he might have walked away from the crash. Unfortunately for Jarrod, he preferred to drive the classic Plymouth Barracuda that he'd restored in his spare time.

So on his way back to the college after his visit to Gilmore Galas, Lachlan decided to swing by the hospital to check on the teen.

"Chocolate still your favorite?" he asked, offering Jarrod the milkshake that he'd picked up.

The boy managed to nod. "Thanks, Mr. Kellett."

"How are you feeling?"

"Like I've got cracked ribs and a broken collarbone."

"Don't forget the concussion."

Jarrod took a long pull from the straw. "The doctor mentioned something else, too, but I'm having trouble remembering some stuff, on account of the knock I took to the head."

"Glad to see your sense of humor is still intact."

"I think they've got me on some pretty good drugs."

"Your mom's not here?"

"She is. Somewhere." He drank some more of his shake. "I guess she called my dad, because he flew back from New York. He got here a little while ago and suggested they go somewhere to grab a coffee. I think they didn't want to fight in front of me."

"Or maybe they just wanted coffee."

Jarrod offered a wry smile. "My mother doesn't drink coffee, and I don't think my dad wanted a hot beverage so much as he wanted to know who put the hickeys on his wife's neck."

And how the hell was Lachlan supposed to respond to that?

He'd seen the marks on Marcia's throat the previous evening and realized that what Aislynn had said about her friend's mother having a boyfriend was likely true. Still none of his business, except in that it had led him to reflect on his own determination to keep his romantic relationships separate and apart from his time with his daughter. Of course, he now suspected that he might have sheltered her too much, as she seemed to be under the impression that he had no life outside of being a father and a teacher.

"Sorry," Jarrod said now. "It's the drugs letting my mouth run ahead of my brain."

"You don't have to apologize to me," he said. "I'm sorry that you're going to go home to turmoil."

"Yeah, but probably not for another three or four days."

"We don't live too far away," Lachlan reminded the teen. "If you ever want to talk—or just need a break—you know where to find me."

"'S'all good," Jarrod said. "But thanks."

"Take care of yourself."

The boy nodded as he took another pull on the straw.

"Oh. I almost forgot." Lachlan pivoted at the door. "Aislynn asked me to give you this."

Jarrod looked wary. "What is it?"

"A 'Get Well' card, I think."

He accepted the envelope with obvious trepidation.

"I don't think it's anything you need to worry about," Lachlan told him.

"Then you don't know that your daughter's got a crush on me," the boy said.

"Actually, I do know." He'd had his suspicions prior to Sunday night, but the way Aislynn had sobbed for hours, even after being reassured that her best friend hadn't suffered anything more serious than a broken wrist, had confirmed it. "But I also know you're a good kid who wouldn't ever make a move on his little sister's best friend."

Jarrod swallowed visibly. "No, sir."

Lachlan walked away feeling relieved that he'd had a chance to clear the air with Jarrod—and worried that his little girl was growing up too fast.

Teenage crushes were normal. His own high school years weren't so far in the rearview mirror that he didn't remember the excitement and intensity of young love. And while he believed Jarrod had meant it when he said he wouldn't make a move on Aislynn, he knew the boy would likely have more difficulty deflecting any moves she might make.

Obviously he was going to have to talk to Deirdre, to find out if she'd talked to their daughter about boys and hormones and safe sex.

And man, did it make him feel old to consider that his daughter might be thinking about sex, but it wouldn't do him any good to keep his head in the sand.

Still, given a choice, he'd much rather think about his own intimate prospects. And thanks to Finley's forgiveness, they were definitely looking up.

* * *

After the meeting with Monica and Peter, Finley checked her phone for recent messages. There were five texts—one from the mother of her May 18 bride, one from the bride herself, and three from Lachlan.

She forced herself to read them in order.

Just got a very late RSVP from Gina's aunt. Apparently the whole family is planning to come from Spokane for the wedding, so we need meals—and chairs—for six more guests.

PLEASE seat my Aunt Cheryl, Uncle Rick and their 4 kids FAR AWAY from Aunt Diane and Uncle Ron. Long story short: I don't want my dad having to post bail for his sisters the day after my wedding.

Because there were always snags, Finley reminded herself as she opened an email window to communicate the revised final number to the caterer.

She was all too aware that complicated family dynamics could lead to conflict at inconvenient times. While most guests were on their best behavior at formal events, it wasn't unheard of for simmering tensions—fueled by free-flowing alcohol—to boil over. Thankfully her team had proven skilled at reading body language, zeroing in on the source of potential trouble and tactfully de-escalating before fisticuffs erupted. Still, she appreciated the heads-up from the bride and added a note to the file.

With that taken care of, she finally shifted her attention to Lachlan's messages.

Can you give me a call when you have a minute?

Only if it's before 3. After that, I'll be in class.

But class is done at 5.

It was a little disconcerting to Finley that all it took was seeing his name on the display to have her heart skip a beat. Especially as she hadn't been this excited about a new man in her life since…Mark. And in light of how *that* relationship had ended, the comparison wasn't exactly a comfortable one.

But she liked Lachlan, dammit, and she wasn't going to let the ghosts of her romantic past spook her this time.

And since he'd asked her to call, she did so.

"It's two forty-five," she noted. "Am I cutting it too close?"

"My three o'clock class is just across the hall, so this is fine."

The low timbre of his voice in her ear raised goosebumps on her flesh.

"I assume there was a reason you asked me to call."

"There was," he confirmed. "Because I realized, as I was driving away, that we didn't actually set a date for our re-scheduled date."

"I guess we got distracted, didn't we?" she said, her cheeks growing warm again at the memory of his kiss.

"And while I have to say, it was the very best kind of distraction, I'd really like to know when I can see you again."

"Me, too," she said.

"I know you said you were booked all this week, so how does Sunday look?" he asked.

"Like an all-day corporate event at the Fairmont."

"Monday?"

"Usually a good bet," she acknowledged. "But there's a bridal expo in San Jose next week. I'll be there Monday and Tuesday and half of Wednesday. But I should be back by three o'clock. Definitely no later than four."

He sighed regretfully. "Unfortunately, Wednesday doesn't work for me."

She waited for him to tell her what plans he had, as she'd

done to explain why she wasn't available Monday or Tuesday. Not that he owed her an explanation, but his unwillingness to offer one seemed to be a red flag.

Or maybe she was being paranoid because he'd stood her up once already.

And yes, she knew that he'd had a good reason for forgetting about their dinner plans, but that knowledge didn't automatically erase the sense of rejection she'd felt as she'd sat at home watching the clock move past seven o'clock then eight and nine and ten.

It was possible that he had a standing date to play poker with his buddies on Wednesdays. But if so, why wouldn't he just tell her that? Was he trying to be mysterious? Or was he hiding something? Like a standing date with his girlfriend on Wednesday night?

Of course, it was more likely a girlfriend would demand Fridays or Saturdays—and maybe he was unavailable those days, too, but Finley wouldn't know because she never was.

She sighed. "You can probably see now why I don't date."

"We'll figure this out," he promised.

"Maybe we shouldn't even try," she said. "Maybe this is too hard."

"Nothing worth having comes easy," he told her. "And I believe we're worth the effort."

"Okay," she said, because she wanted to believe it, too. "Skipping ahead—how about Tuesday, April 16?"

"I have a lecture at noon, followed by office hours until five, but nothing after that."

"I should be finished around the same time," she told him.

"Do you want to come over for dinner?"

"Are you going to cook for me?"

"I've been told that my enchiladas are legendary."

"Legendary?" she echoed dubiously.

"You can judge for yourself when you try them. How's seven o'clock?"

"I'm putting it in my calendar right now."

"I'll text my address."

"And I'll look forward to your enchiladas on the sixteenth."

"Damn, that seems far away," he said.

"You could use the number I gave you to call sometime between now and then, if you want."

"I'll do that."

The next morning, Lachlan was working on grading the last few essays for his sociocultural and linguistic anthropology class when Stephanie Corrigan knocked on his door. Steph was the head of the math department and also the wife of one of Lachlan's best friends.

He took off his glasses and set them aside to give her his full attention. "What are you doing on this side of campus?"

"I was on my way to the dean's office for a meeting and decided to drop in to find out if the flowers worked," she told him.

He scowled—an expression that didn't faze her in the least because she knew she was one of his favorite people in the whole world.

"Does he tell you everything?"

"Of course," she said easily. "Rule number four in the *Guide to a Successful Marriage.*"

"How come I never heard of any such guide when I was married?"

"I have no idea," she said, helping herself to a can of Mountain Dew from the mini fridge in the corner of his office. He kept it on hand for when Aislynn visited him on campus, but his friend's wife was equally addicted to the sugary soft drink. "But the fact that you didn't might explain why you're no longer married."

"Touché."

She popped open the can. "Now answer my question."

"The flowers got me in the door."

"And your Irish charm did the rest?" she guessed.

"I seem to have been forgiven."

"So when are you seeing her again?" She lifted the can to her lips, took a long swallow.

"We're having dinner on the sixteenth."

"The sixteenth? That's two whole weeks away."

"I know," he said glumly. "But she's an event planner, and her schedule is pretty tight this time of year."

"Gilmore Galas." Steph nodded. "Ethan told me. And also that he told you they did my sister's wedding, so I know they're good—and very much in demand. But it's April. Is she really busy every day of the week this early in the season?"

"She's actually free tomorrow night. And next Wednesday."

"Ahh. But you have other plans on Wednesdays."

Now he nodded.

"What are your plans for the sixteenth?" she asked. "Maybe Ethan and I will crash. Check her out."

"And that's why I'm not telling you," he said.

"Come on—it's been a long time since you've been so obviously infatuated with a woman," she pointed out. "Naturally I'd be curious about her."

He glanced pointedly at his watch. "What time is your appointment with the dean?"

She looked at the fitness band on her wrist and swore. "Gotta run," she said, and brushed a quick kiss on his cheek before she did just that.

His phone rang as he settled his glasses on his face again to return his attention to the essays on his desk.

It was Ben's wife, sharing the news that Lachlan had expected as much as he'd dreaded.

Life really was full of ups and downs.

* * *

Finley was pleased that Lachlan took her advice and used the number she'd given him. In fact, he called almost every day, just to say hello and ask about her day. And when they didn't talk, they at least exchanged text messages. Even better, they managed to get together for coffee twice before their official date—once when he was in the vicinity of her office and once when she had an appointment near the college.

Each of those coffee dates had concluded with a quick kiss that gave no outward indication of the heat simmering beneath the surface, but which made Finley wonder if the sixteenth was ever going to come.

Finally the day arrived, and since Lachlan wasn't expecting her until seven, she had time to stop home after work to swap her usual business suit for something a little more informal. She opted for a flirty skirt that hit just above the knees and topped it with a short-sleeved V-neck sweater. Of course, shoes were always the biggest dilemma, and she spent several minutes considering and discarding various options.

If they'd been going out to eat, she would have gone with the wedge sandals with the laces that wrapped around her ankles. But they weren't exactly easy to get on and off, and obviously she'd be taking her shoes off in his home, so she set those aside in favor of Kenneth Cole T-strap sandals with the zippers at the heel.

She made a quick stop on the way to his address, noting that she passed Merivale College en route. It was a nice neighborhood, with established homes, old trees, neatly manicured lawns and well-kept gardens. The kind of neighborhood more suited to families, in her opinion, than a single (albeit divorced) college professor.

Lachlan must have been watching for her arrival, because he opened the door to greet her even before she had a chance to knock.

"Hi." His smile was warm, his gaze warmer.

"Hi," she answered back.

He took her hand and drew her over the threshold, then closed the door at her back and leaned down to kiss her.

It was a casual kiss—light and just a little bit lingering—but like a well-crafted appetizer before a meal, it whetted her appetite for more.

"I brought beer," she said, holding up the six-pack of Dos Equis for his perusal when he drew away from her again.

"Hmm... I had you pegged as a wine drinker."

"I like wine," she confirmed. "But I thought this would go with Mexican food."

"It would," he agreed. "But so would sangria."

"You made sangria?"

He grinned. "Come on into the kitchen and I'll pour you a glass."

She left her shoes and purse by the front door and followed him through the living room to the kitchen.

"Something smells amazing," she said.

"Legendary enchiladas," he reminded her.

She grinned. "I can't wait."

He poured the wine from a cobalt blue pitcher into a stemless glass of the same color.

Through a double-wide arched doorway, she could see into the dining room, where the table was set with woven placemats in bold stripes of orange, pink, green, purple and blue. Green linen napkins were tucked in beaded purple rings, and there were even chunky pink candle holders with fat orange candles.

"It looks like Cinco de Mayo in here."

"Did I go overboard with the theme?"

"No. I'm just surprised. And impressed."

"My mother's influence," he said. "She sells real estate and, though she usually brings a professional in to do the staging, she's picked up a few tricks over the years. And she's adamant that a table always looks better with placemats and napkins."

"And Fiestaware," she noted.

"This is where I have to confess that I borrowed the dishes—and the décor—from her," he said.

"Did she ask why?"

"My mother's pretty smart. I think she figured out that I was trying to impress a woman."

"When you return them, you can tell her that you succeeded."

"And in case you're wondering—no, I did not name names. Not because I didn't want her to know, but because I didn't want her to tell my grandmother, who would be far too smug."

"Aren't your grandparents on an anniversary tour of Europe right now?"

"Not yet. According to my grandmother, they got married in March because they were madly in love and didn't care about the season. But she had no intention of risking a broken hip by taking a once-in-a-lifetime trip in potentially snowy weather."

"That sounds like something Catherine would say," she agreed with a smile.

"Anyway, dinner's ready—whenever you are."

"I'm ready."

He held her chair for her, then topped off her glass of sangria before taking her plate to serve up the food.

"This is a really nice place," she said, when he rejoined her at the table.

"My mom again," he told her. "She knew I was looking for something not too far from the college, but of course, there's almost nothing to be found near a college in the budget of a professor. This one needed a ton of work, so the price was right for me. Of course, all that work required more money, but it didn't all need to be paid up front, and my mom had contacts through her business to put me in touch with the right people."

"How long have you lived here?"

"Almost ten years."

She cut off a piece of enchilada. "So you bought this house when you were…twenty-six?"

"That sounds about right."

"I don't know a lot of twenty-six-year-olds who want the responsibility of home repairs and lawn maintenance."

"Then you don't know a lot of twenty-six-year-olds with parents who constantly espoused the benefits of investing in real estate."

"You're right about that." She lifted another forkful of tortilla stuffed with shredded chicken. "And you're right about these enchiladas, too."

"Legendary?"

She nodded, because her mouth was full.

"I probably shouldn't admit this, but it's a really simple meal to make. I cook the chicken in the crockpot while I'm at work, then throw the rice in the instant pot when I get home, then shred the chicken, assemble the enchiladas and slide them into the oven."

"Simple or not, I'm impressed," she told him. "Most of the guys I know don't know how to do much more than throw burgers or steaks on a grill."

"I can do that, too," he said.

"Of course, you can."

"There's more rice—and more enchiladas. If you want more."

She shook her head. "I couldn't possibly eat another bite."

"Are you saying that you don't have room for dessert?" he asked, removing a bakery box from the refrigerator and setting it on the table.

She immediately recognized the embossed logo on the top. "You went to Bliss."

"After I tasted the cake at my grandparents' anniversary party, I had to check it out."

He opened the lid to reveal—

"Dulce de leche cheesecake," she said, unable to hold back the moan that slipped through her lips.

"You like their cheesecake?"

"I *love* their cheesecake."

"So that's a *yes* on dessert?"

"That's a definite *yes* on dessert," she said. "If we hold off until after we've cleared up these dishes."

"You want to tidy up?"

"I'm certainly not going to leave the mess for you after you did all the cooking."

"Finley, I've been waiting two weeks for this night—I don't give a damn about the dishes."

"I just thought it would give us something to do before dessert."

"I've got another idea," he said, and drew her into his arms.

She linked her hands behind his neck and smiled at him. "You want to tell me about this idea?"

"Why don't I show you instead?" he suggested, just before his mouth covered hers.

She knew what to expect from his kisses now—or thought she did.

But every time he kissed her, it was somehow even better than she remembered and even more potent than she anticipated.

She wondered if, being such a well-educated man, he'd studied the act. He certainly seemed to have perfected his technique.

He nibbled on her lips, teasing her with playful strokes of his tongue that made her tremble and ache and want. But he didn't deepen the kiss. Not yet.

Instead, he drew back and took her hand.

She was a little disappointed when he led her into the living room. She'd thought he might take her upstairs, because she guessed his bedroom was somewhere on the upper level. She hadn't accepted the invitation to dinner at his place expecting that it would lead to sex, but she hadn't been opposed to the possibility, either.

And she definitely didn't protest when he eased her back onto the sofa.

He kissed her again. This time parting her lips with his tongue, deepening the kiss. At the same time, his hands slid beneath the hem of her sweater. She shivered as his callused palms stroked the bare skin of her torso, an instinctive reaction that caused her breasts to rub against the wall of his chest, sending arrows of pleasure streaking from her already peaked nipples to her center.

It was only their first date.

Or maybe, if she followed Lachlan's logic, it was their third.

And wasn't there some unwritten rule about sex on the third date?

If not, there should be, because she was more than ready to get naked with him.

She tilted her hips, rocking her pelvis against his. She could feel his erection straining against his jeans and gloried in the friction of the denim against the silky fabric of her skirt.

He shifted—and nearly tumbled onto the floor.

"I need a bigger sofa."

"A bed would be even better," she said.

"I have one of those," he told her. "A king-size mattress with fresh sheets on it and a brand new box of condoms in the nightstand...and I just realized how incredibly presumptuous that sounded."

"As a woman whose business relies on precise scheduling, I can appreciate a man who plans ahead."

He rolled off the sofa and rose to his feet, then offered a hand to help her up.

He kissed her again—more promise than passion this time—

using his tongue to give her a preview of what they both knew was going to happen when they moved upstairs to the bedroom.

Suddenly he drew back, his brow furrowed. "Did you hear that?"

"What?" The pounding of her heart made it next to impossible to hear anything else.

"It sounds like…"

She heard it then, too.

Footsteps in the kitchen.

Not light footfalls, as if someone was tiptoeing around, trying to go unnoticed, but clomping treads, as if whoever was there had every right to be.

And then a female voice called out.

"Dad? Are you here?"

Chapter Twelve

Dad?

The word froze Finley in place for a moment.

Lachlan swore softly.

She looked at him, waiting for an explanation, because her mind was refusing to compute the obvious.

"Finley—"

"Dad!"

He took her hands, as if to prevent her from fleeing, before he responded. "We're in the living room, Aislynn."

"Who's we? And why are you in the dark?"

"We were just, uh, hanging out."

Suddenly the lamps on the end tables that flanked the sofa were illuminated. Finley blinked in the brightness, then took a minute to study the girl standing in the doorway.

A girl who could only be Lachlan's daughter.

She had the same dark brown—almost black—hair, though hers fell in loose waves to her shoulders, and the same deep blue eyes. Eyes that were fixed on Finley and filled with equal parts suspicion and animosity.

"This is Finley," Lachlan told the girl. Then he turned to Finley, "And this is my daughter, Aislynn."

He said it as if the name was the only revelation.

But he'd never mentioned having a child. Not once in any

of the numerous conversations that they'd had over the past few weeks.

And she wasn't really a child.

She was a teenager.

So why had he never mentioned that he had a teenage daughter?

It seemed to Finley that was the kind of information you'd share with someone you were starting a relationship with.

"You're new," Aislynn said bluntly, breaking the uncomfortable silence that had fallen. Then her gaze narrowed. "So why do you look kinda familiar?"

Finley had to clear her throat to be able to speak. "I'm an event planner—Gilmore Galas," she said. "You might have seen me at your great-grandparents' anniversary party a couple weeks back."

The girl shifted her attention back to her father. "You picked up the party planner?"

"Don't be rude, Aislynn," Lachlan admonished his daughter. "And no. I met Finley when I was in Nevada."

"Is she why you stayed away so long?" Beneath the suspicion in the question was a subtle note of hurt.

"I met Finley the day before I came home."

His daughter didn't look appeased.

"As much fun as it is to be talked about as if I'm not in the room, I think I should be going," Finley decided.

"You don't have to," Lachlan protested.

"Actually, I do. I've got early meetings in the morning."

He nodded then. "I'll walk you out."

"I can find my way," she assured him.

"I'll walk you out," he said again.

She shrugged, as if it didn't matter.

And it didn't, because she wasn't going to let it matter.

And she wasn't going to waste another minute with another guy who'd lied to her.

But she turned to his daughter and said, "It was nice to meet you, Aislynn."

Then she made her way to the front door, slipped her feet into her shoes and retrieved the purse she'd left beside them.

Lachlan walked out beside her. "Will you at least give me a chance to explain?"

She unlocked her door with the key fob. "A piece of advice—if you shared information beforehand, you wouldn't have to explain after the fact."

"I was going to tell you about Aislynn."

"Aislynn isn't the issue. Your dishonesty is." She opened the door and slid behind the wheel. "Thank you again for dinner."

Then she closed the door and drove away.

"Well, that was awkward," Aislynn said, when Lachlan returned to the house and tracked her down in the kitchen.

Often when she stopped by to see him, her first stop was the kitchen. Because apparently teenagers needed to eat almost constantly. Right now, she was digging into a generous slice of the cheesecake that he'd left on the counter.

The cheesecake he and Finley had been saving for later.

"A little bit," he agreed, trying not to resent that he was in the position of having to smooth over the situation with his daughter instead of Finley, who he suspected was even more upset than Aislynn—and justifiably so.

He squirted soap into the sink and began filling it with hot water. "Did I know you were planning to stop by tonight?"

"*I* didn't know I was planning to stop by," she said. "I was just out for a walk and decided to see what kind of ice cream you had in the freezer." She held up a forkful of cheesecake. "This is even better."

He slid the dishes into the soapy water. "You're not supposed to be out walking alone at night."

"It's a seven-minute walk from Mom's house to yours."

"Alone. At night," he said again.

"I have my cell phone."

He rinsed a plate under the tap and placed it in the drying rack. "And the GPS might help the police locate your body— if whoever kidnaps you didn't think to toss it out the window of his windowless van."

"How could my kidnapper toss it out the window if the van is windowless?" she asked cheekily.

"There are windows in the front." He rinsed the second plate. "Just none in the back."

She shoveled another bite of cheesecake into her mouth.

"I know you think I'm overprotective, but you're a teenager and not nearly as street savvy as you think you are."

"Are you really mad that I was out walking by myself? Or are you mad that I came here?"

"Of course I'm not mad that you came here," he said, scrubbing the cutlery. "This is your home, too."

"But the new girlfriend didn't know that, did she?"

"No." He sighed. "I've always tried to keep my personal life separate from my time with you," he confided. "But now that you're older, maybe it was inevitable that those parts would overlap."

"Overlap how?" she asked suspiciously.

"Like what happened tonight," he said. "You might decide to drop by and discover that I have company."

"Company meaning Finley?" she guessed.

"Well, she's the only woman I'm seeing right now." And, considering the way she'd left, even that was in question.

"But not Wednesdays, right? Wednesdays are *my* night."

"Wednesdays are your night," he confirmed. "And our weekends will still be our weekends."

Of course, that had always been his rule—and a source of contention with some of the women he'd dated in the past. But he didn't imagine that his lack of availability every other weekend would be a problem for Finley, who was booked up almost every weekend.

"But aside from our Wednesdays and our weekends, you have to be prepared for the possibility that Finley might be here—and you have to be polite to her."

Aislynn finished her cheesecake, then carried her plate and fork to the sink. "You can't make me like her."

"I didn't say you had to like her—" though he was certain she would, once she had a chance to know her "—only that you can't be rude to her." He looked at her. "You were rude tonight."

"I was caught off guard," she said in a defensive tone.

"I know," he acknowledged. "But next time you won't be."

"You're sure there's going to be a next time?"

"I hope there will be."

"She's pretty," she noted begrudgingly.

"Yes, she is." He washed and rinsed her dishes.

"Not as pretty as Mom, but still pretty."

He didn't agree with her assessment, but he respected her loyalty to her mom.

"I'm guessing you really like her, if you made your legendary enchiladas for her."

"We're still in the getting to know each other stage," he said, silently acknowledging that there was much Finley hadn't known because he hadn't been ready to tell her. Hadn't wanted to take the chance that she might choose to walk away rather than get involved with a man with a teenaged daughter.

Which is exactly what she'd done.

But to be fair, he was at least partly to blame for what had happened. He hadn't given Finley a chance to decide whether or not she wanted to date a single dad because he hadn't told her he was a single dad.

Aislynn isn't the issue. Your dishonesty is.

And he wasn't sure that there was any way to make up for his snafu—but he knew that he had to try.

* * *

"I didn't expect to hear from you until tomorrow," Haylee said, when she accepted her sister's FaceTime call.

"I'm sorry," Finley's apology was automatic. "Am I calling too late?"

"Only if you expected to talk to the kids."

"No. I just needed to talk to you. I didn't even look at the clock."

"I take it the night didn't go according to plan?"

"Not my plan," Finley said.

"What happened?"

"I found out that he has a child. A daughter."

"You like children," her sister pointed out.

"You're right. I do. I love kids. Especially yours."

"So what's the problem?" Haylee wondered.

"There are two problems. The first is that he never mentioned that he had a child. The second is that she isn't really a child. She's a teenager."

Her sister's eyes went wide. "Oh. Wow."

Finley nodded. "Yeah."

"But if he never mentioned that he had a child—how did you find out?"

"She walked in on us."

"Walked in on you…in the bedroom?"

"No." Thank God for small favors. "In the living room, just as we were about to move things up to the bedroom."

"Well, that was…lucky," Haylee said.

Finley narrowed her gaze on her sister's face. "Are you *smiling*?"

"I'm actually trying very hard not to."

"I'm glad you find the situation amusing."

"Can you blame me? I can only imagine how flustered you must have been—and you're almost never flustered."

"I was completely blindsided," she admitted. "How could he have failed to mention that he has a teenage daughter?"

"In all fairness, you haven't known the guy that long."

"I was ready to sleep with him." And he was obviously ready, too, with his clean sheets and new box of condoms.

"And not for the first time."

Finley chose to ignore her sister's teasing remark.

"I really liked him, Haylee. For the first time in a long time, I met someone that I really liked. Someone who made me think that a relationship might be worth the effort."

"And now that you know he has a teenage daughter, you suddenly don't like him?"

"It's not the daughter—it's the lying."

"Did he ever tell you that he didn't have a child?"

"A lie of omission is still a lie."

"Maybe."

"At the very least, it's a secret. And you know how I feel about secrets. And why."

"I know," Haylee confirmed. "But you've got to stop assuming every guy you meet is like Mark."

"But I didn't assume that Lachlan was like Mark—and then it turned out that he was."

"And you ran out without giving him a chance to explain," her sister guessed.

"I didn't run," Finley denied. "I thanked him again for dinner and walked out at a dignified pace."

"And blocked his number, I'll bet."

She hadn't. Not yet.

But it was a good idea.

"He lied to me," Finley said again.

"When was he supposed to tell you?"

"Any point in time prior to his daughter walking through the door would have been good."

"Give him a chance to explain, Fin."

"I can't believe you're saying that to me. I thought you'd be on my side."

"I am on your side. One hundred percent. All the time. And it's because I'm on your side that I don't want to see you shut out the first guy you've really liked in a long time."

"It's not what I want, either," Finley said. "But I'm not going to be duped again."

He sent her a cheesecake.

Finley might have thought it was the cheesecake they hadn't had for dessert the night before if she hadn't been there when it arrived and saw the delivery man with the Bliss logo on his shirt.

There was no note. No personal—if brief—apology this time, only her name on the delivery slip.

And it made her wonder what kind of game he was playing.

Did he think he was being clever?

That she'd feel compelled to call him to ask if he'd sent her a cheesecake?

Of course, she knew it was from him.

Who else would send her favorite cheesecake from her favorite bakery?

Or maybe he was counting on her sense of propriety urging her to make a call, to thank him for the thoughtful gesture.

If that was the case, she had a gesture for him.

She stared at the bakery box in the middle of her desk, trying to decide what to do with it.

Her bruised heart urged her to dump it into the wastebasket beside her desk.

Her logical mind was appalled by the idea of such wastefulness.

Her empty stomach voted for grabbing a fork and digging in.

It was just a cheesecake. In the grand scheme of things, the fate of the cheesecake was irrelevant.

Except that she knew whatever decision she made about the cheesecake was really a decision about Lachlan. And if experience had taught her anything, it was that she always seemed to make the wrong decisions when it came to her personal relationships with men.

Did that mean that she'd made the wrong decision in walking away?

Give him a chance to explain.

With her sister's voice echoing in the back of her head, she grabbed her purse and headed for the door—then turned back to pick up the cheesecake and put it in the refrigerator for safekeeping.

Lachlan had office hours between two and four on Wednesdays for students to drop in at their convenience, but the reality was that students who wanted to chat usually contacted him via email first to make sure that he was available.

No one had made an appointment for today, so he wasn't expecting any particular students to stop by. Still, the knock on his door wasn't a surprise.

The surprise was when he looked up and saw Finley standing there.

He removed his glasses and rose to his feet. "Finley."

"I should have called first. But I didn't, because even though I left my office with the intention of coming here to see you, I wasn't entirely sure I would follow through.

"And I very nearly didn't make it," she continued her explanation. "The layout of this campus is ridiculously confusing, and I had to stop three different people to ask for directions."

"I'm glad you're here," he said. "I'm not sure why you're here, but I'm glad you are."

"I decided to give you a chance to explain."

"Why don't you sit down?" He gestured to the pair of leather club chairs facing his desk.

"I'm happy to stand."

Which he interpreted to mean that she had no intention of letting down her guard enough to get comfortable, so he remained standing, too.

"Can I start by saying I'm sorry?"

"What exactly are you apologizing for?" she asked. "The fact that your daughter interrupted what was happening? Or the fact that you never told me that you had a daughter?"

"Both."

"So why didn't you tell me? And don't you dare say that it didn't come up in conversation, because while that might technically be true, having a child is the type of thing that you should make darn sure comes up in conversation."

"You're right," he agreed. "The truth is, I haven't dated a lot in recent years. And before that, when Aislynn was younger, I was careful to keep my personal life separate from her, because I didn't want to confuse her by introducing her to women who might or might not stick around."

"You said when she was younger—how old is she?"

"Almost sixteen."

Wow.

"So you were twenty when you became a dad?"

He nodded. "Deirdre got pregnant when we were in college, when safe sex was more of a guideline than a rule, especially when alcohol was added to the mix. We both wanted the baby, so we got married and managed to stay together for almost four years before we realized that neither of us was happy. Not only that, we were taking our unhappiness out on each other, constantly sniping and finding fault, forgetting that we'd been friends before we became parents.

"So we decided to go our separate ways and share custody of Aislynn, and we've been co-parenting amicably since then."

"I'm sure you both deserve credit for that," she said. "But right now, I'm still wrestling with the fact that you lied to me."

"I might not have told you the whole truth about my failed marriage, but I didn't lie. If you'd asked if I had any kids with my ex, I would have told you."

"So because I didn't ask, you didn't have any obligation to tell me that you had a teenage daughter?"

"That's not what I'm saying," he protested.

"Then what are you saying?" she challenged.

"That it was…a failure to communicate."

"A failure to communicate?" she echoed.

"And that I'm sorry. Really, really sorry."

She sighed. "So where do we go from here?"

"Where do you want to go?" he asked cautiously.

"I want to have a baby."

His brows lifted. "With me?"

"No!" Her response was immediate and perhaps a little too vehement. "I mean, I don't know. I only meant that, someday I'm going to want a family of my own and obviously you've already been there, done that, so maybe you won't want to do it again."

"Are you asking me if I want to do it again?"

"I guess I am," she admitted. "But in a conversational way, not a propositional way."

"Then, in a conversational way, I'd say that I need to give the idea some thought. Or maybe not. Because now that I am thinking about it, I feel confident that, if I was planning a future with a woman, I could imagine children in that future."

She frowned.

"Not the answer you were looking for?"

"I guess I thought that, if you said you didn't want any more kids, it would justify me walking away."

"And you want to walk away?"

"I don't know what I want."

His brows lifted.

"I haven't had a lot of success with relationships," she reminded him.

"You've mentioned that once or twice," he acknowledged.

"My sister thinks that I look for excuses to end relationships before they have a chance to run their course."

"And I just took away the excuse you were planning to use to end this one."

"Maybe you should be looking for an excuse to end this relationship. Obviously, I've got some issues to work through."

"Everyone has issues."

"That's probably true," she acknowledged.

"So what's our next step? Assuming that you'll give me another chance and there will be a next step."

"I'd like to try the date thing again. But we're going to have to work on our communication," she told him. "And you need to understand that secrets and lies are a hot button for me."

"Then, in the interest of full disclosure, I'll tell you that the night I stood you up, it was Aislynn's best friend who was in the car accident."

Her cool façade melted a bit further. "Of course your focus would have been entirely on her."

He nodded.

"And your Wednesday plans?" she prompted.

"I pick Aislynn up from band practice after school on Wednesdays and then we have dinner together."

"Well, that's a lot better than what I was thinking."

"You thought I was seeing someone else?" he guessed.

"It didn't seem out of the realm of possibility."

"I'm really not that kind of guy," he told her.

"Well, I hope I have the chance to get to know what kind of guy you are."

"And I hope I won't have to wait another two weeks to see you again." His phone emitted a sound like an old-fashioned alarm clock. "That's my reminder to leave campus so I'm not late getting to the high school."

"And I don't want you to be late on my account."

"Can I walk you to your car?"

"You could, but then you would be late," she told him. "I'm parked on the opposite side of campus."

"Why would you park on the opposite side of campus?"

"Because I had no idea where the Social Sciences building was."

"I could drive you to your vehicle," he suggested as an alternative.

"Not necessary," she said. "But if you want, you can call me later tonight."

"I will."

"In that case, I should unblock your number." She pulled out her phone then and swiped across the screen a few times.

"You blocked my number?"

"It was my sister's idea."

"Your sister told you to block my number?"

"Well, no. She assumed that I had already blocked your number, which gave me the idea. But she's also the one who told me to give you a chance to explain."

"In that case, I'm glad you listened to her."

"Me, too." She kissed his cheek. "And thank you for the cheesecake."

Chapter Thirteen

In the two weeks that had passed since the night of the legendary enchiladas (and the teenage daughter reveal), Finley and Lachlan had managed to get together once more for coffee, once for lunch and once for drinks before a Friday night wedding rehearsal. Though they continued to talk almost daily, Finley wanted more. She wanted face-to-face time with him.

Naked face-to-face time would be even better.

She scrolled through her calendar on her way back to her office after an emergency meeting with a couple who wanted to move up their wedding date—by five months!—because they'd just learned that the bride-to-be was also a mommy-to-be. And while Finley prided herself on being very good at her job, there was simply no way she could expect the venue to be available on the earlier date and all the third-party vendors that she'd secured to provide services (flowers, cake, music and more) to be able to accommodate an earlier date. Because it was not and they could not.

And now she was likely going to be late for a site visit on the campus of Merivale College, after which she was meeting Lachlan for another coffee date.

Finley hated being late—even if it was only a few minutes. And having to answer a call from her mother while she negotiated the traffic between Oakland and San Francisco did nothing to improve her mood.

She was three minutes behind schedule when she parked at the college. But at least she arrived before the bride and groom, who showed up five minutes later with their respective mothers. The plan was to tour Alumni Hall as a potential venue for the upcoming nuptials, as Pamela and Mason had met at Merivale College, had gotten engaged on campus (Mason proposed at the very spot where they'd shared their first kiss) and wanted to be married there, as well. Their mothers had other ideas, so Finley's job was to help them see the potential of the setting and tactfully remind them that the day was about their children.

An hour later, she walked into the campus coffee shop to find Lachlan waiting.

"I'm sorry I'm late."

He glanced at his watch. "Yeah, a whole three minutes. I was just about to walk out the door."

"I hate being late."

"I know." He touched his lips to hers briefly. "Should I order you a decaf?"

She frowned. "When have I ever ordered decaf?"

"Never," he admitted. "You just seem a little...wound up."

"It's been one of those days," she confided.

"Let me get the coffee and then you can explain."

He returned a few minutes later with two oversized mugs.

"Thanks." She wrapped her hands around the cup. "And sorry. I guess I am a little wound up."

"Difficult bride?" he guessed.

"Difficult brides, I can handle," she said. "My mother is another story."

"You were in a great mood after shoe shopping with her last week."

"Well, shoe shopping always puts me in a good mood," she said. "But also, that was Colleen. My stepmom."

"I was sure you told me you'd been shopping with your mom."

"I usually refer to Colleen as 'Mom,' because she's been a part of my life since not long after my parents split."

"How old were you when they did?"

"Nine." And she'd been certain it was the end of her world—or at least her family. Because when you're a kid, your family pretty much is your world.

"I think the hardest part, for me, was that Sandra didn't think about Haylee or me or Logan, she just decided that she didn't want to be married anymore and walked out. And it didn't seem to occur to her to take us with her."

Maybe her kids would have balked at leaving the only home they'd ever known, but the fact that she just walked away...

"You felt abandoned," Lachlan guessed.

She nodded.

"My dad seemed as confused as we were. I mean, I was a kid, so what did I know about what went on between them when we weren't around? But he seemed sincerely baffled to discover that she wanted out of their marriage.

"I know he asked her to stay, because I overheard bits and pieces of that argument one night. He told her that even if she didn't love him anymore, she owed it to us to try to make the marriage work.

"Obviously she wasn't persuaded by his argument, and for the next few years, Haylee and me and Logan shuttled back and forth between our dad's house and our mom's apartment, as they tried to do the shared custody thing—a lot less successfully than you and your ex-wife."

"So your mom lives in Oakland, too?"

Finley shook her head. "Not anymore. She moved to Florida after she and Dalton were married."

"You did mention a brother in Palm Beach," he recalled now. "So I guess you don't see your mom very often."

"Maybe once or twice a year. And that's only been since Haylee's wedding. Prior to that, it was more like once every two or three years."

"And she's in town now?"

"Yep. She called completely out of the blue today, wanting to go for lunch, never considering the possibility that I might be unavailable. Because for so many years, I was so desperate for any little bit of attention from her, I would drop whatever I was doing to spend even a few minutes with her."

"You could have skipped coffee with me if you wanted to catch up with her," he said.

"I know I could have," she said. "But I wanted to have coffee with you. Because spending time with you—even if it's only thirty minutes in the middle of the day—makes me happy."

"I'm glad to hear that."

"But what would make me really happy," she continued, "is if you said that you didn't have any plans tonight."

"As a matter of fact, I don't," he told her. "But I thought you had something on your calendar."

"A consult," she confirmed. "Canceled. The bride and groom decided that instead of spending their hard-earned money on a fancy wedding, they're going to put it toward a down payment on a house and have a private ceremony at city hall."

"So what do you want to do now that you have a free evening? Dinner and a movie?"

"How about pizza at my place? We can Netflix and chill—and not worry about being interrupted."

"Sounds promising," he said. "I remember there was a pizzeria around the corner from your place when I drove you home from Haven—do you order from there?"

"Carlos's," she said, nodding.

"Why don't you order whatever you want for seven o'clock and I'll pick it up on my way?"

* * *

Lachlan told himself not to read too much into her invitation. He was pleased that she had a free night and wanted to spend it with him, but when she said "Netflix and chill," it was possible she just meant watching TV and relaxing.

And he'd be okay with that, really. Considering the missteps he'd made at the beginning of their relationship, he decided to let her set the pace going forward.

And if that meant more cold showers in his future, well, he was starting to get used to them, anyway.

He carried the pizza (and the bottle of wine he'd picked up to enjoy with the pie) and made his way up the stairs to her carriage house.

He knocked—and winced when the back patio lights of the main house came on.

Maybe they were on a timer. He certainly hadn't knocked loudly enough to attract the attention of anyone inside the house. But maybe Finley's dad had some kind of paternal instinct that warned him when someone was sniffing around his daughter. And Lachlan had definitely been sniffing—and hoping to do a lot more—but now he was having second thoughts about anything more with her parents so close by.

Then Finley opened the door.

She was standing behind it at first, so he couldn't see her until he crossed the threshold and she closed the door at his back. And then, when he could see her, he couldn't seem to do anything but stare.

"You're not saying anything," she noted.

"I'm…speechless."

Her lips curved.

Lips that were painted the same cherry red color as the satin babydoll she was wearing.

"We agreed that we needed to work on our communication," she reminded him. "So I thought a visual aid might help illustrate why I invited you to come over tonight."

He swallowed. "It wasn't only because you wanted your pizza delivered?"

"It was not." She took the box and the bottle out of his hands and set them on the coffee table. "And one of the best things about pizza is that it tastes just as good cold."

"I want to respond with something clever, but all the blood seems to have drained out of my head."

"Is that because you like what you see?"

"More than you can know."

"I don't often wear red," she said. "I'm not sure it's my color, but I saw this in the window of a little lingerie shop not far from my office and thought you might like it."

He swallowed again. "You were thinking of me…when you bought that?"

She nodded. "And when I put fresh sheets on my bed. And when I tucked a box of condoms in the nightstand."

"A whole box?"

"I don't expect we'll use them all tonight," she said.

"I'll give it my best effort," he promised.

She smiled at that, then took his hand and led him to her bedroom.

She'd set the scene in there, too. With candles flickering around the room and music playing softly in the background.

"I must say, I appreciate your clear communication."

"I didn't want there to be any doubt about how much I want to be with you."

"Do I need to tell you how much I want to be with you?"

Her gaze slid down his body, to where his erection was clearly straining the zipper of his jeans. "I don't think so."

He lifted a hand to toy with the bow tied over one of her shoulders, hooked the loop of satin with his finger and tugged. The bow loosened, then released, the ends of the tie falling apart, leaving her shoulder bare and exposing the curve of her breast. He dipped his head to press his lips to her skin.

She shivered.

"Cold?"

She shook her head.

He repeated the process with the other bow, kissed her other shoulder.

He could see the points of her nipples straining against the fabric. He cupped her breasts in his hands, stroking the turgid peaks with his thumbs. She made a sound low in her throat that was almost a whimper, then lifted her hands to frame his face and draw his mouth down to hers.

It had been a long time since Finley was intimate with a man. She usually enjoyed sex—and even more so when it was with someone she felt close to—but it had been a long time since she'd dated a man she liked and trusted enough to take that next step with. And now that Lachlan was finally here, she had no intention of being a passive participant.

She hastily unfastened the buttons of his shirt, desperate to touch him as he was touching her. The rest of his clothes—along with her babydoll and matching thong—followed, then he eased her down onto the mattress and covered her naked body with his own.

His tongue slid between her lips, to tease and tangle with hers as his palms moved over her torso, stroking her body, stoking her desire. Her hands slid up his arms, tracing the muscular contours. His shoulders were broad and strong—more indicative of the football player he used to be than the college professor he was now.

His whole body was lean and tough, and she wanted to explore every inch of it. She started by reaching down and wrapping her fingers around his rigid length.

He groaned in appreciation as she stroked him slowly, from base to tip and back again.

He let her play for another minute before he captured her wrist and pulled her hand away. "I'm not sure I can take much more of that."

"So take me," she said.

"I'm going to," he promised. "But first…"

He lowered his head to nibble on her throat, the scrape of his unshaven jaw against her delicate skin raising goosebumps on her flesh. She moaned softly as his hands roamed over her body in a leisurely but very thorough exploration.

He continued the exploration with his mouth, tracing the ridge of her collarbone, nuzzling the hollow between her breasts, licking and suckling her nipples. Sparks zinged through her veins; liquid heat pooled at her center. His hand slid between their bodies to part the soft folds at the juncture of her thighs and test her readiness. He groaned again when he found her wet.

Her breath caught in her throat as he lowered his head and touched the sensitive nub at her center with his tongue, a slow, deliberate lick that made everything inside her tighten in glorious anticipation.

"Lachlan…please…"

He didn't respond to her plea, except to continue licking and nibbling her ultra-sensitive flesh, pushing her perilously close to the edge of climax.

She closed her eyes and fisted her hands in the sheet, biting down on her bottom lip as she tried to hold it together.

She didn't want to come apart like this. She wanted to wait until he was inside her.

But he was relentless, tasting and teasing, demanding nothing less than her complete surrender. As he continued his intimate exploration, she couldn't fight the desires and demands of her body any longer. The tension inside her built to a breaking point, and she shattered into a million pieces.

Lachlan held her close while her body continued to shudder

with the aftershocks of her pleasure, then he sheathed himself with a condom and rose up over her.

She gasped as he filled her, then lifted her hips to take him even deeper, the action drawing another low groan from him. Finally he began to move—slow, deliberate strokes that had anticipation building inside her again. Then the pace quickened. Harder. Faster. Deeper.

Her body moved in tandem with his, her fingernails biting into his shoulders as he drove them both toward the ultimate pleasure. As her muscles clenched around him, he tumbled with her into the abyss.

It was a long time later before either of them summoned the energy to move. When Lachlan finally rolled off her, he wrapped his arm around her middle and pulled her close, spooning her like they'd done at the Dusty Boots Motel the night of the storm. Except that they hadn't been naked then.

"Who were the bride and groom who canceled their appointment tonight?" Lachlan asked.

Finley twisted her head to look at him. "Is that really what you're thinking about right now?"

"Only because I want to send them a 'thank you' card."

She chuckled softly. "In that case, you can sign my name, too."

"Done."

She snuggled back against him. "I suppose you want your pizza now."

"I'm not in a hurry," he said—at the same time her stomach growled. "But apparently you are."

"I didn't have time for lunch today," she reminded him. "And that wasn't just an excuse to avoid sharing a meal with my mother."

"Then I guess we'd better feed you, because I want to ensure you have energy for round two."

"You don't have to worry about me," she told him. "I have energy for round two—and I can prove it."

Since her back was snug against his front, she knew that he could, too.

So they did.

And it was a long time later before they dragged themselves out of bed to refuel with pizza.

Chapter Fourteen

"Where's this mysterious Simon that I've heard so much about?" Lachlan asked, as he uncorked the wine.

"Most likely hiding under the bed in the guest room."

"Hiding from what?"

"You. Not you personally," she clarified, carrying plates and napkins into the living room. "But you being someone he doesn't know. He doesn't really like strangers."

"I hope I won't be a stranger for long."

"I do, too," she said, scrolling through the Netflix menu.

"There's a ball game on tonight." He settled on the sofa beside her. "The A's and the Orioles."

"I'm not in the mood to watch baseball tonight."

"Not in the mood for baseball," he echoed, with a shake of his head. "I might have to rethink this relationship."

"While you're rethinking, think about the red thong that you removed with your teeth," she suggested.

A slow smile curved his lips.

"Now what was it you were saying about baseball?"

"Is that the game where you kick the ball for a field goal?"

She chuckled. "Eat your pizza."

"So what are we watching?"

"Four Weddings and a Funeral."

"Because you don't see enough weddings in real life?"

"Because it's one of my all-time favorite movies."

"You have a secret crush on Hugh Grant, don't you?"

"It's not really a secret."

Lachlan, having accepted that he wasn't going to win the battle for control of the TV, focused on his pizza.

Not fifteen minutes into the movie, Finley nudged Lachlan with her elbow.

"That's Simon," she said, as the cat ventured cautiously into the room.

"Does his presence mean that he's accepted me as a friend?"

"No, it means he's hoping I'll slip him a slice or two of pepperoni."

"Do you do that?"

"Sometimes," she admitted. "I know I shouldn't, but I feel guilty that I get to eat whatever I want, and he's stuck with the same chicken and rice every day."

Lachlan peeled a slice of pepperoni off his pizza and held it out to the cat.

Simon turned his head away and gave a dismissive flick of his tail.

"I thought you said he likes pepperoni."

"He likes when *I* give him pepperoni," she clarified. "He doesn't accept attempted bribes."

"Why would I be trying to bribe him?"

"Maybe because you think I'll be more likely to let you back into my bed if you make friends with my cat."

"I don't need to make friends with your cat, I've already made friends with your—"

She lifted her hand to his lips, her eyes narrowed. "Don't go there."

"I was going to say *pastry chef*," he told her. "I've already made friends with your pastry chef."

She had to laugh at his quick retort. "Are you referring to Domenic Torres at Bliss?"

He nodded.

"I don't think buying two cheesecakes from his shop constitutes a friendship."

"How did you know I bought two?"

"I was at the reception desk when the cake was delivered. What I don't know is why you bought a second cake rather than dropping off the one you'd bought the day before."

"Because Aislynn cut into that one."

"You only promised me a piece—not a whole cake. You could have just dropped off a slice."

"But a whole cake seemed like a grander gesture—and I felt like I owed you a grand gesture."

"Well, I did enjoy the cake. So did Julia, Rachel and Taylor."

"I'm glad." He topped off both their wine glasses.

Finley set her empty plate aside and settled back to watch the movie. And even if Lachlan wasn't paying much attention to what was happening on the screen, she appreciated that he was being a good sport about it.

At least until Gareth's funeral, when he decided to nuzzle her throat. The rasp of his unshaven jaw against her skin sent delicious tingles down her spine, but she managed to keep her voice even when she asked, "What are you doing?"

His lips skimmed over her jaw. "Moving on to the 'chill' portion of the evening."

"But…" she closed her eyes when he suckled on her earlobe "…the movie isn't over yet."

"How many times have you seen it?"

"So many that I lost count," she admitted.

"Then I'd guess you know how it ends."

"I know how it ends," she agreed, turning her head to meet his lips.

He captured her mouth then, kissing her long and slow and deep.

"And I think I can guess how this ends," she mused, when his hands slid beneath her top. (Because, much to his disappointment, she'd insisted on getting dressed in actual clothes for dinner rather than sitting around and eating pizza in a barely there babydoll.)

"A happy ending?"

"Very happy, as I recall." His thumbs brushed over her nipples, making her sigh. "Very satisfying."

"Well, tonight's feature might surprise you."

Her eyes popped open. "I'm not really big on surprises."

"You'll like this one," he told her. "Consider it a director's cut."

"An extra thirty seconds of previously unseen footage?" she teased.

"At least an extra thirty seconds," he promised. "And a brand new climax."

"I think I will like this one," she agreed.

He eased her back onto the sofa—or tried to, but there were too many cushions in the way. So he picked up one and tossed it aside.

The pillow hit Simon, who'd been snoozing on the back of the sofa. The startled feline screeched as he began to fall, paws scrambling for purchase—and finding it on Lachlan's back.

He swore ripely.

Finley gasped. "Ohmygod. Are you okay?"

"I'd be better if you could get your cat off my back."

"Right. Sorry." She carefully lifted the cat into her arms. Simon mewed pitifully.

"I know, baby. I'm sorry."

Lachlan swiveled his head. "Are you actually apologizing to *the cat*?"

"You scared him."

"He clawed me."

She gently deposited Simon on the seat of the chair to turn her attention to Lachlan's shoulder, where little drops of blood were seeping through his shirt.

"Come on," she said, taking his hand and leading him to the bathroom.

"Are we going to play doctor now?" he asked hopefully.

"I think you're already well on your way to recovery, but I'll clean it up and give you a Band-Aid."

She surprised him by turning on the shower.

"You want to wash my back in the shower?"

"Do you have any objections?"

He shook his head. "None at all."

He quickly stripped off his clothes as she did the same with hers, and they stepped under the spray together.

She squirted liquid soap onto a bath puff and instructed him to turn around.

He did as he was told.

"Shirla was right about you," Finley mused, as she lathered his back. "You are a bad boy and you've got the tattoo to prove it."

"It was supposed to be a skull and crossbones, but I didn't realize how much it would hurt to get a tattoo, so when I pleaded for mercy, that's what I ended up with."

"You wanted a skull and crossbones but ended up with an infinity symbol?"

"My regret is endless."

She chuckled softly as she continued to rub gentle circles on his back. "There's a date inside your tattoo."

He immediately stilled, holding his breath as he waited for her to ask about it.

A piece of advice—if you shared information beforehand, you wouldn't have to explain after the fact.

He opened his mouth, fully intending to heed her advice, but she spoke first.

"What's the significance of August second?"

The question gave him pause.

"It's Aislynn's birthday."

"I think it's really sweet that you have your daughter's birthday inked on your back."

"Well, it's no skull and crossbones," he said lightly.

"No, it's not," she agreed, moving in front of him to soap his chest…and stomach…and lower.

A piece of advice…

"The thing is—"

The rest of the words stuck in his throat when she dropped to her knees in front of him.

Finley had looked like a fantasy come to life when she'd opened the door in that sexy babydoll the night before. This morning she was no less of a fantasy, standing at the stove in the kitchen, wearing nothing but his shirt, her hips gyrating to the music spilling out of the speaker on the counter.

She did a twirl, halting abruptly when she saw him.

"Oh. Hi." Her cheeks flushed prettily. "Good morning."

He breached the distance between them and kissed her lightly. "Good morning."

"I probably should have asked you if you like pancakes before I mixed up the batter," she said. "But I can make eggs, if you'd prefer."

"I love pancakes." He reached for a strip of the bacon that she'd previously cooked and set aside. "And bacon."

And, as he nibbled on the bacon and watched her flip the cake in the pan, he realized that he could very easily fall in love with her, too.

In fact, it felt as if he was teetering on the precipice, as if all it would take was a tiny nudge and he'd be a goner.

In songs and poems, love was described as uplifting and exhilarating—the reason for being.

In real life, at least in Lachlan's experience, it was terrifying.

Because loving someone meant opening yourself up to the possibility of heartache.

But maybe what he was feeling for Finley wasn't love but lust. After the amazing night they'd spent together, it was understandable that his mind—and his heart—would be muddled by the surge of endorphins in his system.

"Then you're in luck," Finley said, oblivious to the tumultuous thoughts spinning in his mind. "Because those are both on the menu this morning."

"As much as I appreciate the home-cooked meal, I would have felt even luckier to wake up with you beside me," he said, nuzzling her throat.

"I thought about waking you," she confided. "But I figured that you deserved to sleep in after working so hard last night."

"That wasn't work. That was pleasure."

"A very definite pleasure," she agreed, smiling at him as she turned the pancake onto a plate already stacked high.

He took the plate and carried it to the table.

"Do you want juice? Or just coffee?"

"Just coffee, please."

She poured two cups.

"You have class at two today?"

"Nope," he told her. "I'm off this week. Summer term starts on Monday."

"Just when I was starting to learn your schedule, you had to go ahead and change it."

"I didn't change it, the college did."

"So what are your plans for the day?"

"I don't have anything specific on my agenda," he said. "Why?"

"Because it so happens that I was able to clear my schedule for the morning."

He looked at her in mock surprise. "Call CNN—I didn't think that was possible."

"Neither did I," she admitted. "But I'm finally realizing that I don't have to micromanage every detail of every event."

"Really?" Lachlan sounded a bit skeptical. "What's brought about this sudden change?"

Finley sipped her coffee. "I guess I've finally realized that I have an amazingly creative and hardworking team who are more than capable of doing the heavy lifting—when I let them. Which they proved when I was in Nevada, and which I'm letting them prove again this morning."

So they enjoyed a leisurely breakfast, then made love again and followed up with another shared shower—in the interest of water conservation, of course.

"Is it an early night for you tonight?" Lachlan asked, as they were toweling off.

He'd offered to help her dry, but Finley knew that if he did so, the chore would turn into something else, and she really did need to put in an appearance at the office today.

"It is," she confirmed.

"Would it be okay if I brought over some chicken to cook on your grill?"

"I'm never going to object to a man offering to cook for me," she told him.

"Six o'clock?"

"I'll be here."

When they were both dressed, he reached for the keys and phone he'd left on her nightstand, frowning as he looked at the display on his phone.

"What's the matter?"

"I missed three calls from Aislynn."

"Did she leave any messages?"

He shook his head.

"Then it probably wasn't anything important."

"You're probably right," he said, still staring at the log of missed calls. "But she never calls. She texts, sometimes too frequently, but she never calls." He tapped the screen to attempt a callback and sighed. "It's going straight to voicemail."

"Maybe because she's in class?" Finley suggested.

He glanced at his watch. "She should be."

"Then I'm sure she'll get back to you when she's on a break."

"Her next period is lunch," he noted. "If I head over to the school now, I should be able to catch her on her break."

Though Finley suspected that the phone calls were a deliberate effort by Aislynn to manipulate her dad, she wasn't going to say so. Because he wasn't likely to believe her and would probably question why she thought she had any insights into his daughter's mind when she'd only met the teen once.

But she probably understood the girl better than either of them could guess, because she'd been that girl—devastated by the breakup of her family and desperately wishing she could put the pieces back together again.

Instead, she only kissed Lachlan goodbye and said, "See you later."

When Finley got home at the end of the day and found Lachlan sitting on the steps, waiting for her, her heart did a happy little dance inside her chest. It might have been even nicer to come home and find him in the kitchen already, but she suspected it was far too soon—for both of them—to show him where she kept the spare key hidden.

After he'd assured her that everything was okay with Aislynn—a relief if not a surprise to Finley—they worked side-by-side in the kitchen to prepare dinner. Then they ate the chicken along with grilled baby potatoes and a green salad on the deck, enjoying a bottle of crisp sauvignon blanc along with the quiet spring evening.

"I could get used to this," Finley mused. "Unfortunately, the closer we get to June, the fewer opportunities I'm going to have for nights like this."

"Then we'd better make the most of them while we can."

"First—" she rose from her seat to stack their plates and cutlery "—I'm going to put these in the dishwasher."

"I can help."

"No. Sit." She gave him a quick kiss. "I'll be right back."

She wasn't gone more than five minutes, and when she returned Lachlan handed her the phone she'd left on the table.

"Mark called."

She frowned. "You answered my phone?"

"No. His name showed on the display when your phone rang."

"Oh." She set the phone down again and reached for the bottle of wine to refill their glasses.

"You're not going to listen to the message? Call him back?"

"Not right now."

"Are you going to tell me who he is?" he pressed.

"A friend."

"A childhood friend? A friend from work? A friend who's seen you naked?"

She lifted her glass to her lips, sipped.

"Mark and I did go out for a while, a few years back," she finally admitted.

"Wait a minute—are you talking about Mark Nickel? The ballplayer?"

"Yeah. But how did...you Googled me!" she said accusingly.

"Honey, I did a lot more than Google you last night—and this morning—and you didn't seem to have any complaints."

"That was different," she said. "I invited you to my bed last night. I didn't say you could snoop into my private life."

"It's not really private if it's on the internet, is it?"

"Which is one of the things I hated about dating Mark," she admitted now. "We were hardly A-Rod and J.Lo, but Mark was almost as popular with the photographers as he was with the fans, so even the most casual date ended up in somebody's column or blog."

"Wasn't he traded to a team on the East Coast?"

She nodded. "Baltimore."

"But you keep in touch?"

"Occasionally."

"And you see him when the Orioles are in town?"

"Sometimes. But not in the way you mean."

"That's why you didn't want to watch the game last night," he realized.

"Can you blame me for not wanting to snuggle up with my new boyfriend to watch my ex on TV?"

"So I'm your new boyfriend now, am I?"

She cringed. "Sorry. I didn't mean to slap a label on you. I know our relationship is very new and—"

He leaned across the table to silence her with a kiss.

"I don't have a problem with the label," he assured her. "Now what do you say about taking the rest of this wine into the bedroom, girlfriend?"

Of course, she said *yes*.

Finley said *yes* again when Lachlan called her the next day to ask a favor. He'd gone to Santa Cruz to have lunch with a friend and gotten stuck behind an overturned tractor trailer on the 85, which meant that he wasn't going to make it to the school to pick up Aislynn. (He'd tried calling Deirdre first, but his calls kept going to voicemail.)

It would be a stretch to say that Finley was happy to help—the truth was, she was more than a little wary, as Lachlan's daughter had given no indication that she might be warming up to her. But she did think it might be a good opportunity for her to chat with Aislynn without her father there as a buffer between them.

Of course, a conversation required the participation of two people, and the most she was able to elicit from Aislynn were monosyllabic responses to her questions—at least until she pulled into the driveway of Lachlan's house.

Then Aislynn dutifully intoned, "Thanks for the ride."

"You're not getting rid of me just yet," Finley said.

The teen's gaze narrowed. "I'm not a child—you don't have to wait with me for my dad to get home."

"He didn't ask me to babysit," Finley assured her. "Only to preheat the oven and then put the lasagna in."

"I can do that," Aislynn said.

"I'm sure you can, but your dad asked me to do it."

Aislynn pushed open the passenger side door and stepped out of the vehicle. "Did he ask you to stay for dinner, too?"

"No," Finley said. "And I didn't expect him to. I know Wednesday is your night with your dad."

"Every Wednesday *and* alternate weekends."

Finley just nodded as she followed the girl to the door.

"He spends a lot of time with me," Aislynn said, as she used her key to disengage the lock. "And some of his girl-friends didn't like that."

"Those girlfriends obviously didn't know him well enough to know how much his time with you means to him."

"You think you know him better?" Aislynn challenged.

"I'm hoping to know him better," Finley replied, aware that she was treading on boggy ground. "And I'd like to know you better, too."

"I don't really see that happening."

"I guess time will tell," she said lightly, refusing to let herself be offended by the girl's dismissive tone.

Aislynn was scowling as Finley moved past her to the kitchen.

She found the lasagna in the refrigerator, where Lachlan had told her it would be, and checked the heating instructions on the packaging before programming the oven temperature.

While the oven was preheating, she opened the crisper drawer and found romaine lettuce, cucumbers and red peppers.

"What are you doing now?" Aislynn demanded from the doorway.

"I thought I'd make you guys a salad to go with the pasta."

Aislynn watched her tear up the lettuce and divide it into two bowls, offering no help or instruction as Finley rummaged around until she found a cutting board and chef's knife.

When the oven beeped to indicate it had reached the desired temperature, Finley placed the lasagna on a baking tray and slid it into the oven, then set the timer before returning her attention to the salads.

"I don't like red pepper."

"Then I won't put red pepper in your salad," Finley said.

"Why are you doing this?"

She shrugged as she began to slice the cucumber. "My mom always insisted on a vegetable at every meal."

"Dad says the tomato sauce on pasta *is* a vegetable."

"An interesting perspective."

She finished with the salads and returned the leftover vegetables to the refrigerator.

"I have homework to do," Aislynn said.

"Okay."

"I can't go upstairs to do it until I lock the door behind you."

Subtlety was definitely *not* the girl's strong suit.

Finley wiped her hands on a towel. "If your dad's not home when the timer goes off, remove the foil lid and put the lasagna back in the oven for another fifteen minutes."

Aislynn nodded. "Okay," she said, then added a begrudging "thanks."

"Anytime," Finley said easily.

Lachlan's daughter followed her to the door. "Goodbye, Finley."

"Good night, Aislynn."

She'd barely crossed the threshold when she heard the click of the lock at her back, an audible reminder that she was on the outside looking in.

Chapter Fifteen

It had been difficult to make plans with Finley in April, and May was proving to be an equal challenge. June, she cautioned Lachlan, was even more tightly scheduled. But now that their relationship had progressed to the next stage and the question of "will we or won't we" had been answered very much to his satisfaction—and apparently hers, too—Finley seemed comfortable asking him to meet her after an event or stopping by his place if she was on the other side of the Bay.

But she'd warned him that he wouldn't see her at all on the third weekend in May, as she had a rehearsal and rehearsal dinner on Friday, followed by a wedding with two hundred and fifty guests— "actually, two hundred and fifty-six now"—for which she'd contracted several additional helpers, and then a "morning after" brunch for the same number on Sunday. As it was Lachlan's scheduled weekend with Aislynn anyway, he decided to pick up the hint she'd dropped several weeks earlier.

"Planning a romantic weekend, I see," Ethan remarked, looking at the screen of Lachlan's phone over his shoulder when he met him at the campus coffee shop. "Don't you think a trip to Anaheim is a little… Mickey Mouse?"

"Ha-ha. Finley is going to be working all weekend, so I've decided to take Aislynn to Disneyland. I was thinking of splurging on an on-site hotel this time, but this late in the game, all that's available are suites and they're a little on the pricey side."

"A little?" Ethan echoed. "Jesus—is that the price *per night*?"

"No, that's the cost of a two-bedroom suite for Friday and Saturday."

"Still not much better," his friend said.

"You and Steph want to come? You could have the room with the king-size bed, Aislynn could take the one with the two queens, and I could sleep on the pulldown in the living area."

"Unfortunately—or maybe not—my wife and I have adult activities planned this weekend."

"You can spare me the details," Lachlan assured him.

"Not *those* kinds of adult plans," Ethan said. "Though after the wine tour, I'm sure things will move in that direction."

"I didn't think you were a fan of wine."

"I'm not really, but Steph is. And I'm a fan of the fact that wine lessens her inhibitions a little—" he waggled his eyebrows "—if you know what I mean."

"Nope. Don't know and don't want to know."

"Anyway, while you're snacking on churros and slurping Coke, we'll be sampling charcuterie and sipping chardonnay."

Lachlan was still staring at the number on his phone, as if he might will it to change. "I really shouldn't pay that much for a hotel room that we won't spend more than a few hours in, should I?"

"Knowing your daughter, I'd say that Aislynn would be happier with another pair of Minnie Mouse ears to add to her collection. And though it's really not any of my business, I'd also like to say that you shouldn't feel as if you owe her anything more than that just because you've been spending so much time with Finley recently."

"How do you know I'm feeling guilty?"

"Because you're a divorced single dad, and guilt comes with the title. Trust me—I'm Catholic, so I know about guilt.

Divorced Catholic single dads?" Ethan shook his head. "They have no hope of ever getting out from under that burden."

It turned out his friend was right—Aislynn was so excited to hear that they were going to Disneyland, she didn't even care that they were staying at a budget motel offsite.

"We're really going to Disneyland this weekend? Just you and me?"

"Unless you want to invite Harmony to come along?"

She considered for a minute, then shook her head. "I don't think so."

"Kendra?" he suggested as an alternative.

Another head shake. "No."

"I thought you said you wanted to bring a friend."

"I changed my mind," she told him.

"Any particular reason?" he asked.

"I guess I realized that I'm probably going to be going away to school in a couple of years, so we don't have a lot of father-daughter weekends left."

It was a fact of which he'd been painfully aware for some time now. And more specifically, every time she blew him off to hang out with her friends. He didn't ever complain, because he knew it was a reflection of her growing independence— and because he still saw her a couple of times every week. Wednesday nights, of course, but also on random occasions when she decided to stop by.

It was only recently, though, that Aislynn had given any indication that she valued those father-daughter weekends as much as he did. Since he'd started seeing Finley, in fact, and she'd realized that she wasn't always going to have his undivided attention.

Which made him wonder if she saw his new girlfriend as a threat to their father-daughter relationship—or as a threat to her fantasies of a reconciliation between her parents. But that, he decided, was a question for another day.

"Okay," he said now. "It's just going to be you and me. But you remember my rule, don't you?"

"I remember," she assured him. "No more than one ride a day on 'it's a small world.'"

"And you're okay with that?"

"I'm not a kid anymore, Dad. I'd be happy to skip 'it's a small world' altogether for another ride on Space Mountain."

"I don't know about skipping it altogether," he protested. "It is a tradition, after all."

She hugged him, laughing, and he found himself looking forward to the weekend, even if he wasn't going to see Finley at all.

By the time the "morning after" brunch was finally over, late in the afternoon on Sunday, and the last of the guests had departed, Finley's exhaustion went all the way to her bones.

It had been a fabulously successful weekend, and she was proud that Gilmore Galas had pulled off three days of back-to-back events without a hitch—or at least without a hitch that anyone else could see—and she had no doubt that more business would come their way as a result of the Parker-Chesney wedding.

But she would bask in that glory another day, because right now, she was too tired even for basking.

Julia and Rachel were similarly wiped out. And while the rest of their weekend staff had taken off at the earliest opportunity, the three partners decided to have a drink at the bar and do their usual debriefing of the event there rather than in the office the following morning.

Of course, they'd been so busy with the event, none of them had eaten throughout the day, so they ordered food to go with the drinks and ended up hanging around because that required a lot less effort than getting up to go home.

But eventually Rachel's husband came to pick her up and then Julia's fiancé did the same, leaving Finley alone, because her boyfriend (and it still gave her a little bit of a thrill to think of Lachlan as her boyfriend) was in Anaheim—or probably on his way home—with his daughter.

It was just starting to get dark when she finally summoned the energy to slide her feet back into the shoes that she'd kicked off under the table when she sat down and head out to her vehicle, unwilling to jeopardize the sterling reputation of Gilmore Galas by falling asleep in the hotel bar.

She'd just buckled her seatbelt when her phone chimed with a message, and her heart did a foolish little leap inside her chest when she saw Lachlan's name on the screen.

I'm back.

She immediately replied:

Did you have a good time?

It's hard not to have a good time at Disneyland. But I missed you.

I missed you, too.

I thought you might be too busy to miss me.

My days were busy. My nights were lonely.

Are you up for some company tonight? I could be at your place in twenty minutes.

Actually, I'm just leaving the hotel, so I could be at your
place in ten.

Then I'll see you in ten.

She pulled out of the parking lot, suddenly not feeling so
tired anymore.

R u home?

Harmony immediately responded to her text with a thumbs-
up emoji.

Aislynn wanted to follow up by asking if Jarrod was home,
but recently Harmony had accused her of only wanting to hang
out at her place when her brother was there, and Aislynn suspected that it might be true.

She'd known Jarrod forever—and for most of that time as
Harmony's annoying brother. But then, almost overnight, her
feelings for him had changed. It was during the summer of her
fourteenth birthday, after she returned from her annual camping trip with her dad and immediately raced over to see her
BFF. Because she hadn't seen Harmony in a whole week and—
thanks to her dad's stupid rules about unplugging to commune
with nature—they hadn't even exchanged text messages.

When she arrived, Jarrod and a couple of his friends were
in the pool. As she watched, he rose up out of the water, exposing surprisingly wide shoulders, a hard, flat stomach, neon
orange swim trunks and muscled legs covered with dark hair.
Her mouth went dry and her heart started to pound really fast.
Then he gave a toss of his head, to flip his wet hair out of his
face, and spotted her standing there.

His lips curved and her knees trembled.

Was it possible that he was feeling the same things she
was feeling?

The hope had barely begun to blossom when he crushed it with a casual, "Hey, Squirt."

It was what he'd been calling her since she was eight years old. Not because she was little, even if she was in the eyes of a ten-year-old boy, but because she'd accidentally squeezed a juice pouch while trying to jam the straw in it and squirted fruit punch halfway across the room.

Shoving that embarrassing memory to the back of her mind, she slipped on her shoes and snuck out the back door. She didn't really need to sneak out. It wasn't as if her mom would have refused a request to go visit her friend, but she would have insisted on driving her, because her mom was as paranoid as her dad when it came to Aislynn being out on her own after dark. And anyway, it wasn't completely dark yet. Yeah, it would be, when it was time to go home, but she could call her mom for a ride if she needed one then. Or maybe Jarrod would walk her home.

He'd sometimes given her a ride in his Barracuda, if she'd stayed late to hang out with Harmony. But that wasn't an option now, as his beloved car was in the body shop while the insurance company decided whether or not to pay for the repairs. Jarrod assured Aislynn that he'd fix it himself if they wouldn't, but considering that his arm was still in a sling, she figured he should concentrate on fixing himself first.

"What's up?" Harmony asked, when she opened the door for Aislynn.

"I brought you this." She offered her friend a bag of Main Street popcorn—the Mickey Fruity Mix that she knew was Harmony's favorite.

"Thanks. You wanna come in?"

She nodded.

"How was Disney?"

"The Happiest Place On Earth."

"So why don't you sound happy?"

"Because when I got home, my mom and Philip were talking about their wedding plans."

"I want a destination wedding, so I can get married barefoot in the sand," Harmony told her, obviously having given the matter some thought.

"I'm not thinking about my wedding yet," Aislynn said. "And I don't want to think about my mom's, either." In fact, it hurt her stomach to think about it.

"I know you wanted your mom and dad to get back together," her friend said, not unsympathetically. "But maybe your dad will find someone, too. It certainly didn't take my dad long after he found out about my mom and Fernando."

"Actually... I think maybe my dad has found someone already," Aislynn confided.

"Really? When did that happen?"

"I walked in on them kissing a few weeks ago."

"And you're only telling me *now*?"

"I didn't want to talk about it. I *don't* want to talk about it."

Because while her dad had been great the whole time they were at Disneyland, she knew that when he dropped her off at home with a hug and a kiss and a lightning quick goodbye, he was rushing off to see Finley.

"You wanna play some *Mario Kart*?" Harmony asked, honoring her friend's request.

Aislynn nodded and followed her to the gaming room in the basement.

"Good morning."

Finley had hoped to sleep a little longer—especially as it was a rare opportunity for her—but she decided that waking up to Lachlan's sexy voice whispering in her ear was better than sleeping in any day.

She rolled over to face him. "Good morning."

He dipped his head to kiss her—a lingering kiss that led to leisurely lovemaking.

"I think I love waking up with you in the morning even more than I love falling asleep next to you at night."

"The two events kind of go hand in hand," she pointed out to him.

"They do," he agreed, linking their hands together. "Kind of like you and me."

"Somebody's in a poetic mood this morning."

"I really did miss you when I was away."

"I missed you, too, but even if you'd been here, I wouldn't have been able to see you."

"I know." He held her gaze for several seconds before he spoke again. "I think I was a goner the minute you walked through the doors of the Dusty Boots Motel."

"I'm not sure I believe that's true. You certainly didn't look too impressed that day."

"Because I knew you were there to take the last room."

"And then I shared it with you."

"Not just the room but your bed."

"And now we're in your bed," she noted.

"Which is much bigger than yours."

"More important, last night it was closer than mine."

"That is more important," he agreed.

"This morning, though, my priority is coffee."

"My coffee maker has an automatic timer, so it should be ready in the kitchen."

"You're not coming down?" she asked, surprised.

"I just need a couple minutes to shave first," he told her.

"I hope you're not doing so on my account."

"Only because I don't like putting marks on you," he said. "And you've got beard burn on your throat and probably... other places."

"Yes, I do," she confirmed, a smile tugging at her lips. "But I'm not complaining."

"Go pour the coffee," he urged. "And I'll be down in three minutes to scramble some eggs for you."

"An early orgasm and breakfast?" Finley's smile widened. "This is a very lucky day."

She was still smiling as she made her way down the stairs toward the kitchen, then halted in mid-stride when she spotted a woman standing by the counter, pouring what Finley coveted.

"Good morning." The woman—a stunningly beautiful woman with blond hair in a messy knot on top of her head, wearing spandex leggings and a matching sports bra, the strap of which was visible because her oversized T-shirt was worn off-the-shoulder, *Flashdance* style—greeted her.

"Um… Hello."

"I'm Deirdre—the ex-wife." She offered a smile along with the coffee she'd just poured. "And I'm guessing you're Finley."

Finley nodded as she accepted the mug.

Deirdre reached into the cupboard for another, obviously at home in her ex-husband's house. "You're the party planner, right?"

Finley nodded again.

"You did a wonderful job with the grandparents' anniversary party."

"Thank you."

Because the mug of coffee was in her hand, she lifted it to her lips and sipped, swallowing the question that she really wanted to ask—which was, what was Lachlan's ex-wife doing in his kitchen at seven thirty a.m. on a Monday morning?

Then the man himself was there, stopping short in the doorway, as she had done.

"Deirdre." His gaze jumped from his ex-wife to his current lover and back again. "What are you doing here?"

"I wanted to talk about Aislynn's birthday, as I said in the text I sent to you last night."

"Did I respond to your text message?"

"No," she admitted, handing him the second mug of coffee. "But I know you don't have an early class on Monday, so I figured you'd be home."

"Still, you could have called first," he pointed out.

"Why would I bother to call when I drive right by your house to and from band practice?" Deirdre filled a third mug from the carafe.

"And when you drove past the first time, did you not notice that there was another vehicle in the driveway?" Lachlan asked her.

"Of course, I did—and naturally I was dying to know who it belonged to," she said unapologetically.

"Now you know," Lachlan said. "And now you can go."

"Don't be rude," she chided.

"I don't think I'm the one being rude."

"Drink your coffee, Lach." Deirdre shifted her attention to Finley again. "He's always grumpy before his first cup. Though I'm sure you've figured that out by now."

"I wasn't grumpy until I walked into my kitchen and found my ex-wife here," he retorted.

"Aislynn's birthday is in ten-and-a-half weeks," Deirdre said. "And we need to figure out what we're doing for her party."

"I'll call you later to discuss it," he said.

"But I'm here now."

"And I should probably be going, anyway," Finley said, suddenly regaining her voice.

"You're not the one I want to leave," Lachlan told her.

"But I'm the one on a schedule," she reminded him. "And I need to stop at home before heading into the office."

"But you haven't had breakfast," he protested.

"I'll grab something on my way."

Lachlan followed her out to her car. "I'm sorry about Deirdre," he said. "I honestly had no idea she was planning to stop by this morning."

Finley turned to him then, and he could see that she was troubled. "How often does she do that—drop in unannounced and uninvited?"

"I don't know." He shrugged. "Once or twice a week."

"You see your ex-wife once or twice a week?"

"I realize it probably seems like a lot, but we've worked hard to maintain a cordial relationship for Aislynn."

"There's cordial and then there's codependent," Finley said.

He was taken aback by her blunt response. "What's that supposed to mean?"

"Just that it seems easier for you to apologize for your ex-wife's lack of boundaries than to actually set any boundaries."

"I've told her countless times to call before stopping by," he said.

"Have you tried taking away her key?" she asked him.

"I can't do that," he protested.

"Why not?"

"Because this is Aislynn's home, too."

"I'm not suggesting that you take away your daughter's key."

"You don't understand."

"You're right," she said. "How could I possibly understand when I don't have an ex-spouse with whom I share a child?"

Which was kind of his point, but something in Finley's tone warned Lachlan that what she was saying wasn't actually what she meant.

"Can we talk about this later?" he asked cautiously.

"I'd rather there wasn't anything to talk about, but sure," she agreed.

"Please don't go away mad."

"I'm not mad." Then she sighed. "I'm really not. I just didn't realize this relationship would be quite so…complicated."

"I know I've got baggage, but I've also got all the ingredients for my legendary enchiladas," he said, hoping to make her smile.

She gave him half of one. "Are you offering to cook for me tonight?"

"Well, you're running off without the breakfast I promised you, so it seems the least I can do."

"Enchiladas sound good to me," she agreed. "But we're sleeping at my place tonight."

He'd figured that was a given and kissed her gently before opening the door of her SUV for her.

He watched her drive away, then headed back into the house.

"You can't just use your key to barge in here whenever you want," he told Deirdre, who was sitting at the island now, drinking her coffee and thumbing through a Merivale College course calendar.

She closed the book to give him her full attention. "It's never bothered you before."

"You've never done it when I had company before."

"Maybe because you've never had overnight company before."

"I have so."

"Very rarely. And not in a long time."

He couldn't deny that was true.

"You really like her, don't you?"

"I'm not discussing my relationship with Finley with you," he told her.

"That's okay," she said. "You don't have to say anything. I can tell by the way you look at her—because it's the same way you used to look at me."

He sighed. "Dee—"

"No." She held up a hand. "It's okay. I know that was a lifetime ago. Aislynn's lifetime, to be precise. And, as I already mentioned, her birthday is the reason I stopped by."

"I don't know why you think we need to talk about her party, because you're going to do what you want to do, anyway."

"Because shared custody requires talking about the important decisions that affect our child."

"I'm not sure a birthday party falls into the 'important' category, but okay," he relented.

"The first thing we need to decide on is the venue. Kendra's sweet sixteen was at August Hall."

Lachlan was familiar with the Victorian Playhouse in Union Square. It was designed by celebrated architect August Headman and renowned for hosting the premier of Alfred Hitchcock's *Vertigo* in 1958, when it was known as the Stage Door Theater. He also knew that the hall came with a hefty price tag.

"No."

"I'm not suggesting August Hall," Deirdre assured him. "Having Aislynn's party at the same venue would be as tacky as suggesting she wear the same Bottega Veneta dress that Kendra wore."

"What are you suggesting?" Lachlan asked.

"Perhaps The Cliff House or Presidio Golf Club or—going in a completely different direction—a City Cruise."

"Let me further narrow down the options for you," he suggested. "Your backyard or mine."

Deirdre frowned. "It's her sweet sixteen."

"And I know everyone in her social group was talking about Kendra's party for weeks after the fact, but our daughter needs to understand that Silicon Valley executives are in a whole different tax bracket than college professors."

"Why does everything always have to be about the money?" Deirdre demanded.

"Because it doesn't grow on trees."

"I don't mind paying for the party."

Of course, she didn't. Because she came from family money, and even indulging her penchant for upgrading her vehicle every year, redecorating her house to follow the trends and filling her closet with exclusive designer labels, she didn't need to worry about burning through the trust fund set up by her grandfather.

"Just because you can afford to give her an elaborate party doesn't mean you should," Lachlan argued. "Or that I shouldn't be contributing. I'm her father, Dee."

She pouted. "She's only going to turn sixteen once."

"The same argument could be made for eighteen and twenty-one and—"

"And she's our only child."

"Who will hopefully be going off to college in a few years," Lachlan reminded her. "If you want to throw some of your money away, throw it into her college fund."

"This party is a big deal to her."

"Keeping up with Kendra Thornton is a big deal to her," he noted dryly. "And she needs to understand it's just not realistic."

"Okay. We can have the party at my place," Deirdre decided. "But I don't even know where to begin with the planning after that. Maybe Finley—"

"No," he said firmly.

She frowned. "You can't know what I was going to say."

"I can guess," he told her.

And Finley was right—their relationship was already complicated enough without letting her get tangled up in any birthday party drama with his ex-wife and his daughter.

Chapter Sixteen

Finley understood and accepted that Wednesday nights belonged to Lachlan and his daughter, and she never imposed on that precious time. The same was true of his weekends with Aislynn. Of course, she was usually busy with other things, but even when she had a free night or an early evening, she didn't intrude.

She didn't expect Lachlan to reserve the rest of his nights for her, but she would have appreciated Aislynn showing at least some consideration for the fact that her dad was involved in a relationship. Instead, it seemed to Finley that the opposite was true, because every time she was at Lachlan's house, his daughter just happened to find an excuse to drop by.

Tonight Aislynn had arrived as they were tidying up the kitchen after dinner. She claimed that she needed something for a school project and brushed right past them to head up the stairs to her bedroom.

She hadn't reappeared by the time dishes were put away, and Lachlan excused himself to participate in an online chat with the students in one of his summer classes.

Since he'd mentioned that there was ice cream for dessert, Finley opened the freezer to survey the options. She decided to go for the black cherry and began scooping it into a bowl.

She was nearly finished when Aislynn returned to the kitchen.

"Do you want some of this?" she asked, ready to give the girl her bowl and prepare another for herself.

Aislynn's only response was a scowl.

"I'll take that as a *no*," Finley said, putting the lid back on the container.

"I can get my own ice cream," the teenager said, removing a container of chocolate peanut butter cup from the freezer as Finley reached past her to replace the black cherry. "Where'd my dad go?"

"His office. He had an online chat scheduled with a group of students."

"A group of students? Or Zoe?"

Finley lifted a spoonful of ice cream to her mouth. "He said a group."

Aislynn dipped the scoop into the container of chocolate peanut butter cup. "Have you met Zoe?"

"I haven't met any of your dad's students." Though she'd been tempted to ask if she could hang out in his office during the chat—because she really liked how he looked in the glasses he only seemed to wear when he was reading or on the computer.

"Zoe's one of his grad students," Aislynn told Finley. "She's taken almost every course he teaches."

"I'd say that's a testament to his skill as a teacher."

"Or the fact that she's got a huge crush on him."

"Another possibility," Finley acknowledged.

"It doesn't bother you that another woman might be after my dad?"

"No. Because if your dad was interested in Zoe, he wouldn't be dating me."

"He might just be waiting for her to finish school," Aislynn said, adding another scoop of ice cream to her bowl. "So he can date her without getting fired."

"Would that make you happy?" Finley asked. "If he was dating Zoe instead of me?"

"As if you care what makes me happy."

"I don't want to be the cause of your unhappiness."

"Don't worry about it," Aislynn said. "You're not that important to me. Or my dad. You're just someone he's dating at this moment in time."

Finley dipped her spoon into her ice cream again. "Do they still teach Shakespeare in high school?"

"Yeah." Aislynn's gaze narrowed suspiciously. "Why?"

"I wondered if you might be familiar with the phrase, 'the lady doth protest too much.'"

The teen considered for a minute before responding, "That's from *Hamlet*, isn't it?"

Finley nodded.

Aislynn dropped the scoop in the sink and returned the container of ice cream to the freezer. "But what does that have to do with the price of Lego in Denmark?"

Finley appreciated the cleverness of her idiom. Lachlan's daughter was obviously smart—which made her a potentially dangerous rival. Finley had hoped they could be friends instead, but she wasn't going to keep setting herself up to be knocked down.

"It seems to me that if your dad had really had so many girlfriends, you wouldn't be so bothered by me being here."

"You don't know anything about my life or what bothers me."

"You're right," she agreed. "I just remember how I felt after my parents divorced, when my mom introduced us to her boyfriend. And how much I hated seeing her with anyone who wasn't my dad."

That revelation finally seemed to snag Aislynn's attention. "How old were you when your parents split?"

"Nine."

"I was three." She pulled a spoon out of the drawer and stuck it in her ice cream.

"Which might be even harder, because you likely can't even remember a time when they were together."

Aislynn lifted her chin. "They're always together. Every holiday and birthday and family event, they're together."

"Then you're lucky, because your mom and dad obviously put your needs first. Not all parents do."

Something else the girl obviously hadn't considered before now.

"Just some food for thought," Finley said, as Aislynn flounced out of the kitchen with her ice cream in hand.

"This is a nice surprise," Finley said, when she opened the door Tuesday night and found her stepmom standing there.

"You know you can send me away if it's a bad time."

"If that's a bottle of wine in your hand, it's definitely not a bad time."

Colleen chuckled as she stepped over the threshold. "Your dad's working late tonight, and I didn't see Lachlan's vehicle in your driveway, so I thought I'd take a chance that you were free."

While her mom uncorked the bottle, Finley set out some cheese and crackers and fruit to nibble on along with their wine.

They settled on the sofa in the living area and chatted casually for a few minutes, about some of Finley's recent events and her mom's volunteer work at the children's hospital.

"Something's on your mind," Colleen realized, when Finley had been silent for several minutes.

She shifted to face her stepmom. "I was just wondering if Haylee or me or Logan gave you a hard time when you were dating Dad?"

"Not at all," Colleen said. "And I'd braced myself for it—to be shunned and hated as a potential evil stepmom."

"That is how we depict second wives in fairy tales, isn't it?" Finley mused.

"Now, I'm not saying that Haylee and you and Logan didn't hate me behind my back, but you certainly never gave me any indication that I was unwelcome."

"I'm glad," Finley said sincerely. "Because you were the best thing that ever happened to Dad. And to us."

Colleen's eyes grew misty. "I feel exactly the same way about all of you. And I have no doubt that Lachlan's daughter will someday realize the same thing about you."

Finley sighed. "I wish I shared your confidence."

"She's giving you a hard time?" Colleen guessed.

"I can't blame her," Finley said. "She wants her mom and dad back together and sees me as an obstacle to that happening. I'd argue that the two-carat diamond on her mother's left hand is a bigger obstacle, but teenagers don't always think about things logically."

"And if she's always been daddy's little girl, then of course she sees you as a threat—especially if he hasn't dated much, and her mom is now remarrying."

"I don't know how much he dated, but I know he didn't usually introduce the women he dated to Aislynn."

"Which says something about the depth of his feelings for you."

She smiled and tipped her head back against Colleen's shoulder. "You really are the best mom."

"It's easy to be the best mom when you've got the best kids," Colleen replied.

Finley topped off their wine. "Can I ask you a personal question?"

"Of course."

"Did you and Dad ever consider having a baby of your own?"

Colleen nibbled on a grape. "As a matter of fact, we did."

"So why didn't it happen?"

"You mean, other than the fact that our hands were pretty full with the three kids we already had?"

It wasn't really an answer, and the way she didn't meet Finley's gaze told her that there was more to the story.

"Other than that," Finley said, pressing for more details.

Colleen tipped her head down to rest it on top of her daughter's. "The truth is, we did try. When Logan started school full-time, we decided it was the right time to add to our family. I got pregnant pretty quickly, and your dad and I were overjoyed.

"And then, at about seven weeks, I had severe pain in my abdomen. The doctor ordered an ultrasound and discovered it was an ectopic pregnancy.

"It wasn't a good time for me," Colleen admitted. "They managed to remove the fertilized egg and save my fallopian tube and promised I could try again. But I…struggled…afterward. So much so that, for several months, I couldn't care for the kids that I had. And when I finally got myself together, it seemed like too much of a risk to try again."

"I'm so sorry," Finley said sincerely.

"I was, too. But when my body healed… I realized your dad and you and your sister and brother were more of a family than I ever expected to have, and I know that I'm truly blessed."

"This seems to be the week for surprises," Finley noted, when Lachlan poked his head around the door of her office Wednesday afternoon.

"Taylor said it was okay to come back."

"To Taylor you will always be the sender of the cheesecake we gorged on, and she warned me that she'd snap you up in a second if she wasn't in a committed relationship."

"And if you hadn't snapped me up already," he said.

"I did do that, didn't I?"

"Yes, you did," he agreed, drawing her into his arms for a kiss.

"So what brings you out this way today?" she asked.

"I just wanted to see you. And to…" His words trailed off as he spotted the mail on her desk. "You got a postcard from Barcelona."

"Yeah." She glanced at the glossy image of the stunning La Sagrada Familia sitting on top of a pile of envelopes on the corner of her desk. "A lot of our clients send us postcards from their honeymoons or anniversary trips."

"Apparently they don't understand the purpose of a honeymoon," he noted dryly.

She rolled her eyes. "It only takes a few minutes to write a couple lines on the back of a postcard."

"But then you have to find a post office to buy a stamp and mail the card."

"Some people enjoy sharing information about their travels with friends and family back home."

"You mean some people like to show off that they're on vacation to those who aren't."

"And most people love getting postcards," she said, choosing to ignore his scathing remark.

"My grandparents were going to Spain as part of their European tour."

"I know," she said. "The postcard's from them."

"They sent *you* a postcard? They didn't send *me* a postcard."

"Probably because they figured you'd just toss it in a drawer."

"And you're planning to do something different with it?" he asked skeptically.

"We have a bulletin board in the conference room where we tack up all the cards our clients send to us. It's a tangible reminder to all of us at Gilmore Galas that what we do matters—maybe not to the world, but to the people who let us celebrate the important events in theirs."

"Speaking of events—I was wondering if you were free for dinner tonight."

"I'm not sure dinner qualifies as an event," she chided.

"It wasn't a good segue," he acknowledged. "But it is the reason I stopped by."

"To ask me if I was free for dinner tonight?"

He nodded. "I know it's short notice."

"It's also Wednesday," she pointed out.

"All day," he confirmed.

"You have dinner with Aislynn on Wednesdays."

"Also true."

"Did she bail on you for tonight?"

"No. In fact, it was her idea to invite you."

"And that wasn't a red flag for you?" she asked, her tone skeptical.

"Why would it be?"

"Because she doesn't like me."

"She doesn't *not* like you—she just doesn't know you. But if you have dinner with us tonight, it will give her a chance to get to know you. And for you to know her. Assuming you don't already have other plans, of course."

He was giving her an out.

If she didn't want to hang out with Lachlan and his daughter, she could simply say that she had a consult or an appointment or an event. And she was tempted to do so, because she was a little intimidated by Aislynn—embarrassing to admit but true nevertheless.

She was usually good with kids. She loved them and they loved her. The problem was, Aislynn wasn't a kid. She was a teenager, filled with angst and attitude like any other teenager, with an extra dose of attitude thrown in because she was the daughter of a single dad and understandably protective of that relationship.

But if Finley harbored any hopes of a potential future with

Lachlan—and she did—then she needed to not only get to know but get along with his daughter.

"What's on the menu?"

"Does it matter?"

"Not really," she decided. "But it might influence what I bring for dessert."

He grinned. "Aislynn is partial to cupcakes."

"Cupcakes it is."

Lachlan didn't blame Finley for being skeptical of his daughter's motives. He'd been a little taken aback himself when Aislynn suggested extending an invitation for her to have dinner with them. Prior to that she'd been...less than welcoming to the new woman in her father's life. Sometimes her attitude had been cool; other times it had bordered on hostile.

"Nobody likes change," Ethan had pointed out, when Lachlan expressed concern about his daughter's attitude toward Finley. "Add to that the fact that Aislynn's a teenager, with raging hormones and divorced parents, and it's understandable that she'd be resistant to welcoming someone new into your life."

But dinner had gone well. They'd had burgers and potato salad and then the cupcakes for dessert.

"Oh. My. God." Aislynn took another bite of the Black Forest cupcake she'd chosen from the assortment Finley offered. "I don't think I've ever tasted anything so good. Except maybe the cake at Great-Grandma and Great-Grandpa's anniversary party."

Finley smiled. "The cupcakes are from the same bakery."

"I'd love to get the cake for my birthday party from there," Aislynn said.

"That might not be in the budget," Lachlan warned.

Not wanting to get into the middle of a personal discussion, Finley got up to clear the table. Aislynn immediately jumped up to help her, but Lachlan insisted that he would take care of the cleanup so they could hang out and chat.

"I appreciate you letting me come for dinner tonight," Finley said, when Lachlan had disappeared into the kitchen. "I know your time with your dad is precious."

"It is," Aislynn agreed. "But I realized it's selfish of me to want to keep him all to myself when I'm going to be going away to college in a couple of years and he'll be on his own."

"That's very magnanimous of you," Finley said, not entirely sure she believed the girl's explanation but willing to give her the benefit of the doubt.

"Can I ask your opinion on something?" Aislynn asked, reaching into the bakery box for another cupcake.

"Of course," she immediately agreed, eager to grasp whatever olive branch Lachlan's daughter might be offering.

"I have to decide what kind of cake I want for my birthday, and I keep going back and forth between vanilla cake with raspberry mousse and chocolate cake with chocolate ganache."

"If you went with two tiers, you could have both," Finley said.

"I'd love that," Aislynn said. "But as you might have guessed from his earlier comment, Dad set a strict budget for the party and, based on prices I've seen posted on various websites, it's unlikely I can afford more than one tier."

"Cupcakes are always another option," Finley noted. "They're typically less costly, easier to serve, and they can be displayed to look like a cake."

Aislynn seemed to consider this. "These cupcakes are amazing, but cupcakes seem more middle school than high school."

"If you wouldn't think I was overstepping… I have some contacts through Gilmore Galas. I could maybe make some calls to inquire about a possible discount on your cake."

Blue eyes so much like Lachlan's went wide. "Really? You'd do that for me?"

"I'm not making any promises," Finley cautioned. "But I'm happy to see what I can do."

"That would be great. Thank you."

"Do you know how many guests you're going to have?"

They spent another hour discussing color schemes, decorations, flowers and food, after which Aislynn excused herself to finish her homework.

"What did you and Aislynn have your heads together about for so long?" Lachlan asked.

"She asked for some advice regarding her birthday party."

"She's not happy that I set a limit on the guest list—and the budget," he admitted.

"It's hard at that age," Finley noted. "Knowing her friends are going to be making comparisons and feeling as if there's no way her party is going to be as awesome as Kendra Thornton's."

"It's certainly not going to be as splashy," he agreed. "Her parents rented August Hall."

"There's one of those in every group," Finley noted.

"Did you have a friend like Kendra when you were a kid?"

"I knew girls like her," she confirmed. "But I was fortunate that my best friend was my sister."

"You hung out together at school?" he asked, surprised.

"It would have been strange if we didn't, considering we were in the same class."

"I thought she was older than you."

Finley nodded. "But only by eleven months. Her birthday is in January, mine is in December."

"December what?"

"Third," she said. "When's your birthday?"

"June fifteenth."

"That's in a couple of weeks," she noted.

"Yeah."

"Why didn't you tell me?"

"I just did," he pointed out.

"I meant, why didn't you tell me before now?" she clarified.

"Because I didn't want you to feel as if you had to make yourself available to celebrate with me."

"Maybe I want to celebrate with you."

"That's really not necessary," he told her.

"You already have plans," she realized.

"Not renting August Hall kind of plans," he said lightly. "Just the usual, low-key, family kind of plans."

"And you don't want me there."

"It's a Saturday. In June."

"I could make arrangements," she said, albeit not very convincingly.

"Which would only create more stress for you, and that's the last thing I want to do."

"Will you come over later that night—after your family celebration?" she asked hopefully.

"How many events do you have that day?"

"Just the Bracken-Ross wedding."

"That's your biggest one this summer, isn't it? With more than three hundred guests?"

"Close to four hundred," she admitted.

"You'll be exhausted."

"But I can sleep in on Sunday," she said. "It's one of those very rare summer Sundays when Gilmore Galas has nothing on the books."

"Then let's plan to do something Sunday," he suggested.

Lachlan was right. June fifteenth was a busy day. Still, Finley found herself occasionally peeking at her phone, because she was certain Aislynn would post photos on her Instagram account. And she was right.

When Lachlan said it was to be a family celebration, she'd

assumed that meant his daughter and maybe his parents. Possibly even his sisters and their families. And maybe they were there to celebrate with him, but in the dozen photos that Aislynn posted (#celebrating #bestdadintheworld #birthday #family), the only people she saw were Lachlan, his daughter and his ex-wife.

She was too busy to dwell on the pictures and speculate, but she couldn't seem to block the echo of Aislynn's words from the back of her mind.

They're always together. Every holiday and birthday and family event, they're together.

She texted Lachlan when she got home that night, to let him know it was okay if he wanted to come over. He didn't respond, which wasn't really a surprise considering that it was after midnight, but she was still disappointed.

So she got ready for bed, and she almost managed to convince herself that she didn't mind that he'd rather spend his birthday with his ex-wife than with her. Because she understood that Deirdre wasn't only Lachlan's ex-wife, she was the mother of his child. But when the knock sounded on the door, she knew it was a lie.

She wanted him to want to be with her. And she was so glad that he was here—because it meant that he'd chosen her.

She went to the door with a ready smile on her face.

Except it wasn't Lachlan she found at the threshold.

It was Mark.

Chapter Seventeen

"I like that kind of *hello*," Finley said against his lips, when Lachlan greeted her with a kiss the following morning.

"In that case, *hello* again," he said, and captured her mouth again.

He wrapped his arms around her and pulled her close, deepening the kiss. Her tongue danced and dallied with his as her scent, something fresh and distinctly Finley, stirred his blood and clouded his mind.

"You're out of bodywash, Fin."

The deep, undeniably masculine voice came from the hall, and Finley winced before she stepped out of Lachlan's arms—just as a towel-clad figure stepped into view.

"There's more in the cupboard under the sink," she responded to her apparent houseguest.

"I looked but couldn't find any."

"Then I guess I'll have to add it to my shopping list."

The mostly naked man deigned a glance in Lachlan's direction before commenting to Finley, "When I said I was up for a threesome, I was hoping you'd invite a girlfriend to come over."

"Don't be a dick, Mark," she admonished.

"Ah, the infamous Mark Nickel," Lachlan realized.

"Infamous?" Finley's ex echoed.

"Mark showed up here late last night and more than half-drunk, so I let him crash on the sofa," Finley explained.

"That's the story you're going with?" Mark said dubiously.

"It's the truth," she said, her gaze on Lachlan. "As you can see by the blanket and pillow on the sofa."

A neatly folded blanket and pillow, he noted. On top of which the cat was curled up, snoozing contentedly.

"It really doesn't look like anyone slept there," Mark remarked casually.

Finley glared at him. "I should never have opened the door when you showed up here last night."

Lachlan wanted to ask why she did, but he wasn't going to give her ex the satisfaction of questioning her in his presence.

She answered the unspoken question, anyway. "I only did because, when I heard the knock on the door, I thought— hoped—it might be you."

"You snooze, you lose, buddy." Mark's tone was smug.

Finley whirled to face him. "I will boot you out right now, wearing nothing but that towel, and call the *East Bay Times*."

He held up his hands in surrender. "I'm going to get dressed," he decided. "I have to head back to Los Angeles soon anyway."

"Good idea," Finley agreed.

"Would you really kick him out without letting him enjoy the breakfast you made for him?" Lachlan asked.

"I made breakfast for *you*," she said. "Pancakes."

He couldn't help but smile. "I have very fond memories of your...pancakes."

A faint flush colored her cheeks. "Why don't you help yourself to coffee while I get you a plate?"

He found a mug and filled it from the carafe on the warmer.

"Are those sprinkles in the pancakes?"

"Of course," she said. "That's how you know they're birthday pancakes and not just everyday pancakes."

"Do I get whipped cream, too?"

She lifted a brow. "For your pancakes?"

"Sure." He wrapped an arm around her waist and drew her close. "I could use it on the pancakes, too."

"Oh, honey, you didn't have to go to so much trouble," Mark said, striding back into the kitchen.

She smacked his hand when he reached for the pancake on top of the stack. "Those aren't for you, and you know it."

"I do prefer to avoid heavy carbs on game days," Mark confirmed, stealing a strip of crisp bacon from the tray on the table instead.

"That's not for you, either," she admonished.

"So how long have you two been together?" Mark directed the question to Lachlan.

"I don't see how that's any of your business," he replied evenly.

"Not long, I'm guessing," the other man continued. "Because you left her to sleep alone on a Saturday night, which suggests that you're not yet at the stage of regular weekend sleepovers."

"Ignore him," Finley said.

A honk sounded from the driveway.

"That's your Uber," she told Mark.

"I didn't order an Uber."

"That's why I did it for you."

"Okay, I can take a hint," he said, stealing another slice of bacon before heading to the door.

"I'm not so sure," she said.

But she walked him to the door and hugged him goodbye.

"So that's your ex," Lachlan mused when the man had finally gone and Finley returned to the kitchen.

She eyed him warily. "Not the only—or even the most recent—but probably the most recognizable one."

"Did you know he was in town?"

"He wasn't supposed to be in town. The Orioles are in Los

Angeles this weekend, but he hopped on a plane following their afternoon game yesterday."

"He just hopped on a plane and showed up at your door—confident that you'd let him in?"

"He's used to getting what he wants."

"And apparently that includes you."

"No." Finley shook her head. "It doesn't."

"Then why was he here?"

"I'd guess because he's been in a bit of a batting slump and trade rumors are swirling and he wanted his ego stroked."

"I don't think it's his ego he wanted stroked," Lachlan said dryly.

"He might be spoiled and self-absorbed, but I don't believe for a minute that he'd cheat on his wife."

"And yet he showed up here in the middle of the night."

"Because he knew that I'd deflect any passes he made."

Which seemed to confirm that the man had made passes.

Lachlan clenched his teeth.

"If he'd really wanted to step out on his wife, he would have stayed in LA and crooked a finger at a ball bunny or walked into a downtown sports bar."

"Do you really think it would be that easy?" he asked dubiously.

"I know it would," Finley assured him. "Because I saw the way women threw themselves at him when we were dating—even when I was right there."

"That must have sucked."

She shrugged it off.

He should have taken that as a hint to change the subject, but there was one more question that he needed to ask.

"Were you in love with him?"

She sighed. "You're not going to let this go, are you?"

"I'm only asking because I care about you and it occurred to me that I really don't know much about your past."

"Because it's not relevant to our present," she told him.

"Or maybe it is," he countered.

"Okay, if you really want to know—we were talking about a future together, and we wouldn't have been having that conversation if I hadn't believed I was in love with him."

"Then he got traded," Lachlan guessed.

"Then he *asked* to be traded," she clarified.

"And you didn't want to go to New York with him?"

"I wasn't invited."

He frowned at that. "But if you were talking about a future together—"

"He asked for the trade because he realized he was still in love with his ex-girlfriend—now his wife—who'd moved to Baltimore for a job."

"Oh."

"Yeah."

"I'm sorry."

She shrugged again. "Anyway, thank you for not fighting with me in front of Mark."

"Are we supposed to be fighting?" he asked curiously.

"I don't think it's necessary, but I thought it might be inevitable."

"I can't say I was happy to find him here, but you've never given me any reason not to trust you," he pointed out. "Besides, if you'd really tangled the sheets with him, I doubt very much you would have opened the door for me while he was in the shower."

"A very reasonable analysis of the situation."

"Don't get me wrong, when I saw him strutting around in that towel, I had some very unreasonable thoughts that might have involved my fist and his face."

That revelation seemed to surprise her. "You would have fought for me?"

"Absolutely," he said. "I mean, he's a professional athlete

and I'm a college professor, so I probably would have lost. Badly. But I'd have given it my best effort."

She kissed him lightly. "Thank you for that."

"Can I have my pancakes now?"

"I have a better idea," she said, picking up his plate. "What do you say to breakfast in bed?"

He grinned. "I say, don't forget the whipped cream."

Over the next few weeks, Lachlan spent more nights in Finley's bed than his own. In fact, he was at her place so much that he'd half-jokingly suggested moving his bed, so that they'd have more room for their nocturnal activities. Unfortunately, Finley nixed that idea, pointing out that a king-size bed wouldn't leave room in her room for anything else.

He didn't really mind her bed—and it certainly wasn't a hardship to snuggle up with her—he just wished she wasn't so opposed to sleeping at his place. He understood that she had concerns about Aislynn seeing her vehicle parked in his driveway overnight, but he suspected that she was even more uncomfortable with the possibility of facing his ex-wife over coffee again in the morning—despite his assurances that Deirdre hadn't used her key since the incredibly awkward morning after the first night Finley had stayed at his place.

So he was fast asleep in Finley's bed when his phone vibrated against the nightstand, jolting him awake. (He never activated "do not disturb" mode because he wanted to be sure that Aislynn could always reach him—anytime day or night.)

Beside him, Finley remained thankfully undisturbed.

And naked.

He loved that she slept in the nude, because he loved sleeping with her bare skin against his—and not because they were sharing body heat.

But he pushed those thoughts aside now, because middle-of-the-night text messages were rarely a good thing, and a chill of trepidation snaked down his spine as he reached for his phone.

Are you there?

Those three words identified the sender of the text even before he saw Deirdre's name above the message. His daughter never spelled out a word when a single letter would do.

But, of course, there was only one reason he could think of for his ex-wife to be reaching out in the early hours of the morning.

Aislynr?

She's fine. Sleeping.

His heart rate slowed to something approximating a normal rhythm.

What's up?

The three dots hovered on his screen, as if she was typing a really long reply. Then they disappeared, suggesting that she'd deleted her message. Finally she responded:

I just really need a friend right now.

He wanted to ask where Philip was.

Shouldn't her fiancé be the man that she turned to when something was bothering her in the middle of the night?

But he and Deirdre had been there for each other through all the highs and lows and milestone events over the past eighteen years, and he couldn't turn his back on her now.

On my way.

Of course, he had to find his clothes before he could dress—
not an easy task in the dark when they were scattered all over
the floor, a testament to the haste with which he'd shed them
in his eagerness to get into bed with Finley.

He heard her shift now, and the sound of her hand sliding
over the sheet as she reached for him.

"Lachlan?" she murmured sleepily.

"Sorry. I didn't mean to wake you."

Finley lifted herself on an elbow to peer at the glowing
numbers on the clock on her bedside table.

2:18.

"What are you doing?"

"Looking for my sock."

"Why?"

"Because I have to go." He stood up to fasten his jeans.

"If you were the type to skip out in the middle of the night,
I would have expected it to happen the first time we slept together, not three months later."

"I'm not skipping out," he denied. "I got a text message
from Deirdre—"

She was immediately wide awake. "Is Aislynn okay?"

"She's fine," he said.

Finley exhaled a sigh of relief. Though she and Aislynn had
gotten off to a rocky start, she thought they'd made progress
in recent weeks and even bonded—kind of—during their extended discussions about her birthday party.

"So what's the problem?" she asked now.

"Can we talk about this in the morning? I mean, later in
the morning—when I have the answers to your questions?"

"Let me get this straight…you have to go because your ex-
wife sent you a text message and you're not even sure what
the supposed crisis is?"

"I know she needs a friend," he said.

"You're serious," she realized.

He'd apparently located the errant sock, because he sat on the edge of the mattress to tug it on. "Why are you upset?"

"Are you honestly asking me why I'm upset that the man I'm sleeping with is running off, in the middle of the night, to be with another woman? And not just any woman, but his ex-wife with whom he clearly has a dysfunctional codependent relationship."

"You know it's not like that," he chided. "Dee and I have a history."

"As if I could forget."

He scooped his keys off the dresser, then hesitated. "If you really don't want me to go . . ."

She waved a hand. "Go. Be your ex-wife's knight in shining armor—you're good at that."

He leaned down to brush a quick kiss over her lips. "I'll call you later."

She wished she could tell him not to bother, but there was no point in fighting with him at two o'clock in the morning. She didn't want to fight with him at all, but she didn't know that she could tolerate always coming in second place to the ex-wife of the man she loved.

Because she could no longer deny that she'd fallen in love with Lachlan.

And even if she hadn't said the words to him, she couldn't ignore the yearning in her heart.

A yearning for more.

For a commitment. A future. A family.

Her desire for those things wasn't new—she'd wanted them for a long time. But now she wanted them *with Lachlan*.

But she was afraid to tell him. Afraid that he might not want the same things. Or maybe not with her.

Mark had told her he loved her, but he'd loved his ex-girlfriend more.

Lachlan hadn't made any declarations, and he still ran to Deirdre when she called.

Once again, Finley was in second place.

She honestly didn't mind taking a backseat to his daughter. In fact, his commitment to his relationship with Aislynn was one of the things she loved about him.

But she resented playing second fiddle to his former spouse.

For just once in her life, she wanted to be with someone who put her first.

Deirdre met Lachlan at the door, her face streaked with mascara and tears.

"What happened?" he asked, automatically enfolding her in his embrace.

She sobbed against this chest. "Philip and I...we had a big fight."

He'd never seen her so distraught and felt a surge of protectiveness rise up inside him. "What do you mean by a big fight? Tell me what happened."

Deirdre drew in a shuddery breath. "Ever since we got engaged, he's been pressuring me to set a wedding date and... I'm just not ready. So tonight I finally told him that, and he said that if I didn't actually want to marry him, why did I accept his proposal?

"I said maybe I shouldn't have and I gave him back his ring and...and he left." Her voice broke and she buried her face against his chest again. "He just tucked it into his pocket and walked out...without so much as a backward glance."

Lachlan drew back to look at her. "Are you telling me that you texted me—*in the middle of the night*—because you had a tiff with your fiancé?"

"Didn't you hear what I said? It was more than a tiff. I gave him back the ring. He left."

"Jesus, Dee. I thought something really bad had happened."

"He. Left," she said again.

"And he'll come back."

"How do you know?"

"Because he loves you."

Her eyes filled with fresh tears.

"Tell me," he said to her now. "Why did you accept Philip's proposal?"

She sniffled. "Because I love him."

"So maybe that's what you should have told him when he asked the question?" Lachlan suggested.

"Maybe." She rubbed the wet streaks on her cheeks with the heels of her hands and let out a long sigh. "He accused me of still being in love with you."

"And to prove him wrong, the first thing you did when he walked out was…call me?"

"Nobody else knows me the way you do."

"Probably because you don't overshare with anyone else the way you do with me."

"I don't overshare."

"Yeah, you do. But that's not the point. The point is that you've been with Philip for more than three years, and it's past time you opened up and let him know what you're afraid of."

"Who said I'm afraid?"

"I did. And I know that you are because I know you."

"Maybe Philip's right. Maybe I'm still clinging to hope that you and I might get back together."

"You're not," he told her.

"I loved you once," Deirdre said.

"I'm not sure you ever really did."

"I married you, didn't I?"

"We got married because we thought it was the right thing to do. But it wasn't. Not for you, not for me, and not for Aislynn. We made each other miserable."

She sighed again. "We did, didn't we?"

"The best thing we ever did—after having Aislynn—was get divorced."

"So why am I so reluctant to marry a man that I really do love?"

"Because you're afraid that you might get it wrong again. Because being with someone without that formal commitment—even being engaged and living together—isn't quite the same. It doesn't carry the same weight of expectation or the same risk of failure.

"And I suspect that's why he wants to marry you," Lachlan continued. "Because marriage is more. Making promises in front of your family and friends makes it more. It makes it real."

"Are you afraid, too?" she asked him.

"We're not talking about me," he said.

"Maybe we should."

"You were the one who called me in the midst of a crisis," he reminded her.

"And you're the one who came running," she countered.

"Because you said you needed me."

"I did say that. Because whenever I've encountered an obstacle in my life, I've turned to you. And for eighteen years, you've let me.

"And it has to stop," she decided, sounding uncharacteristically determined. "We've been in a codependent relationship for too long."

"That's eerily similar to what Finley said," he admitted. "Though she added the word dysfunctional."

"Well, she's right. And you're lucky to have her in your life."

"Yes, I am. Though she wasn't too happy when I told her I was coming over here tonight."

Deirdre's brows lifted. "You were with Finley when I texted?"

"Yeah."

She shook her head. "For a smart man, you really are an idiot sometimes."

"Are you saying that I should have ignored your message?"

"Yes." She sighed. "But also that I shouldn't have sent the message."

She picked up her phone.

"Who are you texting now?"

"Philip."

"It's after three o'clock in the morning," he felt compelled to point out to her.

"I need him to know that I want my ring back. And that I want to get married before the end of the year."

Only seconds after sending her message, she got a reply.

She smiled. "He's on his way."

"Then I should be on mine," he said. "I don't think your fiancé would be too happy to find me here when he gets back."

"Probably not," she agreed. "But I'm going to tell him that we talked. I don't want any secrets between us."

He kissed her forehead. "Congratulations on your upcoming nuptials."

"I'll make sure you get an invitation. Hey, do you think—"

"No," he told her.

Soft laughter followed behind him as he walked out the door.

Finley was distracted during her morning meeting with the linen rental company. Thankfully, the vendor didn't have an opportunity to notice, because Julia took the lead in the discussion to adjust the terms of their current contract. But the fact that Julia had taken the lead told Finley that her friend was aware of her preoccupation.

At the end of the meeting, smiles and handshakes were exchanged all around, then Julia escorted the vendor out. Finley didn't dare breathe a sigh of relief, because she knew that her friend would return with questions.

When she did, she also brought two mugs of coffee.

"I thought you could use this," Julia said, setting one of the mugs in front of Finley.

"Thanks."

Her friend sat across from her and sipped her own coffee. "I dropped the ball today. I'm sorry."

"The ball didn't drop," Julia said.

"Because you didn't let it."

"Because we're a team."

Finley stared at the dark liquid in her cup. "I hate not being at the top of my game."

"I know," her friend commiserated.

"I should be able to keep my personal life separate and apart from business—and when I'm at work, I need to focus on work."

"That's a great theory," Julia said. "But it doesn't translate to the real world, because we're people, not machines, and people have feelings and feelings are messy."

"Maybe too messy."

"Do you want to tell me what he did?"

Finley gave her friend a brief summary of her middle-of-the-night argument with Lachlan. "It seemed like a huge deal last night," she confided. "But now, in the light of day, I wonder if maybe I overreacted."

"Really?" Julia said. "Because I think you *under*reacted. If that had been my boyfriend, I would have told him that if he walked out the door, he shouldn't ever expect to walk in it again."

Finley had wanted to say something very much along those lines—to force him to make a choice. But in the end, she'd been afraid to give him that kind of ultimatum. Afraid that he still would have chosen Deirdre over her.

"But maybe your professor is smart enough to have seen the error of his ways, no ultimatums required," Julia mused.

Finley followed her friend's gaze to where Lachlan was standing in the doorway.

Julia stood up with her coffee. "Should I finish this in my office?"

She directed the question to Finley, letting her know that she'd stay to provide backup if her friend needed it.

Finley gave a small nod of assent and Julia headed to the door.

Lachlan took a couple of steps further into the room. "I know you're probably tired of hearing me say that I'm sorry, so I'll tell you that I'm glad I went to see Deirdre last night, because we had a long overdue talk about some things—most notably our dysfunctional codependent relationship."

"Okay," she said cautiously.

"The bottom line is that she's always going to be part of my life because she's the mother of my child. And I can appreciate that it's inconvenient and maybe even frustrating to have to factor my daughter and my ex-wife into our plans, but if we're going to be together, that's something we're going to have to deal with on occasion.

"And I really want us to be together. When I'm with you, it's because I want to be with you. And when I'm not with you, I'm thinking about you and wishing I could be with you, and I'm sorry if at any point in time—and especially last night— I ever gave you reason to think otherwise."

"It's kind of hard to stay mad after an apology like that," Finley admitted.

"Does that mean I'm forgiven?" he asked hopefully.

"You're forgiven," she confirmed.

He took her hands and drew her to her feet, then lowered his head and brushed his mouth over hers. "Now we've officially kissed and made up."

"Not quite."

He drew back to look at her quizzically.

"The only good thing about fighting is the make-up sex that follows."

His gaze slid to the conference table.

She laughed. "No. Still no locks on the doors." She glanced at her watch. "Plus, I have another appointment in twenty minutes."

"And I'm definitely going to need more time than that," he promised.

Finley smiled. "I finish at eight tonight."

"I'll pick up the pizza."

Chapter Eighteen

Lachlan was on his way home, thinking about his plans with Finley for the night ahead, when his mom called.

"I need a favor," Marilyn Kellett said without preamble.

"Good thing it's my day off," he noted.

"That is why I'm calling you," she confirmed. "I need you to pick up your grandparents from the airport."

"I can do that."

"I told them that I'd be there, but I've been working with a couple who have viewed the same property in Hunter's Point three times and are finally ready to make an offer. The seller's agent is expecting another one to come in tomorrow, so I want to get in first."

"No worries," he assured her. "Just text me their flight information and I'll be there."

He'd had some reservations when his grandparents first mentioned their plan to tour Europe in celebration of their six-tieth anniversary. After all, his grandfather was eighty-one and his grandmother two years older than him. But they'd both remained active since their retirement—Douglas golfed at least twice a week, and Catherine participated in water aerobics—and were determined to celebrate in a big way.

"How was Europe?" Lachlan asked, after they'd exchanged hugs at the arrivals gate.

"Je suis tombé amoureux à Paris," she told him.

"You fell in love *in* Paris?"

She frowned. "*Avec* Paris?"

"*De* Paris," he said. *"Vous êtes tombé amoureux de Paris."*

"Show-off," she grumbled.

He grinned. "I'm happy to see you, too. And pleased to know that you had a good time."

"It was fabulous," his grandfather chimed in. "And something we both wish we'd done twenty years ago."

"Twenty years ago, you weren't retired," Lachlan pointed out.

"Fifteen years ago then," Douglas amended.

"In any event, we're already planning our next trip," his wife said.

"Well, hopefully you're going to stay put for at least a few weeks. I'm not sure Aislynn would forgive you if you missed her sixteenth birthday."

"Of course, we wouldn't miss her birthday. Are you planning a big party?"

"We're planning a party," he confirmed. "The size and other details are still being negotiated."

"You should get in touch with Finley Gilmore at Gilmore Galas," Catherine suggested, then she frowned. "But summer is prime wedding season, so she might not be able to fit another event into her schedule.

"Still, you should call her anyway," she decided. "She's really a lovely girl and I was so disappointed that I didn't get a chance to introduce you at our anniversary party."

"I appreciate the thought," Lachlan told her. "But I don't need my grandmother to introduce me to women."

"Apparently you do," she said. "Because as far as I know, you haven't dated anyone since Victoria and that was…how many years ago?"

"Four," he admitted.

"Four years." She shook her head. "Now I'm not naïve

enough to believe that there haven't been other women in that time, but clearly no one that you liked well enough to introduce to your family."

"Catherine." Her husband's tone was both admonishing and indulgent.

"I know you think I'm interfering—"

"You *are* interfering."

"—but I only want our grandson to find someone special to share his life with. To someday travel Europe with, strolling hand in hand across Tower Bridge, picnicking in Jardin des Tuileries, making love all night to the sound of the waves in Torre del Mar."

"Way too much information," Lachlan told her.

"I don't know why young people always think they're the only ones who get to have any fun."

"I never thought any such thing," he assured her. "But I wouldn't mind a change in the topic of conversation."

"You're the one who said you wanted to hear all the details of our trip," she reminded him.

"Have some pity on the boy and stick to the PG details," her husband suggested.

"Alright," she relented. "Why don't you tell us what's new with you, Lachlan?"

"Well, apparently you'll be surprised to hear this, but I've been dating someone."

"Why didn't you say something?" his grandmother demanded.

"Probably because he couldn't get a word in edgewise," Douglas said.

Catherine scowled at her husband before turning her attention back to her grandson. "So tell us now. What's her name? Where did you meet her? And when I am going to get to meet her?"

"If you promise to stop the interrogation right now, I might be persuaded to introduce you to her at Aislynn's birthday party."

She fell silent, but she grinned the rest of the drive home.

It felt strange, showing up at Deirdre's house, even if she was an invited guest. It might have been a little less awkward, Finley mused, if she'd been able to arrive with Lachlan. But he'd wanted to be there early, and she'd needed to do an airport pickup.

Transportation needs were usually handled by a car service, but this particular father of the bride required a personal touch. While the bride insisted that she wasn't particularly worried about his arrival, that was only because she'd been let down so many times by her father that she didn't actually expect him to show. In fact, she'd made alternate arrangements for a favorite uncle to walk her down the aisle in his absence.

It was a testament to the groom's affection for his bride that he'd made all the arrangements for his future father-in-law's travel and a personal plea to Finley to get him to the church on time for tonight's rehearsal. Once the father of the bride had been delivered to the church and the rehearsal had begun, Finley left Rachel in charge and slipped away to Aislynn's birthday party.

Of course, she was one of the last guests to arrive, forcing her to park halfway down the block, as Deirdre's circular driveway was already overflowing with vehicles. After she parked, she picked up the "bouquet" she'd brought for Aislynn. Wrapped in floral paper were sixteen cardstock "daisies," each with a gift card holder on the back. Finley hadn't gone overboard—she didn't want it to appear as if she was trying to buy Aislynn's affection—but she'd discovered, through conversations with Lachlan and his daughter, where the birthday girl liked to shop or hang out or grab a bite to eat, and so each daisy offered a unique surprise.

Deirdre answered the door herself when Finley rang the bell.

"You made it," Aislynn's mother said, sounding genuinely pleased to see her. "Come in, come in."

She led the way through the house to a wall of French doors that opened up onto a back deck as wide as the house and equally deep. The railing around the perimeter had built-in planters at six-foot intervals, and the royal palms that grew out of the planters had been wrapped for the occasion in twinkling lights, while more twinkling lights had been suspended above the deck to create a ceiling that looked as if it was made of starlight.

An arch of white and pink balloons stood over the gift and cake tables at one end of the deck, and a second marked the location of the food and drink stations at the other. Standing tables were draped with white cloths and wrapped with bows of pink tulle, and at the center of each table was a clear glass jar filled with white and pink peonies.

"The gift table is over there," Deirdre said, gesturing. "But I really wish you hadn't brought anything."

"I was hardly going to show up to a birthday party empty-handed."

"But you've already done so much, using your contacts and connections to help us put this party together—and keep us on budget."

"That was my pleasure," Finley said.

"I really do think you mean that," Deirdre said. "But honestly, it was a lot more work than I'd anticipated, and it gave me a whole new level of appreciation for what you do."

"Well, everything looks absolutely stunning."

"I was pleased," Deirdre agreed. "But more important, Aislynn was blown away."

"Where is the birthday girl?"

Deirdre pointed to a group of six girls near the cake table. "There's my baby," she said. "All grown up."

"You must be so proud."

"I am. I can't take all the credit, though. Lachlan has been there every step of the way. But, of course, you know that already."

"She's lucky to have both of you," Finley said sincerely.

"She's lucky, too, to have a solid group of friends, most of whom have been close since grade school." Deirdre then proceeded to identify Harmony, Kendra, Gabby, Sofia and Joy.

"And I swear Lachlan was around here just a minute ago," Deirdre said.

"Don't worry," Finley said. "I'll find him."

"Bryan and Marilyn are here somewhere, too," she said, naming Lachlan's parents. "And Catherine and Douglas are on their way. And this—" she said, as a man with sandy brown hair and warm brown eyes joined them "—is my fiancé, Philip Cohen."

Philip offered his hand. "You must be Finley."

"I am," she confirmed.

"You're also empty-handed," he noted. "What can I get you to drink?"

"Oh. Um…" She glanced around, not sure what her options were.

"There's nonalcoholic punch, which is what most of the kids are drinking," Deirdre said. "And an adult version with a little bit of a kick. We've also got champagne, soft drinks and sparkling water."

"I think I'll stick with the nonalcoholic punch," Finley said. "There's a slim chance that I might have to duck out to an event and a certainty that I'll have to drive home later."

"Champagne for me," Deirdre said.

"I'll be right back," Philip promised.

Deirdre watched him go, a look of pure adoration on her face that surprised Finley a little. Because Deirdre was a stunningly beautiful woman while her fiancé was handsome enough but not the type of man who, in a crowded room, would draw a woman's eye.

Not like Lachlan, who she'd been drawn to from the very first.

But where the heck was he?

When Philip returned with the promised drinks, Finley thanked him and excused herself, not wanting the couple to feel as if they needed to babysit her.

She added her gift to the pile on the table, then approached the group of teens that included the guest of honor. "I don't want to interrupt," Finley said, "but I did want to wish Aislynn a happy sweet sixteen."

"Thank you," Lachlan's daughter said, before deliberately turning to face one of her friends.

Ouch, Finley thought, and was about to walk away again when Kendra spoke to her.

"I don't think we've met," she said, in a much friendlier tone than the birthday girl had used. "Are you a friend of Aislynn's mom or her dad?"

Aislynn jumped in to answer the question before Finley could. "Finley's the party planner."

So much for thinking they'd bonded.

"Finley Gilmore," she introduced herself with a smile, determined to ignore the sense of betrayal evoked by Aislynn's words.

"As in Gilmore Galas?" Joy looked at Finley with renewed interest.

"You've heard of it?"

"Are you kidding? Since the Memorial Day party for Reese Scott at Venice Beach, *everyone's* heard of Gilmore Galas," Kendra said, dropping the name of a chart-topping pop star.

"I did a Memorial Day party at Venice Beach," Finley confirmed. "But it wasn't for Reese Scott."

"But she was there," Sofia insisted. "And she posted a ton of pics on Insta."

That part was true, and for a whole week after that event, Finley and her colleagues had barely been able to keep up with the requests and queries that had come into the office at Gilmore Galas.

"I saw those pictures," Harmony chimed in, sounding suitably impressed.

Aislynn stood by sullenly while her friends peppered Finley with questions about the event and the pop star. She was obviously annoyed that they were paying more attention to "the party planner" than the guest of honor, and while the situation was of her own making, Finley didn't want to be the cause of any distress for Lachlan's daughter—especially not on such a special occasion.

"It was nice meeting you all," she said, extricating herself from the group. "But I need to check on something in the kitchen."

She headed back toward the house, but she hadn't made it more than half a dozen steps before Lachlan caught up with her.

"There you are," he said, offering her a smile that warmed everything inside her.

"Here I am," she confirmed.

"Everything go okay with the airport run and the rehearsal?"

"Father of the bride did indeed arrive as scheduled and the rehearsal was just getting started when I snuck away."

"Does that mean you're free for the rest of the evening?"

She held up crossed fingers.

"Good," he said. "Because I have plans…"

"Don't look now, but your dad's flirting with the party planner," Harmony said.

"I'm definitely *not* looking," Aislynn assured her, though she couldn't resist sneaking a glance in their direction.

"Wait a minute," Harmony said now. "She's not just the

party planner, is she? She's your dad's new girlfriend. The one you said you walked in on him kissing."

"Yeah." She wouldn't have admitted it in front of Gabby, Sofia and Joy, but they'd wandered off to the food table, leaving her with only Harmony and Kendra, and they were her very best friends. The ones she didn't have any secrets from.

"So why didn't you say that she was his girlfriend?" Kendra asked.

She shrugged.

"Well, anyway, she seems really nice."

Aislynn shot her traitorous friend a look.

"I'm just saying—maybe you shouldn't be so quick to judge," Kendra said. "Especially considering that she knows people."

"I don't *not* like her," Aislynn said. "I just don't think she's right for my dad."

Kendra glanced over at the couple, whose heads were bent close together. They weren't actually holding hands, but Aislynn's dad was stroking the back of Finley's hand with his fingertips, a subtle caress that somehow seemed even more intimate.

"Obviously he disagrees," she said.

Aislynn turned away. "I'm going to get some more punch."

"Me, too," Harmony said, immediately falling into step beside her.

"Ignore Kendra," Harmony said, when they were far enough away that their friend wouldn't overhear them. "She only thinks she's an expert about this stuff because she's got a new stepmother."

A twenty-two-year-old gold digger, according to what Aislynn overheard her mom telling a friend.

"At least I know Finley isn't after my dad's money, because he's not rich."

"No, but he's hot," Harmony said.

"Eww."

"I mean, for an old guy," her friend was quick to clarify.

"Still *eww*," Aislynn told her.

"Did I tell you how much I love all the fairy lights?" Harmony asked, obviously desperate to change the topic of conversation. "They make the deck look magical."

Finley's idea, Aislynn remembered.

But almost everything had been the party planner's idea. The lights, the balloons, the flowers, the cake. Finley had spent a lot of time talking to Aislynn—and later her mom, too—about what she wanted for her party, and then she'd helped make it all happen.

But that was her job, wasn't it?

So Aislynn hadn't been lying when she said Finley was the party planner.

But she hadn't been telling the whole truth, either.

She'd treated Finley badly and now she had knots in her stomach and it wasn't fair.

It was *her* birthday.

And not just any birthday—her sweet sixteen.

A special occasion, her mother insisted. A day that was supposed to be all about celebrating her.

But suddenly Aislynn wasn't in a party mood anymore.

Finley would be lying if she said that Aislynn's dismissive attitude didn't hurt. But she understood. She'd been that sixteen-year-old girl once, eager for parental attention and peer approval, desperate to feel as if she mattered.

And it didn't bother her to take a step back, to focus on helping with the party and support Aislynn's designation of her as the hired help. She appreciated that Lachlan tried to stick close, but the fact was, most of the people here were his friends—or at least parents of his daughter's friends that he'd known for years—and it was inevitable that he'd be drawn away to have a word with this person or confer with that one.

But he introduced her to Ethan and Steph—who were friends as well as colleagues of his at Merivale College—and, within five minutes, she felt as if she'd known them forever. She also spent some time chatting with his parents, who were both genuinely lovely people, and then with Catherine and Douglas, when they arrived.

Lachlan's grandparents were understandably surprised to find Finley in attendance at the party—and then overjoyed to discover that she was the mystery woman their grandson was dating.

"I knew you two would hit it off," Catherine said smugly.

"But you didn't know they'd hit it off before you had a chance to maneuver them together," Douglas remarked.

"Which proves that fate wields an even stronger hand than a grandmother."

"Unless that grandmother has a wooden spoon in hers," Lachlan said, wincing as he rubbed his derriere.

"Don't you dare," Catherine admonished, shaking her finger at him. "I *never* paddled your bottom with my wooden spoon."

"But you threatened often enough."

"And those threats kept you in line, didn't they?" she said.

Finley smiled, enjoying their banter, proof of the easy and sincere affection between Lachlan and his grandparents.

Before he could respond to Catherine's question, Deirdre came by to steal Lachlan away "for just a minute." It was the third such interruption in the forty minutes that had passed since his grandparents' arrival.

"You're being an awfully good sport about his ex-wife," Catherine remarked to Finley, after she'd sent her husband off to refill her glass of punch.

"I'm trying," she said. "The fact that I actually like Deirdre makes it a little easier."

"They've been partners in raising their daughter since she was born, so they don't always think about how other people fit into the equation—or even realize that they should."

"There have been a few bumps," Finley acknowledged. "But so far, nothing that's really thrown us off course."

"I'm glad to hear that," his grandmother said. "Because I've known Lachlan since he drew his first breath, and in all his years, I've never seen him as smitten with any other woman as he is with you. And it makes my heart happy to see that you're just as smitten with him."

"Is it that obvious?" Finley asked worriedly.

"Maybe not to everyone," Catherine said. "But a woman in love can recognize another."

"After three glasses of punch, I'm a woman in need of a bathroom."

His grandmother chuckled softly. "While you head off in search of one of those, I'm going to see where my husband is with my drink."

On her way back to the party, Finley took a wrong turn and found herself in what she imagined the architect of the home had referred to as a family room to distinguish it from the more formal living room she'd passed by earlier. This one was filled with comfortable-looking furnishings grouped around a massive flat screen TV, but what caught her eye was the array of framed photographs on the mantel of the fireplace.

She couldn't help smiling as she examined the photos of Aislynn through the years. Finley knew that every mom thought hers was the most beautiful baby in the world, but she suspected that Lachlan and Deirdre's daughter might actually have been worthy of that crown. Even as an infant, she'd been a gorgeous child, with dark wispy curls and big blue eyes.

There was a "First Day of Kindergarten" photo. A picture of Aislynn in a soccer uniform with a ball tucked under her arm and a wide grin that showed her front two teeth missing.

Then a "First Disney Trip" snapshot, with the little girl wearing Minnie Mouse ears and flanked by both of her parents. Fast forward a few more years, and there was Aislynn with her hair in a tight chignon, wearing a pink leotard and tutu. And then a more recent photo of her lounging against a doorjamb with a bass clarinet in hand.

"Did you get lost?" Deirdre teased from the doorway.

"I took a wrong turn," she admitted. "And then I got nosy."

The other woman smiled. "If I didn't want guests looking at the photos, I wouldn't have them lined up on the mantel."

"Did you take these?"

"Most of them."

"You've got an eye for photography."

"A hobby." Deirdre shrugged. "I have lots of hobbies, no real vocation. What's the saying—jack of all trades but master of none?"

Finley smiled—then her attention was snagged by a framed pencil sketch hanging on the wall.

"Do you dabble in art, too?"

"Goodness, no. Even paint-by-numbers are beyond me."

"So who did the sketch?"

"Oh. That was done by some street artist in Seattle when Lachlan and I were on our honeymoon."

"Dee?" Philip beckoned her from the doorway. "The birthday girl wants pictures with her parents before cake."

"On my way," she promised, following him out of the room.

Finley knew that she should go, too. Instead, she took a step closer to the drawing, her attention snagged by the date below the artist's scrawled signature.

Lachlan found her in that exact spot half an hour later.

"I've been looking all over for you," he said, offering her a plate with a wedge of vanilla cake with raspberry mousse filling. "What are you doing in here?"

"Developing an appreciation for art."

"You'd be better off at the Franklin Bowles Gallery," he told her. "Deirdre's taste is somewhat pedestrian."

"Interesting that you'd say that, because I got the impression her taste was similar to yours."

He followed her gaze to the sketch on the wall and winced.

"In fact, that looks like an exact replica of the infinity symbol inked on your shoulder."

"Actually, the tattoo is a replica of—never mind," he decided.

"I read the date as August second—assuming the standard format of month followed by day—which you said was Aislynn's birthday. And yes, I know it is. But the date is actually spelled out on the sketch as Feb 8."

"What do you want me to say?"

"I want you to tell me the truth—is February eighth your wedding date?"

"Yes."

The single word landed like a blow to her stomach. She closed her eyes, struggling to draw in a breath after all the air had been knocked out of her.

"God, I feel like such a fool."

"I didn't intend to mislead you," he said. "You asked me about the significance of August second, which *is* Aislynn's birthday."

"How convenient for you."

"And I realized, as soon as I said it, that I should clarify, but then…"

"Then *what*?" she demanded.

"Then you dropped to your knees in front of me in the shower and every other thought slipped out of my head."

Her cheeks burned. "So it's my fault?"

"No. Of course not. I'm just saying that there were…circumstances."

"You've had plenty of opportunities since then to tell me the truth, but you didn't."

"Because I didn't want to make it seem like a bigger deal than it is."

"The date you married your ex-wife is inked on your shoulder—I'd say that's a pretty big deal."

"Come on, Finley. It's not as if I'm your first boyfriend."

"No, you're not. But I didn't marry any of my previous boyfriends or have a child with any of them, and I certainly didn't tattoo my body with dates significant to our relationship."

"We were young and stupid," he told her. "Each of us barely twenty years old and expecting a baby. On top of that, Deirdre was freaking out about the fact that she was going to get fat and end up with stretch marks, so she wanted me to have a permanent memento too."

"I understand why you got the tattoo," Finley said. "What I don't understand is why you still have it—and why you lied to me about it."

"Because it's a lot easier to remove a wedding band than body ink."

She shook her head, not sure whether she was feeling completely humiliated or just really angry. "All this time, I thought it was your ex-wife who couldn't let go. Now I know it's you."

Chapter Nineteen

"And then she walked out on me."

"That sucks," Ethan said sympathetically.

"It does suck," Steph agreed. "But it's not as if you really gave her a choice."

Lachlan looked at his friends, who'd followed him home after Aislynn's birthday party to find out why Finley had done a disappearing act.

"Can't you show some compassion, Steph?" her husband said. "The guy's obviously hurting."

"It's his own fault," she retorted. "He lied to her."

"She's right," Lachlan admitted. "Finley didn't ask for much from me, but she did ask for honesty."

"So why didn't you tell her the truth?" Steph asked now.

"Because I was afraid I'd lose her."

"And somehow, that's exactly what happened."

"Not helping," Ethan said.

"He needs to realize that he's getting in his own way."

"Huh?" Lachlan said.

"I know you haven't dated a lot of women," Steph noted. "And some of your missteps with Finley might be attributed to treading on unfamiliar ground, but from my perspective, your biggest problem is that you're afraid to let yourself be happy, and so you've been sabotaging your relationship with Finley every step of the way."

"That's ridiculous," he said.

"Is it?" she challenged. "Maybe you legitimately lost track of time the night you were at the hospital with Aislynn, but even so, you could have sent her a quick text message as soon as you realized you'd stood her up. And inviting her to your house without telling her that you had a teenage daughter who is in the habit of dropping by at random times? Then jumping out of her bed in response to a summons from your ex-wife? And lying about the significance of the date on a tattoo on your back?"

"Laid out like that, the evidence is pretty damning," Ethan agreed.

"I know I've screwed up, but none of it was on purpose."

"Self-sabotaging behavior is often unconscious. You grew up in a traditional family with loving parents, so you think you must be responsible for the failure of your marriage and don't deserve another chance at happiness."

"I'm sorry—isn't your doctorate in mathematics?"

"Psychology is a hobby."

"Well, perform your armchair analysis on someone else," he suggested.

"I don't know anyone else who is such an obvious textbook case," she retorted.

"So what's the textbook solution?" he asked.

"Forgive yourself," she said simply. "And open up your heart."

Finley didn't have time to wallow.

She had a job to do, so she put a smile on her face and did it, pretending all the while that her heart wasn't shattered into a thousand pieces.

After Saturday's wedding, both Julia and Rachel tried to talk to her, but she brushed them off. She wasn't ready to tell them what happened with Lachlan, to admit that she'd been fool enough to fall in love—again—with a man who couldn't let go of his past to move on with her. He'd claimed he wasn't still in love with Deirdre, but it seemed to her that permanent ink spoke louder than words.

On Sunday, after all the post-wedding hoopla had died down, she FaceTimed her sister. It was early evening, before the twins went to bed, and they were both eager to talk to "Auntie Fin."

"I can't believe how big they are now," she said.

"Growing like weeds," Haylee agreed.

"Wike fwowers, Gwamma says," Ellie announced, jumping up and down to see herself on the screen.

"That's right," her mom agreed. "Like beautiful flowers."

The little girl beamed.

Finley felt her heart pinch.

"I don' wanna be a fwower," Aidan protested. "I wanna be a dinosaur—Woar!"

"You are indeed a ferocious dinosaur," Finley told him.

The conversation lifted her spirits immensely.

And then, three days later, she opened the door and her sister was there.

"This impromptu trip was Trevor's idea," Haylee said, returning Finley's hug.

"And that's why he's my favorite brother-in-law."

"He's your only brother-in-law."

"Another reason he's my favorite." She looked past her sister. "But where is he? And Aidan and Ellie?"

"They'll be here on the weekend, because he knew that I wanted some one-on-one time with you first."

Finley's eyes filled with tears. "Can we have wine with that one-on-one time?"

"We can have whatever you want," Haylee promised.

So Finley opened a bottle and put out some snacks while her sister carried her bag into the guest room. When she came out again, Haylee had Simon snuggled against her chest.

"He's not happy with you," Finley warned.

"What are you talking about? Why wouldn't he be happy with me?"

"Because he knows you're getting a dog."

"It's Trevor who wants the dog, not me," Haylee said, speaking directly to the cat. "And we don't have one yet."

Simon didn't look impressed with her explanation.

Then again, he rarely looked impressed.

"Now tell me what happened with Lachlan," Haylee said, when they were seated on the sofa with their wine.

"Maybe I should tell you what didn't happen," Finley suggested. "Which is that he didn't have the tattoo with his wedding date removed."

Her sister winced. "When was he supposed to have that done?"

"Any time in the twelve years that have passed since his divorce."

Haylee sipped her wine. "Was this tattoo a recent revelation?"

"No," Finley admitted, and briefly explained to her sister her misreading of the date and, therefore, misinterpreting the significance.

"And you think the fact that he hasn't had the tattoo removed is a sign that he still has feelings for the ex-wife that he divorced a dozen years ago?" Haylee sounded dubious.

"It's at least a sign that he can't let her go," she said.

"Have you spoken with him since you left the party?"

"There's nothing to talk about."

"Fin." Haylee set down her wineglass to take her sister's hands. "I know you better than anyone else in the world, and I know—"

"*Knew*," she interjected to clarify. "You *knew* me better than anyone else in the world. Then you got pregnant and got married and moved five hundred miles away. Now I hardly ever see you."

"Is that why you're freezing me out?"

"No. I mean, I'm not..." She blew out a breath. "Maybe I am freezing you out."

"I know things have changed since Trevor and I got married," Haylee acknowledged, "but you'll always be my sister and my best friend, and even when I'm five hundred miles away, you're always in my heart."

Finley teared up again.

"And because you're my sister and my best friend, I'm going to remind you of what you once said to me."

"What's that?"

"When you're dealing with a boatload of stuff, I'll be right there with you with the life jackets."

Finley was surprised—and just a little bit wary—when Taylor buzzed to tell her that Catherine Edwards was on the line for her.

"Catherine—how wonderful to hear from you." And it was true, because despite what had happened with Lachlan, Finley had nothing but sincere affection for his grandparents.

"It would be even more wonderful to see you," Lachlan's grandmother said. "When can we get together for lunch?"

"Lunch sounds lovely," Finley told her. "But before we make plans, there's something you need to know."

"If you're going to tell me that you're no longer seeing Lachlan, I'm aware."

"And you still want to have lunch with me?"

"I realize that I'm old enough to be your grandmother, but I liked you from the first moment we met. And since I'm at an age where a lot of my friends are dying, I could use some newer—and decidedly younger—ones."

Finley had to chuckle. "I'd be honored to be counted as a friend."

"Of course, as a friend, I'm going to expect some kind of discount when Douglas and I hire Gilmore Galas for our sixty-fifth wedding anniversary celebration."

"And you'll get one," Finley promised.

"Wonderful. Now when can you come for lunch?"

"You want me to come to your home?"

"Would you mind terribly?" Catherine asked. "On my way back from the spa last week, I had a minor fender bender. It really wasn't a big deal, but Douglas doesn't want me driving again until I have my eyes tested."

"I don't mind at all," Finley assured her. "In fact, why don't I pick up lunch and bring it to you?"

"I may be temporarily without transportation—by choice—but I'm perfectly capable of putting together a meal in my own kitchen."

"In that case, does Monday work for you?"

"It does," Catherine confirmed. "What time should I expect you?"

"One o'clock?"

"I'll look forward to seeing you then."

At the end of the summer term, Lachlan took Aislynn camping, as he'd done every August for the past twelve years. When she was a kid, she'd loved their summer retreats, but in recent years, she'd been a lot less enthusiastic about spending any time off the grid that fueled not only her electronic devices but apparently her very existence.

They spent the first few days in town with Ben's family, before heading up to his friend's cabin. Lachlan knew the first trip back after his friend's passing would be the hardest, and so he was grateful to have his daughter's company.

And he had to give her credit, she made it all the way to the evening of day four when they were playing cribbage by solar-powered lights before she said, "We don't have to stay the whole week, you know. If you want to go home, that's fine by me."

"This is our week," he reminded her, selecting two cards from his hand and setting them aside. "And I'm in no hurry for it to end."

She added two cards from her hand to his crib. "You're not missing Finley?"

It was the question he'd been simultaneously waiting for and dreading. And while he didn't always share the details of what was going on in his life, he tried to at least be honest about what he did share.

And yes, he didn't miss the irony of the fact that if he'd applied the same guideline in his relationship with Finley, they might still be together.

"Finley and I broke up."

"Oh." Her brow scrunched as she cut the deck. He flipped the top card, revealing the queen of spades. "When did that happen?"

"A couple weeks ago."

She led with a jack of diamonds. "Was it because of me?"

"No, honey." He tossed down a five and pegged two points. "It had nothing to do with you."

She added another five and pegged two for the pair. "Are you sure? I know I wasn't always very nice to her."

He added to the count with a king. "Except when you wanted her help with your party."

A guilty flush colored her cheeks as she dropped an ace on the table and pegged two more.

"So what happened?"

He started the count again with another king. "You mean between me and Finley?"

She nodded as she played a third king, securing two more points.

"Sometimes things just don't work out," he said, dropping his last card—an eight—on the table and pegging a single point for it.

"That's a totally lame answer," she told him. "If you don't think it's any of my business, just say it's none of my business."

"Okay, it's none of your business."

She scored her hand—nine points including the queen start card. He pegged eight from his hand and another four from his crib.

"Was it because you're still in love with Mom?" she asked, as she gathered the cards to shuffle.

He sighed. "Honey, I know this might be hard for you to accept, but I'm not still in love with your mom. She's in love with Philip and…"

"And?" she prompted, when his answer trailed off.

"And… I'm in love with Finley." It was the first time he'd said the words out loud. The first time he'd admitted the true depth of his feelings for her.

Unfortunately, it was too little, too late.

Not to mention that he'd made the admission to the wrong woman.

Aislynn frowned as she began to deal. "I don't understand. If you're in love with Finley, then why did you break up?"

"None of your business," he reminded her.

"Actually, I don't think that's true," she said now. "Because you're my dad, which means that what affects you, affects me."

"My breakup with Finley doesn't affect you."

"I don't like seeing you sad."

"I'll get over it."

She set the deck aside and picked up her hand. "Are you sure?"

"I'm sure."

"Because in the past five—maybe ten—years, I can count

on one hand the number of your girlfriends that you've introduced me to—with three fingers left."

"And I can count on one hand the number of my girlfriends that you've liked—with five fingers left."

She rearranged the cards in her hand, selecting two for her crib. "I might have been wrong about Finley."

"It doesn't matter now," he told her.

"It does matter," she insisted. Then, when he failed to respond, she asked, "Did you tell her you love her?"

He continued to examine the cards she'd dealt to him.

"You didn't, did you?" she pressed.

"I'm not talking to you about this, Aislynn."

"You need to talk to *someone* about it."

"Maybe I do." He tossed two cards down for her crib. "But it's not going to be my sixteen-year-old daughter."

"Then talk to Finley," she advised. "Because if you don't tell her how you feel, how will you ever know if your feelings are reciprocated?"

"You brought me flowers," Catherine said, smiling with pleasure when she opened the door in response to Finley's knock.

"Based on what you chose for your anniversary arrangements, I figured that dahlias were a favorite flower."

"They are indeed," Catherine confirmed. "And this color is absolutely stunning."

"It's called Frost Nip," Finley told her. "And I'll admit, I like the name as much as the white-edged pink flowers."

"They're going to look lovely in the center of the dining room table. Come," she said, taking her guest's arm and drawing her inside. "Let's eat and catch up."

And that's what they did. Over spinach salad with strawberries, toasted pecans and feta, Catherine regaled Finley with tales from her European travels with Douglas. The salad was followed by roasted lemon rosemary chicken with potatoes and anecdotes from recent Gilmore Galas. By the time they polished off their key lime tarts, more than two hours had passed.

"I can't tell you how much I enjoyed this," she told Catherine, as she carried the dessert plates to the kitchen.

"Hold onto that thought," the old woman said, as the back door opened and her husband came in, followed by his grandson.

Finley felt her heart squeeze inside her chest when she looked at Lachlan, who was looking back at her with an unreadable expression on his face.

Douglas, having quickly assessed the situation, sighed heavily. "You're meddling again, aren't you, Catherine?"

"I can see how it might look that way," she acknowledged. "But this wasn't my idea."

"And it wasn't mine," Finley said, so that Lachlan wouldn't think she'd set up this meeting in the hopes of crossing paths with him. Because why would she want to see him when doing so only made her heart ache again, longing for what she'd had and lost?

"I know it wasn't your idea," he said, taking two steps toward her. "Because it was mine."

"Yours?"

He nodded.

"I think I left…something…in the dining room," Catherine said, exiting in that direction.

The other three people in the kitchen didn't move.

"Douglas?" Catherine prompted. "I could use your help."

"With the…something?" he queried.

"Exactly," she said.

Sending an apologetic glance in Finley's direction, the old man followed his wife out of the room.

"So this was all your idea?" Finley said, when she and Lachlan were alone.

"Not the lunch part," he said. "My grandmother mentioned that she wanted to get together with you—because she really does enjoy your company—but she wanted to make sure that I was okay with it first. I suggested that she invite you to come here, so that we could talk after."

"If you wanted to talk to me, why didn't you just call?"

"Because I figured you'd blocked my number. Again."

"I didn't."

"Oh."

"I was upset when I walked out of Aislynn's party that day, but that didn't mean I wanted it to be over between us."

"There really should be a manual," he muttered.

"A manual?"

He gave a slight shake of his head. "I'm not good at this stuff," he confided. "Flirting is easy. And sex is pretty straight-forward. But when it comes to relationships, I clearly don't have the first clue what I'm doing."

"I thought it was just our relationship."

He shook his head. "The truth is, Deirdre was my first se-rious girlfriend and, when she got pregnant, we got married."

"You told me that part already."

"What I didn't tell you is how much I hate to fail at any-thing, and failing at my marriage—something that was sup-posed to be forever—was major. So I put all my energy into being the best dad that I could be.

"I've dated since the divorce, obviously, but none of the women I've gone out with has tempted me to risk my heart again. Until you. And I hope I'm not too late in telling you how I feel, because the last few weeks have been hell, and I don't want to imagine the rest of my life without you in it. Because I love you."

Finley had always found it annoying when the heroine in a romantic book or movie would willingly forgive all kinds of transgressions simply because the hero uttered those three little words. Because she hadn't understood, until that very moment, how those words could change everything.

Because when Lachlan said, "I love you," her heart swelled inside her chest so that all the bumps and bruises it had suffered—recent and distant—were forgotten.

"You're not too late," she finally said, emotion filling her voice.

He breached the distance that separated them and lifted his hands to frame her face.

"I love you," he said again, looking into her eyes so that she could see the truth of his feelings reflected in the depth of his. Then he lowered his mouth to hers in a kiss that was filled with love and promise.

"I love you, too," she said, when his lips eased away.

He tipped his forehead against hers. "I'd almost given up hope that I'd ever hear you say those words," he admitted. "It was Aislynn who pointed out that if I wanted to know what was in your heart, I had to be willing to open up mine."

"Do you think your daughter's going to be okay with this?"

"She's already started to come around," he said confidently. "Oh, I almost forgot... there's something I want to show you."

"Have you forgotten that we're in your grandparents' house?" she asked, as he began unbuttoning his shirt. "And that they're probably just beyond that doorway listening to every word of our conversation?"

"Following the advice of my grandfather, I'll keep it PG," he promised, sliding one sleeve of his shirt down so that she could see the tattoo on his shoulder.

He hadn't had the ink removed—which she knew could be a time-consuming process—but had, instead, covered the date of his wedding with tiny flowers.

She tipped her head for a closer look. "Are those...?"

"They're violets," he told her.

Her heart skipped a beat.

"An unconventional choice," she noted.

"Do you really think so, Finley Violet Gilmore?"

She blinked. "How did you know my middle name?"

"It's on the diploma in your office."

"So...not a random choice?" she guessed.

"Not random at all," he assured her. "I didn't want to get rid of the infinity symbol, because it was always more about Aislynn than Deirdre, but I wanted to add something that represented you, to show how much I want a life and a future with you."

"Because you love me?" she prompted, wanting to hear him say it one more time.

"Because I love you," he confirmed.

Finley's heart swelled again in response to the words, so much that it almost hurt, and it was the very best feeling in the world.

Epilogue

In March, Finley made her annual trip to Haven to celebrate Aidan and Ellie's birthday. But this year, she had company on her journey. On previous visits, she'd always stayed at Haylee and Trevor's place, but this year, in addition to the twins, her sister and brother-in-law had a new dog and—surprise!—another set of twins on the way. Haylee had assured them that there was still room, but Finley and Lachlan decided that a hotel might be more peaceful for all of them.

Finley had voted in favor of a room at the Stagecoach Inn, because it was conveniently located in town, but Lachlan apparently had a sentimental streak, because he insisted on making a reservation at the Dusty Boots Motel.

"You know, this little trip down memory lane would be a lot more romantic if we'd met at five-star resort on a tropical island," she told him.

"I don't disagree," he said. "But we can only work with what we've got."

And what they had was the key to Room 6—handed over by Shirla herself—and a large pizza from Jo's.

"I'm experiencing the weirdest sense of déjà vu," she murmured, as she followed Lachlan into the room.

"Except that it's not snowing this year."

"I'm almost disappointed," she said, hanging her coat on

a peg by the door. "Because what possible excuse will I have to invite you to share my bed if the power doesn't go out?"

"Hmm...you could maybe try a more direct approach and say that you want to have your way with me."

"Do you think that would work?" she asked dubiously.

He set the pizza box on the desk and discarded his coat beside hers. "I guarantee it."

She turned to him and slid her hands slowly up his chest. "I want—"

That was as far as she got before he lifted her into his arms and tumbled with her onto the bed.

Afterward, they ate cold pizza and washed it down with (plastic) glasses of cabernet sauvignon, and Finley felt certain that she couldn't be any happier than she was in that moment— not even if they were at a five-star resort on a tropical island.

"This is a definite upgrade from last year," she said, gesturing with her glass of wine.

"Over the past year, I've learned a few things about what you like."

She had to smile. "And my favorite wine label, too."

"Speaking of upgrades," he said, taking the opening she'd given him. "I was wondering how you might feel about upgrading our relationship status?"

Her heart bumped against her ribs. "What kind of upgrade did you have in mind?"

"From girlfriend to fiancée seems like a logical progression to me."

"Very logical," she agreed. For the past several weeks, he'd been dropping hints that this moment was coming, and she was excited for it to finally happen.

"But most women seem to have specific ideas about how a man should propose," he continued, in a conversational tone.

"Certainly some women do."

"And what do *you* think would make the perfect proposal?"

She sipped her wine. "In my line of work, I've heard a lot of engagement stories, all of which have led me to the conclusion that the when and where and how aren't nearly as important as who's doing the asking."

"You're saying you wouldn't turn down a guy who got down on one knee in a roadside motel so long as he was the right guy?"

"Are we going to talk in hypotheticals all night or are you actually planning to get down on one knee?"

"I'm undecided," he admitted. "It doesn't look as if this carpet has been cleaned in the past decade."

"The one knee thing isn't a requirement," she said, silently urging him to move things along.

"What are the requirements—aside from him being the right guy, I mean?" Lachlan asked.

"Well, I'd want to know that he loves me."

"I do." He leaned forward to kiss her. "I definitely do."

"And I want a ring."

He reached a hand into his pocket. "How's this one?"

Her gaze never strayed from his. "That works."

"You didn't even look at it," he protested.

"Because I honestly don't care if it's stainless or silver or plastic or platinum," she told him. "I only care that you have a ring, because it proves that you're serious about wanting to marry me."

"I'm very serious," he said. "And FYI, it's a platinum halo engagement ring with a princess-cut center diamond."

She had to check it out then—and it was absolutely stunning.

"So what do you say, Finley Violet Gilmore? Are you ready to start planning *our* wedding?"

"I say, *yes*, Lachlan Patrick Kellett. Because the one thing I want even more than that ring is *you*. For now and forever."

After he slid the ring on her finger, they shared a lingering kiss, and it was a long time later before either of them noticed the fluffy white flakes that were falling outside the window.

* * * * *

Special EDITION

Believe in love. Overcome obstacles. Find happiness.

Available Next Month

The Rancher Hits The Road Melissa Senate
Her Second-Chance Family Elizabeth Bevarly

....

A Cape Cod Summer Jo McNally
It Started With A Secret Tif Marcelo

Keep reading for an excerpt of
THE PRICE OF HIS REDEMPTION
by Carol Marinelli — find this story
in *The Tycoon's Fake Fiancée* anthology.

PROLOGUE

'Hey, *shishka*.'

Daniil Zverev stiffened as he walked into the dormitory and heard what his friend Sev had just called him.

It would seem that *shishka* was now his new name.

Russian slang could hit just where it hurt, and tonight it did its job well.

Big gun.

Bigwig.

Big shot.

Daniil watched as Sev put down the book he had been reading.

'We were just talking about how you're going to go and live with the rich family in England, *shishka*.'

'Don't call me that again,' Daniil warned, and picked up the book and held it over his head. He made to rip the pages out but, as Sev swallowed, Daniil tossed it back on the bed.

He wouldn't have torn it—Sev only occasionally had a book to read—but Daniil hoped he would heed the warning.

'Did you find any matches?' Nikolai looked up from the wooden ship he was painstakingly building and Daniil went into his pocket and took out the handful that he had collected when he had done his sweeping duty.

'Here.'

'Thanks, *shishka*.'

Daniil would do it; he would smash Nikolai's ship. His breathing was hard and angry as he stared down his friend.

The four boys were, in fact, far more than friends.

Yes, Daniil and Roman might be identical twins and Nikolai and Sev no relation, but all four had grown up together. With their dark hair and pale skin, they were the poorest stock amongst the poor. At the baby house they had stood in their cribs and called to each other at night.

Daniil and Roman had shared a crib.

Nikolai and Sevastyan had slept in their own on either side of the twins.

When they had graduated to beds they had been moved to the children's orphanage and placed in the same dormitory. Now, in the adolescent wing, they shared a four-bedroomed room.

Most considered them wild boys, troubled boys, but they were no real trouble to each other.

They were all they had.

'Touch my ship…' Nikolai threatened.

'Don't call me *shishka*, then. Anyway, there is no need to—I've decided that I'm not going to live in England.' Daniil looked over at Roman, his twin, who lay on his bed with his hands behind his head, staring at the ceiling. 'I'm going to say that I don't want to go. They can't make me.'

'Why would you do that?' Roman asked, and turned his head and fixed his brother with the cold grey stare that they shared.

'Because I don't need some rich family to help me. We're going to make it ourselves, Roman.'

'Yeah, right.'

'We are,' Daniil insisted. 'Sergio said…'

'What would he know? He's the maintenance man.'

'He was once a boxer, though.'

'So he says.'

'The Zverev twins!' Daniil was insistent. 'He says that we're going to make it...'

'Go and be with the rich family,' Roman said. 'We're not going to get rich and famous here. We're never going to get out of this hole.'

'But if we train hard we'll do well.' Daniil picked up the photo by Roman's bed. Sergio had brought his camera in one day a couple of years ago and had taken a photo of the twins and, because the others had nagged, he had then taken one of all four boys.

It was the photo of the two of them, though, that Daniil now held up as he spoke to his brother. 'You said that we would make it.'

'Well, I lied,' Roman said.

'Hey...' Sev had got back to reading but, even though he had just teased Daniil, he cared for him and could see where this was leading. 'Leave him, Roman. Let him make up his own mind.'

'No.' Roman sat up angrily. Things had been building for months, since they'd first been told about a family who wanted to give a good home to a twelve-year-old. 'He wants to blow off his one chance because he has this stupid dream that he can make it in the ring. Well, he can't.'

'We can,' Daniil said.

'*I* can,' Roman corrected. 'Or at least I could if I didn't have you dragging me down.' He took the picture of the two of them out of Daniil's hand and tossed it across the floor. There was no glass in the frame, but something broke then. Daniil felt something fracture somewhere deep inside.

'Come on,' Roman said. 'I'll show you who can really fight.'

He got up out of the bed and there was a buzz around the dormitory as the twins eyed each other.

Finally they would fight.

The Zverev twins trained all day.

Sergio put them through drill after drill and they pushed through all of them. The only complaint they ever had was that they wanted to spar. Sergio had refused to allow it until a few months ago, but even then it was always under Sergio's watchful eye. As an ex-boxer himself, he knew better than to start the boys too early.

These boys were beautifully built. Tall and long-limbed, they were fast, light on their feet and hungry.

He knew that with the right training the twins would go far.

What a package!

Two peas in a pod, two pitched minds and two angry youths.

All Sergio had to do for now was contain them.

But he wasn't there tonight.

'Tell the others,' Roman said, and the room started to fill, beds were pushed back to make floor space and the gathering spectators knelt on them.

'Show me what you've got,' Roman jeered, as he came out fighting. He had Daniil straight on the defensive, blocking punches and moving back.

No headgear, no gloves, no money to get them.

Not yet.

Roman gave him nothing, no rest, nowhere to hide, and Daniil, with everything to prove, fought back with all he had.

The other boys were cheering while trying not to, as they did not want to alert the workers.

Roman was at his fiercest, and though Daniil did his best to match him it was he who tired first. He moved in and took Roman in a clinch. He just needed a moment to rest but his brother shrugged him off.

Daniil went in again, holding on to his twin so that Roman couldn't punch him, doing his best to get back some breath before he commenced fighting again.

Roman broke the clinch and the fight restarted, both blocking punches, both taking the occasional hit, but then Daniil thought he was gaining ground. Daniil was fast and Roman rarely needed to rest but it was Roman who now came in for a clinch and leaned on his twin. Daniil could hear his brother's angry breathing but as he released him, instead of giving Daniil that necessary second to centre, Roman hooked him, landing an uppercut to Daniil's left cheek and flooring him.

Daniil came round to stunned faces. He had no idea how long he'd been knocked out but it had been long enough to have everyone worried.

Everyone except Roman.

'See,' Roman said. 'I do better without you, *shishka.*'

The staff had noticed that some of the dorms were empty and, alerted by the mounting cheers, had started running to the room where Daniil now lay, trying to focus.

Katya, the cook, took him into the warm kitchen, calling to her daughter, Anya, to bring the box of tape. Anya was in there, practising her dance steps. She was twelve and went to a dance school but for now was home for the holidays. Sometimes she would tease the twins and say that she was fitter than them.

Anya still had dreams and thought she would dance her way out of here.

Daniil had none now.

'Hey, what on earth were you doing?' Katya scolded. She gave Daniil some strong, sweet black tea and then she tried to patch up his face. 'The rich family don't want ugly...'

DANIIL SAT ON a bed just a few days later, seemingly a million miles from home.

In the car he had looked at the small houses and shops as they'd passed them and when the car had turned a corner he had seen in the distance a large imposing red-brick residence. They had been driven down a long driveway and he'd stared at the lawns, fountains and statues outside the huge house.

Daniil hadn't wanted to get out of the car but he had, silently.

The door was opened by a man in a black suit who looked, to Daniil, to be dressed for a funeral or wedding but his smile was kind.

In the entrance Daniil stood as the adults spoke over him and then up the stairs he was led by the woman who had twice come to the orphanage and who was now his mother.

At the turn of the stairs there was a portrait of his new parents with their hands on the shoulders of a smiling dark-haired child.

He'd been told that they had no children.

The bedroom was large and there was only one bed, which looked out to vast countryside.

'Bath!'

He had no idea what she meant until she pointed to a room off the bedroom, and then she had gone.

Daniil had a bath and wrapped a towel around himself, just in time, because there was a knock at the door. It opened and she approached him with an anxious smile. She started to go through his things and kept calling him by the wrong name.

He wanted to correct her and tell her his name was pronounced *Dah-neel*, rather than the *Dae-ne-yuhl* she insisted on using, but then he remembered the translator explaining that he had a new name.

Daniel Thomas.

That woman, his mother, had rubber gloves on, and his clothes, his shoes were all being loaded into a large garbage bag that the man in the suit was holding. She was still talking in a language he didn't understand. She kept pointing to the window and then his cheek and making a gesture as if she was sewing and after several attempts he understood that she was going to take him to get his cheek repaired better than Katya had done.

He stared at the case as she disposed of his life and then he saw two pictures, which Daniil knew that he hadn't packed. Roman had slipped them in, he must have.

'Nyet!'

It was the first word he had spoken since they had left Russia and the woman let out a small worried cry as Daniil lunged for the photos and told her, no, she must not to get rid of them and neither could she touch them.

His mother had fled the room and the man in the suit stood there for a while before finally coming to sit on the bed and join him in looking at the photos.

'You?' He had pointed to Daniil and then to one of the boys in the picture.

Daniil shook his head. 'Roman.'

The old man with kind eyes pointed to his own chest. 'Marcus.'

Daniil nodded and looked back at the photo.

Only then did Daniil start to understand that Roman didn't hate him; he had been trying to save him.

Daniil, though, hadn't wanted to be saved.

He had wanted to make his way with his brother.

Not alone, like this.

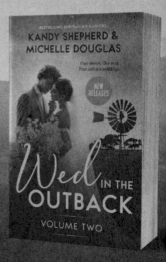

ubscribe and
all in love with
Mills & Boon
eries today!

ou'll be among the first
 read stories delivered
 your door monthly
 nd enjoy great savings.

WE
SIMPLY
LOVE
ROMANCE

MILLS & BOON

JOIN US

Sign up to our newsletter to stay up to date with...

- Exclusive member discount codes
- Competitions
- New release book information
- All the latest news on your favourite authors

Plus...
get $10 off your first order.
What's not to love?

Sign up at **millsandboon.com.au/newsletter**